MW00641943

RIVER

RIVER

WHERE FAITH AND CONSECRATION CONVERGE

A HISTORICAL NOVEL

BOOK TWO

DEAN HUGHES

SALT LAKE CITY, UTAH

Visit us at deseretbook.com

Library of Congress Cataloging-in-Publication Data

Names: Hughes, Dean, 1943– author. | Hughes, Dean, 1943- Muddy.
Title: River : where faith and consecration converge : a historical novel. Book two / Dean Hughes.
Description: Salt Lake City, Utah : Deseret Book, [2020] | Includes bibliographical references. | Summary: "Morgan Davis and his family have moved, along with many of their fellow Saints from the Muddy River Mission, to Long Valley in southern Utah. There they are invited by their prophet, Brigham Young, to embark on a new venture: the United Order. But creating Zion is not an easy task when so many personalities and needs come together"— Provided by publisher.
Identifiers: LCCN 2019054639 | ISBN 9781629727448 (hardback)
Subjects: LCSH: Mormons—Utah—Kane County—Fiction. | Consecration—Mormon Church—Fiction. | Consecration—The Church of Jesus Christ of Latter-day Saints—Fiction. | United orders (Mormon Church)—Fiction. | Kane County (Utah), setting. | LCGFT: Historical fiction. | Novels.
Classification: LCC PS3558.U36 R58 2020 | DDC 813/.54—dc23
LC record available at https://lccn.loc.gov/2019054639

Printed in the United States of America
Lake Book Manufacturing, Inc., Melrose Park, IL

10 9 8 7 6 5 4 3 2 1

For my granddaughter
Katherine "Katie" Russell

A NOTE TO THE READER

River is a sequel to *Muddy,* but the books tell different stories. The main characters continue through the two-part series, but the setting changes dramatically. *Muddy* was set in the Muddy River Valley of southern Nevada, not far from present-day Las Vegas. Early Latter-day Saint missionaries were called to settle that region in 1865. By 1871, for a complex set of reasons, those missionaries were released from their mission, and many of them moved to southern Utah, to Long Valley, north of Kanab. The story of the Muddy River missionaries continues in a new location and greatly different circumstances.

The murky river in *Muddy* symbolizes the unclear choices these early settlers faced. The clear stream known as the East Fork of the Virgin River was a huge contrast for the settlers who moved to a higher altitude and a moderate climate. The clarity of the river symbolizes the pursuit of a higher purpose, the unity and peace that the people struggled to achieve. They established Orderville, where the longest-lasting version of the United Order persisted for ten years.

Modern Church members often speak of the United Order as a failed system, and they make sweeping assessments that have become clichés in classroom discussions. The fact is, when Brigham

Young began to establish the law of consecration in the form of real-world organizations, he allowed each community to write its own bylaws and develop its own procedures. No two Orders were exactly the same. Diagnoses about the so-called failures of these organizations inevitably oversimplify actual events.

United Order organizations actually took many forms. Brigham Young liked the idea of a "family" approach, in which the people shared all their possessions, ate together in a common dining room, farmed large community fields and gardens, and raised animals as community herds. But in some places, including Salt Lake City, unity was sought only in the creation of cooperative businesses. One goal of the United Order was to build self-reliance and to avoid dependence on products being imported from outside the Utah Territory, but the ultimate purpose was to create a society in which there would be no rich or poor and all members would work together as equals.

The United Order relied on an agrarian way of life. It's hard to imagine how the systems developed in the nineteenth century could operate in our complex, interrelated business world. Our way of supporting one another now is through fast offerings, the Perpetual Education Fund, welfare programs, humanitarian missions, and other similar programs. Within each ward or branch of the Church, we work to bless each other's lives. We minister to one another individually, and we use the ward and stake organizations to teach, encourage, and support.

But do we have both rich and poor among us? Brigham Young, in the final years of his life, preached throughout the Church that we were not yet living the full spirit of the law of consecration. I would hope that this book might offer some insight into what the Saints of the nineteenth century attempted to do to combat those problems. United Orders all dissolved in time, and this novel, based on history, might help us understand some of the reasons why. But I would hope that it might also raise a question: Are we doing all we can to bless one another's lives and build that elusive society we call Zion?

—Dean Hughes

CHAPTER I

Angeline Davis felt like herself again. Her confidence, even a sense of peace, had returned to her. She was actually surprised that she could be so happy.

It was a warm August morning, but not blazing, not oppressive like the summer days on the Muddy River, where she and her husband, Morgan, had lived the last three years. She liked this new place—Long Valley—with its pine-covered hillsides, broken here and there by white or rusty bluffs. She especially loved the river—the East Fork of the Virgin. She had walked to the steep bank this morning and followed a little trail down to the edge of the stream. She had dipped and hoisted out a pail of cold water, but now she was lingering, enjoying the coolness of the shade under the willows and cottonwoods. The clear, flowing water symbolized for her all that was best about this valley. The years she had lived by the murky, smelly Muddy River now seemed like time spent in an alien land.

But much of her joy was coming from inside. She now knew for certain that she was expecting a baby. She was feeling a bit of baby sickness this morning, and that was part of why she waited before she began her walk back to the house. Her uneasy stomach was a discomfort she welcomed. Her little Morgy had been saved for her during the exodus from Nevada—brought back to life by a priesthood blessing when she had thought she had lost her only child to a fever. Now that son was more than a year old and toddling about on strong legs. Nothing could please her more than to provide him with a little brother or sister. Angeline had wondered, early in her marriage, whether something wasn't wrong with her, that she would miscarry her first babies, but now she believed she could bear more children, and she was certain that Ruth, her sister wife, would too. She trusted that their family would grow and thrive. She loved to hear her husband talk optimistically about the fall harvest and about the improvements he was planning for their house.

The river was not far from their home—less than a quarter of a mile—but Angeline decided to take the walk in segments, with a few stops to set down the heavy bucket. That was partly to be careful, but even more to be able to tell Morgan that she hadn't exerted herself. She did appreciate that he worried about her health and the baby she was carrying, but she didn't believe that she should be easy on herself. Many of the women in Mt. Carmel—their newly renamed settlement—were pregnant, some of them greatly so, and she saw them working hard every day. She refused to think of herself as frail. She had believed from her childhood that she was strong, able to do anything she put her mind to, and that self-assurance was returning now.

When she stopped to rest a third time, she stretched her back and looked about the valley. She loved the grandness of the mountains, all the shades of green that she had missed in the Muddy Valley, and she relished the sound of songbirds. She was listening to the birds when a movement caught her eye. Something was in the sky, roiling up the valley from the south. It was like a cloud—except that it wasn't dark. It was sparkling, like thousands of raindrops glistening and undulating in the morning sun. But the cloud, or whatever it was, was moving fast, and she heard a whirring noise as it plunged toward her. By then it was engulfing everything, blocking the sunlight.

Angeline's impulse was to run, to get away, but she kept staring, waiting, trying to make sense of what she was seeing. Then something struck her sunbonnet, and she began to be pelted on her shoulders and down her front. She thought of rain or hail, but when she looked at the ground, she saw huge, brown grasshoppers. They were bouncing off her dress, dropping onto the grass beneath her feet. The air was full of them, all around her. She grabbed up her pail of water—which was filling up with the hoppers—and turned to run toward her house.

Just then she heard a voice, and she looked back. Little Sarie Handley was running toward her, her blonde pigtails flying out behind her. "Sister Davis! Sister Davis," she was calling. "They're eating everything up, and . . ." She stopped running, gasped.

"What?"

"They're eating up the wheat and corn down on our farm." She drew in air again. "The bishop said, tell everyone to come 'n help. We gotta stop 'em before they eat up all our crops."

"But they're everywhere." Angeline took a sweeping look around. The air was buzzing, dense with all the wings, and a writhing layer of insects was blanketing the ground, the grass, the fences, the trees.

Grasshoppers were sticking to Sarie's dress, and she was swatting at them to get them off her face and out of her hair. The plague had surely struck the farms close to town first and then rolled on north. "Are we supposed to help in town . . . or what?" Angeline asked.

"I don't know. They're here now. Maybe the bishop thought they wouldn't come this far."

Sarie was ten or so, usually buoyant, but she looked panicked now, her face red, her eyes wide. She took one more gulp of air, hoisted her skirt above her ankles, and said, "I better go back." She set off running. Angeline was trying to think what to do. She knew that Morgan had gone into town early. Maybe he was trying to help the people there.

Angeline hurried to the house. "Ruth," she shouted, as she approached, "grasshoppers." It was all she could think to say.

But Ruth was already at the door, watching what was happening. "I know," she said. "What can we do?"

"They're eating up the Handley farm. I'll go help."

"But they're eating up our farm, too."

Angeline knew that. But maybe the Saints had to fight together. Maybe they could save some farms, if not all of them. "I'll go ask what I can do," she told Ruth. She grabbed the hoe that was leaning against the house.

"Angeline, stop. You can't walk that far in all this." Ruth swung her open hand in a gesture to indicate the horde that was all around them. "You're in no condition to—"

"We have to stop them." But even as she spoke, she saw what the grasshoppers were doing. The humming had diminished, but a crackling noise had taken over as the insects consumed the dry grass close to the house. The limbs of nearby willow trees were now covered in brown, like swarms of bees.

"I'll fight them *here,*" Angeline said. She ran to the field just west of the house, where acres of planted wheat had become golden in recent days. But as Angeline reached the fence, she saw the stalks bending in waves, falling to the ground, and she heard the incessant clatter of a multitude of jaws nibbling, consuming.

She stopped, watched, tried to think what to do. And then she heard a voice behind her. “We can’t stop them.” It was Morgan.

Angeline turned toward him. When she saw the despair in his face, she broke down. “Why this?” she asked.

Morgan didn’t answer. He only took her in his arms and held her while the grasshoppers landed in Angeline’s hair and worked their way into the collar of her dress.

“Let’s get you inside,” Morgan finally said. “I’ll do what I can to fight them, but—”

“I’ll help you.”

“No. It’s mostly a useless effort. It’s not worth straining yourself.”

Morgan walked with Angeline back to the house. Inside, Ruth helped sweep the grasshoppers off their clothes. Angeline pulled her dress and petticoats off to rid herself of the insects that had gotten into her underwear.

“Your dress is covered in brown spots,” Ruth told her.

“It’s tobacco juice,” Angeline said. “That’s what we used to call it. It comes out of grasshoppers’ mouths.”

Morgy was watching all this, wide-eyed, looking from one adult to another, and Jefferson, Ruth’s five-year-old son, had been asking over and over, “What’s happening? Where did they come from?”

“They just do that,” Morgan said. He knelt by the boy. “But it’s all right. They won’t hurt us.” Then he looked up at Ruth. “The farms south of us, near town, are mostly eaten up. I tried to help fight ’em with shovels and hoes, but it was only a few of us against millions of them. Some people are burning fires, but smoke doesn’t seem to stop the things. I’m going to go back out and keep after them, but the most we can do is pray they’ll leave before everything’s gone.”

"And then what?" Angeline said.

Morgan shook his head. "I don't know. It's too late in the year to plant again. And the gardens and fruit trees will be gone. We'll just have to get by somehow."

The thought that came to Angeline's mind was: *Just don't tell me the Lord will provide. He could have stopped this if He had wanted to.* But she didn't say the words out loud. She didn't want to go back to her doubts and her anger.

Morgan stood up, straightened his back. "We'll be all right," he said. "Somehow."

Angeline saw how broken he looked, but she also knew he meant what he said. He had grown in faith; he was a changed man. He was trying with all his might to overcome the rebelliousness he had struggled with these last few years.

Angeline knew she had to resist the resentment she was feeling, but she had been so happy just an hour earlier, and now they had to "get by" again—as they had had to do so many times before. Surely, the Muddy River settlers had earned a season of peace and at least a small taste of prosperity.

• • •

The grasshoppers stayed for three days and ate up almost every living thing. They not only ate the crops, they chewed leaves off the trees and even gnawed the bark away. They filled up houses and barns, sheds and outhouses. And if people stood still too long, the hoppers actually ate holes in their clothing. But the insects finally lost interest in Mt. Carmel, rose up in great clouds again, and swarmed farther north. What Morgan learned by the end of the week was that the farms all through Long Valley were devastated.

The Saints who had now settled in Glendale, a few miles north, were wiped out too.

A few days after the grasshoppers departed, Bishop Ewan Morrison called a meeting at the newly completed church building in Mt. Carmel. Most of those who attended were men, including those who came down from Glendale. The women were too busy looking after their children and cleaning all the filth out of their homes and off their clothes.

Morgan sat next to his friend Eb Crawford toward the back of the church. When Morgan looked around at the men who had become his brothers, he remembered the days on the Muddy when they had dug out the irrigation canals time and again—and gradually lost hope. But this was something new. They had put their complete trust in this valley and had simply not foreseen a reversal like this.

"Was anything left of your crops?" Morgan asked Eb. Eb had also moved into an abandoned house near Mt. Carmel, partly to stay near Morgan. Their friends Lyman and Alice Hunt and Art and Susan Brooks were living in Glendale, where most of the St. Thomas Saints had settled.

"Not much was left," Eb said. "Only a few rows of corn. My other grains are gone. But I did better than a lot of people—just to have a little corn left."

"Patches of grain survived on quite a lot of the farms, about the same as with you," Morgan said. "For some reason, I have about a quarter of an acre of wheat that didn't get chewed up."

"Every little bit helps," Eb said. "But I'm worried about Mary Ann. She was getting stronger during that last year on the Muddy, but the trip up here was hard on her. And now, this loss has knocked her off her feet again. I guess you know, she's expecting, and she's not doing very well."

"I'm glad you're close to us. Angie will help her all she can."

"I know she will. But how many more setbacks can we take, Morgan?"

"I don't know. I'm telling myself that we've got to have faith, but . . ." He stopped himself. There were things he didn't want to say. So he only added, "It's just hard for all of us right now."

Bishop Morrison, who presided over both Glendale and Mt. Carmel, walked to the podium, and everyone quieted. Morgan was relieved that he didn't have to answer Eb's question any more than he had. In the darkest moment of his life, Morgan had asked the Lord for help, and his son had been restored to him. He had promised on that day to accept God's will, to commit himself to the work of the kingdom, not to question everything Church leaders asked of him. But he couldn't change something basic in himself—an awareness that life wasn't fair, and a feeling that somehow it ought to be, that God ought to make things right more often than He did.

"Let's start this meeting with a prayer," Bishop Morrison said. He called on Brother Fitzgerald, who was a crusty little man, but one known for his faith. He offered a mighty prayer. "We are thy people," he said. "Please, Lord, see our plight and reach down to us. Lift us into thy bosom and caress our broken spirits."

The bishop stood again, looked out at everyone for a few seconds, and then quietly said, "Some of you heard me complain while we were fightin' the grasshoppers. I mighta even cursed a few times. I suppose we all said a few things we need to repent for, and we all asked why we had to face another setback. But the damage is done now, and it's time to look ahead, not back."

Morgan thought he had never heard the bishop sound quite so disconsolate. But Bishop Morrison raised his head and pounded his fist on the podium, as if to say, "enough of that." And then he said, "The grasshoppers did finally give way, and they left us with a little grain and some garden produce—not enough to last 'til spring, but somethin' to use for the next little while. I want to start out by asking around the chapel for a report from each head of household. Take a guess, as best you can, and estimate the bushels of grain and the particular vegetables you think you can salvage."

He started at the front, calling on each man by name. There were about fifty families in the two settlements, and almost all of them were represented. The estimates about bushels of grain were guesswork, the men admitted, but only a few said that they had been wiped out entirely.

When the bishop called on Hosea Marchant—a man who had returned to the valley recently but had not been part of the Muddy River Mission—he stood and removed his hat, then spoke in a surprisingly loud voice. "I've got a few potatoes still in the ground, and some turnips. But my grain is pritty much wiped out."

Isaac Humboldt spoke up immediately. "Hosea, you better take another look. A lot of your corn got through just fine."

"Look a little closer, Humboldt. The stalks is standing, but the ears is et up inside the husks."

"I did look at them, and—"

"Wait, brothers," the bishop said. "We have to trust each other. Let's all be honest about what we have, but let's not accuse anyone of holdin' back."

Brother Marchant said, "I say we each do the best we can to get by, and if some have surplus, they can help the ones who lost everything."

"And according to you," Isaac said, "you're the one who needs help. But you're telling a bald-faced lie."

The chapel was suddenly silent. It was a bare little room, a pine-pole structure with rough boards nailed on for siding. Sound carried well inside, but these harsh words—the first stark anger ever expressed within those walls—seemed to hollow out the place.

Brother Marchant pointed at Isaac Humboldt. "I'll tell you what," he said. "I'll sink or swim with what I've got. And there ain't no law that says I have to report to any of you. The first thing for me is to feed my family. And Humboldt, if you come around my house begging for food this winter, I'll have my shotgun ready. I don't feed begging Indians, and I'm not going to feed you." He walked down the aisle and out the back door.

"That's all right," Bishop Morrison said. "Let 'im go. We're all sayin' things we shouldn't right now. But I'll tell you what: if Hosea's family is hungry, I'll share with him, the same as with any of you. That's the only way we can think about this."

Brother Humboldt wasn't satisfied. "And if he has more than the rest of us, and my family is hungry, I just might take a rifle with me and go see whether he don't want to share after all."

"No, no, Isaac. We can't have that. Calm down."

"I'll calm down when he stops lying."

"Brother Humboldt, go home tonight and tell the Lord that you're thinking about using a weapon against one of your brothers. Ask God if He approves of that idea."

Isaac didn't answer, but Morgan could see the side of his face, could see that his jaw muscles were still set tight.

The reports continued, and Brother Carrington, from Mt. Carmel, added the totals, which he handed to the bishop on a sheet of paper. The bishop studied the numbers for a time and then said, "Brother Marchant does have a point. Even if we all share, I doubt we can make what we have last more than a few weeks, maybe two months. So what are our choices? How do we manage this?"

August could be hot in Long Valley, even if it didn't seem very bad to those who had lived on the Muddy. With the room crowded and the afternoon sun beating down, the little church was stifling. Still, the stronger discomfort for Morgan was to see how disheartened everyone looked. They had struggled so hard to get to this valley, and then to open the land and make a start. It was devastating to lose everything they had worked for and now to face a winter without enough food for their families.

Brother Riddle stood. He wiped his face with a red bandanna before he said, "I come out better than most, but I also know how to get by better'n most. There's things in these woods around here we can harvest: roots and berries. And there's fish in the river. We can make many a meal from fish, and I'd rather fish than farm anyhow."

There was a burst of laughter, the first relief Morgan had felt since the grasshoppers had struck the valley.

"Besides that," Brother Riddle added, "those who have guns and ammunition can hunt, and we can share rabbit meat, deer, geese, pheasants. That'll help us get by."

"We have to be careful about that," the bishop said. "The Indians consider deer as their cattle. We've promised them that we won't shoot any for ourselves."

Morgan thought another point should be made. He raised his hand, and then stood when the bishop acknowledged him. "I also came out a little better than some of you did," he said. "But here's how I look at it. Eb's my old friend. I could share with him, and I could pick and choose a few more friends. But if I do that, all I do is set us against each other. People would have every right to ask me why I helped some and not others. I think the only way to do this is to share as a group. We could each bring in all that we have; then we could dispense food according to family needs. And we can also do what Brother Riddle said: we scrounge and we fish, and we add to what we have that way."

"That's exactly right," a man in the back of the chapel said, and the bishop added, "Thank you, Brother Davis. That's the spirit that will get us on through. And it's what I had in mind too. But it won't be enough. What I need is for some of the younger men—'specially some of our unmarried sons—to go work in places where good crops are expected, and to take their pay in wagonloads of grain. I'll also talk to Elder Snow. I suspect that not every settlement outside Long Valley has been hit the way we were. Some of our brothers and sisters in Dixie might be able to send provisions."

And then he said in a softer voice, "I know when these grasshoppers showed up that we all wondered when the Lord was ever going to intercede and smooth our path for us a little. I don't know why that didn't happen, but I do know this. We put up with almost everythin' the sun and wind could throw at us down on the Muddy, and we came out of it a stronger people. And unified. Brother Marchant wasn't there with us, and maybe that's why he wants to go it alone. But once a man has been beaten down a few times, and he understands that he can only thrive and prosper *with* his brothers, not by fightin' against 'em, he changes the way he thinks. Hosea will see that in time."

There was quiet for a moment, and then Brother Evans, a wiry little Welshman, asked, "But could you tell me this, Bishop? How come the Lord couldn't send a few seagulls?"

Brother Evans's voice was full of laughter, and the bishop smiled. "I guess we're too far from the sea," he answered.

"I know that's true. But up in Salt Lake City, when the crickets come, the Lord sent a cloud of seagulls, and they et up them crickets. I know there's no big lake here, but I kept praying for hawks or eagles or jays—or some sort of bird—to fly in and help us, and they didn't come. So here's my question: what do we have to do to get on the Lord's bird list?"

Everyone was laughing now, but the bishop said, "It's actually a good question, Brother Evans." He waited for quiet to return. "Sometimes the Lord does intervene, and sometimes He doesn't, and we always wonder why. But we'll never know the answer. What I do know is that we have to be worthy of the Lord's blessings at all times, and, even more, ready to accept His will, no matter what we face. I suspect the Lord still wants us to learn more about loving our brothers and sisters and blessing one another's lives. Maybe we'll know before long why that's so important."

Brother Alexander Hart raised his hand. "Bishop," he said, "I've been around longer than most of you, and I remember 1854 and 1855, up in Nephi. The true name of these grasshoppers is Rocky Mountain locusts, and they've eaten up many a crop, long before now—more than crickets ever did. But they come and go. Most people believe that plowing kills off their eggs, and that's why they sort of disappear after you've settled a place and stayed for a year or two. The best answer we found was to plant a lot more than we needed and let the hoppers have their share. The Lord's with us; we don't need to question that. And most of all, we don't have to shed tears and think we got a bad deal. There's many in this world a whole lot worse off than we are."

There was a rumble of agreement in the congregation. Morgan was one who was nodding and saying, "That's right, Brother Hart." And Morgan told himself that it was the attitude he needed to take.

• • •

During the following days, Morgan thought often about the optimism he had felt when he and his family had first arrived in

Long Valley half a year earlier. He had found hope in the valley itself, with its moderate weather, and even more, he had liked the change he felt in himself. He had always clung to his own independence—didn't like to be told what to do. But after the miracle that saved his son, he had offered his will to God. And he liked what that had done to him. The move to Long Valley had been arduous, but Morgan had devoted himself to helping everyone in their company. He had always taken pride in his practical skills, and he had always been willing to help people, but more than before, he felt connected to the entire group, and he believed that that was what God had wanted of him all along.

The Muddy River settlers had arrived in Long Valley in March 1871. They had made a seemingly impossible climb up the long dugway over the Hurricane cliffs—a passage many times more difficult than the ascent onto the Mormon Mesa in Nevada—and then they had continued across the desert of northern Arizona to Pipe Springs and Kanab. Travel in the sand had tested the draft animals to the limit, and many of the wagons had broken down. Then, after the settlers had dealt with heat for many days, Long Valley, north of Kanab, had been cold in March. Angeline, Ruth, and Jefferson had wrapped themselves in quilts in the wagon, and the two mothers had held their babies close. They had worried about the measles that had broken out among the children in the wagon train. Two of Bishop Gibson's daughters had died. These deaths were heartbreaking to the entire company, and Angeline and Ruth inspected Jefferson and the little ones every day, fearing signs of the disease.

But the babies—Morgy, Angeline's son, and Ella, Ruth's daughter—had survived, and when trees began to bud out and grass began to green, everyone became more hopeful. Green was something they hadn't seen much of in recent years. And when the men turned over soil with their shovels, the dirt was dark and loamy. That was the kind of land they could understand.

Long Valley was narrow. It would never sustain a big population. But the cream-colored cliffs, set off against the junipers and piñon pines on the hillsides and the willows along the river, all made the place look like the sort of country Morgan was used to. Even the tightness of the valley seemed cozy after the newcomers had looked out across flat stretches of sage and mesquite for three years. Still, it was that soil they loved most. Morgan had grabbed a handful and smelled it. "We'll have a short season here, compared to the Muddy Valley," he told Angeline, "but we'll have good crops, good gardens. This feels like a reward, after all we've been through."

The settlers had camped in the south part of the valley, and John R. Young, Brigham Young's nephew, had called a meeting that night. Brother Young, on assignment from the First Presidency, had led the wagon train to the valley from St. George, and he would help them get resettled. He assigned those from New St. Joseph, West Point, and Overton—towns on the Muddy—to occupy an area where the canyon opened up, just a short distance north of their camp. Those from St. Thomas would move farther north, through a narrow spot and into another, wider section of the valley.

Brother Young instructed each group to locate a site for a town center where a church would be built. The plan was for the people to build houses close to the church, and five-acre farms, assigned by lottery, would surround the town. "It's all good land," Brother Young told the people. "It doesn't matter too much which parcel you receive. There are also quite a few houses scattered nearby, built by Saints who lived here earlier and got driven away during the Indian war. Some of the folks who got pushed out of here a few years back have let Apostle Snow know that they want to come back, so we'll stay away from their farms. But the places that aren't spoken for could be repaired and occupied, and that would save you some time in getting your families inside."

Morgan liked that idea, so he spoke to John Young after the meeting. "How do we choose one of those existing houses you talked about?" he asked.

"Some of that is still up in the air," Brother Young said. His manner of speaking reminded Morgan of his uncle Brigham, and he was practical in the same way, but he seemed more measured in his responses. He took hold of Morgan's arm and turned him a little—as though to keep the conversation only between the two of them. "I know of one farm that's in rough shape, but it's one you could have for the taking—and the land nearby has been plowed and planted before. Later, if your family gets bigger, you may want two houses anyway, and you could build another place on a town lot."

"That sounds good. Where is it?"

Brother Young, a man not yet fifty, had a well-trimmed beard and a somewhat longer mustache. He touched his fingers to that beard now and seemed to consider for a few seconds. "That's just the thing," he finally said. "It's a little north of the town we're calling Mt. Carmel, but I believe you lived in St. Thomas. Those folks are going north to Berryville."

"I only lived in St. Thomas toward the end of our time down there. I could go with either group. But maybe someone else should take the house you're talking about. I can surely build a house and break ground as well as the next man. It's just that our baby—Ruth's little girl—has suffered from this move, and I'd like to get her in out of the cold as fast as I can."

"Sure. That makes sense. I'll have Brother Carrington draw you a map so you can find the place, and if you want it, we'll call it yours. The only thing is, it might be best to see what you can learn about the owner. He says he's not coming back, but he may want some compensation for his place."

"Where does he live?"

"As I understand it, his name is Joshua Burt, and he took his family over to Washington, by St. George. Apostle Snow, taking direction from Brigham, told people that if they're not returning, they should give up all claim to their property. Still, if it was me, I'd make a trip over there before too long and maybe get something down on paper."

"All right. But I think I'll move in for now."

"You can't get in immediately, Brother Davis. The report I got is that it needs a lot of work."

As it turned out, John Young's words were an understatement. On the following day, Morgan had driven his wagon out onto a flat lot still covered with patches of snow. He liked seeing that the grubbing of brush had been done, and he liked the location, under some pink cliffs, with the Virgin River not far away. But the house was even worse than he had expected. The roof had fallen in, and one wall had collapsed.

"Oh, dear," Angeline said when she saw it, and he heard her draw in air as though she were trying to hold back what she actually wanted to say.

"Don't make up your mind yet," Morgan said. "Let me have a look." He got down from the wagon and approached the house. But what he could see through a window, he didn't want his wives to see. When he rubbed the glass to clear some dirt, the sound sent mice scattering inside. He could see larger droppings, too, and he wondered what sort of critters had been living in the place: skunks? porcupines?

He walked around and checked the walls that were standing. The house had never been well built. It was thrown together with rough poles as studs and rafters. He might have to tear much of it down before he started rebuilding.

When Morgan returned to the wagon, he could tell that Angeline and Ruth had been talking, and he had a pretty good idea what they had been saying. "Listen," he told them, "the house is almost worthless, no question, but this land has been plowed before. I can get it planted without all the grubbing I'd have to do on a new farm. Even if I tear the house down and start over, we're way ahead this way."

"But how long will we be outside?" Angeline asked.

"Not as long as if I started trying to get the land cleared first, the way I'd have to do in other places. I'll work on this old house today and salvage what I can. But in a week or so, we can get inside. Maybe after that, we can build a new house next door—or in the settlement. But don't look inside, all right? Let's get our tent set up, and we can get by with that for now. You're used to cooking outside."

He watched them both nod, as if to say, "It's just one more thing to deal with." He was proud of them that they held back any complaints they may have felt.

• • •

Ruth had learned not to expect too much. She had never been indulged as a little girl, had never had any luxuries in her life. But living in a tent, even for a short time, worried her because of her daughter. Little Ella had proven herself a fighter at first, tough in her own way, but something had happened in the move, first from the Muddy to St. George, but even more on the hard climb into the mountains and in the desolate desert between the Hurricane cliffs and Kanab. Ella had seemed to lose some of that tautness in her little body. She had stopped crying and begun to whimper. She had stopped sucking as if desperate for sustenance, and she sometimes lost interest entirely. She didn't seem sick, exactly, but maybe battered, perhaps by the heat and then the sharp cold. Ruth's only thought now was to keep her warm, feed her well, and get her through these next few weeks until gentler weather would come on.

Morgan got the tent staked while Angeline and Ruth and the little ones sat in the wagon. Angeline had protested that she could help, but Morgan had told her to help Ruth with the children, and she had given way to his request. But after the women carried their things into the tent, arranged quilts for beds, and made little stacks of their belongings, Angeline said to Ruth, "Are you all right for now? I want to have a look into that house."

Ruth laughed. "Morgan told you not to do that."

"Morgan tells me lots of things. But I'm not moving into that house until all the 'critters,' as he calls them, are *exterminated.* If there's a snake in that disaster of a house, I want it gone—with all its brood of little snakelings."

"I don't like rattlesnakes," Ruth said, "but garden snakes don't bother me."

"As far as I'm concerned, every snake is Satan himself. I don't trust any of them."

Jefferson was sitting in the center of the tent with his legs crossed in front of him. "I'm not scared of snakes," he said.

"Well, aren't you a big brave boy?" Angeline said. "Your aunt Angeline is not so brave as you."

"I know."

"Is that because you're a little man, Jeffy?"

Jefferson nodded. Ruth liked hearing some confidence from him. He was still small for his age, but he was stronger than he had once been, and she had noticed lately how much he tried to model his behavior on Papa's. Morgan was not his real father, but Jefferson had accepted him fully now. Jefferson had even taken on some of Morgan's mannerisms, pressing his shoulders back when he had something he wanted to say, and slowing the pace of his words when he wanted "his mothers" to pay attention to his opinion. Ruth liked to see him do that. Morgan's example was so much better than anything Jefferson might have learned from her first husband, who had died when a wagon had turned over on him.

Angeline wrapped the boy up in her arms. "Well, you're not too big for hugs. I know that much."

He giggled. And Ruth felt happy. She always felt Angeline's love for her children, and Ruth loved little Morgy the same way. That was something she had never expected out of plural marriage. She was now preparing herself for another change, another year of hard work and big adjustments, but she was better off than she had been when she had first met Angeline and Morgan and had envied Angeline for having such a fine husband.

• • •

Angeline did look into the house, and she did tell Morgan that she wanted to clean every inch of the place before they moved into it. "That's fine," Morgan told her, and he laughed at the way she pinched her nose at the smell of the place. "Let me tear things down first. I'll have to cut some timber, too, and get something temporary put together. But when I can, I'll find a way to have some timber milled, and we'll finish things out nice inside."

She believed that. One thing she could always trust was that no one would work harder than Morgan, and no one could ever care so much about making her happy.

• • •

Over the next few days, as he tore the little two-room house apart, Morgan would look up and see Angeline pulling out refuse from inside, which she would carry off and dump well away from the house. He told her she didn't need to do that, but, as always, he was proud that she liked to work alongside him.

In two days Morgan had salvaged what he could of the house, and then, for two more days, he had cut tall pine trees from a canyon nearby, trimmed them, and hauled them back. He had begun to assemble something that was more a shack than a house, but he reused the sideboards from outside and daubed the openings with mud, making the house as tight as he could. The fireplace had disintegrated in places, so he used rock and mud mortar to patch it together. It was nine days, not a week, before he moved the family inside, but he was pleased—and very thankful—that they had enough of a house to get by with. He was glad, too, that he had bought a plow in St. George. As soon as the snow was gone and the earth warmed a little, he began to plow the ground. Ben and Buck, his oxen, were getting old, but they could still put in a good day of work. While passing through St. George, Morgan had also managed to trade a few belongings for what seeds he needed, and by April he had planted his fields—no cotton this time, but corn, wheat, barley, and oats.

He had also plowed a garden spot, and while he was working in his fields, Angeline had done most of the planting in the garden. He gave her a little reprimand for that. "I don't want you to work so hard," he told her. "I think you do better when you don't push yourself quite so much."

"Do better at what?"

"You know what I'm talking about. Better at making babies for us."

"You're the one who hasn't done much to make that happen lately, Morgan. Don't blame me."

"But I'm working hard to get us out of that tent—and then maybe some opportunities will come along."

She smiled mischievously, and he liked that. He remembered that look from the early days of their marriage.

• • •

Good days followed. It seemed as though the Lord had finally decided to bless the efforts of the settlers who had stuck out their mission on the Muddy. He was giving them a gift of mild days, flourishing crops, and lovely cool nights for good sleeping. Morgan spent all his spare time that summer improving the house, hauling lumber and having it milled in Kanab so that he could plank over the open studs inside. He put down a puncheon floor and repaired all the windows and doors. But most important, he added one more room. For the first time, Angeline and Ruth had a large room they could share—a kitchen plus sitting room—and they also each had a small bedroom where they could have their own privacy or spend the night with Morgan. Jefferson slept in one corner of the big room, and Ella and Morgy slept in cribs in their mothers' rooms. What the family needed, of course, was more furniture, and they needed clothing to replace the bedraggled apparel they had brought with them from Nevada. But all that would come. The corn was soon growing tall, and the garden was looking lush and green and productive. Morgan said that once the harvest was in, they should have a little extra to buy chairs and better beds. He would make a fall trip to St. George and come back with some of the items they could afford. And in future years, things promised to improve ever so much more.

The best news was, Angeline whispered to him one night that she was expecting again, and with that, Morgan felt quite sure that life couldn't get much better.

And then the grasshoppers had come.

CHAPTER 2

With most of his crops destroyed, Morgan was left with little work to do on his farm. He and Angeline gleaned what wheat kernels they could, and then he plowed the field under, but he still had some time before he needed to plant his winter wheat. Bishop Morrison received word that the Saints in St. George had seed and other provisions they were willing to donate if men from Long Valley could bring wagons to haul the items back. Several young men had been called to travel north to Nephi and Payson, to work in the fields and haul back grain and produce. Morgan had volunteered to go with them, but Bishop Morrison asked him to head up the group that would make the hauling trip to St. George. So they planned the trip for late September, once the remains of the harvest were in.

Morgan's harvest of corn was less than a wagonload, but on the morning he drove it into town, he saw his friend Willard Branwell, an immigrant from Preston, England, and a neighbor to the Davises. Willard was one who had fought the desert in the Muddy Valley and always found a way to keep smiling. But he looked less cheerful this morning. He was sitting by the barn, leaning back against it. He seemed to pay no attention to Morgan at first, merely stared ahead. As Morgan got down from his wagon, however, Willard stood, and then he did smile. "Them grass'oppers took all I planted. I only brought in a few squash and turnips. So I been stayin' over 'ere, helpin' to unload wagons. It's 'bout the only thing I can do to help out."

"Well, thanks. I appreciate it," Morgan told him.

"I have lots of mouths to feed, you know," Brother Branwell said. "It's a worrisome time for me."

Willard had come to Utah with his wife Margaret and six children, and the following year he had married his wife's sister, who had migrated late. Each wife had since given birth to two children, so they had ten in all. "Both my wives is great with child again. If someone would tell me what causes that, I'd surely see that it doesn't happen no more." He laughed.

"It's a matter of the birds and bees, Willard. Or so they tell me. Chase down a hive of bees and maybe you can learn something."

Brother Branwell grinned. "Let me tell you something, Morgan. If Angeline has a sister, don't ever marry her. Margaret and Hannah love each other as sisters, and they hate each other the same way. At my house, it's always bickering and blaming, and all those children put up a noise louder than a steam engine pullin' a boat upriver. I have to stay out of the house as much as I can, just to hear myself think."

"But you always look happy."

"That's because I stay away from the house most of the time."

"I think you get along all right with those sisters—even if they quarrel a little from time to time."

The smile faded from Brother Branwell's face. "I'll tell you the truth, Morgan. Margaret asked me to marry her sister, and it wasn't what I wanted to do, but my bishop said it would be the right thing. Still, if I had it to do over, never would I do it. I'm a man who likes peace, not noise, not confusion, and I've known no peace at all these last few years."

"Build another house. I'll help you."

"Next season I will. But for this winter, the only thing I can think about is not letting my children go hungry."

"We'll all help with that, too, Willard. Don't worry." He clapped a hand down on Willard's bony shoulder and looked into his face. "We'll make it through."

"One more time."

"Yes, one more time."

But Morgan did worry, more than he wanted Brother Branwell to know. There were other troubles in the settlement that concerned him. There had been sickness going about—fevers and measles again. Morgan always worried what would happen if any of his children got sick and died—especially Morgy. Many of the women had lost little ones these last few years. That seemed to be part of life. But Morgan knew that Angeline would struggle more than most to deal with something like that.

• • •

Morgan used the next couple of weeks to cut more timber and build a storage shed and chicken coop. He even built a shed for his oxen. Then, toward the end of September, he set out with three other men, each with a double team of oxen pulling the wagons. The plan was to stay only two days, but Morgan had a plan of his own. When the little wagon train arrived in St. George, he hurried to load his wagon and take care of business the first day, and then he pushed on to Washington to find Joshua Burt, the man who had once owned the house the Davises had taken over. He had arranged to meet his wagon-train partners at the foot of the Hurricane cliffs before they made the ascent out of the valley.

When Morgan found Brother Burt, after asking around for directions to his farm, the man was out in a field plowing through wheat stubble, turning it under. Morgan walked out to him and introduced himself. He explained that he had moved into Long Valley. "We're building up a little settlement near the house you left behind up there. We've renamed the town Mt. Carmel."

Brother Burt was still standing behind his plow, one hand on the handle, but now he turned toward Morgan. "What was wrong with our name—Winsor?" he asked, and he sounded annoyed.

"I'm not sure how that happened. I think one of the Brethren said it looked like Mt. Carmel in the Holy Land."

"And not one of 'em has ever been there."

"You're probably right," Morgan said, and he laughed.

But Brother Burt didn't laugh. Instead, he asked, "So ya think I walked away from that farm, do ya?"

"I guess you didn't have much choice."

"That's 'zactly right. The Indians was stealin' everythin' in sight—killed some of our people, too. Brigham told us we better git out. We din't have enough settlers to defend oursel'es."

"That's what I heard. But they also tell me that you aren't planning to return."

"Who tol' ya that?"

Morgan didn't like the tone of this. Brother Burt was a little man, stocky, with a stubble of beard and heavy black eyebrows. One cheek bulged with a chaw, and his teeth were brown from the tobacco. His voice was tight and hard. He wrapped his reins around his shoulders, stood sideways, and stared at Morgan. His two big chestnut horses were waiting, flipping their tails but standing stiff.

"According to what John Young told me," Morgan said, "Elder Snow questioned all the old settlers from the area, and you were one who didn't express a desire to come back."

"I din't say I would, but I din't say I wouldn't, neither."

"Well, we need to talk about that. Your place had fallen in—the roof and one wall—and the chimney was breaking down. But I've fixed things up pretty well, and we've moved into it. According to Brother Brigham, those who didn't return were supposed to release all claim to their property. But I'm willing to—"

"You come out smellin' like a rose, din't you? You got ya a place, plowed and ready to farm, and a house to boot—all for nothin'."

"Not if you plan to come back. What do you have in mind?"

"I have in mind to stay right here and not go back and fight Indians agin." He turned his head and spat on the ground. "But I guess I thought if some feller took my property, at least he might pay me somethin' for the improvements I made and the ground I grubbed and plowed."

"That sounds fair to me."

"What does?"

"That I pay you something for it."

"Then how come yer talkin' about Brigham sayin' I was s'posed to hand it over an' just say, 'There you go. Have at 'er'?"

"I just want to do the right thing. I did benefit from your work, so I want to make that right with you. The only thing is, I don't have ready cash right now. We gave up everything when we left the Muddy, and maybe you heard about the grasshoppers that wiped out our crops. But, I'll—"

"Thass about what I thought. You'd like to pay somethin', but you jist can't."

"Not right now. But how about I make a payment after the

harvest next year, and then another one each year until we're right with each other?"

"How much?"

"What's fair?"

"You oughta owe me a hundred dollars, at th' very least."

"Well, Brother, the land up there is free to us, and that house was worthless, so I'm only paying you for the grubbing and plowing you did."

"See, thass what I knowed agin. You sound all righteous, but you ain't goin' to pay me a red cent. We might as well both admit to it right here. Take my land, do what you want with it, but admit to me straight out that yer a thief."

Morgan had to take a breath. There was a time in his life when he would have knocked the man on his back and walked away—with no regret. But this man was his brother, at least in name, and he didn't want to take on his nasty attitude.

"All I'm saying is, let's settle on a price. But a hundred dollars would make you the thief, not me."

"Git off this land, right now. I don't have to listen to ya talk that way to me."

"Fine. And I'll build me a new place when I get back. You can keep that land you never plan to live on, and maybe you can tell yourself it's still yours and feel good about that."

Morgan turned, so angry he knew he needed to get away before he said something even stronger.

"Fifty."

"What?"

"I'll take fifty."

Morgan didn't turn back yet. He was staring away. He still thought that was too much, but he also knew how little he wanted to go back and tell his family they would have to move again. So he did turn back. "All right. I'll pay you ten dollars a year, first payment next year."

Brother Burt nodded, spat another brown stream on the ground, and turned back toward his horses.

"We better put something in writing, Brother Burt."

"I don't write. You write it down if you want to."

"Will you sign it?"

"I don't sign. If you ain't a man of yer word, jist tell me right now. I'll shake yer hand on it, if thass what you want, but I don't need to sign nothin' to make a promise and keep it."

So Morgan walked back to Brother Burt, and he did shake his hand. "Fifty dollars. Ten dollars a year paid after each harvest, starting next year."

They both nodded, and Morgan left.

• • •

Morgan walked ahead of his oxen to Hurricane, where he met his friends on time. The train of wagons ascended the steep climb over the cliffs, but quadruple teams were required to get the wagons—now laden with heavy loads—up to the ridge. Only one wagon at a time could make the climb, and then the cattle had to be brought back and rested before they could pull another wagon up the grade. It took the better part of a day to pull all four wagons over the top. It took three more days to reach Mt. Carmel, and when they got there, Morgan told his wives only that he had "made an arrangement" with Joshua Burt, and they could plan to stay in the house he had rebuilt.

Bishop Morrison reported on the following Sunday that the total harvest in Mt. Carmel and Glendale had not been quite so lean as predicted, and the Saints had been honest in bringing in what they harvested. The additional provisions sent from St. George would also help, as would the loads expected from northern Utah. Still, supplies were not abundant, and the high hopes that the Saints had felt as they had entered the valley were muted now. Morgan sensed a hint of discouragement as he spoke to other farmers, and he saw the worry in everyone's eyes, even the children's. Young people were already being told to be sparing in what they ate, and most of them remembered how hungry they had sometimes been during their time on the Muddy.

• • •

Christmas was coming, and Ruth wished that she could do something special for her children. Jefferson had turned six that fall, and he had never known a Christmas with nice presents or a Christmas feast. Jefferson was friends with Aaron Branwell, Willard's son, who lived not far down the road from them. Aaron, who was older than Jefferson, had been talking for weeks about Christmas coming soon. The Branwells liked to keep Christmas according to their traditions in England—to the degree they could. What Ruth knew was that she and Angeline had little they could use to cook a fine meal, and the Branwells had less. She had talked to Morgan about that, and he had only said, "I'm afraid Christmas will be a day like any other, Ruth. If we eat too much now, we'll have nothing left by spring. Let's not say much about presents. Let's teach Jeff that the best things about Christmas are remembering Jesus and hearing His story."

"We will do that, Morgan. But if we could just do something a little nicer, that would cheer us all up."

Morgan had nodded, hadn't agreed, hadn't argued.

It was Angeline who said, "Could you shoot a goose or a pheasant—something we could roast?"

"I've not had much luck at that," Morgan told her. "I have no shotgun, and not as many bullets for my rifle as I really need. I waste too many, trying to hit a dodging rabbit, and when I do shoot something, the bullet ruins most of the meat."

"Well, that's fine. We'll have our mush and milk, and maybe a slice of bacon with it."

Ruth heard the sarcasm in Angeline's voice, and surely Morgan did too. "I don't know what you want from me," he said. "I'd kill a hog if we had one. I'd trade some of our carrots for a fine turkey—if anyone had one—but we can't change what is, not this year. We'll just have to get by on what we do have and know that everyone else is in the same situation."

"We understand," Ruth said. "We really do."

But Angeline was never as easily placated, and Ruth thought she detected a bit of belligerence in her sister wife's silence. Later, when Morgan had left the house, she told Ruth, "I know how to use that rifle. My father taught me to shoot, and I was good at it. I also know that Morgan still has some bullets he keeps in the shed. I'm going to walk down to the pond this afternoon and see if I can't shoot one of those geese I've seen there."

"Angeline, you shouldn't do that. Morgan won't—"

"I know everything Morgan will say. I shouldn't be out roaming around the banks of a pond in *my condition,* and shooting might deafen my poor little baby. Also, I'm well aware that if I shoot and miss, he'll notice some bullets gone and take me to task for wasting them."

"And what would you say to that?"

Angeline was churning butter. In the spring Morgan had plowed a man's field as a trade for a sorry-looking old cow. But

Ruth and Angeline were glad of it now, with fresh milk available every day—and some to trade or sell—and above all, for the butter. But butter took work. Each day the milk had to set until the cream separated and could be skimmed off. About every third or fourth day, Ruth or Angeline—or sometimes even Jefferson—churned the cream, and then the buttermilk had to be squeezed off before the butter could be molded.

Without looking up from her work, Angeline said, "Well, I don't plan to miss, so I'll tell him, 'Look at this fine goose I shot. Now clean it and pluck it and set it out to freeze, so it will still be fresh for Christmas.'"

Ruth didn't like anything about this plan. She wasn't one to defy or to take chances, and she had to agree with Morgan that such behavior was reckless and wasteful. And yet, she rather wished she had the nerve to do such a thing, and somehow, she trusted that Angeline *could* do it. So Ruth said, "Well, if you're going to try to shoot one, let's go now, while the weather is clear and Morgan is gone."

Angeline laughed. "So you're in cahoots with me?"

"No. But I know you'll go whether I go with you or not, so I'd better be there—in case you slip and fall in the pond."

"What about the children?"

"I'll wrap them up. We can't leave them here alone." But Ruth worried about that. She knew she would have to stand back and not let Jefferson see the killing—if it actually happened.

So, while Angeline finished her churning, Ruth bundled up the babies and found Jefferson's warm coat and gloves. Angeline, with the rifle over her shoulder and her belly swelling under her coat, strode down the road carrying Morgy in one arm. Ruth carried Ella and held Jefferson's hand. Jefferson kept asking where they were going, but he was excited; Ruth could hear it in his voice. He had seen the rifle and was surely wondering why Aunt Angeline had brought it along.

As it turned out, the pond was mostly iced over, only the middle still open. Ruth saw no geese or ducks in the water, but Angeline was pointing by then. "They're over there," she whispered, "on the bank." A thin layer of snow covered the mud. Ruth could only think that it was a long shot, and the walk over to retrieve anything Angeline killed would be scary, maybe dangerous.

"I've got to get much closer," Angeline said.

"But you can't—"

"I need to get close enough to have a good shot, but we can't scare them off. Keep the children here."

There were six white geese together in a little flock. All of them were taking in the sun on this cold but pretty day, and they had their heads tucked back against their bodies. Ruth could only imagine the blood that would fly, and the meat that would surely be ruined, even if Angeline made a good shot.

Angeline was stepping carefully over the snow, and the mud was frozen enough that she wasn't sinking in. She took a few steps and waited, then kept edging closer and closer. She was eventually not more than twenty yards away, and the birds hadn't moved at all. She raised the rifle to her shoulder. Ruth kept whispering to Jefferson to be quiet, but he was getting more anxious all the time. "What's she doing, Mama?" he asked.

Ruth decided it was time to retreat. She didn't want Jefferson to see this. But suddenly there was a voice behind her. "Angeline," the voice called, "what are you doing?"

Ruth spun around to see Morgan walking fast toward her. Then she turned and looked back at Angeline. At that moment the geese all raised their heads, and a second later, Angeline fired. One of the geese dropped onto the snow. The other geese were up now, and just as they were stretching to take flight, Angeline fired again, and this time Ruth saw a bird's head explode.

By now Morgan had run past Ruth and was heading toward Angeline. "Angie, what in the world are you doing?" he shouted.

"Getting us a goose for Christmas dinner." She turned and smiled at him. "And one for the Branwells."

Morgan hurried past Angeline and on to the two geese on the ground. He grabbed them both by the neck and hoisted them into the air. "You shot their heads off," he said. "Both of them." He was standing with arms stretched wide, the two geese hanging limply, blood running over their white feathers. Ruth could see how astounded he was as his eyes jerked back and forth, one bird to the other.

"I didn't want to ruin the meat," she said.

"I know. But—"

"I was almost on top of them, Morgan. That's why I got so close. When you yelled, they stretched their necks, and I had a perfect shot."

"But you shot their heads right off."

"I've been shooting all my life. My father taught me to shoot chicken hawks and running jackrabbits."

"Mine, too. But I can't shoot like that."

Ruth couldn't see Angeline's face. She was still looking toward Morgan. But she heard Angeline laugh. "There's lots of things I do better than you. Don't be so surprised."

"What did Aunt Angeline do?" little Jefferson asked.

Ruth knelt down next to him. "She got us some geese for Christmas dinner. Won't that taste good?"

"I don't know."

"Well, it will. And we'll take one to Aaron's house, so they'll have a nice dinner too."

"Did she kill the gooses?"

Ruth thought for a few seconds, and then she said, "Well, yes. We don't kill just to kill. But we kill animals for food sometimes. You understand that, don't you?"

"I saw Brother Branwell kill a chicken," he said. "He chopped its head off, just like Angeline."

Ruth had no idea that Jefferson had seen such things. "Well, yes. It's the same thing—mostly."

Morgan was walking back now, and he seemed quite pleased, but he told Angeline, "You shouldn't be out here, you know. I saw your tracks in the snow and followed you here, but I never thought of anything like this. What if you'd fallen down, for heaven's sake?"

"Well, I guess I would've gotten back up. But why would I fall?"

Now Morgan was laughing. "You go home and rest," he said. "I'll take care of these birds." What Ruth heard was pride in his voice. She was well aware that she would never win Morgan's admiration the way Angeline so often did.

• • •

Christmas wasn't fancy, nor did Angeline enjoy the goose all that much. The meat seemed a little gamy, and she thought maybe a nice chicken would have tasted better. All the same, she was proud of herself, and Morgan told the story of her shooting the geese to Eb and to his other friends.

Morgan had cut a small piñon pine and brought it into the house. They didn't have popcorn or colored paper to make chains, so they decorated it with a few strands of red yarn, which delighted Jefferson and attracted far too much attention from Morgy and Ella.

Jefferson ate very little of the goose, so Angeline and Morgan carried much of it to the Branwells to add to the other goose that Morgan had taken over earlier. Morgan had checked with the bishop, who said the Branwells certainly needed the extra food more than anyone. Morgan had also brought some little sacks of molasses candy back from St. George, and he gave a sack to the Branwell children. There was only one piece for each child; still, they passed the sack among themselves and then savored the taste. But the children made more noise than an entire chicken coop of hens, and Angeline was happy to wish them well and make her escape.

When she and Morgan returned home, it turned out that Morgan had brought, in addition to another sack of candy, little gifts for his own family. Jefferson liked a short rope that Morgan gave him—one he could use to lasso "calves" while riding his stick horse. He was also thrilled that Papa had brought him two books. Jefferson was learning to read. These books were just a little difficult for him still, but they could be read to him for now—until, gradually, he would learn to read them himself. Morgan had also bought a dainty little dress that Ella could wear to church, and for Morgy, a toy wagon with two carved oxen.

Morgan had not told Angeline that he had bought the gifts; he had kept them hidden away. She was a little put out with him for that. "So, if you had those," she asked, "why didn't you say something?"

"Well . . . I wanted them to be a surprise."

"Where did you get the money?"

"I sold something. You don't have to know what."

"I think it was your pocketknife that you said you lost."

Morgan only smiled. Angeline thought he was enjoying this

a little too much. "You told us there wouldn't be a thing for Christmas," she said.

"I know. But I thought if I said anything about presents for the children, you would wonder why I didn't get something for you and Ruth."

Angeline had not yet cleared the dinner plates, so now she picked up a plate in each hand and walked to the dry sink. "I wouldn't have wondered any such thing. It's the children—"

"But I did get you something. Both of you."

Angeline was as astounded as Morgan had been when she had shot the geese. "And why have you kept that a secret all day?"

Morgan stepped closer to Angeline and smiled. His blue eyes were gleaming against his sun-browned skin. Sometimes she forgot how truly handsome he was, but he had shaved today and dressed in his Sunday clothes. He looked wonderful. "I thought I'd wait until you thought you were going to bed without a single gift for Christmas, and then surprise you all the more. But I couldn't stand to wait any longer."

"Well, now, don't you think you're clever?"

"Yes, as a matter of fact, I do."

"We don't have anything for you, so don't think that we do." She walked back to the table and then returned to the sink with more plates. Morgan picked up some knives and forks and brought them to her.

"I know you don't have anything," Morgan said. "You had no chance to—"

"But we *do* have something." Angeline looked at Ruth, who was smiling back at her.

"Why didn't you—"

"Same reason."

"Now, don't you think you're the clever pair?"

"We do," Angeline said. "Don't we, Ruth?"

"We certainly do."

Angeline walked to the kitchen cabinet and came back with a brown-paper package. Morgan hefted it, smiled, and then took his time removing the paper, as though to relish the moment. Inside the paper were two pairs of knitted wool stockings. "Just what I need," Morgan told them. "My feet will stay warm the rest of the winter."

Morgan suddenly stood up and walked to the door and on outside. When he returned, probably from the shed, he was carrying two small packages. He presented one to Ruth and one to Angeline, all the while smiling as though he had just completed a magic trick. Angeline and Ruth opened the packages at the same time. In each was a golden locket on a chain. Angeline thought hers was far too lovely, too delicate for a person like herself—one who had never cared much about pretty things, women's things. But she loved the locket, loved that in their stretched circumstances, Morgan had wanted to give something pretty to her—and to Ruth. It was something that would bind them, the shared gift, each exactly like the other's.

Christmas was as happy as Angeline had hoped, and better than in any of the years on the Muddy, where snow had never covered the sand.

• • •

It was spring, toward the end of March, when Angeline felt her labor pains come on. It was late in the evening when she finally sent Morgan to fetch Sister Ballif. The pains were hard and kept getting worse. Morgan was not allowed in the room with the women, so he went off to Ruth's bedroom. He put Morgy down to bed, and the boy slept through the moans from the other room. But Morgan didn't sleep. He lay on his bed, fully dressed, ready in case Sister Ballif called him in, but on and on went the muffled cries of pain and the soft rumble of women's voices. "That's good. That's good," he would hear them say. "You're doing fine."

But she wasn't doing fine, and finally Morgan was pacing the floor listening to the agony as Angeline resisted screaming but let out sharp, high-pitched little cries. She had always taken on difficulty with stoicism, but this was hurting her in a way that he had never imagined—apparently more than when Morgy had come into the world. And then finally, early in the morning, Morgan heard a little desperate screech, a baby trying out its lungs for the first time.

Morgan stood at the door and waited. He knew there were still things to do. The women wouldn't want him in the room yet. But finally, he didn't care. He opened the door a crack, peeked into the room, and then stepped inside.

Sister Ballif was just placing a little bundle in Angeline's arms. "I was just about to come for you," she said.

"I couldn't stand to wait anymore."

"That's a good sign. Some men go out to the woodshed so they won't have to listen to their wives cry out."

"I thought about it."

Angeline was looking serene and exhausted. "Come look," she said, her voice barely more than a whisper.

Morgan walked to the bed.

"So what was it you wanted?" Angeline asked. "A boy or a girl?"

"A healthy baby. That's all," Morgan replied.

"Well, then, will you settle for a girl this time?"

Morgan laughed. He had another daughter.

Angeline pulled back the blanket from the baby's face, and then she handed the little girl to Morgan. "She's a big girl, like me," Angeline said. "Not a dainty little thing like Ella. I hope she'll be prettier than her mother."

"Don't expect *that much* of her. But how are you, Angie? You look so tired."

"I am tired. But I'm happy. Two children, when I feared I would never have any."

"Yes. Yes." He glanced at Ruth. "Four children. We're becoming a true family."

Ruth walked closer and took her own look at the little girl. "It's been such a long winter," she said. "It's good to have a lovely little blossom come forth in the spring."

"I'll tell you the truth," Morgan said. "I know you both thought I wanted another boy, but it's not what I was feeling. There's nothing in all the world so nice as a little girl to sit on a man's lap and hug him around the neck. Now I have two little girls, and Ella is doing just fine after we worried so much about her last year. It's more than one man deserves." Morgan watched the baby as she grimaced, then almost seemed to smile, her eyes still closed. She was a little blossom, still red as a rose.

"What do you want to name her?" Angeline asked.

"I don't know. You decide."

"All right, then. I want to name her Naomi. Ruth, in the Bible, loved Naomi. So it seems right."

Morgan liked the idea, and when he looked at Ruth, he saw tears well up in her eyes. He knew she liked the idea too.

CHAPTER 3

Morgan knew he was grinning before he even stepped through the door of his house. But once inside, no one seemed to pay him much attention. Angeline was bent over Naomi's crib, apparently having just put her down to sleep. Ruth was at the fireplace, peering into a pot that was emitting a rather foul aroma, and Jefferson was playing on the floor with his little sister and brother, who were laughing at his antics.

Morgan waited, still smiling. Angeline took a step away from the crib but then stopped when she looked at Morgan. "What are you up to?" she asked.

"Up to? What are you talking about?"

"You're looking like the cat that ate the canary."

"Not me. I was just wondering, what's for dinner?"

Ruth was looking at him by then. "You know very well what's for dinner."

That morning Morgan had dug up some sego-lily roots and collected some wild greens in the woods, where they were just beginning to grow. The spring had not offered much in the way of food to be scrounged, and the early garden would not be producing anything for weeks. This was the hardest time now, and everyone in Mt. Carmel was making do with what was left of last fall's meager harvest and donations. But Morgan, more than most, prided himself on what he could dig up along the river or on the mountainsides.

"You know what might taste good with those greens and roots?"

Now Jefferson was standing up, as though he were catching on. Morgan was holding a wicker basket, and surely the smell from it had to be making its way around the room by now.

"Fish!" Jefferson said. "Fish would be good."

"I do believe you're right," Morgan said, and then he reached into his basket and pulled out a big trout—one he estimated to be a foot and a half long. "Anyone want some of this? Look what I've caught." He raised the fish in the air, smiling all the while. He let everyone enjoy the moment before he put the fish back in the basket, and then he knelt down and let Jefferson look inside. Morgan had caught seven trout, the others smaller than the big one he had shown them, but all very nice fish.

"Oh, Morgan, that's wonderful," Angeline said. "Clean them right now and we'll start frying them."

"Well, now, wait a minute. We can't eat them all. Let's keep two—or maybe three—and I'll take the rest to the storehouse. They'll get shared with families that are out of food."

"Why, Morgan?" Angeline asked. "Any of the men can fish. We could make meals of these again tomorrow."

Morgan understood. He had let the thought run through his head as he was walking back to the house from the river. But he told Angie, "We can't start thinking that way. Remember the potatoes the bishop gave us last week. Someone had turned those in. Whoever did that could have kept them for his own family, but he knew there were families who were completely out of potatoes."

"But all the men can start fishing now."

"Maybe, but the water has been high all spring, and today was the first luck I've had." Then he grinned again. "Besides, not every man is as good at fishing as I am. I'll tell you what. I'll keep four and take three to—"

"No. You're right. Just keep two for us, and take all the rest to the bishop."

"I think I'll take one to Eb—even though I said we shouldn't do it that way. Poor Eb never has been the fisherman that I am." He laughed, and then he looked into his basket again, admiring his catch.

"You'll take the big one to Eb—just to show off."

Morgan laughed even harder. She had him pegged. It was exactly what he had thought to do. He and Eb had fished together plenty, and they had always tried to outdo one another. But he didn't admit that to Angeline. "Mary Ann needs something good to eat. She still doesn't look good. I worry what's going to become of her—and whether she has enough milk for her baby."

"I know. I worry about her too. I visit her as often as I can and try to pick up her spirits."

Morgan knew that Angeline had been doing much more than that. She had brought diapers and laundry back with her, washed those things with her own on Mondays, and she had helped tidy up Mary Ann's house. Mary Ann simply had no strength, and the cold weather had been hard for her. She seemed worn down, maybe tired of the fight.

So Morgan cleaned his fish and gave two to Ruth, and then he cleaned the others while she got dinner ready. The trout tasted fresh and wonderful, and little Jefferson ate so much his stomach hurt, but it was a joy for Morgan to watch everyone and see how happy a little extra food made them.

After dinner, Morgan decided to walk to the Branwells' farm.

No one needed food more than the Branwells, so he decided to skip the storehouse and take some fresh fish to them. He knew the bishop would approve. But when he offered the fish, Morgan thought the roof might fall in from the children running back and forth, shouting, "This one's mine. I'll eat it up all by myself."

Brother Branwell chased them about and reprimanded them, but all with good cheer. When he finally had all the fish under his control, he passed them on to his wives and then said, "We had something of a supper already. But now if everyone gets a nice piece of fish, they'll go to bed very happy indeed."

"That's good," Morgan said. "Do you have a fishing pole?"

"Not exactly. I have a stick I've tried to use, with a bit of string. I've had no luck that way."

"I have a good fishing pole you can use," Morgan said. "Come with me tomorrow, and we'll fish together. It might be fish, more than anything, that gets us by these next few weeks."

"Morgan, I can't tell you what you've done to give me hope. And look at this kennel of barking dogs. They're almost too happy, I fear. We'll never have a quiet moment all evening."

"Get up early, Willard. Fish seem to be early risers. Come by my house for me, and we'll see if we can't keep your children just as wild tomorrow."

After that, Morgan walked on to Eb's house. He gave him the big fish and liked hearing Eb ooh and aah about it. "Well, I kept the big ones for myself, Eb," Morgan said. "But this minnow was a little too small for us to bother with. I thought someone like you—who never caught a big fish in his life—might settle for it."

"Now, just a minute. I seem to remember catching fish three times that long—longer than my arm—while you were settling for ones the size of your finger."

"That's the trouble with old age, Eb. The memory goes first. It's a sad thing to see you forget those *whales* I used to pull out of those little canyon streams just above Farmington."

Morgan glanced at Mary Ann, saw that she was smiling. "I think you both remember what you choose," she said. "But Morgan, thank you so much for that beautiful fish. I feel stronger already, just thinking of having a taste of it."

"I'll tell you what," Morgan said, and he looked at Eb. "Get up early in the morning and walk out to my place. Willard Branwell and I are going fishing. Do you still have that bamboo pole I brought you from St. George last year?"

"Of course I do."

"Do you remember anything at all about fishing?"

"I know *everything* about fishing."

"All right, then. Join us, and I'll show you where I took a whole basket of mighty monsters out of the Virgin River. We'll feed our families and share with everyone in town."

And so Morgan walked back to his place, and in the morning, he and Willard and Eb fished together. They did very well, too, with the river finally flowing more gently than it had all spring. Morgan even took some joy in Eb catching the biggest fish—and bragging about it. But what pleased him most was watching Willard get the idea. Morgan let him use his pole, and after missing a few, not setting the hook just right, Willard began to react at the right moment. He took immense joy in his catches. When the morning had passed, they had caught sixteen fish, which they shared through the storehouse. The day after that, more of the men in town were out fishing. The big catch lasted only a couple of weeks before success fell off, but in the meantime, a few more days had been made easier. And every day, the gardens were growing.

• • •

It was during the big fishing spree that Bishop Morrison found Morgan at home one night. Morgan was out at the shed, retrieving some firewood. The evenings were still cool, and a fire felt good in the house. Bishop Morrison had approached the house and then had seen Morgan coming around the corner. "Morgan, I wanted to talk to you for just a minute," he said.

"Sure. Come inside."

"It might be better if we talk out here."

"That's fine." Morgan set his armload of firewood on the ground.

"I've received word that the St. George Saints will send us some added provisions to get us through these last weeks before we start producin' our own food again."

"That's good news."

"Yes, but they want us to come and get it, if someone can take a wagon down to St. George."

"I can go again."

"Good. But I almost hate to see ya leave us. You've done so much to keep everyone agoin' this spring."

"Not really. People have all been good about helping each other."

"Morgan, I'm truly amazed at what a strong, good man you've grown to be. I know you used to worry about takin' advice from your leaders when it didn't fit with your own thinkin', but you—"

"I still do."

"Maybe so. But you don't let it stop you from listenin' and learnin'."

"Well, I'm trying."

"Then let me offer some advice I suspect you don't wanna hear."

"What's that?"

"It's somethin' I've been thinkin' about for a time, but maybe now's as good a time as any to bring it up with you."

"All right."

"You've put a toe in the water on this matter of the principle, but you need to think about divin' in all the way. If you want all the blessings of the Lord, take yourself another wife or two—or maybe more."

Morgan hadn't expected this. "No," he said resolutely. "I'm not interested in doing that. It's been hard enough to get used to the way we are now."

"I understand. I only said it was advice." The bishop laughed. "But I also said you're gettin' better at takin' advice. Maybe I was wrong."

Morgan couldn't think what to say.

"Well, never mind for right now. But think about it. Ask the Lord about it before you make up your mind. It's men like you—good leaders, good husbands, good fathers—who ought to raise up a righteous posterity and help build the kingdom of God." He patted Morgan on the shoulder, still smiling. "For now, there's somethin' else I was hopin' you could do. The St. George Saints will send back mostly wheat and corn flour and maybe some cured meat. But I was thinkin', if we all looked about and thought what items we could spare, you could do some tradin' for some molasses and maybe some fruit. Fruit ripens early in Dixie, and the children need to taste somethin' sweet. They also need fruit in their diet. Wouldn't some cherries or apricots be nice?"

"Sure. I may not have many talents, but if I may brag just a little, not many ever get the better of me when it comes to trading."

Bishop Morrison laughed. "I know that. And that's just why I wanted you to be the one to go."

"How soon shall I leave?"

"The sooner the better, but we need to ask 'round and see what we can find to trade."

So it was a few days before Morgan left town, with the oldest Branwell boy, Ezekiel—known as "Zeke"—by his side. The boy didn't talk much along the way, and when he did, he didn't say things of interest to Morgan. But they got along all right, since Morgan rather liked the time to think and consider what lay ahead for him.

In some ways, things couldn't have been better. Morgan's wives were getting along quite well these days—and that wasn't true in a lot of plural families. Jefferson had become a lively boy, not at all the sad little character he had once been. Ella was becoming a cute little girl who never stopped talking, and Morgy was a strapping lad, almost two. He seemed destined to be a big help on the farm someday. But Morgan had bigger hopes for him. He could surely be a missionary, as Morgan had not been so far. He could travel somewhere in the big world and carry the message of the gospel. Morgan had no doubt that Morgy would be a better speaker than Morgan had ever been. Angeline and Ruth always said he was a "beautiful" boy, but Morgan liked to imagine a good man who had been raised in the gospel and understood what it meant. Now, added to his hopes for his other children, Morgan had a feisty baby daughter, Naomi, who was already showing that she had a will of her own.

Morgan, however, was not so sure about himself. He wanted the farm to prosper, and he wanted more children. He also wanted to be a strength to the bishop and to his people. But sometimes he wondered what the end of all his work would be. If he labored all his days and raised a good family, surely that was all a man should hope to do in life. But he still wondered at times what else there might be. Maybe, if he could pull things together well enough, the prophet could send him off on a mission too, but the idea, in truth, actually frightened more than excited him.

When it came to taking a fish to his neighbors, Morgan was not shy, but he didn't like to dispute, didn't like to preach. Some things he believed but had no idea how to explain. Lately, he had begun to study the scriptures more than ever before—especially the Book of Mormon—and he felt his faith expanding. He thought a great deal about Christ and His teachings. For Morgan, the Atonement had become as real as planting seeds and knowing they would grow—by the grace of God. But he had no idea how he would preach such an idea. What worried him more were things inside him that he knew were not right, not all they ought to be. He gave fish away in spite of what he would have preferred to do, and not because it was natural to him. He resented men who didn't have enough gumption to get themselves out to the river to catch their own fish.

And yet, he knew that was not what Jesus Christ had preached. Nowhere in the scriptures did he see anything about taking care of one's own self and forgetting everyone else. He saw only admonitions to bless the lives of others, to be patient and long-suffering and generous. He knew that was right, so he told himself it was what he wanted to do—wanted to be. But his preference would have been to start a farm in the clearing of some distant woods, make it into the best farm he could, and let everyone else do the same. And if they didn't do for themselves, they could suffer their own consequences.

Still, he thought of Eb, who worked as hard as any man and yet wasn't possessed of great strength or even the instinct to grow things. And what about Mary Ann? She couldn't help it that she was frail and frightened. Morgan wondered why God hadn't made every person equally strong, equally good, equally resistant to temptation. The conclusion he had reached was that people had to forgive each other, acknowledge weaknesses in themselves, and not judge others harshly. Strong people needed to reach out a hand and hoist up the weak ones. But if that was his conclusion, it still wasn't his inclination. He didn't want a hand up from anyone, and deep down, he felt contempt for those who were always expecting others to help them get by.

So Morgan was disappointed in himself. He wondered whether his desire to do right, to help others, would ever become instinctive to him. He saw no sign that it was happening, and yet, it was what he knew he had to accomplish in life.

One thing Morgan refused to contemplate was his bishop's suggestion that he take on more wives. If that was what it took to become more like Christ, he would simply have to let it pass. He had given all his effort to making a life with two wives; he couldn't imagine how hard it would be to expand beyond that.

"How long before we stop?" Zeke asked.

Morgan smiled. "Well, I guess a man goes as far as he can, and then he stops. Not because he gets to where he wants to go, but just because he can only do so much."

Zeke turned and looked at Morgan, clearly confused by his response. "I was just thinkin', the oxen prob'ly need some rest."

That made Morgan laugh. "Yes, that's true. We think we're doing something, and all the while, we're being pulled by another power. That's important to remember."

Zeke looked even more perplexed, but Morgan didn't explain. He did decide, however, that it was time to stop for the day.

• • •

Naomi was crying, and Angeline was walking the floor with her. She wasn't sure what to do. She had sat in her rocker, keeping it rocking at a smooth and even pace while she sang softly, "Lullaby and Good Night." But the shrieking had continued. Naomi seemed to be in pain. Angeline bounced her a little, talked in her ear, told her how much she loved her, but nothing soothed her.

Finally Ruth stepped from her bedroom. She was wearing her long nightgown, the same as Angeline, and her hair was pinned up. That was something Angeline didn't often see, since Ruth always got up earlier than she did and was dressed and busy before Angeline got started. The firelight from the fireplace was playing off Ruth's face now, reflecting from her eyes. She looked concerned. "Do you want me to take her for a time?" she asked. "You need to get some rest."

"No. I can't rest so long as she's crying. I don't know what's going on. I changed her diaper, nursed her, rocked her. Nothing calms her down."

"The way she's squealing, I think it's colic."

"That's what I'm thinking too, but what can I do about it?"

"I wish we had some peppermint," Ruth said. "That's what my mother used to give her colicky babies."

"Where would we get peppermint?"

"We can't. I'm sorry."

Sometimes Angeline wished they weren't so far from everything. Morgan could have brought back some peppermint from St. George, if he had only known. There were just so many things that weren't as close as a store, the way they had always been in northern Utah when Angeline was growing up.

"Did she burp after you nursed her?"

"Not really. I tried, but she fell asleep, and then, when I put her down, she started crying like this."

"Let me try," Ruth said.

This was not what Angeline wanted. Sometimes Ruth implied that she knew more about mothering than Angeline did. Of course, she probably did know more. She was six years older than Angeline and had been a mother much longer. But Angeline resented the sense of superiority she heard in Ruth's voice. All the same, she handed Naomi over—and in truth, she was relieved to sit and rest for a few minutes.

Ruth held Naomi in one arm and rubbed her back in circles, all the while talking to her. "Does something hurt, little one? Do you have a bubble that won't come up? It's all right, sweetheart. We'll make it go away."

Naomi was still crying, but not with the same intensity. And Angeline began to pray. She was so tired, and she wanted to sleep for a while before dawn. But more than anything, she didn't want her baby to be in so much pain.

Ruth lifted Naomi, held her high against her shoulder, and continued to rub her back, pressing upwards, stroking. "Let it out, little one. I know it hurts. Just let it come out."

It didn't happen quickly, but finally Naomi let out a resounding burp and almost immediately began to quiet. Within a few minutes she stopped crying altogether and settled her little head against Ruth's neck. Angeline wanted her now, wanted her warm love, but she didn't want to jostle her and start her crying again. She tiptoed to the crib and got the blankets ready, and then Ruth very gently laid Naomi down.

Her soft breathing continued, and both women held still for a time. Finally, they backed away from the crib. By then, Angeline realized that she was the one crying now. She was just so relieved. She turned toward Ruth and pulled her into her arms. "Oh, thank you, dear sister. Thank you. Sometimes I don't know what I would do without you."

"You'll get the knack of it. Morgy never had colic, so you haven't had to deal with it. You saw what I did, didn't you?"

"Yes. But you have the touch. I don't know that I ever will." Angeline knew she was admitting what she hadn't liked to think—but she did feel that it was true.

"That's not the case at all," Ruth whispered. "Do you have any idea how much Jefferson loves you? He doesn't know the difference between Mama and Auntie. He just knows we both love him."

And that was true. When Angeline finally lay down, she thought she would fall asleep instantly, but she didn't. For a time she thought about Ruth. She still wished she didn't have to depend on her so, or that Ruth didn't make her feel inadequate in so many ways. She cooked better, she had more patience, and she was nicer to Morgan—almost never disagreeing with him. Angeline worried that Morgan would make the comparison and feel more love for Ruth. Angeline still wished that she didn't have to live this way, to share Morgan, but she also knew that if she had to have a sister wife, she would never find anyone dearer to her than Ruth had become. Angeline had no idea what would happen as life went on, whether they could always feel so good about each other, and she wondered how two growing families, joined together, might be able to stay happy. But she recognized—tonight—that Ruth was a blessing. She hoped, in time, she could be as much of a blessing to Ruth.

• • •

When Morgan reached home with his wagonload, he enjoyed showing the bishop what good bargains he had made. "Just what we need," Bishop Morrison kept saying as he looked over the tools that Morgan had thought to trade for. He had also gotten, along with a load of grain and produce, the molasses and the fruit that people longed for.

"I'm glad it's you dispensing all this, not me," Morgan said.

"You might have some fights on your hands. I was able to get some oranges, and everyone will want one."

"Let's get everythin' stored away so that no one knows what we have. I want ta talk to all our people before I hand things out."

So the two, with Zeke's help, carried the grain sacks and the bushel baskets into the storage house, and then Morgan and Zeke headed home in the wagon. But the bishop had let them each take enough fruit to give something to their family members. When Morgan stepped inside his own house, he held up an orange. "Anyone know what this is?" he asked.

"I know," Jefferson shouted. "Can I have it?" There had been a few oranges raised in the Muddy Valley, and Jefferson had tasted them before.

"How many do you have?" Angeline asked.

"One for each of us," Morgan said, and he grinned. "Of course, Naomi isn't quite ready for an orange. I didn't bring her one."

"What did you bring for her?" Jefferson asked. "Mostly, she likes to suck on her thumb."

"Well, she has two of those, so I didn't bring her another one. But the woman in the store in St. George said to bring this to her." He reached in his coat pocket and pulled out a little brown bag. "Sticks of peppermint. I think Jeff might like the taste of this, and Ella and Morgy too, but the woman said to give a little bit of it in water to the baby if she—"

"Has colic!" Angeline said, and she hurried to Morgan. "Oh, thank you. Thank you. It's exactly what we wanted a few nights ago. How did you know?"

"What are you talking about? I know everything."

But Angeline seemed more interested in the peppermint than she was in Morgan's all-knowing mind. She took the bag from him and showed the peppermint sticks to Ruth. And then everyone peeled and ate their oranges—without waiting for dinner.

Morgan was pleased by everything. But he noticed that Angeline and Ruth spent the evening sitting next to one another, discussing various things, just chatting at times. Angeline told Morgan about the terrible night when Naomi had cried for hours, and how Ruth had taught her to bring a burp up. That was nice, and Morgan liked to hear that Angeline could appreciate the help—since she had admitted her resentment at times. He wanted to tell them all about his trip to St. George, though, and all the good bargains he had made—but they didn't ask. Maybe they had gotten used to his trips and his tales of getting stuck in this river or that, or seeing Indians trail him for miles.

"I made some good deals in St. George," Morgan finally told them.

"You always do," Angeline said, and then she and Ruth continued to talk.

Morgan sat down by the fireplace and read his Book of Mormon. Or at least he let his eyes run over the words. He was thinking once again about his family, and about the future. Angeline and Ruth had been growing closer for a long time, but tonight they seemed more connected than ever. That was a good thing, of course, but sometimes he wished he could have more time with Angeline—with no one else around—the way life had been before Ruth had joined them.

• • •

On Sunday, Bishop Morrison spoke during church services in Mt. Carmel. "We now have additional foodstuffs," he said, "and other items we've needed. The good Saints of St. George have offered us flour and grain to keep us going until we can feed ourselves again. We have Morgan Davis to thank for making the trip to bring back some of those things, and for some bargains he struck to acquire some tools and implements."

Morgan saw people turn toward him; he let his eyes drop. He could handle almost anything better than praise.

"Now, here's the problem," the bishop said. "We're still short of almost everythin', and one load of food will be gone quickly, once we share it around. We just can't let up on fishin', diggin' roots, gatherin' field greens, and all those things. If I start handin' out sacks of flour and even some fruit . . ." There was a stir in the congregation. " . . . there's just no way to be entirely fair. Some families are bigger than others, and some have made their food last longer. I don't want to have to judge who's been careless and who hasn't—or who deserves what. Do you understand the problem?"

People were nodding. Morgan glanced at a man on the bench in front of him. He seemed almost panicked, as if he wanted to storm the storage barn right now and grab what his family needed.

"If I put everythin' out here in front of you, would you fight over it, or would you say, 'Go ahead, you take somethin' first and I'll take my share later'? I have a feelin' you would want to do the right thing, but you might also think, 'I've got to get in there and grab all I can before it's gone.' We just can't have that spirit, or we'll all turn on one another. So tomorrow I'm goin' to come around with my counselors, and we're goin' to give you a fair share of the goods, and then I ask you to think more of your neighbors than yourselves. If you've gotten along pretty well, and you don't need wheat flour, for instance, share it with someone who has run out. Please don't try to decide who is more *deservin'*. No one can judge that. Just keep sharin' the way so many of you have done this winter. And then, when some of you start to get some produce out of your gardens, continue to think of everyone else. If we all share, we'll be all right until the harvest comes on this fall.

"I do want to say that a few of you have never caught the spirit of workin' with everyone else. And I feel sorry for you. You may have eaten a little better than others, but you've done damage to your spirits. You've failed your brothers and sisters and you need to repent. We may have a fine harvest this fall, but let's never stop lookin' about to see who might need help to get through a hard time."

The bishop looked around. "That's all I'm goin' to say on this subject, but here's what I want to do. I'd like to ask you to fast tonight and tomorrow, and thank the Lord for the goods that have arrived. And I want everyone to pray, both as we end this meeting and all day tomorrow, that our crops will be protected this year. If we humble ourselves, I believe with all my heart that we'll have a rich harvest."

And then the bishop did something Morgan never expected. "I'd like to call on Morgan Davis to say our closin' prayer," he said. "He's one who understands the things I've just talked about, and we have him to thank, in many ways, for helpin' us get through this winter."

So Morgan prayed, but it wasn't a smooth or pretty prayer. He felt as though he stumbled over everything he said. And worst of all, he shed tears in front of everyone.

CHAPTER 4

Angeline was cleaning up from breakfast while Ruth was looking after the children. Naomi continued to have bad nights from time to time, but she seemed to be growing out of the worst of her colic, and the peppermint did seem to help. It was summer now, and on warm mornings the two wives liked to take the children outside and let them enjoy the pleasant air. After the years in the Muddy River Valley, even the afternoon heat was not anything to complain about. Best of all, there had been nice rains in the spring and enough rain in the summer to keep the crops growing. The men were working on canals and irrigation ditches, which had already come in handy, but the weather had been kind, and all the grains looked healthy. A good many grasshoppers had hatched out and fed on the crops, but they had never come in hordes the way they had the year before; their damage was not severe.

Angeline and Ruth had been taking turns hoeing in the garden, and the truth was, Angeline preferred working in the garden to changing diapers or feeding children. Fortunately, Jefferson was an independent soul and could play by himself for hours. He even liked to play with Ella and Morgy, and he loved to hold little Naomi, so he was a help to the women.

Angeline was musing on how life finally seemed peaceful, and how optimistic the talk around town was now, when a hard knock came at the door. Angeline wiped her hands on her apron. When she opened the door, she saw a shaggy little man with heavy black eyebrows standing in front of her. His hair needed cutting, and his sparse beard was in bad need of trimming—or better yet, shaving. Angeline had never seen the man before, and something in his manner, the closeness to her at the door—and his hard eyes—frightened her a little.

"Yes? What is it?"

"Are you Mrs. Davis?" he asked, his voice tense.

"Yes. And who are you?"

"Joshua Burt. I own this house."

Angeline nodded. She didn't want to correct him and tell him he had owned it at one time before Morgan had bought it from him. He seemed too set on watching her react.

"You'll be movin' out now. I'm takin' it back."

Angeline wondered how this man could be a brother in the gospel. He seemed to enjoy the idea of taking away her home. "I'm sorry, Brother Burt, but it's my understanding that we own the house now. You need to talk to my husband about that."

"Don't worry. That's jist what I'll do. But I'm sorry to tell ya, yer husband is a thief. It's too bad that you and yer childern have to move and start over som'eres else. I regret that it's come to that. But even in the Church, when a man tries to take what ain't his, he has to answer for it."

But the "regret" was all in the man's words. None of it was in his eyes or the tone of his voice. Angeline was not going to listen to any more of this. "You will not call my husband a thief, Mr. Burt. He's an honorable man. It's you who wants to go back on a promise and throw little children out of their home. This place was a trap for rats and snakes. My husband was the one who turned it into a home."

"Ya don't know a thing yer talkin' about," Burt said. "Where's Davis? It's him I need to talk to."

"He's out in the field somewhere. Let me see if I can—"

"Stay right there. I'll find him. But start packin' up. I need to git my own family inside jist as soon as I can."

"I'll do no such thing. And you'd better not come to this door again. I'll have my rifle ready, and I'll tell you right now, I can shoot your nose off from a hundred yards away."

Burt laughed about that, and that only infuriated Angeline all the more.

"Just try me, if you don't believe me," she said. "Now get away from here." She shut the door in his face.

• • •

Morgan was checking his soil for moisture, walking through the grain fields, digging down in different places. He thought he could go another day or two without watering, and he hoped the clouds off to the northwest meant that a storm might work its way down the valley. He always worried that a hard thunderstorm—especially hail—could do some damage now, but that kind of storm didn't hit very often.

He had just dropped a handful of dirt back to the ground when he spotted someone off toward the house, looking across the field. The man was dressed in a frock coat and waistcoat even though the day was getting warm. Morgan waved his arm to let the man see that he was coming his way, and then he walked through a long row of corn. As he came out of the field, he recognized that the man was Joshua Burt. He looked anything but friendly, his gaze steady. Morgan attempted a smile and said, "Hello, Brother Burt. It's good to see you again."

"I'm shore you don't mean that, Davis. Ya know why I'm here. I come to reclaim my farm. You may think ya managed to steal it, but I'm not goin' to let that happen."

Morgan walked closer and stood in front of Burt, trying to look pleasant. "I'm not sure what you mean, Brother. We agreed that I could buy the place."

"There's somethin' ya don't understand about buyin' a house. When ya buy somethin', ya pay for it, and I ain't had one red cent from ya so far."

"What you ought to remember is that I promised to make my first payment this year, after the harvest, and I still plan to do that."

"I don' remember any sich thing. An' I know what yer tryin' to do. Ya tol' yerself, I'll never see that man agin. If I don't pay him, what's he going to do about it?"

"No. Not at all. I was planning to make a payment this fall. I even planned to make a trip to your place, to pay you in person."

"What I know is, ya tol' me you'd pay me fifty dollars and I ain't seen a single dollar of it."

Morgan looked at the ground. He had to handle this right. He was starting to get angry, but he wasn't going to do anything now that would make things worse.

"Brother Burt, I have two wives and four children. You can't throw us out on the ground for no reason. I told you I'd pay you after the harvest this fall, and that's still what I plan to do. Maybe I can pay double on this first payment—give you twenty this year. I'm sure we can find a way to compromise."

"What if ya git out tomorrow instead of today? That's my compermise. If I don' see ya gittin' out by then, I'll head down to

Kanab and bring back the marshal. I know the man. He knows this is my place. Do ya have a deed sayin' that it's yours?"

"You wouldn't sign anything. You said a shake of the hand was all you needed."

"That's 'zactly right. We shook. Ya promised to pay. And ya didn't do it. Tell me if I'm wrong about that?"

Morgan could see there was no use arguing with the man. "I'll tell you what," he said. "Let's take our case before the bishop. We'll see what he says, and I'll abide by that."

"He's yer friend. He's goin' to side with you, shore as anythin'."

"He's a man of God, Brother Burt. You can trust him to think right about this matter."

"Don' try ta pull somethin' like 'at on me. I know what yer up to. Ya wanna lie to yer bishop and git him on yer side. Yer jist a lyin' thief, and—"

Suddenly Morgan grabbed at Burt, got hold of his coat, and jerked him up close. He doubled his fist and was about to drive it into the man's face. But he stopped himself, took a breath. "Don't talk to me that way," he said. "I won't put up with it."

Burt's face was full of terror. He spun and jerked away, and Morgan let him loose.

"I'm sorry," Morgan said. "I didn't mean to do that."

Burt was moving away, walking backwards.

"Listen," Morgan said. "I won't touch you again. But go to the bishop with me, and then, if his decision doesn't satisfy you, go talk to the marshal."

Burt stopped. He stared out across the fields for a few seconds. "Well, I'll talk to him. Maybe he is a good man and he can talk some sense into ya. But I won't be cheated out of my land."

"I didn't mean to grab at you that way, but let's not call each other names. Let's treat each other like the brothers we are."

Brother Burt didn't assent to that. He didn't say anything except, "Le's go. I don' have all day."

So Morgan walked to the house and told his wives that he was heading into town to talk with the bishop. He assured them that something could be worked out. But Angeline pointed a finger at him. "Don't let that man take our house," she said.

• • •

When Morgan left, Ruth found herself calmed considerably. Morgan had seemed confident that everything would be all right. But she couldn't stop thinking how adamant Burt had been. She had heard hatred from enemies before, but she didn't expect such a tone from a fellow Saint. The thought of having to move out, to start over again, was almost more than she could stand, but she preferred that to Angeline with her rifle, getting ready to shoot people.

"Morgan will work this out, Angeline," she told her sister wife. "Let's pray that he'll be guided."

"Don't be so trusting, Ruth. Bad people know how to get what they want—and they run right over good people like Morgan and the bishop. They need me to go with them and keep this rifle handy." She had gotten the rifle out as soon as Burt had walked away.

Ruth walked to Angeline and reached out. "Please, give me the gun and I'll put it away." And then she whispered, "You're scaring the children."

"I'll put it away," Angeline said, and then she took it to the cupboard and put it on top, where it had been. But she didn't say a word about praying.

So Ruth took Jefferson and Ella to her own bedroom, and she

said her own prayer. She prayed for Morgan, that he would solve this problem, and for the bishop, that he would find an answer. But mostly she prayed for Angeline, that she would keep her anger under control.

• • •

Bishop Morrison actually lived in Glendale, but he spent much of his time in Mt. Carmel, and Morgan had seen him earlier that day. What Morgan hoped was that he would find him still at his Mt. Carmel office. The office was in a little lean-to building by the church. It was just a small room, but there was a table inside, along with a few chairs. The door was open, and when Morgan appeared, Bishop Morrison asked him and Joshua Burt to come inside and sit down at the table with him, and then he said, "Brethren, what can I do for you?"

"Let me make it simple," Burt said. "Davis here took over my house and farm. He come down to Washington and tol' me he'd pay me fifty dollars for it. But he never did. I don' want to sell it now anyway. The Indian troubles is over, and me and my family, we've come back. We wanna move inta our place jist as soon as we can. I'll give Davis and his family today to get things packed up, but I want them out by tomorrow. I've got my children in a wagon, and they need to get settled."

The bishop looked over at Morgan. "Brother Davis, what do you have to say about this?"

Morgan had been praying all the way into town that he could say the right things and that he and Burt could make peace. So Morgan explained about the arrangement, and about his promise to make his first payment after this year's harvest. And he repeated his offer to double his fall payment.

"What about that, Brother Burt? Isn't that a reasonable way of working this out? We have plenty of land here, and we'll make sure you have a lot you can build on."

"And start all over agin?"

"We all started fresh when we got here. If you had come back to that place of yours, all run down the way it was, it would have been almost the same as starting over."

Burt stood up abruptly. "Thass jist what I 'spected. Yer gonna side with this robber and let him steal my property. It ain't right—and yer s'posed to be a bishop. I'm headin' for Kanab, and I'm goin' to bring back a marshal."

"Now, wait a minute. Sit down. Let's settle this like brothers. There's no use callin' Morgan names. He's not a robber; I can tell you that right now. And didn't you agree to wait until after the harvest to receive your first payment?"

"He's makin' that up. He never said no such thing."

The bishop leaned back in his chair. "Did you two write down your agreement or just—"

"We shook on it," Burt said. "Thass what a man of honor does. But when one of the party don' keep his promise, the agreement is broke up."

"But missin' one payment—as you claim he did—does not necessarily mean that a man has reneged on his agreement, and he's offered to pay you more than you originally agreed to. I'll tell you somethin' else. We've had a family move away just recently. Maybe we could arrange for you to take over that house. We've got land available, and I'll bet Morgan would even help you get it plowed. In fact, a lot of our men would pitch in and help. It's too late to get much of a crop this year, but you could get a start on it."

"But I've got me a good crop growing out there in my fields. Let Davis here open new land if he's so good at it."

"Wait a minute!" Morgan said, his voice suddenly louder. "You want the crops I've grown this year?"

"It's my land. Them's my crops."

"And you call *me* a thief? You'll have to kill me before you harvest what I planted this year." Morgan slid back his chair. He was thinking that he was going to bust this man's jaw after all.

"I guess we could work it out that way, if thass the way ya want it. I could maybe kill ya. But I'd sooner have a marshal come in here and straighten this out. Good-bye, gentlemen."

Burt stood again, plunked his hat on his head, and walked toward the door.

"Don't go just yet," Bishop Morrison said. "Maybe we can—"

"Just a minute!" Morgan shouted. And then he waited, tried to think what was right, what he should do. Finally, he said, "It's all right. I don't want to do this. This is not what Christ would have us do. I'll move out of the house. We'll move into the Riddle place you were talking about until I can get another house built. And I'll open up new ground." Then he looked at Burt. "But didn't you plant your ground in Washington this year?"

"Shore I did."

"Are you going to reap the harvest or let it go to someone else?"

"I'll be goin' back to harvest my grain. I ain't sellin' out 'til after that."

"All right, then. You'll have a crop. Let me have the crop I planted."

"I can let ya have part of it, I guess. But it's my land. Yer a sharecropper, the way I see it."

"But Brother Burt, that isn't fair, and you know it."

"I agree with that," Bishop Morrison said. "You need to let this man feed his family this winter."

"All right, then, here's what I say. You give me one-half of what you take off my land, and we'll call it square."

"Not half. That's not right. Go get your marshal. I think he'll agree with me."

"I have a better idea," the bishop said. He stood and pointed a finger at Burt's nose. "You leave this valley and stay away. We don't need men like you around here. And if you try to take Morgan's land, I'll get up a posse and run you and your federal marshal out of here. That's the only thing I can think of that would set things truly *right.*"

But Morgan could see nothing but trouble if all this started. "No," he said. "Here's my offer. I'll give you a quarter of what I harvest. And we'll leave the house tomorrow."

"All right," Burt said. "I kin go for that. I used to think I had a good head for business, but I guess I'm gittin' softhearted these days. But git out early. Don't take all day."

Morgan had forced his hands behind his back. His fists were doubled, but he didn't let Burt see that. The trouble was, he had been reading about Christ, about turning the other cheek, about giving a man one's cloak. He needed to bring peace to this valley, not anger and hatred.

What Morgan feared more than Burt, however, was facing his wives—or actually, Angeline. When he left the bishop's office, he walked slowly back to his farm. He tried to think what he could say, how he could explain this to her. What was worse, when he stepped into the house, Angeline stood up and said, "I hope you didn't give this house away."

Morgan knew better than to tell the whole story. He had to say what he had done and let the tirade begin. "I had no choice, Angie. He claimed I had defaulted because I hadn't paid him anything yet. I told him I'd pay him after the harvest, but he denies that's what we agreed to. He was going to bring a marshal up here and have us ordered off his land. To keep the peace, I had to give way. But the bishop says we can move into the Riddle place for now. We won't be without a home."

Angeline didn't say a word for a time. Morgan could see that she was holding all the rage inside, her eyes blazing. "How soon?"

"We have to be out by tomorrow."

"*Tomorrow?*"

"Yes. There came a point where I could see we were going to have an all-out fight—between members of the Church. I just couldn't let that happen. While we're at the Riddles' place, I'll build another house—a better one. He wants a share of our crop, but we'll still have plenty to live on this winter."

"Wait a minute, Morgan. You're giving him our crop, too?"

"Not the whole crop. Just a quarter of it."

Angeline stared him down, her eyes cold. "I'll tell you what you lack, Morgan. You're a nice man, and a good one, but there are times when you need to stand up for your family, and this was one of those times. I married a man with some *backbone*. I don't know what happened to that man." She looked down, shook her head. "I wish I'd handled this whole thing with my rifle."

Morgan thought she was right. He longed to be like Christ, to be gentle and forgiving. Submissive. But maybe this had been the wrong time for that. He thought, now, that he should have knocked Burt down and dared him to get up and go get a marshal. He had let his wives down, and his children. Maybe he should have been like Captain Moroni and gone to war to protect his family.

"I'm sorry," he finally said, and he heard the weakness in his voice. He had been a fighter all his life, so what had happened to him? Maybe Jesus—and King Benjamin—had a good notion about how to live, but maybe it didn't work in a world full of people like Burt.

"I don't doubt that you're sorry, Morgan. But we're still going to move out, aren't we?"

"We have to now. I gave my word."

"Yes. Even though Burt doesn't keep his. Next time you make a promise like that, maybe you ought to come home and see what the rest of us think of it."

Morgan nodded. He couldn't stand to look at Angeline. He glanced at Ruth and saw that she was crying. He didn't want to look at her, either. "I'll take a load over to the Riddle farm tonight."

He grabbed two chairs and walked out the front door, just to get away from Angeline's eyes. When he got to the wagon, he slammed his fist into one of the sideboards. All he could think was that he didn't blame Angeline for her disappointment in him—her disdain.

• • •

Morgan's answer to this new problem was the only one he had ever known. He would work every waking hour to make things right. He hauled everything his family owned to the new house, but it was a little place, with everyone in one room, and they wouldn't be able to make things work there for very long. So he asked the bishop for a lot he could build another house on, and for a piece of land he could farm, and he went to work immediately. He could plow the land in the fall and then plant it for the next season, but for right now there was nothing more important than for him to build a house, and he knew he had to make it nicer, even, than the old one—something that Angeline and Ruth would feel good about.

There was not much room for everyone to sleep in the Riddles' house, so Morgan took a bedroll out to his new lot. He fell asleep half dead at night, out on the ground. At least the nights were not cold now, and by being gone, he was cutting back on the crowding in the little house. But more than anything, he didn't have to face his wives.

He cut timber first, and then he dug out footings for the house. It would have five rooms—a kitchen, a living room, and three bedrooms—all with puncheon floors. Jefferson was getting big enough to need some privacy, and it probably wouldn't be long before they would have more children and a need for more sleeping space.

Morgan worked on the house every day, and once each afternoon he would call on his family at the Riddle house and make sure they were getting by—and check on his fields. What he sensed was that Angeline was regretting what she had said to him, but he didn't want to hear it. She was right in what she had said about him, and he didn't want her to take a single word back.

After more than a week of digging and setting stones for footings, Morgan set the base logs that formed the outside walls of the house. Gradually, the place began to take shape. He had the walls up about three feet before he had to stop to cut more timber and prepare more logs. But after he hauled the new logs to his lot, he knew he had to put in a full day on the crops that Burt had taken from him. He walked to his old lot and turned in the irrigation water from the ditch to make sure all his grains were watered. He saw Burt's family, but not Joshua, so he assumed the man had gone back to Washington to harvest his own crop.

Morgan was tired when he walked the three miles back to his new farm—not just from the day's work, but from all the long days he had put in lately. And he was lonely. This had been a difficult time, facing himself and his inadequacies, and still feeling

Angeline's disappointment in him. Still, he decided there was time left in the day, and he needed to work on his new house. But as he approached the house, he suddenly stopped, not sure he believed what he was seeing.

The walls were up, rafters were set, and men were on top nailing boards across the rafters. The house was almost finished.

He spotted Angeline in the middle of things, handing up boards to the men on the roof. He walked over to her, but he didn't say anything. He was ashamed that she had had to take over the job. He had wanted to surprise her.

As Morgan neared, Angeline glanced back. "Oh, Morgan, I'm glad you're here. Look what your friends have done for you."

Morgan glanced up at Eb, who was looking down from the roof. "We should have helped you sooner," he said. "We didn't even know you were building this place."

"You didn't need to . . ."

"You've helped all of us, Morgan. It's about time we did something for you. It was wrong what Joshua Burt did. But look at what you've done. This place will be better than anything you've ever had."

Morgan didn't want this. He looked at Angeline. "I could have finished this in a few more days," he said.

"You're a man of your word, Morgan. This will be nicer for all of us."

"But I should have—"

"You should have done exactly what you did," Angeline said. "You're a better person than I am. I'm sorry for the things I said to you."

Morgan wasn't sure he believed that. But he was breathing again, and that wasn't something he had felt like doing since he had first told his wives that they had to move.

• • •

Joshua Burt was only the beginning of the parade of settlers returning to Long Valley. Most of the people had been happy living there but had retreated when troubles with the Ute and Navajo tribes had increased to the point of war. Few had thought they would ever come back, but now, with more Saints occupying the area, and with peace having been established with Chief Black Hawk, more and more wanted to return. The trouble was, some who had said they would not return were now hoping to reclaim their property after all. No one was quite so adamant as Brother Burt had been, but those who gave up on getting their farms back were angry, and those new settlers who did as Morgan had done and gave way to the pressure were equally upset.

The returning settlers were very different from those who had come to Long Valley from the Muddy. The previous settlers had been scattered through the valley, and although they had established towns they had called Winsor and Berryville—now Mt. Carmel and Glendale—they had been, for the most part, individuals who didn't think of themselves as part of a mission. They had never pulled together to survive the way the Muddy River Saints had had to do.

What Morgan noticed, soon after these Saints began to return, was that they questioned the way the new settlers had organized into towns, with farms surrounding the settlements. The new settlers had become accustomed to working together, lending equipment, helping one another. Even though the former settlers and the new ones worshipped together on Sundays, Morgan had heard some of the returning people complain that they felt like outsiders in their own towns.

Bishop Morrison finally called a meeting in Mt. Carmel, and all the Saints involved in various disputes were asked to gather and see what could be worked out. Bishop Morrison started the meeting by pleading with all the members to remember what they believed, to humble themselves and negotiate to settle disagreements. Morgan thought he discerned the Spirit resting upon the people; the meeting started well. One of the old settlers, John Daniels, stood up and said, "Bishop, this is what I needed tonight. It's been hard for me to come back and see someone else farming the land I opened, and then to be forced to start all over again on another place. But you know what? I signed papers saying I had no intent to return—and I meant it. Now I'll stand by it. I want to live here, and I want to be a brother to all of you. I'm opening new land and building a house, and my family will make the best of it."

"Thank you, Brother Daniels," Bishop Morrison said. "That's the right attitude. And it's in that spirit that I'm goin' to call on Brother Hart, who now owns the property you opened here—and all others who live in your area—to help you get that house up quickly, and to bring their plows and animals and help you grub out the brush and trees and to plow your ground. Who is willin' to offer that kind of help to Brother Daniels?"

Many hands went up, including Morgan's, even though he didn't live close to the Danielses' place. But this was exactly what he wanted to see happen.

Then Marcus Telford stood. He was the patriarch of a group of families who had settled the valley several years back. Now the Telfords had been arriving steadily and reestablishing themselves. They had dominated the area at one time, and it was not easy for them to accept all the new settlers who now led out not only in the Church but in the town. "I agree with what's been said so far," Marcus began, but Morgan heard something in his voice—just a hint of irony. "The only thing is, I know some men who praise the Lord and claim to be your brother, and then, the next thing you know, they've got a hand in your pocket, pulling at your coin purse. They think it's not stealing as long as they say a lot of pretty words, smile at you, and offer to have a prayer together."

Morgan felt the sudden change. He looked around the room. Most in attendance were men without their wives, and they all looked much alike. They had worked their lands that day and were wearing jean trousers and dirty boots. They had set their hats aside as they had entered the room, but their hair was matted in the shape of those hats, and their faces were bronze from the nose down, their foreheads pale as the underside of a melon. They had rough hands, prickly faces or full beards, and they were mostly lean and muscled. They were just the sort of men Morgan had known all his life, and the sort he liked. But they were divided—the new and old settlers sitting with their separate groups, not interspersed.

"I know what you mean, Brother Telford," the bishop responded. "I've seen that too. But why do you bring it up?"

"Well, some of us left, and others of you took over our land. That might not be so fair and square as you're making it sound."

"I'm merely sayin' that we can be guided by the Spirit and find ways to work things out. Do you have a specific concern, Marcus?"

"Who, me? How could I possibly express any concerns after you've preached to us about behaving like true Saints? I've turned the other cheek, and now I'm working from sunup to sundown to make a go of things. And the man who took my property feels no need to pay me a few dollars for the improvements I left him. So far, I haven't seen him—or anyone else—plowing my ground or helping me cut timber to build a house."

"I'm sorry that hasn't happened. How many could—"

"No, no. That's not what I want, Bishop. I don't want you to shame anyone into coming over to help me. Everyone has a lot of work to do, and being such a devoted Saint as I am, I'm just going to enjoy my work, praise the Lord, and keep my peace. I'll build my own house, thank you. And I'll plant my own fields. Just don't expect me to dig a ditch to another man's farm. You've all talked religion, but you've left me on my own. Now I'll thank you to continue the same way. And I'll take care of myself."

Morgan watched the bishop. He clearly didn't know what to say. He started a couple of times, stopped, and then finally said, "Brother Telford, I fear we've let you down. So many have arrived, and it's been difficult for men, hard at work, to do all that could have been done. Maybe now that—"

"Oh, Bishop, you misunderstand. My heart is overflowing with love for all of my brothers here. I'm as religious as the rest of you—and exactly the same way. All I'm saying is, you farm your land and I'll farm mine. Just forgive me if I'm not too impressed with your sermon tonight. It's *doing* that I like, a lot more than *talking*."

He sat down.

Morgan saw some heads nod, heard some words of agreement, all from the old settlers.

The bishop's face was reddening now. He took a big breath, and then he said, "Brother Telford, did you sign one of those statements that you held no more claim to your land and that you wouldn't be returnin'?"

"Yes, sir, I did. And you're right about that. I have no grounds to complain. If a man has a piece of paper that says he can reach into your pocket, it's only right that I let him reach all the way to the bottom and take anything he finds there."

"I'm not sayin' that. But when you signed the paper, you made the land available. That's why it's a problem to come back and ask that man to move off."

"I didn't ask that."

"But you want to be paid, and most of us who came from the Muddy arrived here without a penny to our names. Then we got eaten up by grasshoppers. We don't have ready cash to buy property that we were told we could have."

"That's fine. Don't pay me. Like I said, I'll look after myself."

"Well, then, I don't know what you want. I've offered to help you get started on your new property, and I apologize that we didn't make that happen sooner, but this animosity you're expressing only makes—"

"Animosity? I have no idea what you're talking about. I've already said, I want to live among you in joy and happiness. But don't stop by and tell me how much you love me. I'll do just fine without any of that."

The bishop was stopped again. He looked around the room. "This is not what I wanted," he finally said.

But Brother Burt was on his feet. "Maybe not. But it's what ya should 'spect. All us people that come back, we all got treated the same way. You folks from the Muddy all joined in an' built Davis a house. Ain't no one buildin' houses for us."

Lyman Hunt was sitting up front, but he stood and spun around. "What you did to Morgan was wrong—kicking him out of his house and taking part of his crop besides. Morgan would never do that to a brother in the Church. We helped him because he deserved help."

Brother Burt pointed a finger at Lyman. "Davis never paid me. He tried to—"

"Stop this," Bishop Morrison shouted. When the room quieted, he said, more calmly, "We can work all this out, if we—"

Marcus Telford's voice suddenly boomed through the room. "I've heard enough," he said. "It's fine to be fellow members of the Church, but when it comes to running our farms, we're better off if you, Bishop, stay out of it. Let's just leave each other alone, listen to fewer sermons and to a lot more common sense. I'll be going home now."

The bishop did make one more plea that decisions be guided by the principles of the gospel. The Muddy missionaries nodded when they heard those words, but the returning settlers were already filing out of the building.

CHAPTER 5

During the following months, most of the individual disagreements between new and old settlers were worked out. What persisted, however, was a sense of community among the people who had moved from the Muddy to Long Valley and an unyielding independence among those who had settled the area individually and then returned the same way. Even though Morgan disliked the attitude Joshua Burt and Marcus Telford were taking, he did understand their desire for personal freedom. Even though the idea of sharing one another's load seemed right to him—and was what he saw in the scriptures—it was still difficult for him to accept help. He appreciated his friends who had gathered and raised his house, but it had embarrassed him.

But life settled down over the next few months, and what lifted everyone was a good harvest. Some of the returning settlers who had gotten their crops in late still managed to produce a decent yield. Others, like Joshua Burt, had gone back to harvest crops at the farms they had planted before moving to Long Valley. Morgan hated giving up a fourth of his crop to Brother Burt, but grasshoppers had not attacked in great numbers, so he had come out quite well. He also made two hauling trips to St. George that fall and was able to earn some extra money, buy some furniture, and bring back fabric for his wives to sew into clothing for themselves and the children. What pleased him most was that he was able to buy a saddle horse. The mare was not young, certainly no racehorse, but with all his trips into town and occasional trips to Glendale, he was glad to ride, not walk. He called the horse Lightning as a joke, but the name stuck and soon became a term of endearment.

Morgan received some other good news that fall. Ruth was expecting again, and, of course, she was pleased about it. And Angeline was pleased for Ruth. They seemed to think of their children as joint ventures now, and he liked that.

Morgan felt much more confident about the coming year, but he was not home very often during the fall. He worked long hours to make time for his freight trips, and there was always more to do. He still liked to work, but when he came home for his noon dinner or returned in the evening after working all day, he had a sense that he was a trespasser coming through the door. Angeline and Ruth and the four children were gradually creating their own little society. They had a routine, a way of doing things, and they didn't really want his opinion about household matters.

Morgan had given up chewing tobacco after Brigham Young had called him to the Muddy. He never missed the stuff now. But lately, after a sermon by Bishop Morrison, he had decided he needed to live the Word of Wisdom more fully. He had bought coffee in St. George and had gotten so he liked a cup in the mornings when he was having his breakfast. But now he decided it was time to quit drinking it—and he thought his wives should too. They didn't care much about coffee, but when he told them it was time to abstain from tea, Angeline bristled. She told him retrenchment was all well and good, and she admired Morgan's willpower, but she and Ruth would make their own decision about tea. They weren't about to go back to Brigham tea, which they had resorted to earlier but had always hated. Morgan never liked to quarrel, so he let the matter go—but he finished off the coffee he had and didn't buy any more.

For Morgan, the problem was not really the tea the women wanted to drink; it was the "Ruth and I" he heard so often. Sometimes he wondered who was married to whom. The two women were a united force, and they operated as a team—like oxen yoked together, adjusting to one another's stride and strength. He remembered a time when Angeline had discussed almost everything with him. Lately there was not only little opportunity for that to happen but, seemingly, little interest. He chided himself for worrying about such things. It wasn't the place of a man to feel left out. But he had long had a notion about family life. Angeline, from the beginning, had asked Morgan to be kind to the children, to be patient with them and with her, but sometimes lately he felt as though he had little to do with his family, and life only meant plowing and planting and hoping to survive another winter.

He didn't say any of this to his wives, though. He had hinted in that direction with Angeline at one time, and she had seemed to understand, but he couldn't escape the feeling that she respected him less when he complained. And Ruth was practical. She had babies to deal with, milk to churn, butter to make, and she never seemed to ask herself whether there was anything more to life.

Morgan knew that these thoughts that ran through his head while he was out on his farm or driving a wagon to St. George were, in the end, mere nonsense. A man should work hard, provide for his family, keep going as long as he could, and then leave this earthly existence satisfied that he had done his best. His children didn't need sermons from him so much as they needed an example of manhood. He looked forward to the day when he and Jefferson and Morgy could work alongside one another, and maybe then he would teach his sons a few things about life—but mostly, he would *show* them things, the way his own father had done.

And yet, he couldn't stop wondering what else life might offer. He sometimes considered buying more wagons, hiring men, and starting an overland hauling company. Maybe he could build up some wealth and establish a fine home in northern Utah, where his children could obtain a better education and experience a more refined society. Ella and Naomi could be part of a culture that included more than farms and town dances, and maybe some of his children would want to attend one of the Church academies.

For now, he ran his farm, and his workload eased with winter. However much he longed to have more time, more rest, he actually disliked snowy days, when he felt locked up inside. What he heard his wives talk about turned out to be trivial most of the time, or flatly practical. He sometimes introduced a notion—about things they might hope for in the future, or some such thing—but Ruth and Angeline were either too busy or too focused on the present to sit and talk with him. He liked to play with the children a little and make them laugh, but he could do that for only so long before he wished he could get outside and chop wood or do something else that kept his muscles active.

Spring did finally come, and Morgan embraced his work again. But times became harder in 1873, not only in Utah Territory but across the nation. As a recession deepened, financial worries set off a panic, and many banks began to fail. Mines throughout Utah lost the financing they needed, and some of them closed. Many southern Utah Saints had relied in recent years on selling produce to miners, sometimes even working in the mines themselves to augment their farm income. The mine closings left some towns in strapped conditions, and what made things worse was a sizable drop in the price of almost all commodities. Farmers who depended on selling their grains lost much of their income. Cotton prices had fallen drastically, which was very hard on the cotton missionaries in St. George.

But none of that had much effect on the farmers in Long Valley. After the grasshopper disaster of 1871, they weren't worried about lower prices for their excess. They were just happy to know that they would be able to feed their animals and, above all, feed their children. Some were able to replace depleted draft animals and even buy milk cows or other animals, and Morgan hauled in additional plows and harnesses.

In June, Ruth gave birth to another girl, and she and Angeline chose the name Suzanne. By then, Angeline had told Morgan that she was pregnant again. That was certainly a good thing, but his sense of distance from his wives became more pronounced. He controlled his desire to be "with" them at such times, but even when Ruth recovered from her pregnancy, she was preoccupied by the little one—and very busy. Morgan was disappointed in himself that he even thought of such things—but he did miss the days when they had all been younger.

• • •

Angeline was happy, but a little too busy to measure her satisfaction. Children and housekeeping kept her attention all day, and she was always tired when she went to bed at night, especially with another baby on the way. What she knew was that Morgan wasn't really as happy as he had once been. He worked as hard as ever, and he liked to talk about the future of the farm, or about starting up a hauling company. Angeline was fine with that, whatever he decided, but she wished he would do more than speculate about the coming years and take some steps forward. She had sensed now and then during the winter that he was withdrawing a little—not only from her but from Ruth and the children, too. It was hard to know how to include him in what she and Ruth had to do, and hard to find time to talk the way they had done when they had first married.

"He's fine," Ruth told Angeline when Morgan had walked outside one summer evening. "He just likes to get outside and see what work he can do."

"He keeps chopping wood when we have enough to last for years. I think he's just tired of crying babies and women's talk." Angeline laughed. "Actually, so am I. I think I'll go chop wood myself."

"Let's you and me chop wood and let him look after the babies for a while," Ruth said. "That'll cure him of his blues."

"Do you think he does feel blue?"

"Something like that. But the harvest will be on us again before long, and then he'll be happy. He's never satisfied unless he's working hard."

Angeline wondered. She liked the weeks when he slept in her room, and sometimes they did share some thoughts, but more and more, he seemed to stay within himself. More often than not, Angeline fell asleep to the sound of his deep voice as he talked to her. She knew she needed to give Morgan a little more attention—and affection—and she told herself, over and over, that she would do that. But she also knew, when she went to bed at night, that at least one of the children would be crying before long—hers or Ruth's—and she heard each one. Morgan could sleep through all of that.

• • •

Morgan took Jefferson to the Virgin River on a cool October day, and while Ruth, Aunt Angeline, and the younger children watched from the bank, Morgan baptized this boy who had become his son. He plunged Jeff into the crystalline water and brought him up in a burst of bubbles as his black hair broke the surface. Morgan watched his face, the smile that appeared almost immediately, and he thought how much he loved the boy.

Jefferson was still not sturdy, but he was stronger than he had once been. He took one long look at Morgan, and then he climbed out of the river and turned back, water running from his hair and down his face. "It's not so cold," he said. "I didn't mind it." But his whole body was shaking as Ruth wrapped him in a blanket.

Morgan was cold too, but he thought of the Muddy, how wrong it had seemed to baptize a person in water so murky, and how much he had longed in those days just to be cold for a few minutes.

Everyone hurried home, and Morgan and Jefferson dried themselves and dressed in their Sunday clothes. Then Morgan laid his hands on Jefferson's head and, in a gentle voice, commanded him to receive the Holy Ghost. He blessed the boy that he would grow strong and noble, that he would serve missions for the Church, that he would be an example to his little brother and sisters as they looked to him as a leader.

Jefferson sat still for a moment after the confirmation, and then he stood and wrapped his arms around Morgan's middle. "I'll try," he said, and Morgan understood. Jeff had taken the words of the blessing seriously.

• • •

In the spring of 1874, Angeline gave birth to a boy: Thomas, named for Morgan's grandfather on his father's side. The spacious house Morgan had built was starting to fill up. This was what he had hoped for, but he hadn't quite realized how demanding such a life would be. Still, it was good to see Angeline pleased with this new boy and no longer worried that she would never be able to have children.

It was in March of 1874 that word circulated that Brigham Young, after having spent the winter in St. George, was now setting up cooperative economic systems in towns along his route north to Salt Lake. The system was called the "United Order of Enoch," and it was partly a response to the recession that had caused so much economic trouble for the Saints throughout Utah. It was a means for people to work together, share, and all survive hard times. But it was more than that. From the word that was coming to the settlers in Long Valley, Brigham Young considered it a holy order.

In the earliest days of the Church, a cooperative system had been tried in Jackson County, Missouri. This "Law of Consecration and Stewardship," set forth in the *Book of Commandments,* granted land to Church members. The people farmed their lands but didn't own them. They lived from their crops, but they consecrated their "residue," their surplus, to help the poor. It was a way of raising a whole community to a higher level and avoiding disparity in wealth. It was a society without rich or poor. Ever since the Saints had been driven out of Independence, Missouri, nothing quite so "leveling" had been attempted. Still, Church leaders had often taught that the day would come when this "higher law" would be reinstituted. Recently, various cooperative enterprises had been tried in Utah, especially in Brigham City, with joint stock companies established and all employees sharing in the profits. From what Morgan had heard, this new Order was going a step further, and he wondered whether Brigham, who was getting older, wasn't out to inspire higher principles of living in his people before he left the earth.

All the Saints in Long Valley were curious about the things they were hearing. They wondered whether Brigham would visit them himself and teach the new principles. As it turned out, however, it was his nephew, John R. Young, who was sent with Bishop Levi Stewart, from Kanab, to teach the new Order.

On March 20, 1874, Brother Young called the Saints, both men and women, to a meeting in Mt. Carmel. He invited the Glendale members as well, asking all to gather at 1:00 p.m. in the little meeting hall. They filled the place to overflowing, with many people standing against the walls. After a prayer, John Young stood before the congregation and said, "I'm sure you know why we're here today. It's President Young's desire that all the settlements in our territory begin to live in greater unity. Our Church leaders have been designing a plan, which was recently introduced in St. George. It's a system that can work for all our people and will help us cooperate with one another so that we all prosper equally."

John Young was built like his uncle Brigham, strong and stout. He was a man in his late fifties, Morgan guessed. He had a full beard that was more gray at the chin than along the sides, but his hair had stayed dark. He seemed all business, and Morgan liked that. The truth was, Morgan was a little worried about a plan that would depend on such complete cooperation—especially with all the hard feelings that had arisen between old and new settlers in the valley. On the other hand, as he studied the scriptures, he sometimes imagined a better world—one in which people lived in harmony. He had been thinking about Zion all the years he had lived on the Muddy River, and at times he had imagined a better way of living, one in which people truly supported one another.

"As you know," Brother Young said, "Brother Brigham has tried to keep us self-sufficient as a people. He's been trying for years to help us develop our own products—cotton, wool, sugar, silk, most everything—so we don't have to pay the prices people in the States want to charge us. Buying from back East ties us to Babylon. Merchants not only import their products, they import the false values that come along with them. You know how much Brigham hates fancy styles in dresses and hats that women—at least in the Salt Lake Valley—all think they have to wear these days."

There was a little ripple of laughter in the room. Everyone knew how Brigham made fun of women who flounced around in their big skirts with bustles and layers of petticoats. But part of the laughter, Morgan knew, was caused by looking about and recognizing that women in this valley were happy just to have a second dress to wear while their first one was being washed.

"So long as we buy from others, pay the shipping to get those things here, and let all the profits return to eastern factories, we'll never have an independent, prosperous economy. And now the railroad has completed its transcontinental tracks, and not only are products coming, but outsiders are showing up who want to establish all sorts of businesses, once again to take away our profits. They sell us their articles at inflated prices and then look down their noses at us because of our choice to live in plurality. The same men who cheat on their wives and try to seduce our young women criticize us for taking more than one wife."

The members of the congregation were nodding now, but Morgan felt—and he thought he saw some of the same impatience in others—that Brother Young ought to get on with his proposal. Everyone had heard Brigham's sermons, or they had read them in the *Deseret News*, which was brought soon after general conference, held twice a year in Salt Lake. John Young didn't need to repeat all those ideas.

"But there's another problem in all this. President Young worries that our people are not as concerned as they ought to be about the poor among us. New immigrants arrive and face hard times, but some members who live very well refuse to offer the poor any assistance to get started. Don't you see that that's not our way, brothers and sisters? When some have more than they need, and others have nothing, we start to separate ourselves, and one man holds his nose in the air and considers himself better than his brother. A woman in a silk dress refuses to socialize with someone who can only afford homespun. I'm sorry, but that's not what Jesus Christ would have us do."

These words struck home with Morgan. He looked to his right at Angeline, who nodded. He was glad to see her agreement.

But Morgan could also see Joshua Burt, who was sitting by some of the Telford men. They weren't complaining and whispering with one another, but they looked stone-faced, skeptical, and he hated to think how they were going to react to all this.

"The time has come, brothers and sisters, for us to enter into a new way of living—or, I might say, an old one. It goes back to the scriptures, and in this dispensation, it was taught by Joseph Smith. We have been hounded from one place to another in our history, and we've never been able to reestablish the proper order of things. But the time has come to live a higher law, and I will tell you frankly, to reject this principle is to bring a curse down upon ourselves."

Finally, there was a reaction. Marcus Telford suddenly stood up. "Brother Young, are you telling us that everyone must accept this plan—which you haven't even explained to us yet—whether we have a mind to or not?"

"I did not say that. No one will be forced to join. You will come into this Order by your own free will or not at all. I'm only giving you my opinion that, as with all the principles taught by the Lord and by our prophets, to reject such teachings is to turn away from divine guidance, and a person ends up reaping the fruits of such a choice."

"But this is an economic plan, not a—"

"No, Brother Telford. It has a basis in economics, but its principles come straight from the teachings of Jesus Christ. After He taught the Nephites, and they chose to follow His direction, what do we read? The people lived in peace and harmony for two hundred years, and what?" He paused and looked around. "And there were no rich or poor among them. How did that happen? They didn't try to rise above one another. They helped the poor get on their feet, and when the poor finally had plenty for their own families, those who had been helped looked about themselves to see who else needed assistance."

"I'm not opposed to helping people," Telford said, "unless the man is a lazy lout who won't do for himself. And it sounds as though you want us to enter into an arrangement where every man reaps the benefits whether he does his share of work or not."

"You're wrong there, Marcus. The whole system depends on everyone putting in all he has—both his property and hard work. Lazy louts will not be tolerated. But you're getting ahead of me. Let me explain a little more how the United Order will operate."

The explaining took a long time. What John Young, on behalf of Brigham, was advocating was that Mt. Carmel's and Glendale's citizens become, in each place, "a family." Each settlement or town would work out its own details. One approach was to form a corporation. All members who decided to join would transfer to the organization their "time, labor, energy, and ability," and such property as they chose to consecrate. The property would be owned and operated by the corporation, and all members would prosper together. Brigham Young had talked in general conference about an ideal he imagined, in which a community would eat together in a common dining room and let a few people do all the cooking. This would free up more women to weave and sew or work in community businesses.

People would live simply, wear plain clothing, and practice "economy, temperance, and frugality." Each community would be self-sufficient insofar as possible, producing its own food and clothing. Departments could be created so that a few men might take care of all the stock, others would grow and harvest the grain, and others would operate mills. Some workers could be assigned to run a cooper shop, a tin shop, a tannery, or a pottery—in each case, producing enough to supply all local needs. And when abundance was produced, products could be exported and sold, the profit coming back to the organization, not to any one individual.

Brother Young also made a strong point of everyone within the Order being energetic and industrious, working hard at assigned tasks and producing income or products not for self but for everyone. Each person would sign a pledge to live the commandments of God, obey the Word of Wisdom, honor the Sabbath day, and live a clean, wholesome life.

Morgan worried when he observed the Telfords talking back and forth, obviously still skeptical. Finally, it was Joshua Burt who said, in his caustic voice, "Brother Young, I've lived a while, the same as you, and I'll tell ya what. I've never seen a group of men work together and all put in the same effort. Some will work 'til they drop. Others slack off. An' if a man works for hisself, he works harder than if he's workin' for another feller. I jist don' see how this can make a whole town come out ahead. It brings the hard worker down an' it raises up the lazy one. Is that what you want?"

Brother Young stood silent for a time. He looked away from Burt, not at him. He seemed to be trying to control himself. Finally, in a calm voice, he said, "Joshua, first of all, we're not talking about what I want, or even what President Young thinks we ought to do. We're talking about what the Lord wants of us. The Lord has admonished us to love our neighbors as ourselves. One way to respond to that is to do our level best to overcome our selfishness, to be charitable in our view of others, to recognize that we all have faults. We must make an effort to rise above our natural selves. If you want, you can tell yourself that the Lord has asked too much of us, but I don't think that's the attitude we should take."

Burt was ready. "Yes, an' people can say, 'I love ever'body,' and make a big show of it. But when my ox gets mired into the mud, that feller's the first one to say, 'I'll give a little tug on yer ox, but don' 'spect me to tire myself out.' People is goin' to say that they buy inta this plan, but when it gits right down to it, it's gonna fall apart afore it ever gits started."

Morgan wanted to shout, "Don't judge by your own laziness. Give people more credit than that." But he held his tongue and waited to see what John Young would say.

Brother Young scanned the congregation, looking disheartened. "Is that how you all feel?" he asked. "Should I just leave and tell the First Presidency that you don't think you're good enough to live this way?"

There was a mumble of disagreement, but no one said anything. Finally Morgan stood up. "Brother Young, I just want to make a simple point. I understand what Joshua and Marcus are saying. No one hates being told what to do more than I do. Most everyone here remembers how angry I was when our leaders told us to farm the sand bench down on the Muddy. But I've had some things happen these last few years that make me worry less about my own independence and a lot more about how we all come out together. I think the way to do this is for each brother or sister to ask, 'Am I willing to put my whole heart and soul into this plan?' Not, 'What if someone else doesn't do as much as I do?' Some may have greater stamina or more ability in certain areas—so some will do more than others. But we can't worry about that. We can each give our full effort. Down on the Muddy, we all would have gone under if we hadn't helped each other. I don't remember a single person saying, 'I've done enough. Don't bother me to do any more.'"

"So you're ready to join the Order, Brother Davis?"

"Yes. No question."

"What about the rest of you?" He didn't call for hands, but there was a resounding "Yes" in the room. The Telford group didn't respond, but almost everyone else did.

"All right," Brother Young said. "That's what I needed to know. What I want to do now is read a letter from President Young, and then I want to read the articles of agreement adopted in St. George. That will give you a lot more to go on. Once you've heard all that—and I know the meeting will be rather long—I want you to go home and have supper with your families, and I want you to talk this over. We'll meet again at seven this evening, and all who want to sign up to enter the Order can do so at that time. Then we'll elect officers. This won't mean any immediate changes in your life. It will take a few months to figure out exactly how you want to set everything up. It might be next season before you put your Order into practice."

Brother Young was right. All the reading took a long time, and some of the articles of agreement were not quite clear to people—which brought on more questions. The meeting didn't end until fairly late in the afternoon, leaving the Saints with barely enough time to go home and eat and then return.

As people filed out, however, most of the comments Morgan heard were positive. "I think it's more efficient," Eb told Morgan.

"If someone who knows all about raising sheep runs the operation, we'll produce more wool than if each farmer has three or four animals and tries to shear them himself. It's the same with stock, hogs, even with farming. We pool our draft animals and plant big fields instead of each one of us farming a little plot of land."

"That's exactly right," Morgan said. "We'll produce more, and everyone will share in the benefit. And if someone gets sick or breaks his leg, he'll know that he'll still be able to feed his family."

"Then he can work all the harder for someone else who gets sick later on."

"I don' think you boys was listenin' very good," someone said.

Morgan looked back to see Joshua Burt. "What do you mean?"

"You heard what they said. People is all goin' to draw on supplies. If they don' work hard enough to earn 'em, they'll jist be forgiven at the en' of the year. Another man earns more than he draws out, an' he just forks over everythin' to the Order. That gits canceled out too. Tell me how thass a square deal?"

Morgan knew he had to watch himself. He said, very calmly, "That's not exactly what was said. We have to trust each other, and all do our best. But you heard what Brother Young said. If, year after year, someone doesn't hold up his end and always falls behind, he'll be asked to leave the Order. So we work hard to be Christians and treat each other right, but if someone takes advantage, he won't get away with it forever."

"Thass interestin', Davis. You don' look stupid. You look like a pritty smart feller. But you don' know the first thing 'bout people. They'll take you for all they can ever' chance they git. I don't care what kind of system you figger out, you won' never beat them kind. They'll beg and cry and promise to do better next year, and no one's goin' to boot 'em out on their behinds."

"Well, you do have a point. There are people who will take

advantage of others. I've seen that firsthand." He didn't point his finger at Burt's face, but he might as well have. He stood his ground and continued to stare at him.

"I know what yer sayin', Davis. But all ya have to do is look in the mirror and see a man who tries to pull a fast one on his neighbor when he thinks he can."

Morgan had to make a decision. He thought of rejoinders, but Angeline, who had hold of his arm, was edging past Morgan, and he thought she might be getting ready to knock the man down. He took two, then three, deep breaths and said, "We can work together, Brother Burt. Let's let the past drop."

Burt smiled. "That's fine. I thought about shootin' ya a few times, an' I never did. I guess I won' shoot ya now. But I'll give this Order a year or two, an' then I'm goin' to ask ya why it fell apart, and thass when I want ya to tell me, 'You was right, *Brother* Burt. And I was wrong.'"

Morgan bit his tongue—literally—one more time, and then he said, "Fair enough. And I want you to tell me the same thing if we make a go of this." He didn't stay to hear any more.

• • •

Ruth had stayed home with the children, and she had supper ready when Morgan and Angeline came in. She was actually fine with not going. She didn't like long meetings, and she wasn't sure what she thought about this whole business with the United Order that she had been hearing lately. She liked to think that people could be kind, that they could be good to each other, but she wasn't sure she wanted that kind of "cooperation" turned into a system. She had come to feel good about the life she had now. She hoped for good seasons, with good harvests, and a simple life here in this beautiful little valley. She loved Angeline more than almost anyone she had known in her life—some days—and she grew so irritated with her at other times that she wanted to tell her that she didn't know everything and wasn't always right just because she thought so. But every circumstance had its challenges, and right now she was a little afraid of changing her life.

Ruth didn't say any such things out loud—not to anyone. As she listened to Morgan and Angeline tell all about the Order, she only listened. She had a few questions, but she didn't ask them. She assumed that smart people would figure everything out. And if it worked, it worked. If it didn't, they could go back to life the way it was.

But Jefferson was interested. He was old enough now that he thought he could understand just about anything. "Papa, what will we do? Grow corn and then give it to everyone else?"

"We'll share it," Morgan said. "But I might not raise corn or wheat anymore. I might do some other kind of work. Not everyone will be farmers. The corn we grow will belong to everyone."

"Won't anything be just *ours?*"

"Well, in a way. We'll have our house, and we'll take care of it. The same with animals and tools. We'll have the use of all those things. But no, it won't be exactly ours. We won't have a cow. Someone will raise all the cows—and milk them, too. And someone else will make butter. There's even talk that we'll all eat together, and not cook dinner at every house."

Jefferson looked confused. "Wouldn't it just be better to keep our own house and our own cow?"

"Sure. In a way. But the trouble is, people want too much. And they think too much about what they want, and not enough about what other people need. With this new way of living, no one will try to be better than anyone else. We'll share everything we have, and no one will be rich, but no one will be poor."

"What about my toys? You made 'em for me. Can't I keep 'em?"

"Sure, you can keep them. But if you see another boy who doesn't have a stick horse, wouldn't you want to give him yours, so he'll have one?"

"No."

"Why not?"

"'Cause then I wouldn't have one."

Ruth laughed, and then so did the others. But she liked what Morgan told Jefferson: "Sometimes it can make us happier to see someone else receive something nice than it does to get something for ourselves. You gave that little horse I carved for you to Morgy, and he loves it. Don't you like to watch him play with it?"

Jefferson considered that before he said, "But I still play with it sometimes."

"Well, that's perfect. It's called sharing, and that's what we want to do. It's what Jesus teaches us we should do."

Ruth thought maybe that was right. Maybe the Order would be good for the people. She had probably been a little too selfish in the way she had been thinking about it. Still, it was easy to imagine that people would think the way Jefferson did. She worried that they might prefer to keep their own toys.

CHAPTER 6

The Glendale and Mt. Carmel Saints met together again that night, and almost all the men—speaking for their families—raised their hands in consent to join the United Order. To Morgan's surprise, most of the settlers who had returned in the last year—even the Telfords—agreed to join. Joshua Burt raised his hand too, although he still looked sullen and doubtful.

What followed was the voting for officers. Most of the elected leaders were Muddy River men: Alexander Hart, president; George Clairmont, first vice president. Morgan was surprised that Tobias Carrington, only nineteen years old, was elected second vice president, but he was wise beyond his years and someone everyone trusted. Robert Houston was voted in as secretary, and Marcus Telford was nominated and elected treasurer with the support of all his relatives. Morgan hoped that would help to bring everyone together.

What surprised Morgan most was that he was elected as one of the four additional members of the board of directors, which brought the total in the leadership to nine.

"All right," Brother Young told the people. "This is now your organization, and you'll have to work out all the details before you incorporate. Don't try to move too fast. This is a big change for people, and it's best if you think everything through before you set your plan in motion. Don't assume you have to do things exactly the way St. George is doing."

That made sense to Morgan, and it did take several weeks to write a set of bylaws. By May an organization was incorporated and approved by a vote of the board, but the arguments had only just begun. The proposed rules for conducting the Order that John Young had offered as a guideline were general, and as board members debated the details, the depth of the division in the community became obvious.

At every meeting, the design of the Order was rehashed. Most everyone wanted to take the "family" approach that, according to John Young, Brigham Young preferred. Alexander Hart and his vice presidents wanted members to sign over their property, possessions, and stored food. With this approach, families would retain stewardship over their previously owned homes and furniture, but possessions would be jointly owned. The board would assign wagons, farm implements, horses, and tools according to the needs of individuals and the work they did.

Marcus Telford was bothered by that idea. "Let me see if I understand," he told the others. "It's my house. I give it to you. And you give it back to me. What sense does that make? Why bother with all that? Let's just keep our own lands and then find a way to support one another."

Brother Hart and his vice presidents were seated at the front of the chapel, but not on the raised stand. The other six members were sitting on the first bench, facing the presidency. Morgan had made a point of sitting next to Brother Telford, and they had greeted each other cordially. Now, however, Morgan felt a stiffness come over the man. He was sitting up straight, his hands gripped together over his big middle. He was older than the other men, his beard fluffy and white.

President Hart was a strong man, but soft-spoken and patient. He was over fifty, Morgan thought, but his hair was mostly dark, and it hung over his ears, seeming to blend with his beard, which he kept quite short. "Marcus, remember," he said, in a measured tone, "no one is going to take your property away. It's your own choice to join or not join. And if you prefer, you might hold back some of your possessions. But if you hold back land and farm it yourself, you haven't truly joined the Order. You'll be holding back not just land, but your time and attention. We'll each have a place to live, on a small lot, but our crops will be grown on large, jointly owned fields. It's much more economical to farm that way."

"It sounds like some of us have nothing to gain and everything to lose in this system," Marcus said. "If a man has worked hard to open more land, why should he be punished for it?"

Brother Hart smiled. "But that's the whole point of what we're trying to do, Marcus. We'll farm together, eat together, work hard together, but no one will consider himself above anyone else. It's a changed way of thinking about each other—equals, brothers in the gospel. If that bothers you, you can drop out right now and go it on your own. Isn't that what you wanted to do in the first place?"

"I'm all for working together," Marcus said. He slowly rolled his head one way and then the other, surveying the men sitting in the row alongside him. "I'm a member of the Church, the same as all of you. So's my whole family. We don't want to be shunned and set aside while all of you go ahead with this . . . plan . . . of yours. But to me, farming is not religion; the Church ought to stay out of our private lives."

"I know exactly what you mean," Morgan said. "For a long time I tried to divide things up the same way: spiritual things and worldly things. In some ways, it's still what I'd prefer. But to Brother Brigham *everything* is spiritual, and that's how I'm trying to think about this. You can build a fine house, own fancy buggies, dress in costly raiment, but when life is over, those things won't mean a thing. When we accept the Order and live its principles, we try to take joy in seeing everyone prosper. And the only way we can do that is to organize and cooperate."

"Those are pretty words, Morgan," Marcus said. "But I'm not sure you even believe 'em. How long are you going to last if someone is telling you what to do all the time?"

"It won't be like that," Brother Hart said. "We'll seek consensus on every decision we make."

But Marcus was still looking at Morgan. "Do you believe that? Do you think we can all agree on everything?"

Morgan took the question seriously. He tried to think how he would feel about being assigned to a job he didn't want, or whether he could give up his wagon and his oxen if the board decided he didn't need them in his work. "Marcus," he said, "some things do run against my normal way of doing things, but I've been looking for something better than just plowing and planting and hoping for a decent crop each year. I want to live in Zion, and that's exactly what the Order offers us. It won't be easy for any of us—especially for me—but I want to make it work. I do believe it's the Lord's plan to establish a true Zion."

Marcus nodded and turned a little more toward Morgan. Speaking slowly and thoughtfully, he said, "That sounds very fine, Brother Davis. I understand what you're saying. And, by the way, when you came back from St. George here a while back, you brought a nice-looking saddle horse with you. Now, to me, that horse is spiritual, not worldly." He paused, smiling just a little. "I'm thinking I would be a happier, more spiritual man if that horse was in my corral, not yours. I want you to experience the joy of giving it to me. And give me your spiritual saddle, too. I like to think how joyous you will be in making me such fine gifts."

Morgan didn't want this fight. He laughed and said, "You've got a string of horses, all better than that old mare I bought."

"Still, having one more horse would bring me joy—and give you even greater satisfaction, since you'd be giving up the only one you own for the sake of a brother."

Morgan knew that Marcus had a point. He liked having a horse and didn't want to give it away. He tried to think what that meant. "Marcus, you know that's not the idea of the Order. We're talking about helping the poor—those in the greatest need."

"Well, all right," Marcus said. "Let's take Brother Shaw as an example. He returned to this valley not long ago, and he's poor. He came here without much of anything. Give *him* your horse. That would make him happy—and me too. I like Brother Shaw and want to see him do well. But you would be the happiest of all. So it works out just right for everyone."

"Now, wait a minute, Marcus," President Hart said. "You're getting us way off the subject. We're not asking you to give your possessions to someone else. We're talking about raising up our whole society so everyone has what they need."

That was true, but Morgan wasn't quite satisfied with that answer. "Still, Brother Hart," he said, "I see what Marcus is saying. We can't care so much about our own possessions that we hold back when someone else is in great need. Brother Shaw may or may not need a horse, but he needs a decent house, and he needs help getting started. We can all do our share to bring him and his family to the same prosperity the rest of us have already reached."

Marcus was still laughing. "You just can't give up that horse, can you? Well, maybe you ought to be the one to drop out of the

Order, not me. I'll tell you what. I'll take Brother Shaw a horse tomorrow."

"Marcus, that's not how it works," President Hart said. "You would love to show off that way and prove your point. But we have to work together. We share the work and we share the production of that work. Some will need horses and others won't. We'll work that out as we go along."

Marcus chuckled as he said, "So it's more important to you that the Church gets in the middle and makes all the decisions than it is that one man helps out another man. Is that what you're saying? Because I don't remember Jesus teaching anything like that."

"You need to read in the fourth chapter of Acts. It says that the disciples of Christ were of one heart and of one soul. No one owned anything; they had all things in common."

"Well, they were called to preach. They probably didn't have any land to parcel out."

President Hart stared at Marcus Telford for a time. He finally said, "I don't understand why you joined with us. You have no idea what it is Brigham Young is asking us to do."

"You're wrong there. I'm just trying to figure out how we can make it work."

"Fine. You take a horse to Brother Shaw. I'm sure he'll appreciate it. But we also want to come to your house and receive from you a list of all your stored goods—grain and produce. And we need to know how many acres of land you're placing in the common bank of land. And how many horses and livestock. That's the first thing we need to do: assess all our holdings, and then consecrate what we have to the Order—and that means, to each other."

Marcus took his own long look at President Hart. Finally, he said, "I'm not sure I want to do that, Alexander. I need to think about it. You may be right. This thing may not be what I want to do."

"That's your decision. Let us know. But before you decide, try to get the vision of what the Lord is asking us. The point is, we won't compare ourselves and measure our worth by our horses or our houses or our clothes and carriages. We'll be brothers and sisters, and that will bring more happiness than any horse could ever give us."

Brother Telford took his time to respond, but finally he said, "Well, it's a pretty picture you're painting, Alexander, but it runs against human nature, if you ask me."

Morgan had heard enough. "How do you know that?" he asked—almost shouted. "You assume the worst about people. And I guess that comes from looking into your own selfish heart. Why not *try* for something better? Why sit here in every meeting and think up reasons why we can't improve ourselves?"

Marcus wasn't laughing now. He pointed his thick finger at Morgan and said, slowly and carefully, "Watch what you say to me, Morgan. Don't pretend you're better than me. I've learned a few things in my life, and I don't have to listen to a *boy* who thinks he's got the world all figured out."

"I'm just saying that we—"

"That's enough, Morgan," President Hart said. "Both of you." Then he looked at Brother Telford. "As I just told you, it's your decision whether you stay with us or don't."

"I know that. I'll let you know what I decide. But all of you ought to do some more thinking before you just jump into this thing."

Other matters were discussed, but the spirit Morgan had felt at the beginning of the meeting was broken, and much of that was his own fault. Morgan wondered whether the Order would ever get started in Mt. Carmel, and whether he would ever be a good enough man to do his part.

• • •

The summer passed away with little progress. Board members were busy on their own farms, and it was not easy to meet as often as they needed to. An assessment did move forward, and each member of the board of directors met with families and recorded all the possessions they would pledge to the Order. The problem was, some—especially the returning settlers—reacted much the way Marcus Telford had, and others had almost nothing to pledge. Morgan made his visits, but he soon found himself frustrated by those who complained, those who seemed to be less than honest about their possessions, and those who couldn't wait to share the harvest—since they weren't expecting much because of their own late planting.

Board meetings became increasingly contentious. The meetings were open, and old and new settlers often attended—and sometimes confronted each other. Marcus Telford opposed most of the views expressed by the presidency, and his family and friends would mumble their agreement to anything Marcus said. What Morgan was seeing was this same split developing in Church meetings, and he heard the same thing about Glendale. Those who had found John Young inspiring and wanted to live the higher law he had advocated—mostly the Muddy River group—were growing impatient with all the wrangling. Morgan had seen people stand outside the church after meetings and discuss the matter. Some grew red in the face as the arguments became intense. Marcus would then show up at the next board meeting and argue that the whole idea was only creating trouble. It was never going to work.

It was September when word came that a new bishop, Harold

Spendlove, had been called and would be arriving from Salt Lake City. It was obvious that Church leaders had heard reports of the increasing conflict and intended to bring order by sending a leader with considerable experience. To Morgan, it was just as obvious that Bishop Morrison was worn out—and his health was breaking down—from presiding over people who felt such animosity for one another.

Morgan couldn't resist asking Marcus at one board meeting whether he had ever taken a horse to Brother Shaw. Marcus had muttered something about being unwilling to give an animal to a man who didn't know how to take care of it, and that was the end of that. But Morgan thought he knew where Marcus's heart really was. And in fact, it wasn't long after that when the Telfords, along with about a third of the people—mostly old settlers—decided to withdraw from the Order.

In some ways that simplified matters, except that those who wanted to continue in the organization were all the more scattered now, and neither town had a great many members to build and sustain such a large operation. Added to that, the wheat crop had been disappointing, not because of grasshoppers but because of "rust," a fungus that had spread through the fields. It would be a challenge to get started when their most basic grain would be in limited supply.

Bishop Spendlove, who had recently served a mission to England, was thirty-six years old. He was trusted by Church leaders, and he was known to be decisive and persuasive. Morgan liked him and was pleased when he assessed the situation quickly. By December, he had reached a conclusion: he recommended that those from both towns who wanted to stay with the Order move to a site between Mt. Carmel and Glendale and make an entirely new start. They could make the move in the spring. That way, the land could be parceled, houses could be built for everyone, and even the shape of the community could be built around a town square that would include a dining hall, offices for leaders, and a storehouse. People could live near that center, and the farms could all be laid out as cooperative land from the beginning. Other land could be set aside for a large community garden, and stock could be pastured in a common area.

• • •

Morgan thought a new town was definitely the right answer. Angeline and Ruth were not so pleased.

Angeline was downright angry. "It's the men who are fighting. They don't want to give in to each other. This whole Order thing is supposed to unify the Saints, and all it has done so far is make everyone angry. I say, let the men all move to the new town and build new houses. We women get along all right. We can live just fine without 'the priesthood' knocking heads with each other."

Ruth laughed. "Well, I know what you mean," she said, "except that some of the women are as upset as the men." And then she said more seriously, "It touches my heart to hear the way Morgan talks about it, though. He really believes we'll all be happier once we get the Order operating the way it's designed."

"I'll tell you something about Morgan," Angeline said. "And you know it's true. He lives his whole life thinking there ought to be something better. He wants angels to come down and carry us off to some paradise where people all love each other and never speak an unkind word. Down on the Muddy, he never stopped talking about building Zion."

Ruth laughed again. "I know. I see that. And yet he has enough of a temper, he just might knock Marcus Telford off his feet one of these days. But that's part of what I love about him. He's like a boy wanting to grow up to be a man, but he can never quite get there."

"That's how they all are. Men. They don't grow up. They play their games when they're boys, and then they turn their lives into games. They're like puppies, all nipping at each other, thinking they're in a real fight."

Jefferson had been entertaining Morgy, the two down on the floor together. "I don't fight like a puppy with Morgy," he said.

"That's because you're nine and Morgy's only five," Ruth said. "He does whatever you tell him to do. But you get mad at him or Ella if they make too much noise when you're trying to do your school lessons."

"That's because they shouldn't bother me."

"They're little, Jeffy," Angeline said. "You weren't always such a grown-up fellow yourself, you know."

Jefferson stood up, as though he had suddenly become aware that he was playing with childish toys. "Well, they have to learn, the same as I did."

"You let me do the teaching," Ruth said. "You should show more patience."

Jefferson shrugged his shoulders. "You just said Papa has a temper. I guess I'm the same way."

Angeline looked at Ruth, and they both smiled. "Well, you both have to do better," Angeline told him.

"You two need to do better too. You shouldn't say Papa's like a boy."

"And you should close your ears once in a while," Ruth said. She waved a finger at him, but she was still smiling.

"Are we going to move and have to build a new house?"

"Maybe," Ruth said. "That might be fun. Don't you think?"

"No. And that's not what you said."

"Never mind," Angeline said. "We'll do what we have to do."

But the truth was, Angeline was fighting off resentment about all the things that were happening. This house was finally comfortable, with furniture Morgan had brought from St. George, corrals built, and even a small barn. It was the roomiest house they had lived in, and she didn't want to lose it. More than anything, she hated to think of everything that a move demanded—again. Morgan said it would be a short move, only a few miles, but she feared it meant living in a wagon or a tent while the men built new houses. The United Order sounded wonderful when Morgan talked about it, but she had a feeling that people were people, and they wouldn't change as much as they needed to in order to live the way he described.

Morgan had still not returned from his board meeting, and Angeline had hoped he would come in soon enough to play with his children for a time, but that didn't happen, so Angeline told a story to all of them—her nightly ritual—and then put Naomi and Thomas down and tucked Morgy into his bed. Ruth took Jefferson, Ella, and Suzanne into their own room and settled them down before she returned to the living room and sat down by the fire with Angeline. These January nights were cold. There had been lots of snow this year, with no melting so far, so it had stacked up high. What everyone knew, however, was that if this move were to be undertaken, it had to happen early in the spring so that crops could be planted.

When Morgan finally came in, he hung his coat on a peg by the door, then plopped his hat on top of it. He didn't look at Angeline or Ruth, and that worried Angeline. "So what was the decision?" she asked.

"I think you know what we have to do."

"Move again, no doubt."

"Well, don't say it like that. We'll get away from all the

naysayers, and we'll build the finest town and the best United Order in the Church. It will mean another hard year or two, but five years from now we'll all be talking about it being the best decision we ever made."

In spite of his positive talk, she could hear in his voice—and feel in his unwillingness to look at her—that he was afraid of what she was going to say. So she didn't say what she was thinking. "It sounds like the right thing, then," she said instead. She smiled at Ruth. "It was what Ruth and I have been saying all evening. It's the right thing, and we're all for it."

Morgan didn't respond for a moment. He walked closer to Angeline and studied her face. "I guess you're making fun of me. I know you two don't want to move."

"Oh, Morgan, you don't give us enough credit. We can't wait to live in a wagon again. We still have fond memories of the last time we did that."

"But it will be good, Angie. I think it's important. I've been saying for such a long time, we need to change our hearts. When we leave this earth, it's what we'll take with us: a willingness to do whatever the Lord asks of us. Broken hearts and contrite spirits."

"It's working already. Our hearts are at least half broken, and we haven't even gotten started yet."

Morgan looked crushed. He glanced down, shoved his hands into his pockets. "I don't mean to lead you on a merry chase over and over. I just really think—"

"No, Morgan. It's all right," Ruth said. "You take good care of us. And we'll follow you wherever you need to go."

"You're a visionary man, Morgan," Angeline said. "Just like Lehi. And sometimes Sariah wished he would come down out of the clouds. But Lehi got her to the promised land. I guess that's what we're looking for, just up the road. At least we don't have to cross an ocean."

"I'm not saying that it will be—"

"It's all right, Morgan," Angeline said. "When do we start the move?"

"Just as soon as spring breaks. But I'll go there by myself at first. I'll work with the men to get houses built and crops planted. You and the children won't have to come until everything's ready for you."

"Oh, Morgan," Angeline said. "You know us better than that. You don't have to baby us along. We can help with the house—and all the rest." She walked to him and wrapped her arms around him. "We'll make this work—the same as always."

• • •

The move didn't take place in a wagon train this time. In fact, it started with a committee, including Morgan, riding up and down through the valley and finally picking the best site, about three miles north of Mt. Carmel. A plat was also laid out, with stakes for building lots. The plan was to build small dwellings next to each other, like row houses, forming a rectangle around the town square, with a large dining hall in the middle. The leaders referred to the houses as "shanties"—to express the simplicity of their design—but they were to be well constructed for permanent living. A two-story house was also planned—the "big house," they called it—where some of the leaders and their families could live, and eventually three similar buildings would be built, one at each corner of the square. Morgan would receive two shanties with an adjoining door, since he had two wives. The total space in the rooms would be somewhat smaller than they had had in Mt. Carmel, but

Morgan promised his wives that if their family continued to grow, they could build bigger houses sometime in the future.

In late February, Morgan did move to the new site ahead of his family. He worked with a crew that was building the structures. They cut timber, had it milled at their newly acquired sawmill, and then started constructing the dining hall and the shanties. Other men began clearing land as soon as the snow was off the ground. Teams of men carried out the projects, and the efficiency of this kind of cooperation was soon obvious. A town took shape faster than anyone could have foreseen.

The shanties were assigned by drawing lots, so some people had to wait longer than others. Morgan held off, letting most everyone move in before he did. By then, however, Angeline and Ruth no longer wanted to wait. They packed the wagon themselves and led Ben and Buck to the new site, with the children, except for Jefferson, in the wagon. But the weather had turned quite warm by then, and camping—some of the family in the wagon, others in a tent—didn't bother them much. In fact, Jefferson and Morgy thought it was a fine adventure.

Angeline wanted to help the men with the work. So while Ruth cared for the children, Angeline joined the building team. At first she carried lumber and tools to the builders, but before long she was hammering nails right next to Morgan. She loved to feel her strength again, to know that she was a woman who didn't have to sit on the sidelines.

There was never enough time for Morgan. All day, every day, he was either working or meeting with the board. All sorts of questions came up now that the town was actually taking shape. And assignments had to be made. Board members knew the families who had joined the Order, and knew the kind of work they could do. The only trouble was, sometimes they knew them too well.

They knew which men might be offended if not assigned as leaders of departments, and they knew those who understood the work but had trouble teaching others. All the same, the many departments and committees took shape, and as people moved into their shanties and the planting continued, the stock needed to be rounded up into common pastures. Hog pens and chicken coops had to be built, and skilled craftsmen needed to start setting up shops.

Morgan had never witnessed anything quite so exciting. There was something deeply satisfying about watching a whole village spring up in a spot that had been nothing more than grass and sagebrush. People were not spread out on individual farms. They were part of work details, and in spite of how hard they worked, laughter and friendly greetings were the normal sound of the place. Those who had joined the Order believed in what they were trying to do, and those who had fought the system had stayed in Mt. Carmel and Glendale. Morgan had no doubt that "Order Town," as people had begun to call the place, would be successful. He was certain that the harmony he saw now would only become stronger with time.

Morgan was assigned by the board to serve as the department head for the cattle operation. He would supervise the men who raised beef cattle for the dining hall and for sale, and for now he would also head up the crew that operated the dairy.

Fencing off the mouth of a canyon for a pasture and then gathering the cattle—about fifty head—and driving them there was more complicated than Morgan had expected. Families sometimes clung to their milk cows, which were like pets to them, and it was not easy for some to give up on the idea of making their own butter and cheese. This had been a way of life for many women, and it was hard for them to be told that milk and cheese would go to the dining room, and everyone would have plenty. Even though this freed up time for them to work on other assignments—carding and spinning wool yarn, or sewing children's clothing—they struggled to think in this new way. And yet, Morgan sometimes saw the women a few days after he had led their cows away, and they would say with a sly smile, "I don't have to get up and milk our cow every morning. It turns out, I don't mind that." Morgan didn't tell them that he was finding it a laborious chore to get up early and, along with his crew of men, milk a whole string of cows each morning—and then again in the afternoon. But the work didn't shake his faith in the plan.

Eb had been assigned as one of Morgan's team members, and that, to some degree, Morgan had arranged. He had felt for a long time that he didn't see his old friend often enough, but now they would work together every day.

"I never thought it would come to this," Eb said one early morning, the sun just coming up. They were both sitting on stools, and the sound of milk shooting into buckets was all around them. A cow barn still had to be built, and a true dairy operation had to be set up, but for now, the cows were lined up at the edge of the pasture, eight at a time.

"Come to what?" Morgan asked.

"You and me, turning into dairy men."

"It's what I did every day growing up. What about you?"

"Same for me. But that doesn't mean I liked it."

"Well, I have to agree with that." Morgan laughed. "But Angeline and Ruth have taken turns for a long time. They've milked our cow ever since I bought it. I'm having to learn the knack of it all over again."

"That's something Mary Ann's never been able to do. So I've kept a hand in the work, so to speak." He laughed. "But one cow was enough for me. I never expected to run a whole herd."

"There's plenty of us. It doesn't take too long."

Eb didn't respond for a time. Morgan was thinking about

the change in his own life, the change in everyone's way of doing things. There seemed to be more work, not less, but it seemed right to him. If he had to milk cows, he liked doing it alongside Eb and his other friends.

"This is going to be good," Eb finally said. "This is going to work. It's better for Mary Ann to be around more women, and it's nice she won't have to cook once we start eating at the dining hall. She didn't want to move again, but I notice, lately, she seems happier than I've seen her for a long time."

"I'll tell you what, Eb. I have the feeling we were meant for this. All the trouble on the Muddy, all the disappointments we've faced, it's all made us ready to sacrifice for each other. I think our group is going to make the United Order what it's supposed to be. Other towns will look to us as an example."

"I'm hearing that some places have given up already."

"I know. Some of the towns jumped into the whole thing, thought they had it figured out, and then the bickering started. From what I hear, St. George is struggling."

"Well, back there on the Muddy, I never would have thought we were receiving training, but that's how it seems now," Eb said. "We got our pride knocked out of us, but now we're ready to live the way the Lord wants us to. I just wish He would send a few angels to help us milk these cows. This doesn't seem a whole lot like heaven, so far."

Morgan laughed. "That's all right. I never did want to sit on a cloud and rest all day." And then he added, "But I agree—we're the right people to make the Order work the way it's supposed to."

And he hoped that was true.

But he understood why other Orders had folded so soon. Such complete cooperation would be a test for people who had been learning all their lives to live independently, on their own.

CHAPTER 7

Order Town was not very orderly for the first few months, no matter how hard the people worked to make it so. Time spent building and planting crops was mixed with hours of planning meetings. The board of directors had chosen department heads, and all members of the community, including young people, had been appointed to work in one or more of those departments. Angeline and Ruth were still cooking at home for now, but they had also both been assigned to card and spin wool. A bugler—Brother Roberts, a blacksmith—had begun to play reveille at 5:00 a.m., and he sounded the curfew each night at 8:00. That probably provided a sense of order, but working in teams was still new to everyone, and hundreds of questions kept arising about how assignments should be carried out.

"Is it really necessary to blow that horn so early in the morning?" Angeline asked Morgan. "You'd think we were in the army."

Morgan laughed. "We've had the same discussion in our meetings," he said, "but if all the committees are going to work right, we need everyone on the same schedule. Or at least that's how some of the men feel."

"Yes, and those men don't have to deal with the babies they wake up at five o'clock—or after you've put them down at night."

"I'll have to admit, no one even brought that up."

"That's because no women attend your meetings."

"Everyone's invited. You can come and tell the brethren how you feel about it."

"And be ignored, no doubt."

The two were sitting at their old table. Ruth had taken her children to her own little adjoining house, and Morgy and Naomi were asleep. Angeline was holding Thomas, who had also fallen asleep after nursing, but she clung to him still. She enjoyed the feel of him in her arms. It was a peaceful time, almost nine o'clock, which was late with that early wake-up call coming in the morning. Somehow Morgan had never found time for his evening meal, but Angeline had kept a lamb stew warm, and he had just finished eating two bowls of it with some thick slices of bread. He didn't have to worry about eating too much when he finally did take time to eat. He was as lean as he had been when he and Angeline had first married, and his muscles were still hard and smooth as river rocks. What she liked especially now, however, was that his blue eyes seemed brighter than they had been for a time. This new undertaking, building a whole town and taking on a new way of life, had fired his enthusiasm.

But Angeline found life rather chaotic. "Are things ever going to settle down, Morgan? I hope you won't always have to be gone so long each day."

"Things are calming a little. We've got everyone into houses now, and the dining-hall kitchen will be ready before long. Once the buildings are finished, we'll settle into a routine. Before long, I'll have only the cattle to worry about."

"And all those cows to milk."

"Not really. I'm the department head for now, but we've already decided that at some point we'll split off another department, just for the dairy. I don't want to milk every day for the rest of my life."

"But I know you. You'll be busy all the time anyway."

"Well, sure. But not quite so much as we are right now. It's all the meetings I go to that keep me on the run. But every day we make a few more decisions. One of these days the Order will start to run itself—with each department head figuring out his own problems."

"I'm sorry, but I don't believe that. Working together may be efficient in some ways, but you're always going to have problems coordinating everything—and making sure that all things are done by consensus."

"Maybe. But I only want to serve one term on the board and then let someone else have the chance."

Angeline reached across the table and took hold of Morgan's hand. "They'll reelect you, Morgan. People trust you about as much as anyone in this whole town. It seems like ten times a day someone's knocking at the door. 'Where's Morgan?' they all say. 'I've got something I need to talk to him about.'"

Morgan grinned. "They don't know me as well as you do. You're the only one who knows I'm making stabs in the dark half the time. I don't have any more answers than anyone else."

"I do know you better than anyone. I know the man you were when we got married, and I know what you've become. You know how to do things, but what's different about you from most men is that you always remember *why* you're doing them. I think people need that. They aren't just looking for answers. They want to be around you and feel your confidence."

Morgan leaned back in his chair. For once he didn't deny what she had said about him. She could tell that he liked her assessment; she also knew that it wasn't something he trusted entirely.

"What about the time I came home and told you I'd given our farm away?" Morgan asked. "I don't think you thought I was such a great man that day."

"No, I didn't. And I wouldn't have done it. But I told you I was sorry about that. You do what you think is right, and you don't forget what you believe."

"But I let my family down that time. Sometimes things are not as clear-cut as I want them to be."

"That's true. You do keep your head in the clouds a little too much. There are times when you shouldn't let people like old Joshua Burt take advantage of you. But at least you'll never be like him."

The two looked at each other, taking more time to do so than they had for a long time. A single candle was burning, tinting Morgan's tawny skin. Most of the men in Order Town wore beards—sometimes lengthy, fan-shaped growths that practically covered their chests. But Morgan still shaved often, especially on Saturday nights. Hardly a day went by without one of the women in town telling Angeline how handsome her husband was. What she thought of now was the morning she had climbed onto a wagon with Morgan and departed from Farmington on their way to the Endowment House in Salt Lake City. It was funny to think how young they had been. Only eight years had passed, but it seemed much longer.

Morgan had begun to smile. "Right after we got married," he said, "I told you that I had never really realized how beautiful you were. But you know what? You're prettier now—prettier than ever."

Angeline shook her head slowly back and forth, but she was smiling. "That's because you see what you want to see, Morgan. I'm not pretty. I never was, and I never will be. But you made me feel pretty back then. That was the great gift you gave me."

"What about now?"

She took her time answering. "I don't know, Morgan," she finally said. "Marriage—and plurality—do things to people. I don't know that we'll ever be like we were that first year. I've turned out to be a difficult woman. I watch the way you look at me now—always a little afraid of my moods and the way I challenge you. I feel like I've lost some of your devotion."

"No, Angie, that's not true. We've just been through some hard times. All the work, all the complications of our lives—they pull us apart. Sometimes I don't see you, to really look at you, for days, weeks, at a time."

"And every other week, I have to give you to Ruth."

"But that hasn't made me love you any less."

"I don't know how to think about that. You can't cut something in half and come out with two wholes. It doesn't work that way."

"What about your children? Do you love them all the same?"

"I do. But I gave all my attention to Morgy at first, and I know he felt the loss when his sister came along. And Naomi has been jealous of Thomas ever since the day he was born."

"Is that what you feel too? Loss?"

"Of course I do. I tell myself I'm doing what the Lord expects of me, and I try to be a sister to Ruth. But I'm still jealous every time you go to her bedroom. I've never gotten over that."

"But you love Ruth. You've told me that. Many times."

"I do love Ruth. But I don't like to share with her. I'm still a child when it comes to that."

"Don't you think the Lord is teaching us to overcome our childish ways?"

"I do. But I'm not very good at it. And I don't think most people are. That's going to be the trouble with the United Order."

"We can do it. We're followers of Christ. We just need to grow and never forget what we're trying to become."

"I'm afraid you believe in people more than I do," Angeline said. "My father's second wife made me a skeptic long ago. I saw her selfishness then, and I see the same thing in myself now. I fear that we're asking people to live a law they're not ready for—both in living the United Order and in living the principle."

"I know what you're saying. I see the same problems—not just with other people but with myself. But if we ask more of ourselves, we'll rise higher than if we give in to our base impulses. I don't think people will overcome all their selfishness, but they'll move in the right direction. That's what I'm trying to do—and you know I'm working against my own nature."

"Maybe that's the problem. I'm afraid we'll wear ourselves out—all of us—trying to be something we're not."

"But for quite some time I've been feeling as though life ought to offer something more. When I read the Sermon on the Mount, I always wonder if Christ was asking too much, but then I tell myself that He wants us to try. And He wants us to teach a better way to our children."

"I'm sorry, Morgan, but you sound as though you're trying to convince yourself. It wasn't that long ago that you were just as sure that you had the right to make your own decisions and not listen to the brethren. I don't think you can dismiss all those feelings by saying the right words to yourself."

"I know. You're right. And it's still my daily fight with myself. But do you want me to go back to all that?"

"No. I guess I don't. But, Morgan, be careful. Don't ask too much of yourself, and above all, don't ask too much of me. I like to keep my feet on the ground, and you want me to walk in the air, my shoes never touching the earth."

"I do get carried away, but—"

Suddenly, someone was pounding on the front door. Angeline let her eyes go shut. "Now what?"

Morgan hurried to the door. Angeline saw Robert Houston from the board of directors. "We've had something come up," he said. "President Hart has called a quick meeting. Come right over. It won't take long."

"All right." Morgan turned around and looked at Angeline. "I'm sorry," he said.

"We're learning to love our neighbors," Angeline said, and she tried to smile.

"I'll be right back."

"No you won't. But it's all right. I'm used to it by now."

• • •

On July 11, 1875, Joseph A. Young, son of Brigham Young, along with John R. Young, presided over a meeting in the not-quite-completed dining hall. Joseph Young was the leader of a United Order in Richfield, Utah, and John was the head of the Kanab Order. The two had been called by the First Presidency to officiate as the Order Town United Order was legally incorporated. But this was a Sunday meeting, and more important than the legalities were the spiritual commitments of the people. Joseph Young was a good-looking man of forty, with dark hair and a trim beard. He possessed his father's enthusiasm for the Order, but his manner was considerably more subdued. He admonished the Saints that they would have to love and care for one another as never before. They needed to put thoughts of self aside. This was a time for all the Saints to prepare themselves for the Second Coming, when peace and harmony would reign upon the earth. The United Order was a step forward in that preparation.

Ruth found herself more inspired than she had been since talk of the Order had first begun. After all the busyness of recent months, she had needed to stop and think again about the society that members in Order Town were about to embrace. After his sermon, Joseph Young invited the members to enter the Order by way of baptism—a means of being reborn into a new way of thinking and acting, and a way of putting petty disagreements of the past behind them.

So, after the meeting, the members walked to a lovely place under the cottonwoods where the river pooled deep and calm enough to offer a place for baptisms. One after another the adults went down to the river, removed their boots, and entered the water in their Sunday clothes to be baptized.

Ruth had heard talk of a baptism today, and she had not really liked the idea at first. The Order had sounded more like a business operation than a religious matter—and besides, she hated the idea of getting wet in front of everyone, coming out of the water with her hair plastered down and her dress clinging to her. But during the meeting she had changed her mind. She thought maybe she, more than anyone, needed to change her attitude and feel the same spiritual commitment to the Order that her husband did. She had always longed to be good—naturally kind and caring—but had always found herself rather halfhearted in her covenants. This seemed a new chance, almost like starting over as a Church member, and a way of showing Jesus Christ that she wanted to follow Him in every aspect of her life.

After Joseph Young baptized her and John Young confirmed her there by the river, Ruth looked at Angeline standing nearby, wet and dripping from her own baptism, and Morgan behind her, his dark hair still wet, his face gleaming. Morgan stepped forward and reached for Ruth's hand. Then he and Angeline embraced her, one on each side. They climbed the bank and found Eb and Mary Ann, who had been looking after the Davis children. They traded children, and then Eb and Mary Ann walked down to the water and were baptized the same way.

After Jefferson had watched, he tugged on Ruth's wet skirt. "Was the water cold?" he asked.

"It is cold, but it feels nice on a warm day. It's such good water—better than we ever had in the Muddy River. Everything's better here."

Jefferson considered that, then said, "Except for lizards. I had more lizards to chase in the desert."

"But more frogs here," Morgan told him. "And frogs are easier to catch."

Jefferson was nodding again. "I know. But they're slick. I don't like 'em as much. I let 'em go after I catch 'em."

Ruth was thinking that he would let them go anyway. He liked to sneak up on frogs and grab them, but once they were in his grasp, he was sorry he had scared the poor things. He had told her that. And now it crossed her mind that she wanted to borrow some of his tenderness as she entered upon a new way of life.

Joseph and John Young stayed in town for a few days after that. They met with leaders and shared their knowledge and experience from the Orders that they had been leading. On Wednesday the community was called together again. The members enjoyed a fine dinner, and then Joseph Young presided again over the official incorporation and acceptance of the proposed bylaws, which he explained in some detail. "After some discussion with your current board of directors," he announced, "we propose that 'Orderville' might be a preferable name to 'Order Town.'" He asked the members to vote, and all approved. Ruth had heard from Morgan that a change of the name would be voted upon, and she was pleased. She had never taken to the name "Order Town."

After the unanimous vote to approve the bylaws, Joseph Young proposed a somewhat altered board of directors. Bishop Harold Spendlove was recommended as the new president of the Order, with Benjamin Wilkins and Woodrow Hinton as vice presidents. Brothers Hoyt and Carrington would stay on as board members, as would Morgan—even though he had said all week that he hoped to be left out of the new leadership. But Ruth knew Morgan well enough to recognize that he was actually of two minds. It was always his preference to avoid the attention that came to a leader, but he also trusted his own judgment and ability to get things done. She suspected he was actually pleased to stay on the board for now.

• • •

Over the next few weeks, life did calm a little. The crops were in, and some nice rains had come. People felt good about the likely harvest that fall. But even more, the dining hall was finished, and the first dinner for the members of the Order was served on the 24th of July. After that, the new eating schedule was set in place. A bugle call summoned the people to meals at 7:00 a.m., noon, and 6:00 p.m., and each breakfast started with a morning hymn and prayer. In the evening, people stayed after the meal for songs and recitations, even spelling lessons. Morgan liked these gatherings, and even more, he found that Angeline and Ruth were freed up more than before. They seemed to like their spinning assignment, at least as a change, and they especially expressed their relief that they weren't cooking all the time.

What Morgan found perplexing were all the decisions that

still had to be made. The ultimate goal of the Order, along with a leveling of economic status, was self-sufficiency. But that meant producing almost every needed household and farm item without purchasing goods from outside. All sorts of businesses common in other towns needed to be established. Clothing had to be sewn from homespun wool, and that required an entire department of spinners, weavers, and seamstresses, along with the sheep raisers and shearers. Hats had to be woven from straw or made by hatters. Barrels, buckets, tubs, candles, boots, shoes, saddles, harnesses, furniture, shingles—almost everything—had to be produced, and that meant calling on people with expertise to open shops, or assigning people to learn those crafts. It was like opening a huge, complex business operation and doing it all at once.

Morgan felt at times as though he had jumped into a deep pool and was in danger of never getting his head back to the surface. When he went to bed at night, he fell into darkness, but within hours, the thoughts seemed to percolate back to his consciousness and wake him in a state of near panic.

If Morgan had felt separated from his wives before, it was worse than ever now. He saw Angeline and Ruth only once the sun had gone down—and the summer sun was up until bedtime. He did love Sundays. He loved to hear the sermons that were part of everything: the admonitions to step to a higher plane and to embrace the pure love of Christ as never before.

All that was inspiring to him—except that he could hear Angeline's voice in his head, reminding the leaders not to ask too much of people.

It was during just such a Sunday meeting one afternoon late in the summer that he noticed a pretty little blonde girl, with bright blue eyes and a sprightly way of moving about. After the meeting, he heard someone say that she was Henry and Aurelia Glover's niece, and she had come to visit from Scipio, Utah. She and her cousin Olive were together at church and inseparable during the following week. He kept seeing the two of them around town. His first thought was that the girl was maybe fifteen or so, and, other than to notice how pretty she was, he didn't give her any further thought.

But something started to happen. It seemed to Morgan that Olive and her cousin showed up wherever he was. In fact, he became a little nervous about that and tried to avoid them. And yet, at a Saturday evening social, he noticed the girl—by then he had heard Olive call her "Mattie"—glancing his way, even smiling at him. He pretended not to notice.

Morgan danced a reel with Angeline—which he still wasn't good at—and then he walked her off the floor and joined Ruth on the chairs that ringed the hall. But once again, Morgan noticed that Olive and Mattie had gravitated to his side of the room, and the two were not only looking his way at times, but talking rapidly. Then he heard Mattie say, in a voice a little too loud, "I can't wait for my birthday. Daddy says I can get a new party dress, store-bought." After glancing toward Morgan again, she added, "I'll be seventeen, you know, and I'll be going to lots of parties and dances."

Morgan watched her a little more closely. She did seem to be older than he had first thought, now that he took a better look. He could imagine the attention she would receive at her dances. She not only had dimples and a quick, bright smile, but she had a way of playing her eyes, letting them bounce and roll. He had never liked girls like that—little flirts who knew just exactly how pretty they were. She was tiny; she had probably never in her life saddled a horse or used a hammer, the way Angeline could do. He thought of Mary Ann when she first married Eb—and what a long time it had taken her to steel herself to life as a pioneer.

But Mattie certainly was pretty, and she was smiling at him again.

One thing Morgan had heard all his life was that he was handsome. He wasn't sure that mattered very much, but he did rather like to hear Angeline, or others, say that about him. Still, he was thirty now, and surely a little girl, not yet twenty, wouldn't think an "old man" was still good-looking.

"I hope you're still here for your birthday," Olive was saying. "We'll have a party for you."

"Oh, no, my birthday's not until October, and I'll be home before then."

Morgan was relieved to hear that. He didn't like the discomfort he was feeling. He spent part of his Sunday evening in a board of directors meeting, and then he worked all day Monday, after milking, at the pasture in the canyon. The makeshift split-rail fence he had helped throw together when the cattle had first been driven into the pasture had taken some damage as some of the cows had pushed against it. There was a good deal of repair work to do. His crew of men was digging a ditch from a spring at the head of the canyon, a means for getting water directly to the pasture and down to watering troughs. Morgan was working on the fence by himself.

He had felled a few lodgepole pines and was stripping them, preparing them to use in the fence, when he looked up to see a horse approaching. He took another look after a few seconds and saw that the rider was wearing light blue—a color only a woman would wear. He watched to see which of the sisters from town would be riding out to the canyon without seeming to be in any hurry. And then he realized there was also a splash of yellow behind the blue. Two young women were on the horse, one behind the other. And the sister in the front, he realized, was Olive Glover. He didn't have to ask himself who the second rider, in yellow, would be. It was the same dress she had worn to the dance on Saturday night.

But this was awkward. Girls, for one thing, had duties, and weren't really supposed to be using horses for the mere fun of riding. More important, he was alone out here, and he shouldn't socialize with single young women. Married men sometimes sought the attentions of young women, and they could ask a father for a girl's hand in marriage. But it was not proper for a married man to show attention, in private, to unmarried sisters. What worried Morgan most, however, was that this seemed no accident. These girls must have known that this was the canyon where Morgan spent much of his time.

Morgan looked down at his work, but he heard the horse trudging toward him, breathing in gentle gusts. "Oh, Brother Davis," Olive was saying. "What are you doing out here?"

He finally looked up at them. He tried to sound businesslike as he said, "This is where I spend most of my days. I'm the department head in charge of our cattle."

"I never remember who does what around here," Olive said. She was very different from her cousin, with darker hair, darker eyes. She had some playfulness in her voice and certainly knew how to smile, but her round little face was rather plain.

Behind Olive, Mattie was leaning out, and her face was alight. She was almost startlingly pretty.

"So what are you girls doing—just taking a little ride?" Morgan asked.

"My mother was tired of us 'babbling on about this and that,' as she puts it. We finished our spinning, so she told us to get out from under her feet. My father said we could take the horse if we wouldn't be too long. So we thought we would like to see what some of these canyons look like."

"It is sooooo pretty up here," Mattie said. "Don't you just love this valley, Brother Davis?"

This all sounded a little too planned, even rehearsed, as though they had ridden along saying, *What shall we tell him about why we're out here?* And Brother Glover may have had a horse assigned to him, but it wasn't meant for pleasure riding.

Mattie was saying, "We ought to give old Buttons a rest, Olive." She leaned around her cousin. "Would you mind helping me down? This horse is so tall. My uncle had to lift me to get me up here."

Morgan really didn't want to do this. "Your horse is probably all right. You could just—" But she was turning as though to slide off on her own, so Morgan grabbed her waist and set her on the ground. Then he did the same for Olive. As he did, Mattie was saying, "You are sooooo strong, Brother Davis. You lifted me down like I was nothing but a feather."

"You are nothing but a feather." He had meant to sound a little sarcastic, as if to say, "Now you're fishing for a compliment," but instead, he had sounded embarrassed. He was almost sure he was blushing.

"So do you take care of all the cows, all by yourself?" Mattie asked.

"Oh, no. Some of the men are up at the head of the pasture digging an irrigation ditch. We have men who milk the dairy cows, too. It takes quite a few of us to run the operation."

"But did you cut down those trees by yourself?"

"Well, sure."

"And carried whole trees down here?"

"They're just young trees, hardly more than—"

"You *are* strong. No wonder I felt like a feather to you." And then she turned to Olive. "Look at the muscles in his arms. He could toss us in the air and catch us the way my daddy used to do when I was a little girl."

This embarrassed even Olive. Now everyone was blushing, especially blonde little Mattie.

"You still are a little girl," Morgan said, and this time he meant to put her in her place. He didn't want any more of this.

"Not really. I'll be seventeen in another two months. I'm fully grown, I think. I'm just small. I can't help it. I wish I had muscles like your wife Angeline. My aunt said that she can work as hard as a man."

"Women have to be able to work when they get sent to settle new towns. That's what it takes." He turned back toward the fence. In his mind, he had dismissed her. He had heard talk about girls who preferred to flirt with married men—men who had established themselves and could offer a new bride a ready place to live. The boys their own age were often unable to provide for a family, and too many of them had not really grasped what the gospel was all about. Some girls thought that if they could marry a man who was perhaps a leader in the Church and had his feet under him, they would be better off. Some girls had grown up in polygamous families; they were used to having "aunts" about, and lots of children. It was what they knew, and what they thought they wanted when they married. But a flighty little thing like Mattie would never be able to hold up under hardships. Being pretty was all well and good, but looks faded and substance didn't. This Mattie, Morgan was sure, was not only light as a feather; she was about as smart as one.

Mattie seemed to know what Morgan was thinking. "I can work harder than you might think. So can Olive." She looked over at Olive, who nodded. "I grew up in a big family, and my mother and my two aunts expected me to help with all their work. When I'm home, I milk our cow every morning and every night." She reached out her hand. "Go ahead, shake my hand."

Morgan turned back toward her. He was confused for a moment.

"Come on. Shake hands with me."

So he took her hand in his, and the truth was, she surprised him with her grip. Still, it was a little hand, a soft hand, smooth. "You can grab on, I'll say that for you," Morgan said, and then he realized she still had hold of his hand, and he pulled away.

"And I'll tell you what," Mattie said, and now the sparkle had come back to her face, "when I take hold of something, I don't let go. My daddy tells me I'm stubborn, but I tell him, when I know what I want, I know it for sure. It's not stubbornness; it's like grabbing on to the iron rod. When you know something is right, you hold tight to it."

Morgan nodded, actually liked her words. She did seem to have some substance to her. Still, she was not the sort of young woman he had ever liked. She probably thought dancing was more important than anything in the world, and she surely loved pretty dresses. In the United Order, the sisters were planning to weave their own cloth and make plain dresses from that homespun fabric. None of that cloth would be bright yellow.

But she was a sunny little girl with those big blue eyes. He liked something about her. He hoped things would go well for her. He also hoped she would leave Long Valley as soon as possible.

"I love the white cliffs set off against the green grass in this pasture," Mattie was saying now.

"You should have seen where we used to live on the Muddy

River," Olive said. "When I was little, I thought a cactus was the only kind of tree. I'd never seen normal trees."

So they talked about that, and Morgan and Olive told Mattie about the hard times their group had experienced in the Muddy Mission. Olive told about being hungry at times, eating cactus and anything else her father could find. Morgan told about the sandstorms and digging sand out of ditches over and over again.

Mattie showed that she could listen, and finally she said, "But I envy you in some ways. All the people down here love each other so much. I guess it's because they went through all that together before they got here. I don't feel that at home—not so much as here."

Morgan thought again that maybe there was something to her. But he finally said, "Listen, I've got to finish up with this fence. Let me hoist you two feathers back on ol' Buttons here, and you can head home. It's not like me to stand around and talk this long."

"It's because you like us," Mattie said. "I take it as a compliment."

Morgan avoided a response. He merely lifted Olive up onto the saddle. She worked her dress into place to allow herself to sit astride it. And then Morgan hoisted Mattie up behind Olive, with the rustle and flash of white petticoats.

Mattie laughed and said, "Don't look. I've got to rearrange my dress."

But he had already looked, had seen her little ankle and the graceful turn of her lower leg.

She really was a pretty little thing.

And yet, he was greatly relieved as they rode away.

CHAPTER 8

A Relief Society organization had been formed in Orderville, and Louise Spendlove, the bishop's wife, was elected president. Each Sunday she stood in Church meetings and invited all the sisters in the ward to join. Since the Order operated without any exchange of cash, she explained that no annual dues would be required of the sisters.

Angeline and Ruth had talked about attending, but with six children underfoot—along with learning to card and spin wool efficiently—they had not yet joined. But after Sister Spendlove's appeal on a Sunday in July, Angeline told Ruth, "One of us ought to join, I think, and you're better at that sort of thing than I am. I'll watch the children while you go to the meetings."

"What do you mean, 'that sort of thing'?"

"I don't mind visiting sisters, or helping when I can, but I don't like meetings, and I don't like *talking* about doing good. I'd rather do what I can on my own time, not when someone tells me to do it."

Ruth laughed. She actually had been thinking of going to the meetings, but she wanted Angeline to go with her. "I don't love meetings either, as far as that goes, but I don't think they tell you when to do good. They just—"

"Of course they do. They organize their projects and make

assignments. I don't fit in with a bunch of women talking about their love of charity and then reporting all the fine things they've accomplished."

"I don't imagine it's like that at all." Ruth was sitting at her spinning wheel, feeding the carded wool off her fingers, watching it wind into yarn as she pumped a foot pedal to keep the wheel turning. She actually liked the work, the simplicity of it and the concentration it required. Most of her daily tasks, especially caring for the children, were not so straightforward.

"Well, maybe it's not like that," Angeline said. "But you go this week. And then tell me what you think. I don't want to drag all the babies over there."

"Sister Spendlove has asked some of the girls in town to take care of the children. Almost all the women who attend the meetings take their babies along."

"Well . . . anyway . . . you go for now."

So Ruth decided she would. She liked Sister Spendlove and considered her one of the most intelligent persons in their town, and she even liked the idea of escaping the house for an hour or two, once a week. What surprised her, however, was to find that she liked the meetings even more than she expected. Sister Spendlove knew the needs of the people—which were greater than Ruth had realized. Many of the families had come away from the Muddy Valley with inadequate clothing and furniture, and then had never really recovered from the grasshopper invasion and the subsequent move and restart in Orderville. Even more, illness and tragedy had damaged some spirits. A number of women had lost children or had seen their own or their husbands' health break. Ruth felt better knowing more specifically whom she could help.

She also liked spending time with the women, most of whom were her good friends. After the meeting, Ruth had a chance to talk with Sister Cullimore. Ruth had been aware that Flora Cullimore resented the harsh way Henry, her husband, treated their sons and their little daughter, but she hadn't realized that he was just as harsh with Flora. During the meeting, Sister Spendlove had talked about the need for love in their families, and Ruth had watched Flora wipe tears from her face. When Ruth had asked whether she was all right, Flora had said, "Sister Davis, I go on from day to day and try to make the best of things, but I feel no love in my home. Henry doesn't hurt the children, but he yells at them and tells them how worthless they are. I watch what it's doing to them, and I don't know how to stop it. I've said things to Henry, but he tells me that I don't know what I'm talking about. Fact is, he thinks I'm worthless, too; he just doesn't use the word with me."

Ruth understood all this, and she told Flora about her first husband, how similar he had been. Ruth's understanding—their shared experience—seemed to make a difference, and tough little Flora broke down and cried. Ruth took her in her arms and held her for a time, and the thought occurred to her that she understood more about Relief Society now.

Sister Spendlove had told the sisters that day, "We mostly talk about Relief Society in terms of service and charity, and that's certainly what we do. Brother Brigham wants us to do all we can to help the Indian people, and that's also part of our mission. But we're here to grow in spirit, and to carry that spirit into our homes. In Nauvoo, Joseph Smith told the sisters they should help the men as well as the women to prepare to receive their endowments in the temple. So it wasn't just a matter of tending babies for a sister who was sick, or sewing shirts for the men working on the temple. It was raising up a generation of true Saints, and we can't do that unless we increase our own level of saintliness."

That seemed right, and when Ruth returned home she

told Angeline, "You need to join Relief Society. Every sister in Orderville should join."

"But I'm not like most of those sisters," Angeline said. "I—"

"That's exactly what we need—many voices, many personalities. One sisterhood."

Angeline nodded, seemed to give the matter some thought, and then said, "Maybe I'll give it a try next week. I guess I should."

• • •

Morgan did all he could during the latter weeks of the summer of 1875 to avoid Mattie and Olive, and he was relieved when he attended Church services one Sunday afternoon and found that Mattie was no longer there, apparently having returned to Scipio. But Angeline saw him looking about at the Glovers and whispered in his ear, "Don't twist your neck off. She's gone."

"Who?"

"Don't pretend you don't know what I'm talking about."

"Angie, I wasn't looking for anyone. I was just—"

"Just trying to spot that pretty little yellow dress—and those *big blue eyes.*"

Morgan decided to say nothing and avoid sounding false in his denial.

"Do you think I don't know she's in love with you? She did everything but fall at your feet to get you to pay attention to her."

"She's just a girl. She doesn't know what she wants."

"She's turning seventeen, and she knows exactly what she wants."

Again, Morgan didn't answer. And when the opening hymn began, he tried to relax and sing—although he wasn't very good at doing either one.

Finally, Angeline took his arm. "I don't blame her," she said. "You're the finest looking man in town. And she knows she can turn any man's head. I just hope someone grabs her up before she ever makes her way back to Orderville."

"That's what I hope too," Morgan said, and he knew that this time he didn't have to pretend his sincerity.

Angeline gripped his arm a little tighter, which seemed to say that she believed him. And the fact was, Morgan was glad to have the whole matter behind him.

Morgan was also pleased when Bishop Spendlove praised the members of the Orderville board of directors for all the hard work they had done. In the course of the last few weeks, all the members of the community had released their various possessions to the Order. Much of what they signed over was then granted them for their personal use. But Morgan had collected cows and calves, sheep and mules, plows and wagons, hayforks, chains, harnesses, yokes, and a host of other things. And he had loaded his wagon—or actually, the Order's wagon—with grains, potatoes, bacon, beef, hay, and produce. He and other board members brought everything to the storehouse in the town center, as they would also do with the harvest to come. Every item had to be assessed for dollar value and then recorded, and corresponding credits would be entered in the books as shares in the corporation. At least for the foreseeable future, no dividends would be issued, but leaders recognized that some members might choose to leave the Order, and that separation might involve compensation for the investment they had made in the beginning.

"I strongly believe," Bishop Spendlove said, "that most of the world would be astounded to see what has happened here these last few weeks. You have turned in your hard-earned possessions, and you've done it cheerfully, joyfully."

Morgan essentially agreed with that—except that the "turning in" hadn't always been quite so simple as the bishop thought it had been. Many of the people retained various animals, wagons, and other possessions. They assumed they would need those things to carry out the assignments they were receiving. But these were not easy decisions to make. Morgan was certain that he needed his horse—or some other horse—to herd cattle and make his daily trip to the canyon. The board had agreed, and he was still using "his" horse, Lightning. So it was not easy to look a man in the face and tell him that he no longer needed a team of mules or a workhorse because his assignment was in the poultry operation. Men liked their animals. They felt devoid without a wagon and team, and not very many were happy with the thought of spending their full days looking after hens or hogs or milk cows.

There were other hard decisions. Vegetables would now be grown in a large garden operated by one of the departments—along with an orchard and vineyard—so it was no longer necessary for people to keep small gardens near their shanties. But it was second nature to people to grow their own food, and some had planted little plots even though there was no plan to do that. They didn't see why it hurt to grow a few things, but that meant that they still needed their shovels and hoes. Morgan made judgments and let people keep certain items. But he didn't always talk such matters over with the entire board. He assumed other board members were making the same kinds of judgments. The bishop probably had no idea how many little matters of that kind had had to be worked out.

Bishop Spendlove already had considerable experience in the Church. He had served a mission to England, and with his well-trimmed chin beard and mustache—and his refined manner—he seemed rather British to Morgan. He was enthusiastic and friendly, already well liked by the people in Orderville, and Morgan loved the man. But he was more a theologian and spiritual leader than he was a manager. He left details to others, which was all right, but he sometimes made decisions about farming or business development without learning enough about the issues involved. Morgan worried that he might not be the man the Order needed. Still, he supported the bishop faithfully. He was just thankful that most of the members of the board were men who had settled towns, had farmed, and had run businesses. They made up for Bishop Spendlove's impulsive nature by bringing facts and reason to every discussion.

What Morgan told himself, and had come to believe, was that more than anything, the people needed the bishop's spiritual approach and his ability to communicate the philosophy behind this new way of living. Everyone needed to keep the larger purposes of the Order clear in their minds. It was going to take that kind of idealism to keep the system functioning.

Bishop Spendlove had come to Long Valley alone the year before, but early in 1875, he had returned to his home in the Salt Lake Valley and brought back his wife, Louise. He had also married a second wife, Patricia, while at home, and he had brought her, too. She was a pretty young woman of eighteen with lovely dark ringlets. She was not the strong leader that Louise had already proven herself to be, but she was gracious, and the truth was, Morgan liked to know that his leaders were willing to embrace the principle. He felt reassured that plurality was persisting in a world that was becoming increasingly critical of that way of life. In recent years, federal government pressure against polygamy had been increasing. Congress had attempted to tighten laws against the practice. Brigham Young had even been arrested and kept one night in jail, and now a test case against George Reynolds, a polygamist, was moving forward in the courts. Church leaders hoped that the Constitution's promise of religious freedom would prevail, but eastern politicians were confident that the case would be the final hammer blow against a great evil. Morgan worried what could come of all this, but he felt certain the Lord was on the side of the Saints and all would be made right in time.

As it turned out, the somewhat late start in planting crops in Orderville that first year seemed certain to result in a limited yield. Bishop Spendlove was already admonishing the people that there would be enough food to last the winter, but only if everyone was careful, not wasteful. Handling beef and dairy cattle, sheep, and hogs in common pens would eventually produce a plentiful supply of meat, but for this year, meat would not often be served in the community dining hall.

In spite of having to face another lean winter, Morgan saw a better future, and he felt sure that the Lord was finally blessing the efforts of His people. They had suffered through hard years, but their desire to live the United Order seemed to be opening the windows of heaven. True prosperity was still a few years off, but Morgan was confident that the Order would create a better life for all its members.

• • •

From the beginning, the Orderville Saints had committed to follow Brigham Young in his admonition to keep life simple. Extravagance had no place in this new society. The plan was to wear "plain" clothes, but now decisions had to be made about what that would actually mean. President Spendlove finally called for a planning session and invited the women in the weaving and sewing departments to meet with the board of directors to establish guidelines.

Angeline had agreed to represent herself and Ruth at the meeting, but only reluctantly. Clothes meant almost nothing to her, and yet she bristled at the thought of being told what she could and could not wear.

The meeting had hardly gotten started when Sister Blanchard, head of the sewing department, asked, "Could you tell us, Bishop Spendlove, whether there will be one pattern for clothing? Will we make everything just the same, except for sizes?"

"Well, I think so," the president said. "That's how I've thought of it. I rely on Louise a good deal to guide me in the clothing operation, and I know she has some doubts about taking that approach, but I don't see any way around it."

Angeline had heard some skepticism in Sister Blanchard's voice and now saw the sternness in the other women's faces.

"The same for little girls, young women, and old women—all just alike?"

"I haven't thought about that, Sister Blanchard. Do you think there should be different patterns for different ages?"

Bishop Spendlove had arranged benches so they faced each other, the men of the board on one side, with women from the sewing committee on the other. Angeline glanced about and noticed that most of the sisters were looking puzzled, maybe even annoyed by the president's question. She thought she knew what they were thinking: *He just doesn't understand these matters.*

"I've never known little girls to dress like their grandmothers," Sister Blanchard said. "But if that's what the Lord wants us to do, we won't question it."

Jerusha Blanchard was a thin woman with pointed features and eyes that communicated even more than her tone of voice did. Angeline heard something of New England in her pronunciation and suspected that she was more educated than most of the women in Orderville. She was wearing a plain dress herself, dark gray, with no ruffles, but she had taken to wearing that dress only lately. Angeline remembered her in a royal blue dress at a dance back in Mt. Carmel, with her hair longer at the time, more curled. She wondered whether Sister Blanchard was doing what she thought was expected of her now—not what she normally would have chosen.

President Spendlove laughed. "Sister Blanchard, I know you wouldn't question the Lord if you heard His voice from heaven, but I have a feeling you wonder whether I'm quite so all-knowing."

"Not at all. If you want us to cut every pattern the same way, that's exactly what we'll do. We accept the authority of the priesthood."

Bishop Spendlove's smile faded away. "Why don't you offer us your thinking, Sister Blanchard," he said. "Would it be a problem, for example, to develop several patterns—one for each age group?"

"There's more to it than that, Bishop. Some dresses are flattering to a slim woman, and yet they do nothing to enhance the appearance of someone . . . not so thin. Most women have learned what looks best on them, and they buy—or sew—dresses that fit their needs. Our women, after living on the Muddy these last few years, have only one or two worn-out dresses, so they'll be happy with almost anything new, but we're setting the standard for years to come. We don't want people to wear something they'll come to hate."

"I see." President Spendlove nodded a couple of times. "You're right. I hadn't thought about all those kinds of things. So let me just describe, if I may, what we're trying to accomplish, and you tell me what you think might help us serve that purpose."

"It's not for me to tell you what to do, President."

"Ah, but that's not the way the United Order works. I don't command. We all work together, in unity. So let's work something out here tonight—something everyone can be happy with."

Sister Blanchard nodded. But Angeline could see that the men were looking solemn, as though they expected an impasse, not a resolution.

"Here's what we're trying to avoid," President Spendlove said. "President Young has advised women not to wear hooped skirts, with acres of fabric in them, and lots of crinolines. He doesn't like dresses that are made from fancy silks and satins with ribbons and bows, ruffles, and all those things. So I think we try to get away from using too much material in the dresses, and we keep the patterns simple and modest. Is there a way to cut dresses that look nice on particular women—and are still not exactly the same as every other dress in town? And can we do that and still hold to the idea of simplicity?"

"I don't think so."

The room fell silent.

"Excuse me?"

"Women don't like to go to church and find that some sister has on a dress exactly like her own. I'm not saying we should wear fancy dresses in bright colors, but some little difference to make a dress distinctive—and her own—would be much more appealing. I've talked to people around town, and they don't want to wear a *uniform*—some plain, dull housedress, worn for every occasion."

"All right. I suppose I can understand that. But could women take a dress you made for them and then add a little something to it, or change it just a little in order to—"

"You mean add some bows and ribbons and ruffles that you say President Young doesn't want?"

President Spendlove crossed his arms over his chest and was silent for quite some time. Angeline didn't like the feeling in the room. Sister Blanchard, whether she knew it or not, was raising questions that were going to be fundamental to the success of the

Order: Could each person be singular, individual, and yet equal to and unified with all the others?

"Sister Blanchard," President Spendlove finally said, "do you understand what we're trying to achieve by entering the United Order?"

"I'm sure you think I don't."

"I didn't say that. Just tell me what you think the purpose is."

"It's for all of us to share what we have and to work together as a community."

"Yes. But why?"

"I don't know, exactly. I guess it's because President Young thinks we'll be better for it."

"But think about why. So long as one woman has a fancy store-bought dress and another has a homespun dress, there's going to be a divide between us. It's like the caste system they have in some countries—in England, for instance, where I served a mission. If we all have clothing that's *similar,* we can stop making comparisons and feel ourselves as one body, all equal before the Lord."

"That's fine. Just tell us how to do that. I'm a reasonably good seamstress, but all the women I know want to look like themselves. If they have a few extra dollars, they like to have a few nice things—like a feather on their hats, or maybe a bit of jewelry. I guess I don't know what's so wrong about that."

Angeline usually kept quiet at such meetings, but she spoke up now. "Bishop Spendlove, homespun cloth is usually quite heavy and thick. We can weave cotton for summer wear—if we bring some in from St. George—and wool for winter, but it's all rough looking, and women who like to wear silk, with hoops and crinolines, may feel as though they look quite common and ordinary. Do you understand what I'm saying? Myself, I've never worn silk in my life, and I'm happy with the plainest dress I can sew for myself, but prettier women—or women who have grown up differently from me—might feel as though they're giving up too much to dress every day in homespun fabrics."

President Spendlove looked over the women's heads, stared off at the distant wall. Finally, he said, "So if I'm hearing right, there's just no answer." His exasperation was obvious. "People want to wear clothes that set them apart as superior—or different—and they never will accept simple homemade clothing. We're just barking up the wrong tree with this whole idea."

Angeline was a little disappointed with President Spendlove. Sister Blanchard may have sounded rebellious to the men, but it seemed to Angeline that she was merely trying to explain the challenge the committee was up against. Somehow, the impulse to be an individual couldn't be such a terrible thing. It was too basic to everyone, as far as Angeline knew. But she had to be careful. "Bishop," she said, "I've seen Brigham Young many times in my life. He likes a well-cut suit of clothes—and a brightly colored waistcoat. And his wives dress very nicely. Maybe he's willing to wear homespun now, but I never thought ill of him because he liked to dress up a little."

"All right. Fine. So just tell me. What do you propose? Could Sister Blanchard bring us some designs, several variations people could choose from, and offer a little individual choice that way?"

"But if we produce our own cloth, all the same color," Sister Blanchard said, "I don't see how women will be happy with that, no matter what patterns we use."

Angeline saw the frustration in the president's face, and she watched as all the men ducked their heads. Sister Blanchard had made her point, but now she was taking a stand and offering nothing more than a stalemate. She saw Morgan raise his head enough to look at her and nod a little, as if to say, "Do something. We can't end the meeting this way."

Angeline agreed. She had to show President Spendlove that she—and the other women—did understand what the Order was all about. "I think women can be happy in homespun dresses," she said. "First, though, they have to get used to the idea. All I was saying before was that the change won't be easy. Women have to find out that it's nice not to worry about outdoing each other, and I think that will happen. Still, if we can offer a little variety in style, maybe that will help the adjustment."

"Thank you, Sister Davis. I suppose that's the only answer we have. Sister Blanchard, will you come back to our next meeting with some examples of men's and women's clothing that would allow for some individual choice."

"I can try." But then she added in a more conciliatory tone, "I've never liked the idea of showing off at Church meetings, turning worship services into a fashion show. I've only been trying to say—as Angeline just said—that it won't be easy to change the way people think."

Brother Spendlove nodded. "Yes, I understand. As you all know, I've entered into a second marriage recently, and my new wife brought with her lots of nice clothes she wore in Salt Lake City. I hate to tell her that she should throw her dresses away—for one thing, that seems a waste. But maybe she can cut off a few ruffles, for now, and in time, she'll have no choice but to wear the clothes provided by your department."

Angeline thought, *And Bishop, you can't get around the fact that she looks beautiful in those dresses, and that's what first caught your eye.* But she didn't say that. She only felt a little thankful that she herself was not pretty and therefore could wear plain dresses without much sense of loss.

"All right," Bishop Spendlove said. "Sister Blanchard, why don't you come to our next meeting with some ideas? You could design a few patterns for different ages, maybe different sizes of people. But we do want simple patterns. Would you try that?"

"Yes. I'll try."

"Wouldn't it be too bad if the Lord gave us a higher law and we couldn't make it work because people cared so much about the clothes on their backs?" He paused, and then he added, "This is all going to take some time. We can't change what's in our hearts in a day or two."

Angeline agreed with that.

• • •

Once the harvest was in, there was more time for meetings—and there were more issues to work out. Board members questioned how work should be credited. Was there a higher value in the work of department heads than for those they supervised? And what about skilled craftsmen compared to laborers? In the rest of the world, people were paid what an employer determined their work was worth. Was it possible for members of the Order to stop thinking that way and to see every assignment as equally important? For now, the men decided to consider all work equal and therefore to credit it all the same. To Morgan, that seemed a way of saying that every man and woman was offering his or her best to the entire society, and all were equally valued.

Ruth was not one to worry about such matters. She was happy with her assignment and didn't care how that work was credited. The fact was, wool would not be sheared until spring, and there wasn't much cotton available yet, so the spinning and weaving operation was moving slowly so far. She and Angeline had both been provided with spinning wheels. For now, though, the demand on their time was not burdensome. Her worry was that she would eventually have too much to do, but she saw nothing lowly about being in the clothing department instead of some other line of work. Most of her attention and concern were directed toward her children—all her children, including Angeline's. And of course, the two new babies that were coming.

It was a cold day in January, 1876, when Ruth's labor pains began. She didn't say anything for a few hours, not wanting a big fuss to start, but Angeline soon realized what was happening. "I'll get Sister Ballif," she said in that matter-of-fact way of hers. Angeline wasn't one to express her support in too many words. She was more likely to ask herself, "What needs to be done?" and then to do it. She found Morgan outside and sent him after Sister Ballif, and then she got the bed covered over with oilcloth and pulled out the white rags she had boiled a couple of weeks back. She began to boil water to sterilize anything else that would need it.

But every few minutes she would ask, "How are the pains? Are they coming faster? Harder?"

They *were* coming faster and harder, but Ruth thought she still had a few hours to wait, so she didn't say too much.

It was late in the night when the pains finally ended and another little daughter was placed in Ruth's arms. "She looks just perfect," Sister Ballif said.

Angeline told her, "She looks wonderful—healthy as you could ever hope for."

"Thank you," Ruth whispered, and it was another of those moments when she felt love for this sturdy, practical woman who had let her into her home and into her marriage.

• • •

Angeline was relieved that Ruth's time was over. She helped her choose the name: Tabatha Emily, after two great-grandmothers. And Angeline cared for the baby while Ruth rested for the usual seven days.

Angeline was feeling confident by then. Her baby was still very active, and she felt strong and healthy. She suspected she would have another big boy. She actually thought she might like to have a girl this time, but she didn't say that to anyone.

Morgan was kind to her. She knew she had felt distant from him all winter, as she had slept by him but not "with him." But he had never shown signs of frustration about that, and she had heard stories about men who were not so careful with their wives. When she had been sick in the mornings, early in her pregnancy, he had tried everything to help her. After working outside for a time, he would always stop back to make sure she was doing all right.

It was almost March, and still wintry outside, when Angeline awoke one morning to her own labor pains. Ruth was very kind about getting help and getting everything ready. Angeline noticed how much softer Ruth was, and she appreciated the kind words, the support she gave. Still, Angeline would have preferred to be alone, at least until the final moment. She didn't like to scream or show weakness in front of these women, or to let Morgan hear her from wherever he was waiting. So she stifled her cries as much as she could, and when the baby finally came, she took a long gasp of relief. She felt tears on her face and quickly wiped them away. She heard the little squeal of the baby trying out its lungs, and she asked, "Is it a big boy, like I said it would be?"

"Not this time," Sister Ballif told her. "It's a big baby, but it's a girl."

"Poor thing," Angeline said. "She'll be big and awkward like her mother."

But it was Ruth who said, "All that awkwardness is in your head. You're as graceful as any woman I know."

It was such a kind thing to say, and Angeline really did like to hear it—although she couldn't find voice to thank her. What she knew was that Ruth was the dearest friend in her life. They had been through so much together. She regretted that she found the woman so annoying at times. The two were so very different, and that was often obvious, but she had learned by now that she didn't have to like everything about the people she loved.

Angeline, with Morgan and Ruth's help, chose the simple name of Jane. Angeline had an aunt named Jane, a woman she had always admired, and that was reason enough for everyone.

Angeline was pleased that she had adequate milk, and little Jane was such a good sleeper, right from the beginning. This was all a little too easy. And then measles struck Orderville and spread to most of the homes.

It was little Ella who brought the measles home—apparently from school—and Morgy got them next. Angeline was up by then, and she and Ruth spent many hours each day comforting the two. But these mothers had babies in the house, and they were terrified. They prayed every night together—the whole family—before everyone went to bed, and always they pleaded that Tabatha and Jane would be spared. Angeline was surprised by the growth of her own faith. She trusted this time. She loved this new daughter who had come to her after a winter of waiting, and now she felt certain that the Lord would not take her away. She had been tested enough, she felt certain now. The hardest days of her life seemed to be behind her.

CHAPTER 9

Jane was a delight to Angeline. She was long and strong from the beginning, and she thrived on her mother's milk. Morgy had wanted another brother, not a sister, but he soon took to Jane, and he liked to hold her. Thomas, who was almost two, was not quite so pleased. He had become whiny, and he clung to Angeline more than ever before, always wanting to be held—especially when Jane needed to be nursed. Angeline understood the way of little ones by now and knew that Thomas, who had always been quite independent, only wanted reassurance. Fortunately, Morgan stepped in to help and spent his evenings entertaining all the children, even after very long days at the dairy and the cattle pasture. And Ruth, as always, was a second mother who could offer Thomas attention when Angeline was occupied.

The best news was, Ella and Morgy recovered from their bout with measles, and the younger children didn't come down with them.

Six weeks passed. Better weather was coming on when Jane began to sniffle and cough. Angeline felt the baby's head and realized she had a fever. Fevers were always a worry, so Angeline asked Morgan to bring Sister Ballif over to have a look at Jane. But Sister Ballif wasn't concerned. "Half the people in town have colds right now," she said. "And I don't see any sign of measles. She'll be fine in a few days." Still, Sister Ballif mixed up a foul-smelling poultice, spread it over a rag, and plastered it to little Jane's chest. Jane shrieked when she smelled the stuff, but after a minute or so she seemed to like the warmth, and she settled down. Angeline didn't know everything that was in the poultice, but she had seen some pine pitch and thought she smelled turpentine. That was already more than she wanted to know.

Angeline was relieved when Jane slept fairly well that night.

And then everything changed.

Early in the morning, the fever came on with a new fierceness. Within an hour, Jane seemed to lose all awareness, her body limp, her eyes unfocused. Angeline sent Jefferson out to the pasture to find Morgan, and then she stripped Jane down and wiped her little body with water. Ruth fanned her a little, but Angeline told her to be careful, not to make her too cold. But Jane showed no signs of awareness; she seemed not to feel comforted or stressed—or anything else. Angeline had been talking to her in soothing words, but gradually she was becoming frantic, and she began to plead with Jane to wake up and look at her. She even slapped the baby's face, just lightly, trying to bring her out of her stupor.

By the time Morgan arrived, Jane's breathing was rough. "Do something!" Angeline pleaded. "She's like Morgy was."

"What's happened? I thought she was doing better."

"She was. I thought she was—but she's going, Morgan. You have to call her back."

So Morgan took her in his arms, folded her little body against his chest, and he blessed her—called upon the Lord to let her return. But Angeline didn't hear the same voice of command she had heard when he had called Morgy back. She sensed what he was feeling—that things were different this time.

When he handed Jane back to Angeline, he said, "I'll go get Priddy Meeks."

That only sounded like doubt to Angeline. What she had wanted to hear was his confidence that her baby would be all right.

Morgan rode his horse away to find Brother Meeks, an old doctor who lived in the valley and was known for his natural cures. While he was gone, Angeline and Ruth continued to cool the fever. "I think she's coming around a little," Angeline said more than once, but she wasn't sure she believed it.

Brother Meeks came back with Morgan, and he administered a plaster of his own. He even used his finger to put some sort of compound on the baby's tongue, but Jane didn't react, and before long the brown powder was drooling down her cheeks. Dr. Meeks seemed careful with his words of instruction, reluctant to offer the reassurance Angeline wanted.

When he was gone, Angeline prayed—though she had been praying, pleading, all the while—but she already knew. She and Ruth continued to bathe little Jane, and the fever seemed to ebb, but her breathing became shallow and sometimes scarcely discernible. It seemed to stop at times, but when it did, Angeline would lift her, bounce her, order her to wake up. And each time, Jane jerked a little and then breathed again.

Morgan and Jefferson were there, keeping the children quiet as best they could and eventually putting them down to bed. After Ruth nursed little Tabatha, Morgan rocked her, then took her to the other room and put her down, too. Angeline wanted him not to be so calm. She wanted him to say, "Let me bless her again. I'll call her back." By then, however, she was sure that he knew what she knew.

It was after ten o'clock when Jane's breathing stopped altogether. Angeline gave her another bounce, tried once more to startle her awake, but Jane was gone. Angeline had to accept that. She wrapped her up in a blanket, and she held her close for a time. She cried, but she didn't say anything. No one did. Ruth was crying too, and maybe Morgan was. At least no one tried to console her.

Angeline had had all night to think, and she told herself that she had been spared from this once, and she couldn't always be. So many other mothers had lost their babies. But it was one thing to talk about "babies" and another to lose *this* baby, this Jane—this sweet soul who had made little sucking sounds at her breast in the middle of the night, who had fallen asleep in her arms, her head light against her chest. It didn't matter that others had experienced the same thing; this loss seemed simply too much.

But Angeline didn't say that to anyone. She told herself that she would not fall apart; she would not call attention to her grief. Instead, she became silent. And after the little coffin had been lowered into the ground in the Orderville cemetery, she continued to stand and look down at it. She would get through this, she told herself. She would not carry on, not pity herself. But inside, a kind of blankness had taken over. She would actually have welcomed a feeling of anguish to replace the hollowness that had taken over. She wanted to cry, wanted to grieve and end her pain, but she couldn't feel, couldn't think of anything to do, couldn't see her way forward.

Angeline stayed by the grave. Morgan told her that the grave diggers didn't want to cover the little box over until she walked away. But Angeline barely heard Morgan's words, as if from a distance. Gradually an understanding was forming. It was not a thought, but a sort of picture in her mind: God was sitting on a mighty throne. He plucked up babies when He chose; He did as He pleased with puny humans. And neither she nor anyone else could do anything about it.

She had pleaded with God. Morgan had done the same. His blessing had been a heartfelt request in the name of the priesthood.

And God had ignored them both.

She had told herself all her life that she was strong. But she wasn't. Ruth and Morgan kept telling her that she still had her other children, and she would have more in the future. But they didn't understand. Yes, she had Morgy and Naomi and Thomas, and she would do everything to bless their lives, but at any moment the Lord could take them, too, if He chose, and she suspected that sooner or later He would strike again. For some reason, God had decided to toy with her, to give her what she wanted and then to pull it back.

Sister Spendlove had helped Angeline prepare Jane for the grave, and she had said, "Oh, Angeline, I'm so sorry. I see so much of this. But we can't give up. Lisbeth Miller lost four of her first five children, not one living past a year or so. But she has a nice family now—six more—and all doing well. It's all just part of what we go through in this world. Lisbeth passed through all that and came out stronger—and you'll do the same."

Angeline had tried to grasp a little solace from those words, but now, as she stood over this dark hole in the earth, she saw no consolation in knowing that God could torment others just as much as or more than He was tormenting her. Others had prayed for bread and been given a rock, just the same as she had. It was only more evidence of His cold unconcern.

Angeline didn't want to say such terrible things to herself. She fought not to do it. But she also didn't want to hear encouraging words from others. She hated the kindness in Morgan's voice, the patience in Ruth's. They wanted something from her she could not give them: acceptance of God's cruelty. So Angeline kept standing by the little grave. She wanted to see the dirt fall on the coffin and cover it over. She wanted finality. She wanted to hate that spot of earth. She didn't want to imagine Jane rising like a little angel, wrapped in her Heavenly Father's arms. She wanted God to see black earth fall upon her little baby, wanted to hold that picture in her own mind. She wouldn't express her resentment to anyone, but she needed to hold on to it as a kind of revenge against the Lord.

When she finally walked away, it wasn't because she took the steps herself but because Morgan and Ruth had hold of her on both sides, and they were pushing her where they wanted her to go. She resented both of them, but she gave way to their force.

When they reached the house, Ruth told Angeline to lie down and rest for a time, so Angeline didn't do it. When the family went to the dining hall for dinner, she stayed home, then walked to the river and simply watched the cold water flow.

In the following days, members of the Church came by to see her—the bishop, the Relief Society president, neighbors. They expressed their sorrow; they offered thoughts about God's love, about the afterlife when she would see her daughter again. Angeline pretended she was listening, but the sounds were like the buzzing of insects at night. She looked at people, but she didn't see them, didn't let them know that she heard anything at all. She had to live for her children, and she would, but she would hold on to her bitterness. It was all she had.

• • •

Morgan had no idea what to do. After the first day or two, he gave up completely on consoling Angeline or offering reasons why she should not despair. Ruth told him that Angeline needed time, and that they both had to support her but not try to tell her how to feel. That certainly made sense, but days turned into weeks, and Angeline had taken on a whole new personality. She would say things that had to be said—the maintenance matters about housekeeping and Morgan's busy schedule—but she expressed no emotions, provided no hint as to what was going on in her mind.

Morgan had learned some patience over the years, but his impulses had not changed a great deal. When a problem presented itself, he liked to attack it, solve it, and move on with life. He knew that Angeline needed some time to recover, but he saw her making no effort to put this latest disappointment behind her. He had a hard time seeing anything but self-pity in the way she was behaving. Sometimes he wanted to shout at her: "Babies die. Every family in this town has lost someone." Angeline had had miscarriages, and she had now lost a baby, but none of that was out of the ordinary. Angeline needed to gain some toughness, not just physical strength. She couldn't always think like a child. Her way was to pray, ask God for things, and then always expect to get them—as though God were a lucky charm. She wanted life to be that simple, and it wasn't.

But then he would hate himself for his own thoughts. He knew how much she had hoped for children—especially to prove herself a good wife to him. And he knew how much she had loved little Jane. She had doted on her, caressed her, for those two months she had had her. She had surely imagined the young woman Jane would become, and she had talked of the love that the children would develop for one another. It was all a sort of dream picture, but it was what a mother did—and in truth, it was what Morgan had done too. He had pictured his little girls in dainty dresses, their hair curled, their little hands in his as they walked to church. All those thoughts were heartbreaking to Morgan, so he knew some of what Angeline was feeling, but he also knew that they had to go on with life. There was no other choice but to continue, to take the weight of the world on their shoulders and not behave like weaklings. It was what the Saints had been doing from the beginning, and it was what he and Angeline and Ruth had to do again to prove themselves worthy of their heritage.

Morgan wanted to say all those things to Angeline, but when he even started to address the subject, she pulled back, remaining silent and distant. Worse, she looked at him as though she were deeply offended. Morgan could understand her grief; he couldn't understand her desire to cling to it.

Morgan went about his work, and he attended his meetings. He continued to believe in the idea of the United Order, and he often expressed that vision when people became petty and complained about the way the organization was being administered. They didn't seem to understand what an enormous change it was for people to think in terms of sharing everything. Sometimes their impulse to better themselves individually came into stark combat with the ideal of carrying the whole society forward, and the board of directors had to guide the entire community through this delicate process of adjustment.

New people were joining the Order now, moving in from other areas out of a desire to be part of a system that was actually up and working. Many of the towns that had started similar organizations had fallen apart quickly, quarrels and jealousy gradually turning into complete dysfunction. The people of Kanab had already given up on the Order they had created. But the Muddy River Saints, who had learned to work together over the years, were doing better, and those who believed in the concept of cooperation were gravitating to Orderville. Still, a myriad of details had to be worked out. When people arrived with little more than a broken-down wagon and an aged team of mules, should they receive the same treatment as those who consecrated considerable means? The Order immediately raised the station of the indigent, or of those in debt, and provided them with a place to live. But were those people really ready to accept all the responsibilities that came with the Order? New members had to commit themselves to be guided by leaders, to practice economy, to live the Word of Wisdom, to avoid backbiting, profanity, quarreling, and abusing "dumb animals," and to work to the utmost of their strength and ability. These requirements were all in the contract they signed upon joining. But it was easy to accept these and other rules verbally, and much harder to live up to their commitments.

One night Tobias Carrington, one of the members of the board, pointed out the difficulty he saw developing. "Brothers," he told the other board members, "I'm not sure we can keep adding people who come to us with nothing to offer. If we take too many in any one season, we won't be able to feed everyone."

The men were sitting, as usual, on two benches, the presidency facing the others. A few people would usually come and sit just behind the board, and more often than not, they had an issue or a question. Sometimes Morgan wished everyone in town would attend so that they would understand the difficulty of fine-tuning the operation.

President Spendlove responded, "I know, Tobias. I know exactly what you're saying. Clearly, we can get too big. The whole idea of the Order is that we live together as a family, and a big city can never operate that way. I don't know how many people we can accept, but we probably need to go a little slower than we have so far."

Morgan agreed, but he also saw the problem. "So who are we going to send away? When people show up here, it's like a beggar at our door. I suppose we can say, 'We helped the last seven, but eight is too many.' But I don't see anything in the scriptures about that. We're taught to feed the hungry and clothe the naked."

"But there are more hungry people in this world than we can possibly feed," Brother Carrington said. "We can't give away all we have and then let our own families go hungry. And you know what Brother Brigham has been telling us. We have to keep a careful record of every possession that members consecrate to the Order—and all the hours of work people put in. If we don't, people will drop out and then sue us in a court of law for what they think they're owed. We may have a problem with too many joining us, but we might have a bigger one if too many quit."

"I understand all that," Morgan said. "But the man who comes with nothing, if he's willing to work, can help us open more fields and put in more crops, or he might have the skill to open up another shop we need. If we give a man a chance, he'll become part of us, and we'll all benefit. I just don't feel good about sending away people who want to join."

"Morgan, I agree," Brother Carrington said, "but we have to be realistic. The Order is built on high ideals, and yet, it has to work in the real world. If we don't control our growth, we'll go under. It's just that simple."

"Yes. I see that. And we all know that some have joined and then dragged their feet when it came to doing their part."

"Well, I have to say," President Spendlove said, "not many have been like that. Most are willing to work hard."

Morgan thought that was true, but he had seen a few families receive a house and food with pleasure but then give back little effort in their work. And what he knew about himself was that he had almost no tolerance for such people. He tried to understand, but he found himself wanting to snap a whip over their heads, the way he did with oxen or mules who balked at pulling their share of the weight. It was all he could do to keep himself from berating them. What he also knew was that he was feeling something similar about Angeline right now. It was time for her to lean into the yoke and start pulling as she always had before.

• • •

Ruth was sitting at her spinning wheel. It was her peaceful time that she enjoyed each day. Gradually, as people needed new clothes, they were turning to the storehouse and to the sewing committee, which was producing sturdy trousers and shirts, housedresses and children's clothes. Most everything was dyed a plain gray, and at first the clothing had looked drab and uninteresting—as the committee had predicted—but as more people had begun wearing the homespun material, it had become, it seemed, the marker of this little cooperative society. People weren't so much proud of their clothes as they were proud of the idea of weaving and sewing their own apparel, and of accepting plainness as a thing to be admired. All the worry about differing styles and individual tastes was turning out to be less of a problem than Sister Blanchard had expected.

Before the loss of little Jane, Ruth and Angeline had chatted during these spinning sessions. They had taken turns, one spinning, one looking after the children, but they had often had quiet times, even quiet hours, when they could talk about their lives, about their children, about their hopes for Orderville.

But all that was before Angeline had stopped talking and Ruth had stopped trying to make her talk. Almost three months had passed since Jane's death. Sometimes Angeline seemed to be sleepwalking. It was not that she was holding back saying things she wanted to say. It was the opposite. She clearly had nothing to say—and, apparently, nothing to feel.

Ruth knew that anger was probably seething under Angeline's silence, but she was never sure what form it was taking. She saw in Angeline's eyes at times a quick response to something that she or Morgan would say, and then she watched as the flash passed away—or was put away. Maybe Angeline resented Ruth for being able to have babies and for not having lost any. Maybe she thought God had been unfair with her in that regard. But that idea was painful to Ruth. It was she who had lost a young husband. It was she who had spent painful, lonely years trying to make do on her own, and it was she who had come into this marriage in a secondary role.

But the standoff, the silence, couldn't last forever, and in the end it was something very small that fired Angeline's temper. Ruth was sitting at her spinning wheel, and Angeline was kneeling on the floor next to Thomas and Suzanne, who had gotten into a dispute about something. And then Tabatha, in her crib, began to cry.

"Oh, not again," Ruth said. "I just fed her and changed her diaper. I don't know what she wants. She's just never been as easy as my other babies."

Angeline stood, was quiet for a moment, and then she suddenly spun around. "What do you want, Ruth?" she asked—almost shouted. "Do you want me to feel sorry for you? Is that it?"

"No. Of course not. It's just that—"

"Bury her in a deep hole and see whether you hear her cry."

Ruth was aghast. She couldn't think of anything to say. A full minute must have passed before she managed to think of a response. By then, Angeline had walked to the window and was looking out, holding still as a statue. Ruth walked to the crib and picked up Tabatha. "I'm sorry, Angie," Ruth finally said. "I know how you must—"

"No, you don't." She didn't sound angry now. Her voice was flat, and she was still staring out the window. "It's what everyone says, but it's not true. No one in this world understands anyone else. We're all locked up inside ourselves. We say words to each other and pretend they mean something, but they don't. We think only of ourselves, and we pretend we care about each other."

Ruth let some more time pass. Once Tabatha had quieted, she said, "Angie, I don't think that's true. I watch you walk around this house, buried in your own pain, and I want more than anything in this world to help you somehow. I do care about you, and I do wish I could take your pain away. But I leave you alone because I know you don't want me to talk to you about . . . what's happened."

"That's right. I don't."

Ruth was afraid to push this. It seemed an opening to say something more, but she didn't know what. She stepped back and forth, rocking her baby. All the noise in the room had stopped. Jefferson had been sitting in a corner, reading a book, but he had stopped and was watching Aunt Angeline. Morgy and the younger children were playing on the floor. But they had all heard the anger, and they were all watching, waiting. Ruth worried what this would do to them, to hear such harsh words from one of their mothers.

Angeline turned around. She looked down at the children, and maybe she was thinking the same thing. When she looked at Ruth, her eyes had changed, lost their fierceness. Then she said the last thing Ruth expected: "Let me hold Tabatha for a minute." That was something she had never done since Jane had died.

So Ruth carried Tabatha to Angeline, who met her halfway, in the middle of the room. The children continued to watch, clearly aware that something important had just happened.

Angeline tucked Tabatha against her gently and made the same rocking motion, stepping forward and back. "It's all right," she said. "We love you, little . . ." But then her voice broke and she began to sob. She held the baby high in her arms, just below her chin, and she turned her face so her cheek touched the blanket. Sobs kept breaking from her in waves.

Ruth put her arms around Angeline's shoulders. "I'm so sorry," she said. "I do care about you."

"I don't . . . know. I'm not sure of anything anymore."

"I remember when you first came to the Muddy, Angie. I never knew anyone who worked so hard and then gave herself to helping others with the same kind of devotion. You do care about people. I know you do. Your pain has been so great, you've lost some of yourself. But you'll come back. You'll be all right."

Angeline didn't say anything, but she didn't deny the possibility, and that seemed to Ruth a step forward. Angeline continued to rock the baby for a time, and then she carried her to her little crib and put her down, softly, and looked down on her. "Babies don't know anything, do they?" she asked.

"They know more than we do. They've just been with God."

"The longer I live, the less I know," Angeline said. "And I'm afraid to hope. That's when God likes to come after me—when I begin to think I have some faith."

"Life is for learning, Angie. When God asks hard things of us, we grow."

"I used to think that. But if He just keeps taking things from us, how can we ever trust Him?"

"Come here." Ruth walked Angeline to the kitchen table and motioned for her to sit down across from her. Then Ruth reached across the table and took hold of both of Angeline's hands. She spoke softly so the children wouldn't hear. "We all go through things, Angie. I married a young man because he was handsome and he said he loved me and told me what a wonderful life we would have together. And then he broke every promise he ever made. He didn't love the Lord, didn't take care of me, didn't hold true to anything. Still, when he died, I was all alone, and I thought I would never survive this life, let alone be happy."

"Then Morgan came along," Angeline said, "and your dark time ended."

This was a bit of a stab, but Ruth chose not to hear it that way. "Yes. In a way that's true. But you're Morgan's love. I'm the one he saved from disaster. He'll never love me the way he loves you. And that's all right. I understand. But my pain is like slow-moving water—flowing along without a ripple, but never ending. I still wish I didn't have to be the second wife. I wish I could have married a man who always loved me—and me alone."

"Ruth, I'm sorry, but I hate you sometimes."

"I know. Because I intruded."

"I gave my permission—because I thought I had to. And because I thought the Lord would bless me if I did. But you could have turned Morgan down. You could have chosen to leave me alone. It's what I can't help thinking—that you knew I didn't want to share my husband, and you said yes to him anyway."

But there was no anger in Angeline's voice. It was as though she felt relieved finally to say all this.

"I understand everything you're saying," Ruth told her. "At first, I only wanted someone to look after me and Jefferson. But then I loved him, and I wanted him for myself. At the very least, I wanted half of him—but marriage doesn't work that way. Half is never enough."

"We're not good enough to do this, Ruth. I don't know if anyone is. We're nasty little creatures. We want what we want—like crying babies—and we resent anyone who doesn't provide what we expect of them."

Ruth thought for a time about that. It was the sort of thing she had considered before, but she had also suggested an answer to herself, and now she felt more than ever that it was true. "Angie, I think God asks more of us than we can possibly do. Jesus tells us to love others as much as we love ourselves—but we really can't do it. Still, He doesn't ask such a thing to make us miserable. He gives us an idea of the ideal, and we try to find it in ourselves. We never get there, but there's worth in the effort. And maybe, in the next life, we'll finally be able to learn that kind of love."

Angeline was nodding, clearly thinking, and her eyes seemed to have taken on some life. Then she smiled. "I hope, in the next life, women are the ones who get plural husbands. I think I'd like to parcel out my love according to my moods, and be the boss of a little harem of men. I'd tell them to take good care of me and satisfy my wishes. And if they didn't, I'd make them stay away from my bedroom."

Ruth smiled. "I'd just say, 'I'll have a new dress, please, and more servants to take care of my house. Remember who's in charge around here.'"

"So all we're admitting is that we aren't ever going to be what the Lord wants us to be."

"I know. But sometimes, when you've tried and tried for a long time, it feels good to give up for a while."

Those seemed to be words Angeline could understand. She bowed her head, and tears began to run down her face again.

"It's all right," Ruth said. "I went through my own silent time, and I felt many of the things you're feeling now. But you need to know, one part of my heart may hate you, but the other part loves you. Do you know what I mean?"

Angeline nodded, but she didn't answer. Still, Ruth felt sure that things would get better now.

• • •

As it turned out, Angeline started to come back to herself after that day, though the process was gradual. Morgan noticed a difference that very night, but he knew better than to ask what had happened. He merely saw some hint of light in Angeline's eyes, noticed some moments when she laughed again. And sometimes, when she walked by him, she would touch his arm or back, as if to say, "I don't want to be distant anymore."

Morgan didn't tell her what she ought to do or feel; he merely accepted the change, and he felt as though life was coming back to his own heart and mind. He had been as lonely and disconsolate as Angeline. He had merely known that he couldn't add to her pain by saying so. And yet, it was the loss of Angie, even more than the loss of his little Jane, that had hurt him the most.

That first night, after the change, Morgan was sleeping with Angeline. In bed, he touched his hand to her waist. When he did, she rolled toward him and embraced him. It was all he needed. He held her for a long time, and he said, "I love you, Angie." He didn't ask her where she had been and whether she was coming back. He only repeated the words as he felt her relax, breathe steadily, and fall asleep. After she was asleep, he continued to hold her, and he prayed, "Father, life seems too hard sometimes. It's all I can do to keep up with all that's expected of me. But I can't manage without Angie. Please bring her back now. And please give her another baby. Give her something to hope for."

• • •

Ruth went to bed that night alone. She would have Morgan again next week, but the meaning of that had begun to change. He wasn't quite as young as he had once been, and he had learned more patience, more gentleness. He made her feel that *she* was important to him.

Still, all she had told Angeline was true. She had dreamed of a certain kind of life and had never had the chance to fulfill that dream. She loved Angeline, but she wished she didn't have to be such an unselfish person. She wished she could indulge herself, not always be reminded that she had to be patient and kind. She wished she didn't have to be careful about bragging up her children because that might set off jealousies. She wished she had her own house, her own family, her own self.

And so she prayed, "Father, give me strength. I'm not as good as I ought to be. I'm not as selfless. Not truly kind. I don't want to be called home to Thee, not with my children to raise, but I hope life won't be too long, either. Please help me keep going for now, and then let me come back to Thee before I wear out entirely. Is that too much to ask?"

• • •

Angeline slipped into sleep, satisfied to have Morgan close to her, and thankful that he hadn't asked anything more of her. She awakened in the night, and when she did, she felt the change in herself. A weight had been upon her for many weeks, but it was easier now, not pressing on her chest. She didn't want to think too much about that. She knew that if she let her thoughts return, her conclusions might be the same as they had been these last few months. She might see that nothing had really changed, and that life was what she had been saying it was since her baby had died. But some force inside her said that she couldn't feel sorry for herself forever. Life was not easy, never would be, and she had finally come to understand that.

She didn't want to think about heaven and some reward for living right. She didn't want to let God off the hook entirely. But she did want to feel that something was right inside her. She had been hating for months—hating those around her, hating even Morgan, and, above all, hating herself. But hate didn't feel right. She wasn't as good or strong as she had once thought she was, but she didn't have to be ugly inside.

She prayed, "Father in Heaven, I'm sorry. I don't understand why my Jane had to be taken from me, and I never will, but I can't always think of myself. I have to notice all the pain others are feeling, and all the pain I've caused Morgan and Ruth." And then, as she felt herself begin to cry again, she pled, "Forgive me. Please, forgive me."

CHAPTER 10

Two years passed—two good harvests and two years of expansion for the United Order—and the people were prospering as never before. The great blessing for the Davises was that Angeline had given birth to a healthy little girl named Patience, and Ruth now had a second son named Andrew. The babies had been born only six weeks apart in 1877, and now, in the spring of 1878, were both trying to take their first steps. Patience was nothing like her name, and she grew frustrated when Andrew could get around better than she could, but she loved her brother and, even more, adored her big brother Jefferson, who was now twelve. He was working outside a great deal now, alongside his father, or on assignments with the cattle crews. He was a good worker, but he was even better at his schoolwork. School sessions lasted only four or five months, in winter, but Jefferson relished those days, and he read every book he could get hold of during the other months.

Morgan had continued to make his long-haul trips, and now he took Jefferson with him, even though Ruth worried that they might be attacked by Indians when they were out in the desert alone. But Morgan was known on the roads, and he had learned to share with the Utes and Pah Utes, even Navajos who approached him. He had learned fragments of their languages so he could converse enough to show his goodwill. He knew Jacob Hamblin, Church missionary and ambassador to southern Utah Indian tribes, and he had accepted Jacob's philosophy of honoring and respecting the people who had lived in Utah Territory long before the Saints had come there.

Angeline and Ruth were busier than ever, with nine children filling up their joined houses. But Morgan saw a change in Angeline that worried him. The hardworking, intense, and interesting Angeline had now, at age thirty-five, settled in as a quieter, perhaps more resolved woman. She could laugh, and she was pleasant enough most of the time, but life had convinced her that she should expect less than she had once hoped for. She was rarely excited, and she admitted at times that she was wary, prepared for new difficulties or some new test of her faith. And even though she had what she had hoped for in her large and growing family, she sometimes expressed her frustrations with all the effort required, day and night, in looking after the children. It was easier not to have to cook and wash dishes, and the weekly yarn quotas for the sewing department were not an unreasonable burden, but work was incessant.

What troubled Morgan was that the vitality Angie had brought with her into their marriage was clearly diminished. He loved her as much as ever, but he missed the idealistic woman she had been. He knew, however, that he had lost something too. He was still firm in his belief in the purposes of the United Order, but it was not easy to take his joy entirely from the progress of the community. The cattle operation was large now, with five hundred animals to care for. He no longer oversaw the dairy, but the breeding, feeding, calving, and slaughtering work never ended, and the biggest undertaking was an annual drive of the herd to winter pastures in Arizona. Though he took pride in growing the herd and being able to sell off some of the cattle to the benefit of the Order, he faced a life that promised little change. He believed in a simple life—plain clothes, modest dwellings, group meals—but in his travels, he met men who had established good businesses, built fine homes, and collected a good many worldly possessions. He didn't envy the homes or the possessions, but he did wonder about the sense of accomplishment that must come from setting personal goals and reaching them.

Ruth, who was forty years old now, had blossomed in some ways. She had been a quiet, unassuming woman at one time, pleased at any little good fortune. She talked more now, was more confident, and she was not afraid to disagree with Angeline now and then. But she was not one to hope for a great deal more than she already had. Life, in her case, had taught her that she should be thankful that conditions were not any worse than they were. She had plenty of work with her family and with the Order, but she also had enough to eat and an adequate supply of small pleasures.

Morgan had always expected to stay close to Eb, his oldest friend, but Eb had been moved to the hennery, where he helped look after the egg production. It was not a job he liked, but it was no worse than many other assignments he might have received. What it meant, though, was that Morgan rarely saw him, other than at church. Eb and Mary Ann had had two more baby boys since moving to Long Valley, Peter and Phillip. Mary Ann was managing the demands of her life. She seemed happy, and Eb reported that her health was better than it had ever been. With their four children and Morgan's nine, it was almost impossible to gather in any one house. Morgan told himself that as summer came on, when evenings were pleasant, they could all gather outside for picnics. But he was well aware that, with their busy schedules, they wouldn't manage to do that very often.

Lyman Hunt worked on a farm that was close to one of the pastures, so Morgan saw him from time to time. Lyman and Alice had three children living; they had lost a fourth, a little girl who had died of whooping cough when she was only a year old. Art Brooks had become the foreman of the sawmill operation, and he was highly thought of by the members of the board. Morgan tried to stop by the mill when he could, just to say hello, but Art was always so busy that Morgan had given up the effort to chat for more than a minute or two. Susan Brooks was expecting her fifth baby and, in truth, looked worn out, as though she had aged twenty years or more in the eleven years since the newlyweds had all left the Salt Lake Valley together.

Morgan hated to think that he was losing some of his own enthusiasm. He kept telling himself that life was better than it had been during their Muddy River years, and he didn't dwell much on the discontent he sometimes felt. He was still serving on the board of directors for the Order, reelected each year, and he was relied on more and more as a voice of reason and especially as a voice of vision. More than anyone on the board, he kept before him a philosophical commitment to what the Order was meant to achieve. And maybe that left him somewhat disappointed. In one sense, Orderville was prospering as much as he had hoped it would. The town had moved a long way toward being self-sufficient. Not only did the Order operate big farms and a huge garden—along with dairy, beef, sheep, and poultry operations and a gristmill and sawmill—but several shops and small factories produced cabinets and furniture, wagons, barrels, shoes, clothing, soaps, brooms, silk, and leather goods. The board had purchased several ranches outside their valley to provide adequate grazing for cattle and sheep herds and had also bought a cotton farm near Washington, Utah. In addition, the Order ran a sugarcane and molasses operation, along with orchards, in Moccasin Springs, Arizona.

A telegraph line had reached Orderville, keeping locals in touch with the rest of the world. A department now maintained canals and supervised irrigation, and another operated all overland hauling. Seven midwives kept busy not only with births but also with nursing the sick. Priddy Meeks, the Thomsonian physician who lived not far from Orderville, was often called on for medical care. A bakery with a brick oven had been added to the dining hall and kitchen, and one hundred pounds of flour were used each day to bake enough bread for the big dinner meal.

So many people had moved to the town that not all could eat at one time, so the men ate in one shift, early, and the women and children followed. This took a rotating group of women to work with a head cook in the kitchen, along with a number of young women who waited on the tables—set out in three long rows. Brother Roberts sounded his bugle for each eating shift.

Each night, after the evening meal, an entertainment of sorts followed. Members would often present comic or religious readings, or the town band would play. And on Saturday nights, the young men cleared away the tables for a community dance. The young people also put on plays and held picnics or watermelon busts, and the Relief Society sponsored quilting or husking bees.

Harold Spendlove had served as a loving and admired bishop, but gradually, Tobias Carrington had shown himself to be a better manager, and he had been elected as president of the board of directors. Brother Carrington hardly seemed old enough for such a position. He was the youngest man on the board, only twenty-four, but he had a presence about him that immediately appealed to people. He was informed and thoughtful and, above all, decisive.

Morgan was pleased with the choice, and entirely willing to support him.

Church leadership had also been reorganized the year before. Bishop Spendlove had been called into the stake presidency in Kanab, and Brother Carrington had been called to serve as bishop of the Orderville Ward. He was immediately forced to deal with some of the growing challenges caused by more and more people showing up in town wanting to join the Order. Board members continued to talk about limiting the number who could join, but they had never settled on a good way to reject anyone. The new members needed houses, furniture, and other household items, and they added to the numbers being served in the dining hall each day. Certain items, such as milk and butter, were often in short supply, and to keep the kitchen crew from overworking, after a hearty meal for noon dinner, supper usually consisted of simple mush and milk.

Of all the United Order organizations in the Church, Orderville had become the most successful. Most of the others were already dissolved. It was not so much that they had failed; in most cases, they had never really gotten started. Brigham Young had gone to his grave in the summer of 1877, preaching to the end that the Order was the Lord's way of living. Now, however, President John Taylor was less concerned about carrying the United Order forward. He recognized the problems and continued to say that consecration was the way of the future but that challenges to the system would have to be worked out. Several leaders suggested that Orderville represented a test case. It was the town that had to prove to other members of the Church that true Christians could accept a life with no rich or poor among them.

What pleased Morgan was that even though he had seen some bickering and some disagreement about the details of the operation, the people had been unified enough to work their way through their problems. He thought their wisest choice, from the beginning, had been to move away from all the naysayers and unite a community of people who had all chosen this way of life.

All that was encouraging, but Morgan had hoped for a kind of spiritual unity that went beyond "prosperity." He saw examples of selflessness that inspired him, but he found in himself—and sometimes in his neighbors—the old human traits that prevented them from achieving a truly Zion society. He wanted to find a place inside himself that took as much pleasure in someone else's success as in his own. He did feel that desire much of the time, but his old impulse to look out for himself, to pursue life as an individual, was something he couldn't quite shed.

• • •

The next year seemed to bring even greater challenges. One night, early in the summer of 1879, the board heard Jud Jenkins and Clement Flynn, the department head and assistant department head of the wool operation, present their annual report. Morgan was well aware that wool production had been down a little lately, and that seemed strange in light of the progress shown in most departments.

But President Carrington didn't say that. He only asked, "So Brother Jenkins, how are things going in your department?"

"Quite good, I think. But there's always something going wrong that we don't expect. This year we lost more lambs than usual when that late snowstorm hit. Things like that you can't do nothin' about."

"Does that account for the lower wool production this year?"

The nine members of the board were spread out in a half circle, with the two brothers seated before them. Morgan noticed that Brother Jenkins was fidgeting and rubbing the palms of his hands on his trousers. He was a rather shaggy-looking man, with loose hair hanging onto his eyebrows and over his ears. "Well, no," he said. "I'm not sayin' that. But it'll make a difference in how things go next year. Sometimes, you have to look backward to see why things have turned out the way they do."

Brother Flynn hadn't spoken, but Morgan watched him open his mouth as though to add something, then duck his head without saying anything.

"Can we hope that the production will keep up with the pace of growth in town? I think we used up most of our wool ourselves this year and didn't have much to sell."

"That's true. But we've done all we know to do. I can't guarantee that we can increase the herd every year, or that we'll end up with more wool. We've rented lots of sheep, then paid for the wool we harvest off of them. Once we build the herd more, we won't have to do that. But the kitchen always wants mutton, so we have to decide how many animals we'll slaughter each year."

Morgan had his doubts about all this. He had produced more beef each year, and yet cattle sales outside Orderville had increased at the same time. On top of that, the money he made from the sale of oxen had turned his department into one of the financially strongest in the Order.

President Carrington had glanced toward Brother Flynn a few times and seemed to be picking up on his uneasiness. "What's your opinion, Clement?" he asked. "Do you have anything to add to what Jud has told us? Can we, in the future, produce more wool and still feed our people?"

"Yes, I think so."

"What would get us to that point?"

Brother Flynn glanced at Jud Jenkins and nodded as if to apologize. Then he said, "Well, I don't want to second-guess anyone, but I've raised sheep all my life, and I've learned a few things. It just seems to me—"

"He thinks he knows more than me," Brother Jenkins said, and there was irritation in his voice. "It don't matter what I do, he tells me I'm doin' it wrong." He didn't look at Brother Flynn.

Morgan felt the awkwardness. There were several townspeople attending the meeting, just listening; Morgan glanced at them and could see how still and stiff they had become. It was unusual for members of the Order to challenge one another in such a personal way.

"That's not at all the case, Jud," Brother Flynn said. He was apologetic, but his voice still sounded authoritative. He was a bigger man than Brother Jenkins, and even in his homespun clothes and well-worn boots, he had a manner that suggested greater importance. "There are ways to plan the season that can make a big difference. Even just training the shearers so they do a better job would help out. We lose too much good wool because some of our shearers don't really know what they're doing."

"This is what I hear all day long," Jud said. "He knows everything and I don't know nothin'. I've sheared a lot of sheep in my life too, and I guess I can get the wool off as good as the next fellow. But you men keep changin' who's on our committee, and then new fellows have to come in and do things they've never done before."

"Well, that's good to know," President Carrington said. "We need to leave your committee alone and let them get better at what they do."

"But, President," Clement Flynn said, "they won't get any better unless we show them how. We have to take time to do that."

Now Brother Jenkins turned and looked at Brother Flynn. "Oh, and don't we have a lot of extra time to stand around and 'talk' shearing when we gotta get the work done?" He looked back at President Carrington. "I'll tell you what. I'll step down from this job. I don't want it anyway. Give Clement what he wants right here and now, and then next year he can answer to you men the way I've had to do these last few years."

President Carrington was holding up both hands. "Wait just a minute. We haven't suggested any such thing, Jud. Don't get so hot under the collar. We're not your accusers. All we asked you was how things were going with the wool production."

"And I told you. Not as good as Clement Flynn thinks they should go. So make him the department head." There was silence for a few seconds, and then Jud stood up. "Am I finished here?"

"No, not at all," President Carrington said. "We haven't asked you to step down. As far as we know, you're doing the best job that can be done. Now settle down and let's talk about this just a little." The president looked at Brother Flynn. "You weren't suggesting that you take over the job, were you?"

"Not at all. Jud's a good sheep man, no question about it. And I don't see that I'm trying to undermine him if I make a suggestion now and then."

"How about, ever' day?" Jud said. He was still standing.

"Please sit down, Jud," the president said. "Let's think about this a little." But Jud didn't sit. His neck was red beneath his beard. Morgan could only imagine how hard he must be to work with. "Here's the thing," the president said. "The United Order is a system that helps us work together and produce more than we could if we were all running our own little herds of sheep. But it's a lot more than that. It's a plan in which all members give their best effort and we all support each other. We've asked you to head up the wool operation for now, and someday someone else might be asked to do it. We rotate jobs from time to time. But I'll tell you something I believe with all my heart: it's more important that you and Clement respect one another and work well together than it is that we produce wool and mutton. This whole system is built on love of God and love for each other."

Jud didn't look pleased at all, but he didn't say anything.

"So keep at it, and talk to each other," President Carrington went on. "Listen to each other. That's all we ask of you. Do you agree to that?"

"Well . . . we'll see how it goes," Jud finally said.

Clement added, "I think I have been too strong in some of the things I've said. I'll try to watch myself from now on."

So that settled that. But Morgan wasn't optimistic. He had known Jud for a long time, and the man did know sheep, but he was also stubborn about holding to an opinion no matter what anyone said to him. What Morgan fully expected was for all this to explode again one of these days, and then some sort of change would have to be made.

When Morgan got home that night, his wives wanted to know how the meeting had gone. "I'll tell you what," he said. "The United Order is perfect. It's the system God has chosen. The trouble is, He put that system in the hands of a bunch of regular folks. What we really need is a chorus of angels at our meetings, singing hosannas—and kicking us in the rear every time we act like mere mortals."

• • •

A few days after that, Mattie Glover showed up in Orderville. Morgan thought he saw her on the street one day, walking with her cousin Olive. He hoped it wasn't her, and he tried not to give the matter a second thought. But then there she was at church, wearing a deep red satin dress among all the gray homespun, and looking like a bright crocus that had sprung up after a long winter. She was prettier than she had ever been, and if he remembered right, she must be twenty now, close to twenty-one. He had assumed that she would be married by now, but he doubted that she would have come to visit Olive all alone if she had gotten married.

What he noticed immediately was that she had changed. She seemed a grown woman, not nearly so quick to giggle with her cousin or to chat during Church services. And when the meeting was over, she walked straight to Morgan and his family and shook hands with everyone. "It's so good to see all of you," she said. "You've had more babies, I see."

"Yes," Angeline said. "We have nine children now." Angeline was polite but reserved. Morgan knew what she must be thinking.

"You're a beautiful family, I'll say that much."

"And you're still not married, Mattie?" Ruth asked. "I thought you would be snapped up long before now."

Mattie laughed, and Morgan saw some of the playfulness he remembered, her dimples and her eyes flashing together. "I will say I've had a few young men come around to make my acquaintance, but they all had pimples on their faces and couldn't quite grow a beard yet." She gave Morgan a quick glance, as if to assure herself of the contrast. "I shooed them all away from my door."

Morgan was almost sure she was flirting—but without the obvious techniques she had used four summers earlier.

Morgan didn't want to think about her. As he walked with his wives back to their houses, he certainly didn't mention her, and he was relieved when Angeline and Ruth didn't say anything. It was

Jefferson who said, "Who was that lady? She's about the prettiest girl I've ever seen."

Ruth said, "She's Olive Glover's cousin. She's just visiting. But you're right. She's pretty as a picture."

Angeline still said nothing, but Morgan knew he had to avoid Mattie, not even think about her.

On the very next day, though, Mattie showed up riding a horse toward the ranch where Morgan was working. It was what she had done four years earlier, but this was entirely different. For one thing, she was alone, and she seemed to be seeking a way to spend time with him, which was considered immoral in Mormon society. He was standing near the hay barn, and no one else was around. But some of the men who cared for the cattle could show up at any minute, and he knew he didn't want to be seen with her.

So Morgan pretended not to see Mattie, and he walked inside the barn. He waited, listened, hoped she had ridden on by. But after a minute or so, the barn door opened and there she was, dressed this time in a simpler dress, almost as gray as the ones the women in Orderville wore. "Hello, Morgan," she said, not "Brother Davis."

"Hello," he said, but he added quickly, "You shouldn't come in here. It's not right for just the two of us to be here alone."

"I know that," she said. "I'll only be a minute. But there's something I need to say to you."

He took a breath, waited.

The light from the open door was shining behind her. She let her arms fall to her sides. She seemed calm, not nervous. "I didn't tell your wives the whole truth," she said in a matter-of-fact tone. "I *have* had many boys coming around, and I was not interested in them, as I said. But I do have a serious suitor. He's a good man, fairly well off, and he professes to love me very much. The only trouble is, he's not the man I would choose for myself. I've tried to stop thinking about you these last four years, but I haven't been able to do it. I'm wondering, have you thought about me?"

Morgan tried to sound neutral. "Well, of course, I've thought of you from time to time."

"And that's all?"

"Yes." He had to get rid of her, even if he had to insult her. He just couldn't go down the road she seemed to be suggesting.

"All right, then. I just want you to know that I fell in love with you back then, and I expected to get over it, but I haven't. At first it was only because you are so handsome, but I also watched the way you treated your wives and your children. You are the kind of man I would like to marry—for all eternity."

Morgan took a breath. What he didn't want to do was to let her beauty become important to him. "Mattie, thank you." Thinking maybe he had sounded a little too appreciative, he worked to take on that neutral tone again. "The thing is, though, I don't plan to marry again. Having two wives is more complicated than I expected, and it's hard for me to be fair and just to both of them. I can't imagine how confusing it would be to marry again." He hesitated, and then said, "I'm very sorry to tell you that." Immediately he wished he hadn't added those words, hadn't seemed sorry about that decision.

"Morgan, my father has four wives. I grew up with a whole throng of brothers and sisters and aunts. It's the way life seems normal to me. I understand why you might hesitate, but I can only say that I like Angeline and Ruth very much, and I would get along with them, even if they were to resent me at first. I would work hard to take some of their duties, cook and mend and watch the children—whatever would make their lives better. And I would respect Angeline's position as the first wife."

"That's easy to say, but—"

"I know. And now I'll leave. I don't want to beg you. I simply didn't want to accept the other offer without telling you, once, that I love you and would like to be your wife."

"Well, that's all right." Morgan looked down, tried to avoid her eyes, but when she said nothing more, he looked up to see her sorrowful face. "So, anyway . . . thanks for saying something," he said. "I don't mind that you did."

She turned a little, and he saw her profile, those delicate features, the pretty curve of her cheek. She took a step toward the door and then stopped and looked back again. "Do you want to think about it, or do you just want to say no right now?"

Morgan knew that he shouldn't think about it. He needed to tell her no and have done with it. And yet, his breath caught, and the words that came out were, "I guess I could think about it. My bishop told me, years ago, it's something I should consider."

"Good. And ask your wives. If they really don't want me, I wouldn't be happy anyway."

"All right."

She stepped outside, then turned around and smiled. "Thanks for considering me, Morgan. I'll be praying about this. I hope you'll do the same."

Morgan nodded, and then she was gone.

"I can't do this," Morgan told himself; and he was sure that was right. No matter what he had said, he would *not* think about it. But Mattie was grown up now, and she was lovely, not just pretty, and she understood about plural marriage and what it involved. Still, he knew she would make life difficult for him, whether she believed she would or not. Angeline would be deeply hurt, and Ruth would feel pushed further into the background.

Morgan doubled his fist and struck it against his thigh, and he made a vow to himself. He was not going to think about her anymore, not even once. He didn't have to pray about it either. His answer was simply too obvious.

• • •

When Angeline saw Morgan come through the door, she wondered what had happened. She could see that he was upset, or troubled, or that something was on his mind. But she didn't ask him. Ruth and the children were all waiting, and it was time to trek across the square to the dining hall. "Have you eaten?" she asked.

"Yes. I went there straight from the pasture. You go ahead now, and I'll look after the babies." That was their usual arrangement.

It was later, when Ruth had taken her children to her side of the shanty and Angeline's children were down in bed, that Angeline said, "So what happened today? You came in looking like someone had hit you over the head with a brick."

"Well . . . yes. Something did come up, and I need to mention it to you, just so you'll know, but I already settled the matter in my own mind. It's not something either one of us needs to worry about."

Now Angeline *was* worried. "Yes, it is. It's still written all over your face."

"Well, fine, I'll make it quick. Bishop Morrison talked to me a long time ago about taking more wives. He said he thought I should, and I told him I didn't want to. You wouldn't want me to take another wife, would you?"

Angeline had seen this coming. She just hadn't expected it quite yet. "Are you talking about Mattie Glover?"

"Well, yes. In a way. But I think you agree with me that it

wouldn't be good for our family for me to take more wives. I think we feel the same way about that."

But he was nervous, embarrassed. So it was coming, and what Angeline knew was that she couldn't stop it. If she told him not to take another wife—especially such a beautiful girl—she would create a terrible gap between Morgan and herself. She would always wonder whether he was pining for that younger woman. But if she said yes, she would have to see that girl every day and compare her own gawky self with such a petite and beautiful young thing. Whatever she said would be wrong.

Angeline was sitting in her rocking chair, but Morgan was still standing. She watched his face, his unwillingness to look at her, the sorrow in his eyes. He was like a little boy, ashamed of himself.

"Did you see Mattie today?" Angeline asked.

"Yes."

"Where?"

"She came out to the barn and spoke to me. She said she would like to be part of our family and asked me to think about it. She said she liked growing up in plural marriage and she would try to be a help to you and Ruth. She likes you, and she would like to be a sister wife to both of you. She asked me to think about it."

"Well, I'll say this much for her. She sees what she wants and goes after it. I thought you were supposed to call on her father and ask for her hand. I didn't know it worked the other way around."

"It doesn't, Angie. She was wrong to come out there and talk to me all alone."

"I guess that's how young women are acting these days. It seems wrong to me, but I have to admire her in a way. She didn't just flirt around with you. She told you how she felt."

"Yes, but that still isn't right. And I told her it would never work. Why would I want another wife?"

Angeline smiled. "Well, I can think of a reason, but I won't suggest it to you. I suppose you've thought about that already." Morgan looked down, avoiding her eyes. "Here's what I know. She told you to think about it, and you're thinking about it."

She watched Morgan's face. He couldn't bring himself to admit that he was, but she knew what was happening inside him. "No," he finally said. "Let's make this the end of it."

"Morgan, we believe in the principle. If I tell you not to marry her, I hate to think what the Lord might put me through. And I need the Lord to be on my side. If you're asking me whether I like the idea, you know better, but don't ask me to be the one to refuse her. You would never forgive me."

"But I—"

"Pray about it and make your decision, and then let me know. But don't put the decision on me. That's not fair."

"I'm not going to give it another thought, Angeline."

"It doesn't work that way, Morgan. The thought is in your head already. And I won't stand in your way if you think this is the right thing. But pray about it. Don't just think about those pretty dimples."

CHAPTER 11

Morgan didn't pray. He decided once again that he didn't need to. But thoughts kept coming back to him, so he finally prayed that he could put those thoughts behind him. Marriage was holy, and its purpose was to raise up a righteous generation. He didn't want to think of Mattie any other way.

But he couldn't settle himself. He didn't really think Mattie would suffer much if he turned her down, but he did think how sincere she had sounded, how sure of her love she seemed. He knew there were other things on his mind when he thought of her, but he willed himself to put all that aside. The fact was, she said she had prayed about the matter, and he did wonder whether she might have been guided to feel the way she did. Finally, he decided he would talk to Bishop Carrington, who had three wives, but who also had great wisdom for such a young man.

Morgan walked to the Big House in the town square. He found President—Bishop—Carrington in his office and asked whether he could have a few minutes of his time. Bishop Carrington was always welcoming. "Of course, Morgan. Come in," he said. "But you look awfully serious. Is everything all right?"

"It's hard to say," Morgan said. "I hope so." But when he sat down in the little office, he felt his face heat up. "I think you know Mattie Glover, who's been visiting her family here in town."

"Everyone knows Mattie," the bishop said. "When she walks into the church, the whole congregation turns to look at her. And I've noticed she pays a great deal of attention to you."

So there it was, out on the table—easier than Morgan had expected. "Well, I've never wanted to take another wife, but, as you say, for some reason she's taken an interest in me." He knew his face was coloring. "She could have any fellow she would like, and yet, she's actually told me that she would like to marry me. I didn't bring it up with her. I've never sought her out. I wasn't pleased that she would seek me out alone, but she took the chance to tell me, straight out, that she wanted to join my family."

"Congratulations. She'll make you a fine wife. Everyone knows she's pretty, but I've had a chance to talk to her since she returned to town. She's a good young woman, and she'll be a fine mother."

"But I'm not so sure, Bishop. Sometimes I think two wives is one too many. It's hard to balance everything just right. And three—I don't know—it seems like more confusion than I can handle."

"It's only hard if you make it hard, Morgan. When I got married, I entered the principle right from the beginning. I married Louisa and Ellen on the same day, and then last year, I added one more when I married Amy. And I'll tell you what. They're all three a little different from each other, and I imagine they disagree from time to time, but I don't worry about that. I stay out of such matters. We believe in plurality, and we've covenanted to make it work, no matter what the difficulties may be."

"I'm sure that's right, but Angeline is a strong woman, and she—"

"Strong is good. My wives are young, but they're not silly little things. Each one has a mind of her own." Then he stopped, and his smile gradually faded. "We've had six babies, Morgan, and three of them, all born to Louisa, have died—three little girls. We had them for a year or two in each case—long enough to love them with all our hearts—and we miss them every day. Ellen just had a new little girl, and Louisa is expecting, so we're looking to the future, but I strongly believe that our grief has brought my wives together as nothing else could."

"I understand that. When we lost our little Jane, Angeline's heart seemed to break, but it was Ruth, more than anyone, who got her through that time."

"Here's what I say, Morgan. There's no reason to make polygamy any more difficult than any other marriage. Love all three, show equal attention to each, and treat them all with honor and respect."

"But don't they get jealous of each other anyway?"

The bishop leaned back in his chair and laughed. He had good teeth under his dark mustache—a big-hearted smile. "Well, sure," he said, "that can happen. But just being man and wife is complicated. Just think of it as three marriages within one, and if you're a man of God, you bless your family with your priesthood and you teach your children righteousness. All the difficulties occur when you let your earthly wants get in the way. A leader in a family has to rise above all that."

Morgan took a long look at the man who was both his bishop and the president of the United Order. He was as good a man as Morgan knew. Morgan found himself thinking that maybe this matter didn't need to be so complicated as he had been thinking. But he couldn't just set aside all the drawbacks he had been considering. "The thing is, Bishop, we live in the real world. Both my wives tell me that when I spend a week with the other one, they feel lonely, and I see them take it out on each other at times. Or sometimes they take it out on me."

"I know all that. But Morgan, you remind the board all the time that the Order is more than an economic system. You tell people they have to see the greater purpose—to understand the Order as a progression toward a real Zion. Plural marriage is the same. You have to rise above pettiness. You don't split your love three ways; you multiply your love and give your whole self to each one."

Morgan wondered about the bishop's calculations.

"I know what you're worried about," Bishop Carrington said. "You're worried that Mattie is too pretty—and young. You wonder whether you won't give yourself over to all the wrong impulses."

"Well, yes, I guess. Still, I'll always love Angeline. From the beginning, I only wanted her. But then my bishop asked me to marry Ruth, and it took a while, but I've grown to be almost as close to her as to Angeline. I don't want to hurt the two of them. It's going to be hard for them to accept Mattie. They'll think I favor her—even if I don't."

"Are you sure you won't?"

Morgan looked down, considering. "I guess I am worried about that. It's not that I'll love her more. I just—"

"But you might want her more."

Morgan crossed his arms over his chest. He looked past the bishop at the whitewashed wall. He tried to think what it was he feared. "That does worry me," he said. "When she started flirting with me, I didn't want to notice it. But I couldn't get her out of my mind. And yet, I don't want to marry her for carnal reasons. I wouldn't blame Angeline and Ruth for hating me if I did that."

Bishop Carrington leaned forward and waited for Morgan to look him in the eye. "But Mattie asked *you,* didn't she?"

"Yes."

"Why do you think she did that?"

"She said she liked the way I treated my family, and she said she grew up in polygamy and it seems, for her, the normal way to live."

"And I know she noticed what a fine-looking man you are. What's wrong with that? Of course we marry people who appeal to us physically. But that doesn't have to make marriage all about carnal desires—not if we're moved upon by the Spirit to treat each wife as a daughter of God."

"I know. That's how I try to think about it."

"All right, then. Here's what I have to say. Mattie Glover could marry some young man her own age, if that were what she wanted to do. But she sees something better in you. She wants the kind of life you've given your first two wives. I see too many of these young men in our Church who want to live like Gentiles. They drink whiskey, curse, gamble—all those things. We don't have a shortage of men. We have a shortage of men who honor their priesthood and put first things first. Mattie is looking for a husband who will not only give her children to raise but will be an example to them and teach them the gospel. I would say that a quality young woman like that deserves a good husband like you. I wouldn't doubt yourself for a moment. Propose to her and then take her down to St. George and marry her in the new temple."

Morgan liked hearing all this. The idea didn't sound carnal at all, put that way. But something was still nagging at him. "Bishop, I read the scriptures just about every night. And I especially like the Book of Mormon. Not long ago, I was reading in the book of Jacob, where he says a man shouldn't want many wives and concubines. He says plural marriage is a sin. What do you think about that?"

"Did you read the whole passage?"

"Yes. I'm sure I did."

The bishop picked up a Book of Mormon from his desk,

thumbed his way through to the book of Jacob, and then read aloud, "For if I will, saith the Lord of Hosts, raise up seed unto me, I will command my people; otherwise they shall hearken unto these things." He looked at Morgan. "That's the exception. Usually, one man marries one woman. But when the Lord commands us to take more wives—to raise up seed unto Him—we obey. The Lord gave Joseph Smith a commandment, and He has continued it into our day. I'm not one who says that you can't be exalted to the celestial kingdom unless you enter plural marriage. Plenty of righteous people have decided not to embrace the principle. But I do believe that when you obey the Lord and live His higher laws, you receive blessings for your efforts, and you find in yourself a capacity to be the kind of man the Lord wants you to be."

"I can see that." Morgan hesitated. All this was making good sense, but he was not ready to make a decision. "I need to pray some more—and think some more—now that I've heard what you have to say. But if I decide to marry Mattie, I just hope that I can help Angeline and Ruth understand."

"Don't preach too much, Morgan. Don't even explain too much. Just show them, by the way you behave toward them, that you're as good a husband as you've ever been."

Morgan wasn't sure he had always been that good. He knew he was not an easy man to live with at times. "All right," he said. "I'll let you know what I decide. We'll need to obtain approval from Brother Brigham."

"I'm sure that won't be a problem." The bishop stood up. He was smiling. "I'm better at the philosophy than I am at the practice, Morgan. That's how we all are. My wives would surely tell you that I've got a long way to go to ever be the kind of man I want to be. But I do my best, and that's what you'll do."

Morgan nodded, shook hands, and then left. But he didn't say anything to Angeline or Ruth yet. He prayed almost constantly for three more days. Even then, he only "felt" he had his answer. He still wondered whether all his motivations were pure—and what Angeline would say.

• • •

Angeline had watched Morgan since he had first admitted that Mattie had proposed marriage to him. He had been pleasant, even kind to her, but he was preoccupied. She didn't think he had settled on an answer, but she had no doubt about what his decision would be. She tried to be angry about that, but mostly she was sad.

Then one night Morgan asked Angeline and Ruth if he could talk to them after all the children were in bed. Angeline could see how nervous he was; she had no doubt what he was about to tell them. What he rehearsed, rather briefly, was his conversation with the bishop. And then he said, "I've done my own praying, but I need both of you to pray, too. We should all be united in our decision, whichever way we go."

Ruth nodded. "I'll do that," she said. "I'll pray about it."

"I'll pray as *long* as you like," Angeline said. "I see no hurry." She heard the resentment in her voice and tried to calm herself. "But let me tell you something. The bishop may use idealistic words and pretend everything will be perfect, but women talk, and I happen to know that his own family has had problems. His first two wives grew up together, and they know each other a little too well. They quarrel plenty, and they also consider Amy a spoiled child. All while Amy was pregnant, she didn't think she had to carry any of the workload in their house. Her sister wives got sick of that."

"I understand. Bishop Carrington told me that things weren't always as he would like. Sometimes they—"

"I don't need to know anything more about that. But *you* need to know that putting three families together may be a spiritual feast—as the bishop describes it—but it's *difficult*, and I don't think we should expect it to be otherwise."

"I know. I told him the same thing. But he's right. If we enter into this, we have to keep our eye on the higher purpose and try to live up to the demands the Lord puts on us."

"You poor man. What a burden it must be to respond to God's *demands* and be forced to marry a beautiful young *girl*." Angeline told herself to be careful. Her words were harsh enough; the anger she was feeling was even stronger.

Morgan sounded hesitant, almost frightened when he said, "Angie, I know she's pretty. I understand how it must look to you. But I would never marry her just because of her outward appearance. Above all else, that's what I've fought to avoid."

Angeline didn't want to laugh—or shout. She decided not to argue the point. "Oh, I'm sure she's very sweet," she said sarcastically.

Morgan was still trying to explain himself—maybe to justify himself. "The bishop told me that Ellen—*and* Amy—helped Louisa through her grief. I know it's easy to lose patience in a marriage—or among sister wives—but we've learned, too, that we can support one another. Plural marriage is hard, but it does have its good side."

Angeline knew that was true; she knew that Ruth had helped her since she had lost Jane. She also knew there was more on Morgan's mind than unity and love among sister wives. "Morgan," she said, "you used to say that you missed me since our lives had changed so much. Now, if you marry her, I suspect I'll miss you forever." But the words had cost her. Her anger melted away, and it was sorrow she was now feeling.

"I promise not to let that happen." But she looked at him doubtfully, and, after a moment, he added, "I'll do my best."

"Oh, Morgan, I wish you could face reality more than you do. You always think we can live with the angels—but I've got devils poking at my heart."

"We all do. And it's good for me to remember—that I have too many theories and not enough sense of reality." He gave a stern nod, as if he had reached a conclusion. "All right. I'm thinking we're coming to a decision. I won't go forward with this. I'll tell Mattie our decision."

The strange part was, Angeline believed him. He meant what he said. But how would he feel the next time he looked at Mattie?

It was Ruth who said, "Let's all pray for a day or two before we decide. We all need to feel the same way."

Angeline didn't trust in that. She would turn out to be the evil one if the other two agreed. But she couldn't say that. How could she speak out against prayer? So she nodded her agreement.

That night, with Morgan in Ruth's bedroom, as Angeline lay awake most of the night, she kept asking herself what she believed. Was plural marriage from God or wasn't it? And if it was from God, could she blame Morgan for choosing a pretty young woman—or could she blame that young woman for choosing him? She had prayed before she had gone to bed and essentially told God she wasn't going to accept this, no matter what He had in mind for her. She was sorry for that now, and, as always, she wondered what would happen to her if she rebelled against God. It was very late in the night when she experienced a half-awake dream, and in it she saw a large family with many children. She was in the middle, looking around at a whole host of children and grandchildren. And she was very happy.

Angeline awoke immediately. She rejected the dream for a few minutes, but gradually she let the happiness come back to her. This wasn't like her. Lots of people had dreams and made too much of them, she thought, but this had come with all those questions on her mind—as though the Lord had sent her peace. And yet, it was uneasy peace. She didn't set aside the painful reality she now faced. But in the morning she went to Morgan and told him, "I prayed last night, and I'm all right with this now."

"Angie, don't just give in to it. Make sure you have your answer—because I came out of the night feeling just the opposite."

She wanted to tell him that she was sure he could deal with the reversal. But she wasn't going to say things like that anymore. Instead, she said, "This is the right thing. The Lord found a way to tell me so. I'm sure Ruth will be all right with it too."

And that turned out to be true.

• • •

Mattie was not exactly surprised when she saw Morgan walk toward her uncle's house, although she had begun to doubt that he would ever speak to her again. She stayed in a bedroom but heard most of what was said in the main room of the shanty. She heard Morgan ask for her hand, and she heard her uncle say, "I'm not her father, but I'll write my brother and let him know that I think well of you. I know already that Mattie has a desire to be your wife. So, as far as I'm concerned, you should go forward and assume you'll receive my brother's blessing."

Mattie walked to the door of the bedroom and waited for her uncle to invite her in. When he did, she didn't act surprised. In fact, she smiled at Morgan to let him know she was aware of what had just happened. But Mattie did have a concern. She didn't want Morgan to marry her because she was pretty. She wanted him to think well of her. Angeline and Ruth were women of substance, highly thought of in the community. She didn't want to be the young wife who had nothing more than good looks to give to the family.

"Would it be all right, Brother Glover," Morgan asked, "if Mattie and I walked out for a few minutes? We have some things we need to talk about."

"Yes, I suppose. Some people may say it isn't proper, but it's broad daylight, and I know you will act appropriately."

So Mattie walked out with Morgan. They didn't go far—just to the riverbank, where the Virgin River was still rather high. "I love this river," Morgan told Mattie. "It's clear and swift this time of year. All the time we were at the Muddy, I missed clear streams and good water."

"I like the wild roses along the banks," Mattie said. "I walk over here almost every day. When I was in Orderville before, it was where Olive and I would sit and talk in the shade with the sound of the water all around us." She had been holding Morgan's arm, walking next to him, but now she stopped and turned toward him. "Mostly, we talked about you. But I never thought all my girlish dreams would turn to this—what's happened today."

"You're getting ahead of me," Morgan said, and he laughed. "I talked to Angeline and Ruth. They have agreed to welcome you into our family. And I talked to your uncle. He seems to think that your father will not be opposed."

"He won't be. I talked to him about you before I came here."

Morgan turned a little more so that he was fully facing her. She was surprised, but charmed, to see that he was blushing. He was wonderfully good to look at with those eyes that seemed bluer than possible and his lean, firm cheekbones and jaw. She knew he was thirty-three—and she not quite twenty-one—but she liked that. She felt protected when she looked into his resolute eyes.

Finally, Morgan said, "Let me ask you, then, will you marry me?"

"You know I will."

"All right, then. We can make the trip to St. George after I get caught up a little on my work—and after we receive approval from Salt Lake City. But before we go, I want to add another little bedroom in our house. You understand, I suppose, that I'll stay with you there every third week, and the other weeks I'll be with Angeline and then with Ruth."

"I understand. That's how it was in my family."

"It's very important that I treat all three of you the same. I think Angeline is worried that you'll be my favorite."

"I don't think that could ever be the case. To tell you the truth, I'm not even sure that you like me. This was all my idea." She laughed softly, and she recognized that she was trying to get him to say what she wanted to hear.

"I do like you, Mattie."

"But I told you that I love you. Do you think you can ever love me?"

She knew he wanted this moment to be spiritual, high-minded, and she could see that he was trying not to concentrate on her face. "I do feel some love for you, Mattie," he said. "But I hardly know you. There's a love that comes only with time, and that's the sort of love I feel for Angeline and Ruth. I feel sure that our attachment will strengthen as we become better acquainted. I don't mean to sound quite so high-minded. But it's important we start out on the right footing."

"I know we will," she said. She touched his forearm. "But I can't wait to get to know you better than anyone I've ever known—to share *everything* with you."

"Yes, of course," he said, still holding onto his serious demeanor.

"Just know, I can never share more with you than I do with Angeline and Ruth. It's—"

"I understand. I didn't mean that. You'll have all three of us, but you will be my all in all—for all eternity."

She saw him take a breath, as though he were a bit overpowered. Then he said, "Let's walk back now. I have a busy day ahead of me. And that's something you need to know. I'm a very busy man, and sometimes you'll be with Angeline and Ruth and the children all day, and I won't be there. I hope you can get used to that."

"It's what I want."

"Well, good."

"Morgan?

"Yes."

"Aren't you going to kiss me?"

Morgan took another breath. "No, not yet," he said. "That's not proper."

"I understand. I'll wait. But just know, I do look forward to kissing you."

There were words she wanted him to say, but he didn't. He turned instead and walked her back home.

All that day, she wondered: was he only marrying her because she had asked, or maybe because he believed in the principle? She had thought she had seen signs that he was taken with her, but now she wasn't so sure.

• • •

Morgan worried that he had been too formal with Mattie. But she did need to know that he wasn't a young boy, excited only by her pretty smile. All the same, he moved up the day of their wedding a couple of times, and finally the two made their trip to St. George. Mattie slept in the wagon and he slept out on the ground for the three nights they were on the road. The following morning, in St. George, they were married in the temple. They stayed a night in a little guesthouse there, as Morgan intended to do his bargaining and trading the following morning. As it turned out, that took him pretty much all day, so they stayed one more night before setting out for home.

The heat in St. George was intense. Even the morning was uncomfortable. "We'll be out of the worst of this heat before the day is over," Morgan told Mattie.

"But we don't have to hurry, do we?"

She was sitting next to him in the wagon, close, with her arm folded into his arm. Morgan was amazed at how natural that seemed to him already. "Well, I do need to get back. It's slower going back, with a load in the wagon, but we can probably make it in four days."

"But maybe we could take five nights instead of four—and make the ride a lot more pleasant."

"Well, that might not be such a bad thing. I told Ruth and Angeline we would be gone ten days or so, but I didn't say exactly what day we'd be back. Five days might be better than four. We loaded up the wagon a little more than I expected we would."

"Maybe we'd better sleep a little more than we have the last two nights—or we'll look all frazzled when everyone sees us."

Morgan was taken by surprise. It was the sort of thing Angie had said years ago, but not anything she would say now. Angie had learned that he didn't like to talk in the daytime about what had happened the night before. "Well . . ."

"I embarrassed you, didn't I?"

"Well, actually, yes," Morgan said.

"All right. I won't say things like that from now on. But it was nice last night, Morgan. I want you to know that—and now I won't say another word about it. You need to know, though, that's the way I am. I usually say what I think. And I want you to be that way with me. I think we should be able to talk about anything."

"Mattie, I'm not like you in that regard. I can't say *everything.*"

"That's all right. Just always tell me the truth."

"I think we need to come to an understanding. Our purpose is to raise a righteous family. Maybe we indulged ourselves a little too much these last two nights, but that won't be our way of life most of the time."

But Mattie was laughing, and she pressed herself close to him. "It's God who invented the way we make babies, Morgan. I think He wanted us to enjoy it."

Morgan decided not to comment on that. He was surprised by the things Mattie said sometimes. Angeline and Ruth both liked to be with him—although the excitement had gradually diminished—but Mattie seemed more eager than they had ever been, and he wasn't sure he wanted that. Still, Morgan wondered about himself. If he weren't careful, he could begin to indulge too much in the enjoyment Mattie was speaking of.

And yet, she had a point. The Lord had granted those pleasures to men and women. It was so they would desire to procreate. That made perfect sense. The only problem was, the world was corrupt, and such pleasures enticed many men into all sorts of misbehaviors. If he thought too much about nights with Mattie, he might forget the things that mattered much more.

"I promise I won't be so forward from now on," Mattie said. "And we can hurry home, if that's what you need to do."

"Well, no." He tried to sound casual when he added, "I think five nights might be better. That way, the oxen won't get so worn out. It's hard for them to make this climb back into the mountains."

"Now, *that* was exactly my concern. We don't want those poor oxen to be all done in." She laughed.

Morgan laughed too, and he decided to stop early that night, after the hard climb over the Hurricane Cliffs.

• • •

The first night home, Morgan slept with Angeline in her bed. She didn't ask him about his trip or his time with Mattie. She didn't ask him much of anything; she turned her back to him and seemed to go to sleep very quickly. He had a feeling, however, that she was awake—and struggling. He knew that deep, heavy breathing that overtook her when she actually fell asleep.

Morgan got up early. He needed to check on the cattle herd after such a long absence. He fed his animals, and then he walked to the corral behind the shanty, patted ol' Lightning on the neck, tossed his saddle up on her back, and flipped the stirrup out of the way.

"So, why are you whistling?"

Morgan turned around and saw Angeline. "What?"

"Why were you whistling? I don't remember the last time I heard you whistle."

"I didn't realize I was whistling. I'm sorry. Did I wake you up?"

"No. I've been awake for a long time. I just want to know what causes you to whistle now? I think maybe you used to whistle, but you stopped a long time ago."

"I whistle sometimes, I guess. I'm not sure." He turned back toward his horse and looped the cinch through the ring.

"Early in the morning when you have a day of work ahead of you? Is that when it seems a good time to whistle?"

Morgan tried again to think whether he had been whistling, and, if so, why. But he truly had no idea. Still, he knew he had made a mistake. "I'm sorry, Angeline. It was rude of me with everyone still asleep. I should have thought what I was doing."

"She must be making you very happy."

Morgan knew that was what Angeline had been suggesting all along, but he had hoped she wouldn't say it. He pulled on the cinch and tightened the saddle.

"It's all right. I understand," she said. "You need someone who can make you happy. I've given you far too many worries, and I've let you down too many times."

"Angeline, don't do this. You know how much I love you, and you know I don't think that you've let me down."

But they both knew that he was leaving out some things. Angeline had changed over time. She wasn't the forward-looking woman she had once been. Morgan understood that life had been difficult for both of them. He wasn't as optimistic as he had once been either. Worries about the United Order, struggles between people in the town, and the burden of constant work had taken a toll on him.

"I don't want to be your old, ugly wife, Morgan. I don't want to complain, and I don't want to feel worried and hopeless the way I have at times. But it doesn't seem fair that you can turn to someone else—and she can bring you back to yourself."

"Angie, she's young. She hasn't known heartache yet. Life will knock her down a few pegs, sooner or later. She's like a happy child right now, sort of carefree, but that doesn't mean that she can make me happy and you can't."

"Maybe not forever. But right now, she's beautiful and exciting, and Ruth and I must look like old hags by comparison. I don't blame you for taking joy where you can find it. But I wish I could be young and carefree. I just don't know how to do that."

"Angie, you're my wife. We've loved each other for a long time. Joy in life doesn't come from being young. It comes from shared experiences, shared hopes. Don't make up your mind about Mattie right away. Let's all enjoy her youth, and let's let her sunny ways cheer us, but we don't need to be like her. That's not something we can go back to."

"You say that, Morgan, and it all makes sense. But I know what she's done for you these last few weeks, and it's something I can't do. I don't hate her for it. I don't even resent you. But it's not easy to be cheery when I feel like a tired old mule."

Morgan hated to hear her say such things. Angeline was still the woman who had fought through twelve difficult years with him, and he still knew her better than anyone else in the world. What he really found himself wishing was that he had never married other women, that he had clung to a simple life with his first love. He wondered now whether he hadn't made a terrible choice to marry Mattie. Maybe, in the act, he had destroyed Angie, and he knew that he owed her the most.

He walked to her and tried to take her in his arms, but she held back. He pulled harder, and then she gave way. She let him hold her close, and he heard her first sobs, then felt her tears work their way through his shirt. He held her for a long time, and he told her over and over that he loved her. What he wondered was whether they could ever be as happy as they had once been.

CHAPTER 12

Mattie was a new complication in the lives of Angeline and Ruth. On the one hand, she was always full of fun. Jefferson, who would soon be fourteen, had fallen devotedly in love with her. She entertained the younger children for hours each day. She had the time and inclination to give them more of her attention than Angeline and Ruth ever could. She had received an assignment to work in the community kitchen on a steady, not a rotating, basis. She supervised the young women who waited on the tables, and she liked that. The assignment did take her away from the house early, but she had time to come home between meals. When she returned home in the evenings, her sister wives had finished most of the household chores, and she was free to play. She was a sort of child herself, and she liked to play outside with the children or make up games to play inside as the fall of 1879 progressed into winter.

In some ways Mattie relieved pressure on the older wives, but Ruth found herself jealous both of the time Mattie had and the love she had gained from her children. Still, all that was nothing compared to the tension Ruth felt whenever Angeline and Mattie were in the same room. Angeline was outwardly kind to Mattie, treating her a little as though she were her daughter. But Angeline surely saw what Ruth saw: when Morgan came into the house, Mattie's personality changed. She was still playful with the children, still quick to laugh, but she was also needful of his attention. She liked to touch him, rub her hand over his back, sometimes whisper in his ear. And on the weeks when Mattie slept with Morgan, Ruth felt envious of the joy she saw in Morgan while, at the same time, she worried about the sadness she sensed in Angeline.

One fall evening, when most of the leaves were down and a bit of snow had been blowing about, Morgan carried in some wood and got fires burning brightly in both shanties. "That should do us for the night," he said. "If it gets too cold, I'll get up and put another few sticks on both fires."

"But it's not time for bed quite yet, is it?" Angeline asked.

Ruth heard, and surely Morgan and Mattie heard, the accusation in Angie's voice. Angeline was sitting not far from the fire with some of the children's stockings in her lap. Darning stockings was something Angeline didn't like to do, and she usually put it off, but she was never at ease just sitting. She was looking down at the stockings now but not stitching, perhaps only avoiding Morgan's eyes.

"Well, it *is* a little early," Morgan said. "But I'm tuckered out tonight. I don't want to be up too late."

"Then make sure you're not," Angeline said, and again, everyone knew what she meant.

But Mattie laughed. "That's good advice, Morgan. Why don't you go to bed if you're so tired? I think I'll stay up a little longer."

This was the first night for Morgan to be with Mattie after his weeks with Angeline and then Ruth.

Mattie was smiling coyly now. Surely she knew that she had placed Morgan in an awkward spot. Ruth didn't think that was a proper way to treat a husband, and yet, she couldn't resist enjoying his discomfort.

"Oh, I didn't mean that I'd go off to bed quite yet," he said.

"Then maybe I will," Mattie said. "I put in a hard day at the kitchen."

This was a little too obvious. She was gaming him, taking pleasure in the dilemma she had foisted upon him. Ruth saw Angeline look up with a sly little smile of her own, as if to say, *Keep him squirming, Mattie.*

Ruth exchanged a glance with Mattie, and Mattie winked. Ruth had to duck her head to avoid laughing. There was, even in plural marriage, a certain power a woman could wield, knowing a man's weaknesses. It only seemed right that Morgan should have to trip over his own feet a little before he found his way into Mattie's bedroom.

But Ruth could see that Morgan had had enough. He surely knew he was being teased, but he must have noticed too that he was being laughed at. Without saying another word, he picked up his Book of Mormon, walked to the table, and sat down. He opened the book at random and, without turning a page, bent his head and read—or at least pretended to read.

Ruth gave Mattie a nod, and now that Morgan wasn't looking, they both smiled rather widely. Angeline looked up and joined them in their little pleasure, and then Mattie stretched and yawned. "Well, then, if Morgan's going to read, I guess I'll go off and get some sleep. Could we have our prayer now? And then I'll go to bed."

Morgan looked at Mattie seriously. "Yes, of course," he said. But Mattie was turning on a different kind of smile. Even Ruth thought how beautiful she was. And the smile was saying, *I'm only teasing, Morgan. Please come to bed with me.*

Morgan formed a little rectangle with his wives, and they all knelt down. Morgan said the prayer himself, surely aware that this was an awkward time to call on one of his wives, just when they were all enjoying his predicament. "Oh, Lord," Morgan said in the middle of his prayer, "forgive us of our frailties. Let us rely on the pure blessings of the Spirit, the higher impulses Thou hast granted us. Help us to be kind to one another, and to treat each other with due respect."

It was an obvious reprimand—as much to himself as to the others—but Ruth didn't doubt his sincerity. Poor Morgan wanted so badly to do what was right. He couldn't help it that he was made of flesh. If he could have stripped his body away and lived wholly in the spirit, she thought that was what he would choose to do. All the same, when everyone stood up again, the situation hadn't exactly changed.

Then Mattie, seemingly moved by the prayer, simply took hold of Morgan's hand and led him off to her bedroom.

The room was a corner of the shanty, set off by a boarded wall with no plaster. What Ruth hated about that little place was that sound carried through the thin wall. Ruth decided she didn't want to stay any longer. She didn't want to sit next to Angeline through this, and she also knew what it was like to be in the opposite situation—when she was with Morgan and the other two wives were awake in the next room. But poor Angeline had no place to go. She looked down at the stockings again, and now she didn't look angry or resentful. She looked heavy, dejected.

"I guess I'll go to my room," Ruth said.

Angeline looked over at her. "Please, stay a little. Let's talk about something."

Ruth understood. So she stayed, and she and Angeline said anything they could think to say, just to fill the room with their voices, but Ruth kept wondering, imagining, even wishing, and she had no doubt that Angeline was doing the same thing.

• • •

As winter came on, Mattie knew she was pregnant. She was glad for that, but she felt surprisingly changed. She wasn't very sick, just a little out of kilter. She did feel tired more often, and she found herself less able to give quite so much time to the children. They still loved her, and she loved them, but she sometimes struggled to be as patient with them as she had been in the beginning.

What bothered her most, however, was that Morgan told her he couldn't be "with her" while she was expecting. She had known that was something he believed—that it was preached in the Church—but she wasn't really ready for the loss of something that had quickly become so lovely for her. She knew that Morgan was struggling with the same loss, and she pitied him, but she was almost certain that her sister wives took delight in the change.

Mattie gradually realized what she had to do. She had to serve Angeline and Ruth more than she had so far; she had to prove to them that she was the person she had promised to be. She noticed things that needed doing in the house and set out to do her share and more. She tried to be cheerful even when she didn't feel happy.

The winter, in that regard, was good for her. She had to create a friendship with Morgan, not just a romance, and especially, she realized how much she could learn from Angeline and Ruth. She made a concerted effort to get to know them, to understand who they were: their backgrounds, their concerns. As she listened to them—and expressed her own feelings—she felt the glimmerings of a connection start to build. Angeline still resented Mattie, and

Ruth always held back a little, but Mattie began to feel some of the strain between them diminish.

• • •

The following spring, 1880, brought problems to the United Order. Almost from the beginning the question had been raised about the credits members should receive for the work they did. The whole idea, it seemed to Morgan, was that all work had value, and no one's contribution should be rated as superior to another's. President Carrington agreed with that, but some members of the board had their doubts. The First Presidency of the Church, under President John Taylor, had warned the Orderville leaders that legal problems could arise when members quit the society and made demands as to what dividends they deserved for the work they had devoted to the organization. Daily wages had been established, with different rates for men, women, young men, young women, and children. But these had only been "paper wages," for bookkeeping purposes. Now, however, settlements made with departing families, along with cash demands to operate the various enterprises that the Order had initiated, left the organization in a strapped financial situation. Fortunately, a new member who had moved to Orderville was able to sell stock he owned for a thousand dollars, and he passed the money along to the board. But this was only a temporary solution, and cash problems continued.

The Order had dealt well in protecting against poverty after the recession of 1873, but now, the silver mines that had opened—or reopened—in southern Utah were creating prosperity in Mormon towns, as people either worked for the mines or sold their grains and produce to the miners. This relative prosperity in other towns was drawing away more members of the Order, and those who were moving to Orderville were mostly people who hadn't prospered and were looking to a society that would support them.

The board spent many hours discussing a way forward, and finally began to work on some changes in the bylaws. For one thing, different wage rates for different assignments had to be considered, perhaps only as credits, but as a way to show on paper how much an individual leaving the order had "earned." Morgan understood the need, but he felt as though the original idealism of the Order was giving way to earthly concerns.

After a long session one night in the dining hall, the board members finally agreed to continue thinking and praying about the issues before them. Morgan left the hall late in the evening. It was a cold spring night, with a steady wind blowing down the valley. Morgan didn't have far to walk, but he pulled the collar of his greatcoat up around his ears and walked fast. When he was almost at the shanty, he saw a man waiting outside. It took him a moment, in the dark, to recognize Samuel Layton, a man who worked on one of the farm crews. He was a slight little man who always struggled to hold firm to a bucking, twisting plow. Others seemed to understand that, and they usually assigned him lighter work, but he was a proud man who had always claimed that he wanted no special favors. He also had a large family: two wives and fifteen children. But what Morgan knew about him, more than anything, was that he was never happy about the decisions the board reached or the treatment he thought he received from his department head. He was not one of the Muddy River Saints, but a latecomer who had arrived extolling the idea of the Order and then had begun, almost immediately, to suggest ways it could be improved.

"So, what come of the meeting tonight?" he asked as Morgan approached.

"You should have attended. We welcome everyone."

"I don't like meetings. But what did you settle on? I heard you was talkin' about wages."

"We did talk about wages, but we didn't make any decisions."

"Yer gonna start payin' some people more'n others. Thass what I heard."

"It's possible. We don't know yet."

"Thass what you say, but I notice, you can't look me in the eye. I know what's comin'. I'll get the lowest scale for a man, and all my children, no matter how much they work, won't git much of anythin'. This all works against a family like ours."

"Brother Layton, think about it. Your family is fed, the same as the rest. All your children have clothing, and you enjoy every social event we put on in town. What more do you want? All we're talking about is how we keep the books. Unless you want to pull out and leave town, none of those figures mean a single thing."

"But thass just the point. It's hangin' over me. If I do decide to move on, what am I gonna take with me?"

"Sam, why even talk about leaving? If you stay, you'll raise up a family among the best people you'll ever know, and you'll want for nothing. If you pull out of the Order, you'll have to open up new land somewhere and work your children harder than they work now just to scratch out a living. How would that make any sense?"

"I'll decide when I hear the scale. Just tell me how you broke it down."

Layton was wearing a beat-up black hat with a wide brim. It was pulled down low on his forehead, and his collar was turned up. Morgan couldn't make out his face in all the shadows. But he knew the man. He would argue any point and never admit that he might be wrong. Morgan didn't want to stand in the cold and have that kind of a conversation. "Listen, Sam, I already told you, we don't know if we're going to set new pay scales or not. And we haven't started talking about what those scales would be."

"My oldest son will be old enough to marry before long, Davis. That's what I'm worried about. How is he going to get started in life? Will you let all the children of the members join the Order, or will you tell them to move on? And if you do that, what will they be able to take with them?"

So Layton did have a point. Morgan had known for a long time that this was a predicament that would have to be dealt with sooner or later. The Order couldn't grow indefinitely. At the same time, every grown child who left couldn't demand so much that the Order itself would struggle to stay afloat. There was considerable expense in feeding a whole town, keeping up adequate numbers of teams and equipment, and helping those who were sick or injured. And as the population aged, and fewer young people could work to take care of the elderly, what would happen?

"I know what you're saying, Brother Layton. We've talked about some of these problems that will come on us eventually. It's something we have to spend more time on. But remember, if you were farming a piece of land somewhere else, and your children were reaching adulthood, how much would you be able to give them when they set out to live on their own? What we give them here is experience and understanding of good farming methods. Maybe we can help establish another Order somewhere, and our children could carry on with what we do here. We've talked about something like that. But trust us, Brother. We're trying to do this right."

"Thass all very easy to say, but I have a feelin' you're looking out for yer own families more than some of the others."

"How can you say that? What do I get that you don't get?"

"Higher pay, if you put in this new scale. You're a department head."

"I keep telling you, it's only higher pay on paper. It won't change anything!" Morgan stepped close to Layton, tempted to give him a shove. "But I might as well be talking to a rock. I'm not going to stand out here in the cold and listen to your accusations. It's men like you who distort the whole meaning of the Order. If you want to drop out and get a settlement, I say, do it, and do it now."

"There's no call for you to—"

"That's all I have to say, Sam. You have your mind made up, and you don't hear a thing I say." Morgan turned, walked to his door, and stepped inside. He knew he would have to talk to Sam again, try to settle matters between them, but he wasn't ready to do that quite yet.

He stood with his back to the door and felt how tired he was. He devoted so much energy to just trying to make the Order work, and he wasn't sure that anyone appreciated his effort. He wondered if maybe he was the one who should leave the Order. He was weary of working with people who didn't understand the purpose behind the organization. He suspected he could make a better go of things on his own anyway. He could work hard, produce, feed his family, increase his acreage, keep cattle, and, in the end, have something for himself. As long as he stayed in the Order, he would always share everything, and maybe that meant he would be left without a single possession—except on paper.

He knew immediately that he was thinking wrong—thinking like Sam Layton. He needed to repent. But not tonight. Tonight he would be as angry as Layton, and then—maybe tomorrow—he would go talk to the man again. At the very least, he needed to apologize for his outburst. Maybe he could still show Sam what brotherhood was all about.

• • •

In June, Mattie began to experience occasional labor pains, but one night the pains woke her and continued to grab. She knew her time had come, but she didn't say anything until she heard someone up and moving about. She got up, dressed, and came out to the kitchen. It was Ruth who was out of bed, and she was feeding little Andrew, who was two years old now. "He wakes up so early," Ruth whispered, "and he's always hungry."

"That's good. That's what a big boy ought to be." Mattie patted Andrew on the head. He was sitting in a high chair at the table, his mother next to him. She had toasted some bread at the fireplace and fried an egg for him. "Good morning, Andrew. Are you happy today?" Mattie asked.

Andrew smiled. "Yah," he said. But he still looked half asleep.

Mattie had not planned to say anything yet, but a pain struck hard and she gasped, bent forward, and waited for it to pass.

Ruth looked up from where she was sitting. "Is it time?" she asked.

"I think so."

"Go back to your bedroom and lie down. I'll get Angie and we'll make sure everything is ready. How often are the pains coming?"

"I don't know. Every ten minutes, I guess. Maybe not quite that long."

"You've waited for a while, haven't you?"

"There was no reason to bother anyone. I've had pains before, and then they've gone away."

Ruth stood up and took Mattie in her arms, bending herself around her big middle. "Mattie, you're a remarkable young woman," she said. "I made up my mind that first summer you came to Orderville that you were a spoiled brat, but I see none of that in you. You always worry about the rest of us. You don't put yourself first."

Mattie didn't know what to say. It simply wasn't true, and yet the words touched her, and she was glad to have Ruth, like a mother, ready to help her. She really was scared. She had been hearing about childbirth all her life, about the terrible pain, and as much as she wanted to have children, she wished she didn't have to go through the things about to happen to her that day. "Thank you," she whispered, "but I'm not so good as you think I am."

Mattie went back to her bed and lay on top of the covers. She heard people stirring about. She kept telling herself that millions of women had gone through this experience, and she could too. It was only when the pains hit her with force that she doubted herself. She tried to hold an image of her baby in her mind. Maybe Morgan wanted more sons, but Mattie had always imagined raising a lovely little girl she could feel very close to. She hoped for a pretty daughter, but only pretty enough to be pleasing, not so beautiful that everyone would think of nothing else when they looked at her.

Sister Ballif came after a time, and she and Ruth and Angeline fussed over Mattie. They put oilcloth under her, then covered her with a sheet and a blanket. Sister Ballif said that everything was progressing well, but she felt sure she had time to go home and get her family up and moving before she would be needed.

Angeline told Mattie, "It's a nice day. I'll take the children outside when the time gets closer."

Mattie knew what Angeline meant: that she could scream if she had to, and not worry about the children being near. But Mattie didn't want to scream. She wanted her sister wives to know she was brave, no matter how young she was.

"Mattie, this will be a hard day," Angeline told her. "Ruth and Sister Ballif and I will help you, but it's a time when you and the Lord meet face-to-face—more than at any other time. You'll need Him, and He'll be there. And when it's finally over, the miracle comes. You'll understand more about life than you ever have before. And about love."

Mattie felt the tears slip from the corners of her eyes. She was moved by the affectionate tone of Angeline's voice. The woman was coming to accept Mattie as part of her reality, but this was the first time Mattie had heard love in her voice. It meant everything to her.

Through the morning hours, Mattie kept her resolve not to scream, but finally she couldn't hold back, and she heard her own voice like something outside herself, crying out against an agony she hadn't been able to imagine. She wanted God to come to her now and take it all away, but that didn't happen, and toward the end, she began to feel anger that this experience had to be so overwhelming. The day seemed twice as long as any day she had known, and when the sun was setting outside and the house was darkening, she thought maybe she was dying, that something terrible was happening that was about to tear her apart. And then there was a gush of relief that suddenly emptied her, leaving her limp and exhausted. It took her a few seconds to think of the baby, but by then Sister Ballif was saying, "What a fine little girl you have, Mattie."

Mattie heard the tiny, desperate squeals and glanced down to see a small red body squirm in Sister Ballif's hands. Mattie shut her eyes and rested while the women took her baby and cleaned it.

Finally Angeline placed the baby in Mattie's arms. Mattie

touched the little one's face, looked at her fingers. She could hardly believe that this baby was whole, an actual miniature person with all her parts and a funny little face, flattened still. But she was a real person, and Mattie was alive. The miracle had come, just as Angeline had promised. What Mattie hadn't known until then was that the miracle was in the powerful surge of emotion she felt for this tiny child: instant love of a kind she had never known.

"You need to rest now," Ruth was saying, but all the women had things to tell her. Mattie didn't quite listen. She only gazed at her little girl. "If it's all right with Morgan, I'll call her Hannah," she said. "I had a little sister who died from whooping cough. Her name was Hannah."

"Morgan will like that, no doubt," Angeline said, and the women agreed that it was the right name—because of the little sister.

But Mattie knew something else. Hannah was the wife of Elkanah in the Old Testament—a man with plural wives. She had originally thought of the name because Hannah was Elkanah's favorite wife. Now she regretted that reason for her choice. Today she had felt hints of love from Ruth and even Angeline, and she knew that Morgan would soon be allowed into the room—and he loved her too. That was what she wanted more than anything—to be loved by her family, and for her family to love her daughter the same way.

• • •

Mattie's life changed during that first year of Hannah's life. She hadn't exactly known it, but she had always been the center of her own world, the beautiful girl everyone envied. She didn't feel so beautiful now, and, most surprising, that didn't seem to matter.

She had a child to care for, a baby who kept her up at night. She loved Morgan more than ever, but he had taken on a new role as the father of her child, not just the handsome man she had fallen in love with.

What also changed was that Angie and Ruth were essential to her now, and she didn't see them as rivals. They knew about caring for an infant, and they showed her what to do. All the children loved little Hannah, and that connected everyone. Mattie had thought of herself as a new part of a big family, but now she felt a sense of acceptance. It wasn't as though sharing Morgan suddenly became easy, but that part of her life seemed subsumed in a larger reality: she was like her sister wives—a mother—and they all had to work together to keep their family well.

Still, as Mattie gradually adjusted to all these changes, she was more aware than ever of what she had asked of Angeline and Ruth. She wondered how she would feel if another woman attracted Morgan's attention. She still saw the uncomfortable glances, especially from Angeline, when she went off to her bedroom with Morgan. She suspected that the discomfort would never disappear entirely, but she understood better now, and she no longer felt a need to prove herself more enticing than the other wives.

• • •

The spring and summer of 1881 were rainier than usual, but it was on an August day—a bright, sunny day—that a dark cloud hung over the canyon and a thunderstorm struck hard. It hardly seemed anything out of the ordinary, but within an hour a deluge of water and mud came gushing out of the canyon above the town and directly into the square. The flood came with no warning, and the rush of water and debris was wild and loud.

When Mattie first heard the noise, she had no idea what was happening. She was in the kitchen cleaning when something seemed to slam against the back door, and then water began to seep in under the door and flow through the house. She ran to look out a window and saw the mud smash into the dining hall out on the square, breaking down the doors. Mattie realized with a jolt that Hannah could be in danger. She hurried to the baby's crib and picked her up.

Mattie knew she had to get to Angeline and Ruth. They would know what to do. But she wasn't sure where they had gone. As she opened the door to the adjoining shanty, she saw only children. Then, just at that moment, the outside door swung open, and her sister wives hurried in. They were covered in mud, and Mattie knew what had happened. Some of the children had been playing outside, and Angeline and Ruth had gone out to pull them in. Angeline was carrying Thomas; Ruth had Tabatha. Morgy had brought Suzanne inside. The older girls—Naomi and Ella—had clearly struggled through the mud and were covered in it, but they had made their way inside. The three-year-olds, Patience and Andrew, were still inside the house, looking bewildered. Andrew had begun to cry.

"We have to get away from here," Angeline said—firmly, but with control. "Let's carry all the little ones we can, and you big children will have to follow us close and walk through the water. Let's take all the dry blankets we can, too. We may not get back in here for a while."

Mattie was still holding Hannah. She ran to her little bedroom, grabbed two blankets, returned and wrapped up Hannah and Patience, and then picked them up, one in each arm. She looked about to see what else she might need to take with her, but Angeline said, "That's all you can carry." Just then Jefferson crashed through the door.

"Oh, Jeff, thank goodness," Ruth said. "I didn't know where you were."

Angeline, holding Thomas, said, "Carry Andrew for me, and Suzanne, if you can."

"All right," Jefferson said. "Where are we going?"

"Up the mountain above the blacksmith shop."

Jeff looked around and spotted Mattie. "Stay with me," he told her. "The mud has stopped flowing, but it's deep. Stay close to me and we'll get through."

Jeff was becoming a man, and Mattie knew he wanted to be someone she could rely on. She was touched that he cared so much for her.

Ruth had picked up Tabatha, and Ella and Naomi were holding Morgy's hands.

As Mattie took Hannah and Patience and started out, staying close to Jefferson, she saw Morgan riding his horse fast, sloshing through the water and mud. "We're going to climb the hill above the blacksmith shop," she shouted to him.

"Good. Keep going. Are all the others still inside?"

"Yes, but they're ready to leave."

"I'll go help them." Morgan rode to the house.

Mattie kept struggling through the water, with mud clinging to her boots. Once she had made it to the base of the mountain, she and Jefferson turned and looked back. By then she could see that Angeline and Ruth were on their way. Morgan was still in the house, his horse waiting for him outside.

It was maybe fifteen minutes later that Morgan caught up with everyone else. Lightning was laden with the things Morgan apparently wanted to save, including his Book of Mormon, which was under his arm.

And then there was nothing to do. The water had already

begun to recede, but Angeline told the others, "We can't go back until things dry out a little, and then we'll have lots of mud to clean out of the house."

"I don't think there'll be too much damage to the shanties," Morgan told her. "I just hope we haven't lost everything in the big garden."

"The dining hall and the kitchen are going to be a mess," Mattie told him.

"I'm sure that's right. We'll have to work out other arrangements for eating for a while."

It was all settling in. Days, weeks, of hard work were ahead, all for a few minutes of high water. Somehow Mattie had never thought of a flood coming out of the canyon, but she heard Angeline say, "It's like being back at the Muddy. Every time we got a little peace, something would happen again."

What struck Mattie was that Angeline and Ruth—and of course, Morgan—had experienced so much together, Mattie would never catch up. She was suddenly thankful for this little test. She could work hard and show her sister wives that she could hold up in hard times too.

But the next few days were tedious—and long. Morgan brought a wagon and a tent to the site on the hillside, and everyone camped out. Angeline and Ruth seemed to know all about that, but Mattie found it difficult. Her sister wives put her and Hannah in the wagon, with quilts under and over them, but sleep wasn't easy. Still, she worked all day, first mucking out the house and then washing everything.

And then, while Ruth watched the children, Angeline and Mattie went to the dining hall to help get the building ready for church on Sunday. In one corner of the room the mud had gathered and settled almost two feet deep, but the whole floor was covered. Most of the men were trying to clean out barns and free up farm equipment that was mired in mud, so the women took over at the dining hall. They used shovels to fill up wheelbarrows, and some of the young men wheeled the mud outside. It was a huge, slow task, and some of the women talked of their aching backs. But Mattie took pride in working hard. She also liked to make the women laugh.

At one point, late in the afternoon, when everyone was running out of steam, Angeline turned and looked at Mattie. Angeline had seemed brighter these last few days, as though she thrived on work, loved to show how hard she could shovel. But when she looked at Mattie, who had sat down on the floor for a few minutes of rest, she said, "Mattie, I'm glad to see you with mud on your face and in your hair. I just wish you didn't look prettier than ever. There ought to be a law against something like that."

Mattie didn't really like hearing that. She ran her fingers over her hair, and some dried mud fell off. Then she looked down at her boots, caked all over. She reached down, swept a little dab of mud into her fingers, and then got up and walked closer to Angeline, who was now looking away from her. "If you think it looks so nice, here's some for you," she said. She reached and swiped the mud across Angeline's cheek and on into her hair.

Angeline spun around, surprised.

"Hey, it's true," Mattie said, and she laughed. "You look prettier yourself with a dirty face."

Angeline seemed confused for a moment, but then she smiled. She actually looked pleased as she grabbed a handful of mud from the floor, and in one motion she came up flinging. The mud splatted across the front of Mattie's dress, some of it hitting her neck and chin.

"Now, that was unkind," Mattie said, sounding entirely serious.

"I didn't think a nice person like you would attack a delicate little thing like me. I'm very disappointed in you." She saw some doubt in Angeline's face, as though she suspected Mattie might be speaking in earnest. But Mattie stepped closer, crouched, and picked up a handful of mud. Angeline jumped back, obviously expecting to be struck by the mud, but Mattie said, "I only regret that these other women are not as pretty as we are." Mattie spun and thrust the mud at Sister Jones, who had been laughing at all she had seen.

Now the whole group liked the fun. In the next few minutes, mud flew in all directions. Even the boys operating the wheelbarrows got involved, mostly smudging one another, but flipping some mud in the direction of the sisters as well.

Laughter filled the room. When the mud finally stopped flying, one of the women said, "The town's going to wonder what kind of cleaning ladies we are."

"We're not afraid to embrace our work. That's all," Mattie said.

Angeline looked at Mattie and beamed. Mattie had never felt so close to her. The day Hannah had been born, she had felt a new, if somewhat temporary, affection between them. But this was as real as mud—just ordinary, everyday friendship.

Things did change after that—somewhat. Angeline continued to thrive on the hard work, and in the days that followed, Mattie saw more enthusiasm in her, more fun. But Mattie couldn't change the fact that she was young, and she couldn't change the way Angeline felt about that. What she knew was that she would have to be productive, hardworking, supportive—all the things a younger wife was supposed to be. And more time would have to pass. But they had this shared experience now. They were surviving something hard together, and they would always have memories of that.

CHAPTER 13

On Sunday the Orderville Saints held Church services in the dining hall. It still smelled musty from all the water and mud, but it was clean from floor to ceiling. Morgan sat with Ruth on his left and Angeline on his right, and at the far end of the bench was Mattie, who always volunteered to sit next to Jefferson, with the younger children in between. Morgan was never sure what was correct in a situation like that. He didn't want to give special consideration to any one of his wives, but he also never wanted to give Angeline the feeling that she was anything less than the honored first wife. What he knew was that indications of his affection could be noticed by one or the other of his wives, and even though the women weren't really easily insulted, they could—for reasons he didn't always understand—become quiet and apparently disappointed. He often wondered about himself, that he couldn't foresee and avoid such hurt feelings.

Still, Morgan felt good about his family right now. Angeline and Mattie had laughed together this last week more than ever before. They joked about casting mud on each other, and he had never quite understood what that was all about, but something good had happened between them, and they had brought Ruth into the story. What pleased Morgan most was that Mattie seemed to be living up to her promise. She did like Angeline and Ruth, and she tried hard to make the best of things, to be a help with the children and assist with all the work around the house. In turn, Angeline and Ruth looked after little Hannah, seemed to love her as much as their own children, and sometimes told Mattie that she had done enough and ought to relax and play with the children, the way she still liked to do.

Morgan knew that Angeline still envied Mattie's beauty. Angie had told Morgan one day recently, "My face looks like an old leather saddlebag, all worn and creased. But Mattie, she's as fresh and pure as an angel. When I look at her, I feel downright homely."

There was no right response to a comment like that. Morgan knew that. If he denied that he thought Mattie was pretty, Angie would know he wasn't being honest, and if he said that Angeline was just as pretty as Mattie, she knew better than that, too. So he had only said, "I think you *are* beautiful, Angie. You know I do."

"But you've stayed so handsome. I look like I could be your mother."

"I think there's something wrong with the mirror you've been looking at," Morgan told her. "When I look at you, I see who you are, and I see all our memories hovering around you—like stars in the heavens."

She laughed. "You had to stretch to come up with that one, Morgan. Half those memories are the times I've put your teeth on edge with my sour moods."

Morgan put his arms around her and said, "I love you, Angie. More than ever. And that's all that really matters."

Angeline seemed to know that she had said too much, that she was fishing for compliments in the wrong stream. Morgan did love her, but he wasn't going to tell her that she looked twenty, or that she never bothered him with her changeable moods. What

Morgan also knew, however, was that he could be bothersome to her as well. He recognized that he held back his feelings, ruminated too much, and theorized about some of his beliefs more than he practiced them. Her practicality was just what he had valued when they married, and he loved her ability to dig in and get a job done. It was what he liked to do too. But over the years, he had acquired the habit of stepping back to think about what he had done—or what he wanted to do—and he always imagined a better world than the one he lived in. Angeline settled for reality; she didn't expect anything else. He was sure that was why the idealized future that he talked about sometimes became annoying to her.

Now, sitting in the dining hall, Morgan glanced at Ruth—tranquil Ruth. He loved what she had become to him: a support, the father of his children, always reliable. She was surely just as aware as Angeline that she wasn't as pretty as Mattie—or, for that matter, as attractive as Angeline—but she accepted such things like the sand and wind she had learned to live with in the Muddy River Valley. She never fussed about the things she couldn't change. All the same, there was a deep well inside Ruth: emotions that rarely touched the surface, rarely even changed the look of her face. But she did feel things, did care. Morgan knew that, and he knew that her experiences had taught her not to be disappointed, not to compare what she had to what she had once dreamed of having. In her way, she taught those things to Angeline and Mattie—and Morgan. She kept life even.

Morgan knew plural families that were like armories full of explosives. Some women absolutely refused to live in the same house with other wives. And some plural wives clashed over cooking, over housekeeping, over cheese making and every other responsibility. But above all, sister wives clashed over their children. Many women accepted the slights that came to them as part of polygamy, but when they thought another wife's child was being favored, they would rise up like mother badgers, ready to scratch and fight. Morgan knew all this from conversations with other men trying to live the principle. Some of those men seemed oblivious to such issues. They stayed out of the house as much as possible and ducked for cover when they saw troubles at home. Some tried to be the masters of their domain, tried to rule and reign—and a few of those even managed to intimidate and demand and come away victors. Or at least they claimed that they did. But most were like Morgan: aware that they had bitten off more than they could ever chew and just hopeful that, day to day, they could balance all the pressing demands they felt. Still, as Morgan looked on down the row, surveying his children, he saw they were polished up as much as possible after all the mud they had worn that week, and Morgan, more than anything, was pleased that his wives cared for—and loved—all the children.

Morgan was also thankful as he looked along the bench and saw three wives and ten children all looking rather mild. There were plenty of wiggles, and, at one point, Tabatha had given Thomas a good whack and said, much too loudly, "Slide over. Quit kicking my leg." But Angie didn't defend her son against Ruth's daughter. She leaned over and told them both to shush. And they had done so—more or less.

What Morgan knew, of course, was that life was always changing. Different circumstances brought out different traits, different worries, even different needs. He had become more of a worrier over time. He tried to imagine what would happen to all these little ones as they began to make more of their own choices. At least for now, though, he thought they were doing quite well.

Morgan was also happy with the spirit he felt in the town since the flood had come. What the Muddy River folks had needed,

Morgan supposed, was a good natural disaster. It was what they knew how to deal with. Deciding on rules and regulations for the Order was tedious and difficult—but cleaning up mud was something that could be attacked. Progress could be measured in shovelfuls. Something about sweating together, battling a common enemy, seemed to bring out the best in people, and the satisfaction of that cooperation and progress filled everyone with joy—not in the work, perhaps, but in the camaraderie.

Bishop Carrington welcomed the Saints and asked them to join in singing, "Let Us All Press On." It was just the right hymn, and the members sang it with spirit. After the passing of the sacrament, the bishop stood again.

"Brothers and sisters, this has been a hard week. But a good one. I'm glad to see you here this afternoon, scrubbed and shiny. But to be honest, you never looked better to me than when you were covered in mud. You sisters worked as hard as the men. And let me say this: there's no people in this world I would rather get down in the mud with than you good folks here in Orderville. We sometimes wonder whether the United Order of Enoch can work in our modern world, but we saw our unity in action this week, and we proved to ourselves that it takes more than a little flood to stop us.

"We do, however, have to make one change in our way of doing things—at least for the present. As I think you all know, the brick ovens in our community kitchen filled up with mud and collapsed. We have always followed President Brigham Young's admonition to eat together as a family in our dining hall—and that's been good in many ways. But there have been drawbacks, too. So maybe it's a good time to try another way. We're going to ask all families, at least for now, to eat in their own homes. Some of you have lean-to kitchens on the back of your shanties. For now, please share the use of those kitchens, and we'll start building a similar addition onto every house.

"What the board has discussed—and we'll want your opinion on this—is that it might be better if we continue this practice rather than to rebuild the kitchen and bakery. Our town has grown very large, and it's getting more and more difficult to feed so many people. Even more than that, some families are feeling that, since their children are eating with the other children, they are losing the chance to sit around a family table where the gospel can be taught and family concerns can be discussed. Some young people eat quickly and then run about together, separated from supervision and, all too often, falling into small temptations. It all feels a little too wild, and the thought is that the traditional family table might bring members of individual families closer to one another. So let us know what you think, but for now, plan on taking a draw of food from the storehouse and cooking in your own shanties or houses. But please, do not waste. There is great efficiency in feeding everyone together, and we don't want mothers to start requesting more food than they can keep fresh and put to use in a way that avoids spoilage."

He then explained that some sort of food voucher would be issued that could be used, like money or scrip, to purchase needed items from the storehouse. Details would have to be worked out and announced later.

Morgan had been in the discussions about this policy change. He actually hated to see common dining come to an end. It was true that families were split apart for those meals, but the community had had a chance to get better acquainted at group meals, and the time spared from everyone cooking really had opened the way to much higher production. Still, he knew what the bishop was saying. This issue was like so many others the Order was facing:

ideals and hopes often looked better in the planning stage than in the practical act of making them work.

After the meeting, the change in eating arrangements was the major subject of conversation. "Here's what I propose," Mattie said as they were walking home. "I'll become the cook. My assignment in the dining hall just ended, and I'm the one with only one baby. Ruth and Angeline can work at their carding and spinning, just the way they do now, and, until I receive another assignment, I'll provide the meals."

Morgan was pleased that she would offer, but a little worried, too. "The only thing is, you've been helping out in the kitchen with all those huge pots and big ovens, but all we'll have is a wood-burning cookstove."

"I know. But I think that might be easier—just a few loaves of bread instead of hundreds."

It was Angeline who dared to ask, "Did you cook a lot at home, Mattie—you know, when you were growing up?"

"Not really. But I know enough to fry meat and roast potatoes—all those kinds of things. And I'll be able to learn much, much more. You and Ruth can tell me what to do, and then I'll carry out your wishes. I can't think of a better way to improve."

"That sounds good to me," Ruth said, and she laughed just a little.

Angeline glanced at her and then laughed too. "We have no complaints," she said.

It was Morgan who was still worried, but he knew better than to say so. "Well, it's settled," he said. "We have a new chef."

But once again, the theory was better than the practice. Mattie did know how to fry things—or cremate them—and she could boil water, but she had no concept of making mush, and the first time she served her mush for breakfast, the children were too innocent to be diplomatic. Even Jefferson, who had always thought Mattie could do no wrong, pushed back his bowl and said, "There's something wrong with this stuff."

But Mattie only smiled. "I know what you mean. I must have done something wrong. It didn't taste good to me, either." She looked around the table. "All right, then, I'll fry some eggs. Everyone pour your mush into the slop bucket. We'll take it to the hogs, and they'll think they've died and gone to heaven."

"Or the other place," Jefferson said, and everyone laughed, even Mattie.

Before the week was gone, Mattie's mush was tasting much better—after some instructions from Ruth. What amazed Morgan was Mattie's resilience. He wondered at himself, that he had proposed to her without really knowing her.

• • •

Mattie was actually not quite so happy as she pretended to be. She had been devastated by the reaction everyone had had to her mush. And she noticed every day that some of the family, especially the children, pushed her meals away without eating very much. Ella was eleven now, and she had always eaten everything on her plate at the dining hall, but she blurted out at the dinner table one night, "When are we going back to eat in the big hall? Everything tasted better there."

"Ella!" Ruth said. "That's not a polite thing to say."

Ella looked at her mother, maybe confused, as though she had no idea what she had said wrong.

"It's all right," Mattie said. "Your aunt Mattie is better at playing jacks than she is at cooking vegetables. I think I boiled the carrots and parsnips too long."

Ella seemed to realize that she had hurt Mattie's feelings. "It was just nice to see all the other girls at the dining hall," she said. "I wish we could still go there."

Mattie knew she had to learn more of the skills expected of a mother. When she was a girl in school, boys had offered to carry her books home, or they had sent folded love notes to her in class, often professing their plans to marry her someday. But some girls could join a snowball fight and throw as hard as the boys. Boys seemed to like that, too. Later, after they had all grown up, it was the girls who had known how to throw snowballs or play at leap-frog who were married before she was. It was as though men kept her at a distance, most of them seeming to think, "I would never dare to spark her." She had overheard young men say those very words. The truth was, she hadn't been interested in them anyway; that was part of the problem. She had always believed that she could have her pick, so she had kept looking about, thinking there might be a better choice.

But she had fallen for Morgan completely. Maybe his charm had been that he paid little attention to her until she had gone out of her way to let him know she wanted him to take a look at her. Even then, if he had been impressed by her looks, he hadn't let her know it.

What Mattie feared now was that it would be the capacity to cook and care for children and take care of a home that would mean the most to him. Once he learned that she wasn't really very good at anything, maybe it would only be the pleasure she could give him when alone that would be her hold on him. But she suspected already that as people grew older, that part of their lives probably mattered less.

So Mattie wanted to be more useful, and cooking at home seemed to open up that possibility. She watched Angeline when she weeded the little garden outside their shanty, trying to gain some understanding of what a well-kept garden looked like. So far, Angeline had had to reprimand her several times for hoeing away the plants instead of weeds. Mattie knew she had to get so she could tell the difference.

Right now, what Mattie wanted was for Ella to think she could provide a decent meal and at the same time be like a big sister to her. When Mattie had first joined the family, she and Ella had played together. Ella had always wanted to be a princess and had asked Mattie to play as if she were an older sister. Mattie had loved that. But lately Ella wanted to be with her friends in town, not play make-believe.

So, after dinner, Mattie whispered to Ella, "Should we go for a little walk? Maybe we can find some of your friends, and you could spend a little time with them before it gets dark."

That pleased Ella very much. So the two walked. But the weather was turning cool, and not many children were outside. "Let's walk to the river," Ella finally said. "I brought some bread. We can feed the ducks."

But there were no ducks in the pool by the bridge, where Mattie sometimes saw them. All the same, the two stood by the river and chatted about the pretty rustling sound the breeze made in the cottonwoods, and they enjoyed the yellow glow on the water as the late afternoon sun filtered through the leaves.

"Water is so nice when it trickles along this way," Mattie said. "It's hard to believe that we had such a flood not long ago."

"My mother loves this little river. So does Aunt Angeline. They always say it's so much better than the Muddy River. I was born down by the Muddy, but I don't remember that. Everyone says life is better here, and I guess it is, but sometimes, to me, it seems too much the same every day."

"What kind of life would you like to have? Do you want to stay here when you grow up, or move away?"

"Move away, I think. But then I'd miss everyone." Ella had an innocent face, pretty eyes, a gentle smile. Mattie could only think that she was just beginning to discover herself and try to understand the world she lived in.

"What do you want to be?"

"What do you mean?" Ella bent and picked up a little stick. She tossed it in the river and watched it float away under the bridge.

"Would you like to be a schoolteacher or a doctor or—"

"A doctor? Girls can't be doctors."

"Oh, yes, but they can now. And not just midwives. Some of our sisters have gone to the East and studied medicine. There are lots of things girls can do."

"What did you want to do, Aunt Mattie—be a mother?"

"Yes. But I imagined other things. I'm not smart enough to be a doctor, but I would like to work in the Church. Maybe someday I can be the president of the Relief Society or something like that."

"Not me. I think I want to go to a city, like Salt Lake City, and go to dances and plays and all those things. I've never seen a play—except the ones people do here sometimes, just for fun. But we don't have a real stage or anything like that."

"You could be an actress, maybe."

"I know. I thought of that, but I don't know where I could learn to do it."

"We could practice together. You could try out for one of the plays the young people put on. You could learn a lot from the other actors."

"Jefferson could be the hero in a play."

"He certainly could." Mattie knew how much Ella looked up

to her big brother, five years older than herself. In fact, lots of girls in town were taking notice of him now, and Mattie had noticed that he paid attention to Harriet Hart. He liked to talk to her after church, although so far he had never dared to ask her to dance at the Saturday night socials.

"Jeff wouldn't like to be an actor, though," Ella said. "He likes everything our dad likes. He wants to work on a farm and raise cows and ride horses."

"I like to ride horses too. Have you ever ridden your father's horse?"

"Not by myself. He says Lightning is getting ornery in her old age and might buck me off. But he picks me up and lets me ride with him sometimes." She found some little pebbles, and she began to throw them into the water, one at a time. She and Mattie watched as ripples, in circles, expanded until they disappeared. "Papa told me once, that's how life is. We all make a little mark in the world—like a splash in the river—and then the water moves on and we're gone—and no one knows we were even there."

"Oh, Ella, our lives mean more than that."

"That's not what he meant. He just meant we can't think we're more important than other people. God knows us, and that's all that matters."

"But it's not wrong to want to do things in this world. Being in a play or riding a horse—those are nice little pleasures. They're gifts from God. Maybe I could take you for a ride on Jeff's horse. Then I could let you ride a little by yourself."

"All right. When?"

"I'll talk to Morgan. We'll see what he says."

"He'll do it for you," Ella said confidently. "He does whatever you say."

"No. Not really. But I'm a pretty good talker when I want to convince someone to accept my opinion."

"Could you teach me to be a good talker? I get scared when I have to say something at school. I forget everything that I had in my head."

"Sure. I can help you. When you have an assignment for school, bring it to me, and we'll practice together."

Ella suddenly turned and put her arms around Mattie. "All right," she said. "I want to be like you. Maybe you can show me lots of things."

Mattie loved the moment, but she doubted herself. She wasn't sure she could help much with school assignments, and, the truth was, she didn't know much about riding horses. Her uncle had had to saddle his horse for her and hoist her into the saddle—and those rides in Orderville were the only ones she had ever taken. Mattie would help Ella all she could, but she wished now that she had learned more when she was growing up.

As the two walked back toward the compound, Mattie spotted some young people coming out of the dining hall. The sun was setting now, and Orderville was at its best, with the day's heat passing away quickly and the sun glowing from beyond the bluffs. The young people were laughing together—three boys and five or six girls—and the sound was echoing through the valley. One of the girls waved to Mattie and said, "Hello, Sister Davis." Mattie knew the girls from working with them in the kitchen. The one who had spoken was Madeline Roberts. "How are you?" Mattie asked. "What are you doing now that you don't have to serve meals anymore?"

Madeline pointed at one of the boys. "Orson, here, wrote a play. We're rehearsing to perform it."

Mattie stopped in front of the group. "My goodness, that's just what Ella and I were talking about. She would like to try acting. Is there a part for her, or—"

"It's all right, Mattie," Ella was quick to say. "I don't know anything at all about acting."

"Nor do we," Orson said. Then he grinned. "It's a madcap play. Its purpose is utter silliness. I can add another part in two minutes of concentrated creativity. I may not be the Bard of Orderville on the Virgin, but nonsense pours from me like honey from a dripper."

"Yeah. Slow and sticky," one of the other boys said.

Orson laughed. "It's true," he said. "But it must be slow and sticky to match Evan's speaking voice, which hobbles along like a three-legged dog."

Evan laughed too; he didn't seem bothered by the insult.

Mattie knew Orson Millard a little. His mother fancied herself a poet, and she had sometimes read her verses after dinner in the dining hall. Orson had liked to drop into the kitchen and tease the girls who served there—these same girls who were laughing now.

"But would it really be too much trouble to add a character?" Mattie asked.

"Not at all. Let's see. Ella, you could play a grandmother, perhaps, or maybe a workhorse with a long, swishy tail."

"I don't think so," Ella said, but now she was laughing.

"How about a ten-year-old girl? Could you try something that remote to your experience?"

"I'm eleven."

"Ah, that's great. You know all about being ten—from past experience. I have something in mind already. I can drop a line in for you in every scene. You'll be the one who says, 'I'm sorry, but this play makes no sense to me.' But you must say it with . . ." He spread his arms and looked to the sky, then, with exaggerated intensity, pronounced the word " . . . *feeling.*"

"But I'm serious," Mattie told him.

Orson suddenly assumed a solemn face. "And I, too. Have you ever known a more somber man than I? I'll write something up tonight, and Ella, you can rehearse with us tomorrow evening."

Ella nodded, and she actually looked quite pleased.

"He really is a good writer," Madeline said. "The play *is* silly, but it's kind of smart, too." All the others were nodding. "Orson wants to write plays and novels and—"

"And farce!" Orson said. "My specialty is farce."

"You read a lot, don't you?" Mattie said.

Another girl, Sariah Peters, said, "That's all he ever does. Read and write."

"Not true," Orson said, but his tone had changed. "Most of my waking hours, I work at a job I truly hate. I only *wish* I could read and write all day." He looked at Mattie. "I milk cows early each morning and evening, and I feed cows, I scrub the mud off cows, and when they fall down and skin their knees, I give them a kiss on the lips and say to them, 'There, there.' They like that. I've never known what 'there, there' means, but it's what I say to them."

He had never smiled through all that, and Mattie heard something like despair beneath the laughter in his voice. He was a gangly boy with big ears and a shock of reddish hair that hung on his forehead. Mattie had known for a time that he was a fish out of water in this place, but she had considered him funny and happy, not tragic.

"But you really do want to be a writer?"

Evan was a rather heavy boy with a childlike face. He put an arm around Orson's shoulders and said, "It's the only thing he wants to be."

"Yes, Evan is right," Orson said. "And my dog wants to be a mountain lion, but his chances are not good. Neither are mine."

"Why?" Mattie asked.

"Never mind. I'm mostly just joking."

"No, you're not. Isn't there some way you can do what you want to do?"

"First, I would probably need to attend an academy, perhaps even a university, and I've looked all up and down Long Valley, even in the canyons, and so far I haven't found one. And how am I—or any of us—going to get out of here? The only thing we know how to do is farm or milk cows or weed the big garden." He hesitated, then added, sounding more serious, "How are we supposed to do something with our lives other than homestead a farm and grub in the dirt to feed ourselves? I read books about the world, but I've never seen it—not any of it."

Evan said, "If we leave Orderville, we won't really take anything with us. We've all gone to school each winter, but we don't know how to live any way but the way we live here."

"I'll tell you what I'd like to take with me," Orson said. "I'd like to take away a beautiful girl." He didn't say it, but Mattie knew from the way he had been looking at her that he was thinking, *like you.* He continued, "See these girls? I like them all. But they think I'm too silly, and, frankly, they don't like my looks—not that I can blame them for that. But that's not the biggest problem. In two or three years, they'll all be taken by older men—men like Brother Davis. And we fellows their age, we'll be kicking a boulder down the road."

"It's not always like that," Mattie said. "You can—"

"Why didn't you marry someone your own age?"

"I don't know exactly. I fell in love with Brother Davis, that's all."

"I'd give everything I have—or ever will have—if someone like you would fall in love with me. But I'm going to have to settle for those cows I kiss and hug every morning."

Mattie had no idea what to say, but she felt tears come into her eyes. When she glanced around at the girls in the group, they were all looking down, as though they couldn't really deny what Orson had said. Mattie hadn't thought about any of this—what the young men were going through as they watched men who already had wives marry the young women their age—but she didn't blame Orson for the doubts he was having about his own life and his own future. For the first time, she wondered what would become of such boys as the years passed.

CHAPTER 14

On a lovely October day, early in the evening, Angeline asked Morgan to walk out with her. A breeze was picking up, whisking leaves about, and birds were making a commotion in the trees as the sun began to set. Morgan couldn't remember the last time he and Angeline had walked together simply for the pleasure of it.

For a time Angeline tucked her arm in his, and mostly they talked about the beauty of the valley and how pleased they were that they had come here. They walked along the river, which was now a gentle stream, and they saw a few friends taking their own strolls. There were more than seven hundred people in Orderville now, and Morgan and Angeline knew almost all of them. They greeted the people they saw, but they didn't stop to talk; instead, they continued beyond the town, out where cut wheat was now stubble in the fields. Morgan talked about the progress in the cattle herd—ten times bigger than the herd he had started with. As he talked, however, it was obvious to him that Angeline didn't take great interest in such matters. He felt quite certain that she had something else on her mind. So he quieted, and waited, and finally she said, "I suppose you know that I'm expecting again."

"Yes. I know."

"Because I'm so grouchy?"

"No. I've noticed the changes starting."

"Yes. You know me well by now."

The two had stopped. The sun was red now and seemed to be sitting on the cliffs above them. The entire valley glowed, as though in lamplight. The peace of it, the generosity, filled up Morgan's chest. "I do know you, Angie, but you're still a mystery to me at times. But then, I don't really understand myself very well."

She laughed in a kind of whisper. "I know what you're saying. I feel the same way. But don't you feel blessed? I thought I would never have a baby, and now we'll have five together—and little Jane waiting for us on the other side."

"I do feel blessed. But when women have babies, their husbands don't matter to them quite the same as before. I guess it's only natural. With three wives, you all seem to join forces to care for the family. You take turns with your chores and all those things, and it's what you talk about all the time. It's like a ladies' club, and I don't qualify to join."

Angie laughed again. "I know. It's true. But I know what else you're feeling."

"What?"

"There for a while, you had a new young sweetheart in Mattie. She cared only for you, and she knew how to please you. Now she's a mother, and things have changed. I think you're lonely again."

Morgan suspected that was probably true, but he felt relieved in a way. He had struggled with feelings toward Mattie that he wasn't proud of, and now he felt more like himself again. "It's just the way of things," he said. "Women have their work to do, and so do men. It's nothing to worry about."

Morgan and Angeline began to walk again, but a blackbird was none too happy with intruders into its nest area. It swooped down toward Morgan's head and broke into wild cries. After the bird made several passes, as frantic as before, Morgan and Angeline gave way and turned back toward town. It was then that Angeline said, "Morgan, I worry that I've been more of a burden to you than a strength. I must sound like that screaming blackbird with all my complaints."

"You're a strong woman, Angie, and you can't change that—nor should you. It's what I first liked about you. When you lose some of your strength, you feel frail, and you don't know how to deal with it. You've suffered some hard disappointments, and you've been down at times, but you always come back to yourself."

"Some women have faced much more than I have and kept their heads up better than I do."

"You're not 'some women,' Angie. And I'm not 'some men.' We are who we are. You take things hard, but who's to say that's wrong? I don't let myself feel as much grief as you do. I guess I'm scared of going under if I let too many things get inside me. So is that the best way to deal with life? Probably not. But we each find our way."

"Thank you for saying that, Morgan. You've been very patient with me. But I am happy right now. Maybe I'm just hopeful because I get a chance to bear another child, and I'm feeling stronger. I just wish I hadn't been quite so knocked off my feet when we lost Jane."

Morgan walked on, still close to Angeline. He liked this time with her; he felt closer to her than he had for a long time.

"There's something else I've been wanting to say to you," Angeline said.

Morgan waited. It was so good to hear the gentleness in Angie's voice. He just hoped that the next thing she said would not change what he was feeling tonight.

"The worst thing I've faced in my life was losing little Jane. But your choice to marry Mattie was almost as hard. I think you know that."

"I do." Morgan wanted to say, *we all decided together*, but he knew better. He had made the choice, and Angie had fit her will to his. He had watched her since then, had been able to see her struggling to make their situation acceptable.

She waited for him to look at her. "I'm sorry about the way I treated her—and you. You're living the law that was taught to us. You didn't chase after Mattie. She proposed to you, and she loves you with all her heart. It's only my jealousy that causes problems."

"But sometimes I wish I had followed my first instinct and avoided her altogether."

"Yes. But you love her, and I understand that. You never have turned away from me and Ruth even though she's so beautiful. You try to be fair to all of us."

"I hope so. It's what I want to be." But Morgan knew he would have to work at that fairness all his life.

"I love Mattie," Angeline said. "I didn't think I would ever say that, but it's true. She's a little too good at enticing you, and she's an expert at getting what she wants, but she's worked like a servant around our house, and she's taken a better attitude toward me than I ever have toward her. What I wish, of course, is that I could have you for myself all the days of our lives—and all eternity—but that's not the plan God has given us. I'm just thankful that my sister wives are people I can love. And I want to love them even more."

Morgan and Angeline were approaching the town square again—all the shanties and public buildings—and twilight was making silhouettes of everything, but a pale glow was still in the air. Morgan forgot to look at the beauty of their valley sometimes, but he felt it now. He was fortunate to have been led to this valley, and he was glad for the blessing of his growing family. He knew he was frustrated at times, and most often not so happy, but he was glad for this moment, to feel this love *for* Angie and *from* Angie.

"But you need to know, Morgan, it's only when I'm thinking right that I can say these things. Sometimes I look at Mattie and wish with all my heart that she would age a little, get some wrinkles, not look so wonderful even when she gets up in the morning. I thought maybe having a child would change her, but she only looks lovelier than ever these days."

Morgan sometimes wished the same thing—that Mattie would start to age a little, but only because he worried whether she wouldn't start to see him as an old man before long and regret the choice she had made. But he was also thinking about Angeline and what it would take to keep her as happy as she was right now. Still, Morgan didn't say any of that. Instead, he said, "We've been through a lot together, Angie. But it has been good, don't you think?"

"I do. I always think of that first wagon ride with you, when we hardly knew what we were getting into. After those days, I knew I could never love anyone the way I love you. I'm so thankful you came looking for me when Brother Brigham told you to find a wife."

But this was difficult, and they both knew it. Morgan could never say to her, "I don't love anyone as I love you." So he said the closest thing he could. "You were my first love, Angie, and you'll always hold that place with me. The rest of . . . our situation . . . I have to figure out from day to day, but I know I want you forever, and I want nothing to come between us."

"Yes. That's what I'm saying, too. That's what I wanted to tell you tonight."

• • •

Autumn of 1881 passed peacefully. Angeline's morning sickness didn't last as long this time. She liked the tranquil voice she had used in the talk she had had with Morgan, so she held on to it, and she observed the difference it made in dealing with her family. She was happy with herself, and she felt a new confidence that her baby would be all right. She prayed about that, as always, but she didn't fear as much, and she wondered whether she was finally gaining the faith she needed. Maybe, she told herself, she was becoming a mature woman, more at peace with herself.

And then she got sick. She felt nauseated one morning and thought it was morning sickness again, but by evening she was feeling feverish, and she awoke in the night burning all over. Morgan was with Ruth that night, so Angeline was alone. It was when she heard Mattie up in the night with Hannah that she called out, "Mattie, can you help me?"

Mattie hurried to her bedside. "What is it?" she asked.

"Fever. I'm very hot."

Hannah was crying hard now, her little shrieks coming in bursts. Angeline knew that that had to be taken care of first. "Nurse your baby, Mattie. I'll be all right."

"I'll get Ruth," Mattie said.

"It's not that serious, I don't think. I'm just—"

"I'll get Ruth."

Angeline was actually relieved. She was scared. She couldn't remember ever having such a high fever.

In a moment Ruth was standing next to her, touching the back of her hand to Angeline's forehead. "Oh, my goodness," she said. "We need to cool you off."

And then Morgan was there too. "What is it?"

"Don't worry," Angie told him. "Go back to sleep. I'll be fine."

But Morgan didn't leave. In a minute or two, Ruth was back

with a rag and a pail of cool water. She wiped the water over Angeline's face, and the coolness felt wonderful. "Let's get this off," she said, and she helped Angeline pull her nightgown up and over her head, then untied the top of her garments. Then she ran the rag over her chest and down her arms.

The cool water felt like love, as did Ruth's soothing words. And Morgan was still there, holding her hand. "I'm worried about the baby," she told him.

"I know. But just relax. We'll get your fever under control."

Angeline drifted a little after that, not sleeping but seemingly floating above herself. She could only think that her newfound faith had been betrayed again. The Lord seemed to have another test in mind. Or maybe He would take her now, just when she was becoming more satisfied with life.

• • •

Mattie finished nursing Hannah and put her down in her crib. Then she went to Angeline. "How is she doing?" she asked Ruth.

"She's cooling off some. She's gone to sleep."

"I'm wide awake now," Mattie said. "Let me take a turn."

"I'll stay with you."

"No, let me be with her an hour or two, and then I'll wake you. Morgan, you go to bed. There's nothing for you to do now."

"I'll stay with her. You go to bed," Morgan said.

"You need to be up early in the morning," Ruth told him. "There's no use all of us staying up. Let's let Mattie take a turn."

So Mattie stayed, wrung out the rag, and then very lightly stroked the coolness over Angeline's head and face, arms and legs. It was dark, and she couldn't see much, but it was strange to her to touch a woman's body this way. She was not one to feel shy about such things, but she knew Angeline was. Somehow, it was satisfying to do something real for Angeline, to look after her, to bless her with her hands. But she was scared. She wasn't sure that Angeline was sleeping. She might have passed out, for all Mattie knew, and she might be in serious trouble. It struck her as never before how much she needed this woman who in some ways now seemed like a mother to her. Mattie loved Ruth, but she was not the force in the family that Angeline was. Angeline was complicated, sometimes difficult for Mattie to be around, but under her harshness there was a kind of nobility and rightness that Mattie had never experienced from anyone else, even her own mother. Angeline struggled with emotions, but she saw life more clearly than most. Mattie's own limitation, she knew, was that she saw only a few steps in front of herself, didn't concentrate on the longer path ahead. She had always looked forward to the next town dance or her week with Morgan, but Angeline's eyes had a depth to them, as though she could see beyond the horizon and keep eternity in her mind.

Mattie prayed. She placed her hands on Angeline's head, just as she had seen her mother do at times when her brothers and sisters were sick. She called on the Lord in the name of Jesus Christ to heal Angeline, to spare her life, to restore her to herself. And she prayed that the baby might live and thrive.

A couple of hours passed after that, and sometimes Angeline roused enough to say, "Thank you, Mattie. Oh, thank you."

And then Ruth returned. "Let me take her now," she said, but Mattie didn't want to leave. She wanted to keep praying, keep swabbing and cooling this sister wife who mattered so much to her.

"Mattie, we have to take turns. Her face isn't as hot as it was, but we have to keep her as cool as we can, and we can only keep that up if we work in shifts."

"I know." So Mattie went to bed, but she didn't sleep. And

when the sun came up, she nursed Hannah again and then went about making breakfast for everyone.

A day and night passed, with Morgan taking turns at night with the women, and all of them sharing what they could tell each other about Angeline's condition. "She babbles things," Ruth told Mattie, "but I don't think she knows what she's saying. I just hope the fever hasn't . . . caused her any damage."

Mattie knew of such things: people who recovered from fevers but never with their minds quite right again. That would be even worse than losing her. But there was also the worry about what the fever might do to the baby.

It was on the third morning that the fever gave way, and with the light, Angeline opened her eyes and looked at Mattie. "You're going to be all right now," Mattie said.

"How long?"

"You got sick on Tuesday. It's Friday now."

"I was talking, wasn't I?"

"Sometimes."

"I told the Lord to save my baby if He couldn't save me."

"I think you're both all right now."

"You blessed me, didn't you? I heard you do that."

"Yes."

"How can you love me, Mattie? I was so mean to you when you came to us."

"No. You tried to be, but it wasn't in you, Angie. You love people too much."

"Oh, my goodness, you silly girl. You don't have an inkling about me. I can be very unkind. I can hate."

"But you don't hate me. I know that."

"No. I don't hate you. I wanted to. But I don't."

• • •

Angeline took a deep breath. She wasn't sure she was back in the present—not quite. She was still suspended in air.

"I didn't want him to be with you," she finally told Mattie.

"I know. And I didn't like him to be with you or Ruth."

Angeline tried to think about that. She had sometimes imagined what pleasures Morgan might find with Mattie, but now it struck her that that wasn't the point. She told Mattie, "What I wanted was him close to me, breathing by my ear, waking up with me in the morning and touching my face, taking me in his arms. All I could think was that he was giving all that to you."

"I know. That's what I want too. No matter how much I love you, I still want him next to me."

Angeline laughed. "Men understand so little about us. They think we're like them, and we're not."

Mattie was nodding.

"Are you sure I'm going to be all right?"

"I think so. Your fever is gone, and you're talking right."

"Yes. Pray with me, then. We need to thank the Lord." And Angeline meant more than thanking Him for her life. She also needed to thank Him for Mattie. And for Ruth.

• • •

As winter came on, some of Morgan's hardest work set in. The Order owned several ranches that provided summer range for the cattle herd, but it was impossible to feed so many animals with the hay that could be cut in Long Valley, so when snow started to fall, it was time to drive the cattle south, beyond Kanab, into northern Arizona. There were crews to drive each of the divided herds down the trek more than thirty miles, but Morgan supervised the whole operation. He rode his horse back and forth and stayed in touch with what was happening with each herd. There were always problems—early snow, coyotes, snakebites—and Morgan ended up hearing about every difficulty and solving as many as he could. But a number of men were assigned to stay with the cattle for weeks at a time, and then to rotate the responsibility. Morgan was gone only a few days after the initial drive to the Arizona pastures, but he sometimes made the trip during the winter, just to oversee the men and the cattle that were staying there. So he was gone from home fairly often, and during those times his wives and children dealt with their own challenges and seemed to become accustomed to doing so. What Morgan noticed was that, with three adults and Jefferson nearly an adult himself, the other ten children had plenty of care and supervision. But they were growing up. Morgy and Ella would both be twelve soon, and they were beginning to take interest in matters other than toys and dolls.

Morgan knew that Morgy looked to him as an example—but he seemed to worship Jefferson, who was sixteen. Jeff had become quite a good horseman. He had been assigned to work with the cattle, so he spent most of his days around Morgan and the cowboys who tended to the herd. A horse had been assigned to Jeff, and he spent many days in a saddle. He had even ridden with the men during the cattle drive, and he had returned with stories to tell the younger children. He had chased down cows that had strayed from the herd, and once he had been riding hard on the chase when he suddenly came upon a little stream he hadn't expected. Barney, his horse, had seemed ready to jump the stream, but instead had suddenly driven his front hooves into the ground and stopped. Jeff had been thrown over the horse's head and had somersaulted into the middle of the stream.

Jeff only laughed as he told the tale, and he reported that he had climbed out of the little river and told Barney that he *would* jump that stream, and then had made sure he did so. Morgan listened to the story, but he didn't comment. He liked to see Jeff gain the attention and admiration from the other children, and he liked to watch Jeff grow in confidence.

"How did you learn so much about horses?" Morgy asked after hearing the story, and Morgan had to duck his head not to laugh when Jeff said, "Well, the men tell me some things, but mostly, when you spend a lot of time riding, you pick up things yourself."

Jeff made it sound as though he had been riding for years, not months, but that was all right with Morgan. In fact, Morgan had sometimes let Jeff take Lightning so Morgy could use Barney and the two could take rides together. Jeff had taught Morgy how to saddle a horse, how to ride at a gallop, and how to care for a horse after it had been ridden. Morgy was catching on, becoming a decent rider himself.

What pleased Morgan just as much was that Mattie had taken some rides with Ella. Morgan had been hesitant at first, but Mattie had convinced him that Ella needed something a little more exciting in her life, and she had reminded him that Angeline had grown up riding all the time. Mattie couldn't saddle a horse, so Morgan or Jeff had helped with that, and Mattie was clearly still learning about horses herself, but she had let Lightning know who was boss—to Morgan's surprise—and Ella had taken to riding quite naturally. She had also performed in a silly play that the young people had put on that winter, and as far as Morgan was concerned, she had stolen the show. She had only had a few lines, but she had entered into the lighthearted spirit of the play and spoken those lines with an enthusiasm that he never would have expected from her.

Morgan liked all that, even though he worried a little about Morgy and Ella both wanting to grow up a little too fast. And he worried that Jeff seemed to look to Morgan, and to his family in general, for his place in the world. He didn't do so well making friends with the young people in town, and Morgan was not sure why. But Morgan was pleased with Jeff's developing self-assurance—and skill—and pleased that all his older children were gaining trust in themselves.

During the coldest time of the year, the children, including Morgy and Ella, returned to school, but Jeff was finished with school and continued to work with Morgan full-time. One night in the spring, Morgan invited Jeff to go with him to a board meeting. When Jeff mentioned what he was doing, Morgy wanted to go too. "Sure, that's fine," Morgan told him. "You young fellows need to know a little more about the way the Order works. It's not easy to keep such a big operation going." He almost hoped that a tricky problem might come up so his boys could start to understand how reasonable men could work out the challenges that came along.

As Morgan and the boys were putting on their coats, ready to leave, Ella asked, "Can't girls go to those meetings?"

Morgan laughed. "Anyone can go. Would you like to go with us?" he asked, and he was pleased that she said, "Sure I do."

So they all walked together to the building that had once been the dining hall. But Morgan hadn't been prepared for the issue that arose at the meeting. President Carrington called on a brother to pray. He greeted everyone, and then he said to the members of the board, "Brothers, I got some news from Salt Lake today—news that could change our lives."

Morgan didn't like the ominous tone of the president's voice. He glanced around at his children, who were all three sitting up straight, looking curious. He could see that they too were wondering what President Carrington was about to say.

"You all know that Congress keeps making a fuss about stopping us from living in plural marriage." President Carrington was surely aware that Jeff and Morgy and Ella, three children of plural marriage, were sitting behind the board members, clearly in his view. He sounded as though he were choosing his words carefully as he continued. "What we call celestial marriage, they seem to think is some sort of sinful indulgence. They don't understand the way we live and the benefits that come from our kind of marriages."

"But what are they saying now?" Brother Houston asked. "Are they trying again to stop us?"

"Yes. That's exactly what they want to do. You all know that we lost the test case in the Supreme Court—the one that ruled against George Reynolds. The Court took a stand against religious freedom, as sure as anything. But it's still hard to prove that a man has more than one wife, since our temple marriages aren't recorded in government records. So Congress has been looking for a way to make things more difficult for us. They passed a law last week that's going to be a serious problem for us if they try to enforce it. This new law—it's called the Edmunds Act—makes 'unlawful cohabitation,' as they call it, a misdemeanor with a jail sentence. If they can show that a man is living with more than one woman, that's all the proof they need. And they're willing to take the testimony of anyone who claims to know that a man has more than one wife—whether the wife admits to it or not. They've also removed all our public officials from their territorial offices, and they're sending out a panel of men to supervise new elections. Any man who even says he believes in plural marriage will not be allowed to vote, to serve on a jury, or to hold an office in the government."

"When's all this supposed to take effect?" George Clairmont asked. Brother Clairmont, an Englishman, had recently returned to Orderville from a mission to his home country. Morgan knew this new law was important to him because he had two wives himself and about a dozen children.

"Well, that's just the thing. The Church is going to appeal all this, and it might end up in the Supreme Court again."

"A law like that can't be constitutional, can it?" Morgan asked.

"I don't know. We said that before, and we lost the Reynolds case. No one knows what the courts might do. But I'll say this much. The pressure on us is going to get a lot worse if they can make this law stick. There are men sitting in this room right now who could end up in prison—and, as you all know, I'm one of them."

"Will they look for us, clear down here?" Brother Clairmont asked.

"It's hard to say. I'm sure they'll start up north, but I doubt they'll leave us alone." He hesitated, glancing in the direction of Morgan's children. "But there's no reason to concern ourselves too much for now. Let's just hope the Supreme Court judges in our favor."

Brother Houston asked the question that Morgan was considering but had not wanted to ask. "If the courts rule for the government, will they merely try to stop future marriages, or will they break up our families?"

President Carrington shook his head. "I don't know, Robert. But God is on our side. I have no doubt about that. We just have to trust that the Lord will fight our battles for us."

"That's what we said back in Nauvoo," Brother Houston said. "And the mob killed our prophet and chased us out of the state."

"Well, I know," the president said, "but . . ." He was silent for a time, and then he looked up and smiled. "We've known hardship before, and we've survived those times, and maybe that's what's coming again. But let's not expect the worst. Let's trust that we'll manage, no matter what the government tries to do to us."

There were other things to talk about that night, but the president's announcement—and the discussion that had followed—hung in the air the entire time. Morgan wondered what might happen to the Church if the United States government threw all its power against it. And he couldn't stop thinking about his children and wives and what might happen to them.

After the meeting, as Morgan walked out with his children, Jeff asked, "What difference does it make to anyone whether someone has more than one wife? It doesn't hurt them—and we're not asking them to do what we do."

"Well, it's hard to explain. Most people outside the Church believe a man should have only one wife, and our way just seems wrong to them."

"Why?" Morgy asked.

Morgan couldn't think what to say. Morgy had been raised by a mother and an aunt—and then two aunts—all of whom loved him. Morgan understood that nothing seemed wrong to Morgy about that. Finally Morgan said, "Sometimes people don't understand what they haven't experienced. They make up their minds about us without really knowing the sort of people we are."

"Are they going to put you in prison?"

"I don't think so. But let's not worry about it for now."

The truth was, however, imprisonment was clearly a possibility for Morgan. He wondered what would happen to his family if the government carried him away and locked him up.

CHAPTER 15

Morgan had tried over the years to improve his dancing skills, but he still felt as awkward as a goose on ice when he walked onto the dance floor. So when he took his wives to the Saturday evening dances in the old dining hall, he usually sat out most of the dance sets. Plenty of men in town were more than happy to give Mattie a swing onto the dance floor, and she dazzled everyone as she danced. Sometimes it seemed to Morgan that every eye was focused on her—but then, who could help it? It wasn't just because she was pretty but because she enjoyed herself so fully, seeming to touch the ground only long enough to prove she was actually human.

It was Angeline who held baby Hannah in spite of the fact that she had no lap now. And it was also Angeline who told Morgan, "I wonder how many know what a lovely person she is."

But Morgan knew the lovely side of Angeline, too, and he put his arm around her shoulders to let her know he felt that way. Ruth, as usual, had stayed home with the younger children. Morgan had begged her not to do that. She needed to get out and have a nice time on a spring evening. He could stay with the children—and wouldn't mind, since he didn't want to dance anyway. But Ruth hadn't listened. She had smiled and said, "Well, clean your boots and black them—just in case Mattie talks you into a dance or two. You don't want to look like an old farmer out there alongside her."

Orderville now had more musicians than the Muddy Mission had ever had. Tonight two men were playing fiddles, along with others playing clarinet, cornet, and trombone. Brother Stoddard called out the various steps of the quadrilles.

The hall was packed with both adults and young people. In the corners, children were bouncing about to the rhythm, creating their own dances, and down the middle of the hall were two sets of dancers lined up and ready to carry out the calls. The music echoed off the walls and low ceiling, and the laughter and shuffling feet added to the sense that the hall was filled beyond capacity. But Morgan liked what he saw, even if he didn't want to dance. People worked very hard in Orderville, and it was always good to see them enjoying themselves.

Bishop Carrington was a fine dancer, and he joined in most of the dances, taking turns with his wives. Others chose his wives as partners as well, everyone changing partners often, enjoying all their friendships. When an older man, Brother Hill, asked Angeline to dance, she seemed genuinely pleased, and it was good for Morgan to see how gracefully she danced, even in her motherly state.

Morgan now had Hannah on his lap. He was giving her most of his attention, but he had noticed a little huddle of young men not far away. They all looked like boys who had done more farming than dancing and even right now would rather wrestle a steer to the ground than get recruited onto the dance floor. But they were certainly watching Mattie, and Morgan wondered how often the older boys in town questioned what a young woman like Mattie could see in an older man like Morgan. This group of boys was known for being just a little rowdier than the town leaders liked. They were a year or so older than Jeff, and they had always held him off even though he would have liked to have been accepted by them. Jeff had been small for his age when they were all growing up, and he had been more compliant than they were to the wishes of their teachers. Morgan was quite sure that was why they didn't include him. But Jeff attended the dances, and even though he danced rather clumsily, he took every opportunity to dance with his friend Harriet Hart.

Morgan was not too surprised when he heard the boys talking about a fistfight that had broken out between boys from Orderville and boys from Toquerville. Then he heard one of the boys, a young man named Harv Jones, say, "When I took that last load of wool up to Nephi, some of them boys up there pointed at me and laughed, right out loud. 'You must be from Orderville,' one of 'em said. 'That's right. What of it?' I told him, and this same fella says, 'If I lived down there, I don't care what they told me, I wouldn't be caught dead in a pair of them ol' homespun pants you got on.'"

This was something Morgan had heard talk about, and it worried him. People had adjusted to homespun clothing over the years, and most didn't seem to mind looking the same as everyone else in town. It was the young people who had begun to express the embarrassment they felt. The board had discussed the matter, and a plan was in place to open a factory that would weave nice fabrics—but it would be a while before that took place.

Angeline returned, looking flushed and a little out of breath, but when she sat down, Morgan handed the baby to her, and he stood up. There was something he wanted to do. He stepped a little closer to the boys, but for now he didn't say anything.

A boy named Jesse Crabtree asked, "What'd you tell him, Harv?"

"I didn't say much." Then Harv laughed. "Well . . . I mighta mentioned that at least I didn't have to wear his ugly face around. And I might have offered my 'pinion that his face reminded me of our old sow that I feed slop to down here in Orderville."

"You didn't say that."

"Oh, there you're wrong. That's 'zactly what I told 'im. Then I stepped up so my nose was right up next ta his, and I said, 'What else you got to say about my pants?'"

"I'll bet he backed off when he saw how big you are."

"He backed off, all right, but once he got a few paces off, he said, 'Them homespun pants is still the ugliest thing I ever seen. Them girls across the street was all laughin' at you.' So I looked over and saw some girls. I don't know if they was laughin' at me, but I think maybe they was."

Another boy in the group—Brother Houston's son, Reggie—said, "I wouldn't blame them if they were laughing at you. The way they cut our pants, we look like we're carrying around two gunnysacks on our legs."

Morgan was well aware what had brought this on. In recent years the Silver Reef mine, near St. George, had been changing the economy of southern Utah. Nephi, up north, had opened a salt mine that was also doing well. The Saints in all the towns around the mines were selling products to the miners, asking high prices and getting them. They were beginning to have enough money to buy things they had gone without most of their lives. Among the "luxuries" were store-bought clothes, the very thing that Brigham Young had always preached against. When Orderville citizens traveled to other towns, they now looked not only old-fashioned but poor.

Harv Jones was more confident than some young people, but he said, "I'll tell ya what. I ain't goin' back to Nephi again 'til I git me some better pants. And when I git 'em, the first thing I'm gonna do is smash that fella's nose flat against his face, and the second thing, I'm gonna walk right up to one of them girls and say, 'How about walkin' out a little with me in my new trousers?' She'll go with me, too." Harv grinned, and his freckled face brightened. "I have to admit, I am good-lookin'."

"Yes, I must agree," Reggie said. "You're about as good-looking as that ol' sow you were talking about."

The boys gave each other some playful shoves—a little more vigorously than Morgan thought proper. "Hey, fellows," Morgan said, "let's not get too wild."

Harv grinned at Morgan. He seemed to know that Morgan had been listening to everything he had said.

So Morgan took the chance to say, "Do you boys understand why we wear homespun clothing?"

"'Course we do," Harv said. "It's been preached to us about a thousand times. 'No rich or poor among us,' the bishop tells us. An' he's right about the rich. We got none of that around here. But we shore got the poor part."

"We have our kind of riches," Morgan said. "The kind that matter most."

"That's all fine and good, Brother Davis, but if you don't mind, I'd like at least one decent pair a pants before I grow old and die."

Harv was laughing, and Morgan laughed too, but he could tell that this was no minor issue for these boys. Younger people hadn't been involved in the thinking and planning that had brought about the United Order.

Morgan put his hand on Harv's shoulder. "I know it's hard to see the things some people have in other towns. I know we're different, but we should be proud of it. Most people in the world think that if they have the fanciest houses or the best horses and buggies—or rings on their fingers and boots brought in from England—they're more important than other folks. But riches don't make people happy. That's Satan's oldest trick to get us thinking wrong."

"That might be right, Brother Davis, but I'd like to have just a few of them things and see whether they ain't half bad. I kinda like to think of myself sittin' up behind a matched set of sorrel horses in a fancy carriage. I don't see why God wouldn't want me to have a rig like that, and maybe a pretty wife—like you got—to ride alongside me."

The boys all liked this response. They were nodding and laughing. Jesse said, "Maybe being rich doesn't make you happy, but being poor has a darn good chance of making you miserable."

"We're not poor, Jesse," Morgan said. "We all live in nice houses."

"Shanties."

"We call them that, but they're warm and safe. And we eat well. We have nice families. We all know our neighbors, and we take care of each other. There never will be a time when things go wrong for you that someone in town won't be there to help you out."

"How long is that going to last?" Harv asked.

"What?"

"That's fine for you and for our parents, but we won't be able to stay here."

Morgan knew exactly what Harv meant. He had seen this problem coming for a long time. All the same, he said, "It'll work out all right for you. This town has to stop growing at some point, but once the valley gets too full, other towns, modeled on this one, can start in other places. And there's no reason we can't all prosper. We're starting our own woolen mills before too long, and we'll be weaving better quality cloth. We can train tailors, maybe send them away to learn from the best tailors anywhere, and they can sew nice-looking suits of clothes for men and dresses for women—even decent work pants. At the same time, we can stay unified, keep supporting each other."

"How come we're the only ones worrying about that, Brother Davis?" Reggie asked. "Lots of Mormons are making good money at the mines, and they're getting ahead in the world. As long as I stay in this town, no matter how hard I work, I won't ever be able to build one of those big houses like I saw when we traveled up to Salt Lake City. There's good Mormons living in brick houses five times bigger than our shanties, and they're all decked out when they go to church like they're lords and ladies. They don't seem to think they're doing anything wrong."

Morgan knew he was sounding way too preachy to these boys—even old-fashioned—but he hated to see them give up on everything they had been taught all their lives. "Maybe they are doing something wrong," he said. "Brigham Young told them over and over not to act like that. He hated to see members of the Church holding themselves above other members—just because they had more money. What we're trying to do here is live a higher law and set an example for the rest of the Church."

"Then you keep doin' it," Harv said. "I'm gonna leave jist as soon as I can, and I'm gonna see what I can do to git rich. Then I'll give to the poor. I'll send some money down here and buy all these ugly fellas a nice set of britches, as nice as the ones I'll have."

Harv was still laughing, but Morgan was worried. It was one thing to create an idealistic society; it was another thing to pass that idealism along to another generation, especially in the midst of a world that made fun of the very things that the United Order stood for.

• • •

Later in the spring, Morgan and his wives were attending another one of the Saturday night dances. This time Ruth had come along, and Angeline, now very great with child, had chosen to stay home. And once again, Mattie was the center of attention. Morgan did agree to dance with her a couple of times, and from that position, out on the floor, he could see the same gathering of boys who had complained about Orderville. But Harv wasn't there. Morgan had asked about him, and one of the boys said he had been on one of his trips to carry surplus wool to sell in Nephi—the same town where he had been shamed before.

Later in the evening, Morgan—now sitting down again—saw a little stir near the door of the building. A lot of the young men were gathered around someone, and then Morgan saw Harv's head above the others. He was smiling in his usual bright way. What was different was that some of the young women began to gather into the circle and even push to get closer to Harv. The tittering mounted, and Morgan heard someone say, "They're store-bought."

Morgan had to see what was going on. He walked closer and looked over some shoulders, and he saw that Harv did indeed have himself a new pair of trousers. They weren't baggy, weren't made of thick fabric. One girl said, "Let me have a better look," and she moved in close to Harv and whispered something in his ear. Then, suddenly, she kissed him a little peck on the cheek. All the young people laughed.

Another girl was saying, "Harv, my card is open for the next dance. Want to try a waltz?"

No waltzes were allowed in Orderville, even though they sometimes were in other towns. Waltzes involved too much touching, too much dividing off into couples.

Morgan knew the girl was only joking, but he also knew a hint of rebellion was erupting. Everyone was treating Harv as though he had done something praiseworthy. So Morgan, as much as he hated to do it, spoke over the others. "Harv, could I speak to you for a moment?"

This brought on more laughter, but also a bit of scattering. Everyone must have heard the seriousness in Morgan's voice.

"Sure thing, Brother Davis," Harv said. "I guess you want to admire my pants too."

Morgan didn't respond to that. "Let's just step outside for a moment," he said. And when others began to follow, he looked back and said, "This is just between Harv and me."

Harv walked a few steps outside and then turned back. He looked pleased with himself when he said, "You don't have to worry, Brother Davis. I bought these pants with my own money."

"And how did you get what you call your 'own money'?"

"I used my head."

It was cool outside, and dark, but a lantern hung by the door. Morgan could see the boy in the dim light, his blondish hair looking yellow. "We don't make money for ourselves in Orderville, Harv. You know that. Any money you earn individually becomes community money."

"What if I used something others were throwing away? Once they don't want it, what does it hurt if I gather it up? Isn't it mine then?"

"I don't understand what you're saying. You sold trash?"

"You might call it that."

"That's still against the principles of the Order. You've used that money to place yourself above others. That's what I was talking about. It's against the spirit of our system."

"Well, other people can do the same. Some of us just have

more gumption than others. Is that what you want to beat out of us?"

It was a stunning question, and Morgan hated the answer. In a certain sense, the Order did take away individual initiative, replacing it with the belief that all people should use their skills for the good of the entire community. What he didn't know was how he could help a young man like Harv understand that he was being selfish.

"So, can you tell me what you collected and sold?"

"Is that one of our rules, too? That I have to report to *you* everything I do?"

Morgan didn't want to get angry. He stood for a moment, took a breath. "No. Not at all, Harv. I like you. I've known you since you were a little boy, and I've always noticed how smart you are—and good-natured. But you will have to answer to the board. We do have rules."

"The last I heard, we live in a free country. I don't remember anything in the Constitution about reporting to a board my own personal actions."

"Harv, this isn't a legal matter. It's a commitment we've all made to each other. It's our attempt—"

"I don't remember making any such commitment. Now, if you don't mind, there's a pretty girl in there waitin' to dance with me."

Harv walked back into the dining hall, and Morgan didn't stop him.

• • •

It was on the following Thursday evening, when the board of directors met, that Harv Jones was called forward to sit before the president and the men of the board. But tonight there were many spectators, mostly young people and their parents.

President Carringon asked Harv to sit across from the board members, who were spread out across a long bench. "Brother Jones," he began, "we're really hopeful that we can have a friendly discussion tonight and clear up a few matters. We're not accusing you of a moral or legal transgression, but only of breaking a rule that we have a feeling you don't exactly understand. You told Brother Davis that you don't have to answer to this board and that you've made no commitment to the United Order. In one sense, that's true. Your parents were the ones who made that commitment, but, as a child not yet of age, you come under that commitment with your family. We do have the right, and we exert that right at this time, to ask you how you acquired the means to purchase your pants." And then the president smiled. "And I must say, they certainly are handsome ones."

Harv grinned, and then he surprised Morgan by saying, "I wasn't tryin' to make no trouble. My father says I need to answer your questions, and I don't mind doin' it. I jist don't think I did anything wrong."

"All right. But could you explain where you got the money?"

Harv's smile returned, and again, he looked pleased with himself. "So I'll tell you how I did it." He looked directly at Morgan, as though he especially wanted to set the record straight with him. "This spring I helped dock the lambs—you know, cut their tails off. The shearers would whack them off and throw 'em in a pile. And it was a big pile; we git a lot of lambs each year. So after all the shearing, them guys was just gonna dig a hole an' throw the tails in. So I said I'd do it. And I did. But before I threw 'em away, I sheared all the wool off those tails. It was just wool that was gonna be stuck in the ground to rot. I decided, if no one wanted that wool, I did. And I knew what I wanted to do with it. I kept that wool in a burlap sack, an' the next time I went up to Nephi, I sold that bag of wool apart from the rest of the load, an' then I used what I earned from my own wool to buy these pants."

He stood up so everyone could see the pants, and he laughed as he turned all the way around.

President Carrington was smiling too. "Well, that was very smart. I'm impressed with your resourcefulness." All the board members were nodding their agreement. It was hard for Morgan not to break out laughing. But he was also well aware that the issue would not end that easily.

"Here's the problem," President Carrington said. "Even though someone was being wasteful and didn't think to harvest that wool, what you proved was that it should have been harvested. Or, in other words, the wool you sold belonged to the Order. I congratulate you on your wise action, but the fundamental mistake you made was to say, 'That wool is mine.' If you had used the money to buy something for all the young people in town, I wouldn't be so concerned, but you used it to deck yourself out in a way that would, in your mind, make you look better than the other young men."

"I do look better," Harv said, grinning again. "You jist said so yourself."

"Yes, but—"

Morgan broke in. "President, Harv has a point. He was wrong to try to place himself above the other young men in town, but we can't really blame him for feeling that he didn't want to be made fun of in Nephi. The homespun clothes satisfy me just fine, but it's a little more difficult for a young person to tolerate the kind of jeering they get outside our own little community. I told Harv and some of the other boys that maybe, before too long, we could weave better fabric here and cut clothing so it doesn't look quite so bulky and baggy."

"I do understand what you're saying," President Carrington said, "but we have to remember why we've chosen to wear simple, plain clothing. Brigham Young taught us not to compete with the corrupt world, that simplicity was better than the 'costly apparel' we often read about in the Book of Mormon."

From somewhere in the room, a woman's voice said, "Where's the harm in looking nice? I'm tired of this scratchy old dress I wear. I never saw Brigham's wives going around in homespun dresses."

That brought a laugh. And Morgan knew he had sometimes thought the same thing.

"Well, Brigham was a prophet, but he was also a man," President Carrington said. "He tried and tried to achieve some retrenchment in these matters, and to get his family—and all our families—to settle for simpler things. He died before he got very far. But it's still what he was preaching right until the last summer he lived."

"President Carrington," Brother Clairmont said, "maybe we can also think in terms of improvement instead of perfection. Maybe we can't refine our weaving too much just yet, but we don't have to make the pants so baggy, either. That probably wastes good material. What if we took Brother Jones's new pants apart and used them as a pattern, and then we started cutting all the pants the same way?"

There was some general agreement in the room, lots of heads nodding and people assenting.

But Harv was laughing. "Wait a minute. After they take my pants apart, can they sew 'em back together and give 'em back to me?"

Most everyone in the room laughed, but President Carrington

gave that question some thought. Finally, he said, "How would you feel about this approach? We start improving on the tailoring of all pants sewn in the future, but we don't throw away any perfectly good pants. Nothing would be more wasteful than that. When a boy outgrows his pants—or when any man or boy wears out his pants—he can submit to the sewing department to receive a new pair, cut in the new way. Does that sound acceptable?"

"Well, I guess it'll have to be," Harv said.

President Carrington seemed just a little troubled with that response. He sat for a time, seeming to think everything over. Finally, he asked, "Brother Jones, weren't you one of the boys who was caught raiding the melon patch?"

The memory seemed to delight Harv. "Yes, I might've been one of 'em."

"Wasn't Brother Palmer the one who caught you at it?"

"Yes. I do seem to remember that."

"And how was that matter settled?"

"Brother Palmer said he din't mind us eatin' a few melons, but when we went trampin' through his garden, we ruined too many vines. So he told us he'd pick some in the evenings and set 'em out by the fence—and we could eat all we wanted."

"How did you feel about that, Brother Jones?"

"It was fair—more than fair. It was a good way to solve the problem. The only thing is, the stolen melons always tasted a little better'n the ones he just put out there for us to take."

This got a very big laugh from everyone in the room—except that President Carrington appeared troubled again. "Harv, I hope you understand, we aren't trying to make life more difficult for you young people. We do want to be fair, and that's why Brother Palmer went the extra mile, just to show you that we're not trying to ruin all the fun you young men might have. I'm sorry, though—I don't like to hear that you would prefer to take what isn't yours. It's the same thing as these pants you bought. Can't you see that?"

Harv seemed to take the question seriously. He ducked his head for a time, and when he looked up, he said, "I was mostly jist jokin' about the melons tasting better, but I do feel like we don't have much freedom in this town. I have a hard time understandin' why a pair of pants—or a watermelon—has to be made so much of. Me and my friends, we're not bad people, President. I've talked to boys in other towns who do a lot worse things than we've ever even thought of."

President Carrington nodded. "I agree. You're not bad people at all. But we're trying, here in Orderville, to climb to a higher plane. Most of the towns that set out to live the Order have long since failed. We're trying to live in harmony. And that's what we hope to pass along to you. Can you accept that?"

"Shore. I know you want what's best for us. So make me a better pair of pants as soon as I wear out the ugly ones you gave me before, an' I won't say another word about it. But the day might come when I move to a place where Mormons don't fuss so much about what we wear."

President Carrington nodded, looking serious. "Fair enough," he said. "I'm glad we could settle this matter. But I hope, if you ever leave, that after a time you'll discover what we stand for here—and maybe wish to raise your own children the same way."

• • •

Morgan was pleased with the outcome of the meeting, but he was less pleased when he talked to Harv outside. "I appreciate your cooperation," he told him.

"It don't matter to me no more," Harv said. "Give me two years, tops, and I'm leavin' this place. You can all be plain and all look alike, and have no rich or poor, but I'm gonna go out and make somethin' of myself. If you don't want to be rich, that's fine for you. But I want to be richer'n a king."

Morgan decided not to preach to the boy. Harv might have to learn for himself, as President Carrington had suggested. Besides, there was something that Morgan had always known: however much he believed in the Order, he always yearned to give his family a better life, to provide not just the necessities but maybe a few special things. That wasn't the higher law, but it was something he could never quite get out of his head. So he understood Harv better than the boy would have suspected.

After that night, what Morgan noticed over the next few months was that the newly cut pants started to show up sooner than he had expected. Apparently some young men in town were wearing out their pants, or outgrowing them, and they had applied and received the new ones. Harv was so far not one of them, but he told Morgan one day, "These old pants of mine are startin' to wear pritty bad. I might have to apply for new ones before long." There was a sly smile on his face, almost as though he were predicting something that he could control.

"I don't see much wear," Morgan told him.

"Take a closer look." Harv spun around and bent over. "The seat is wearin' right through."

The fabric did look worn and thin, but it seemed a strange place for pants to wear out. People didn't do much sitting in Orderville, and Harv didn't have much chance to ride a horse.

So Morgan kept an eye on the young men when he had a chance. He had a feeling something was going on. And then, late one spring evening, he saw Harv and three other boys heading for the toolshed by the town offices. When he saw one of the boys glance back, as though checking to see if they were being watched, Morgan was certain they were up to something. He walked to the shed once the boys were all inside, and he listened. He heard whispers but couldn't make out what they were saying. Just then, though, he heard a rough sound, like something rubbing. "Just a little at a time," he heard Harv say. "We can't make it happen all at once."

Morgan threw open the door and stepped inside. And there was Harv, standing with his backside against a grindstone as another boy turned the wheel. When Harv saw Morgan, he stepped away from the grindstone quickly. But he knew he was caught. His grin came back. "I tol' you these pants were wearin' out in the seat, didn't I?" he said. And he laughed.

CHAPTER 16

In May of 1882 Angeline gave birth to a healthy baby boy. She and Morgan agreed to name him Joseph Brigham Davis. Angeline had worried that the fever she had survived might injure him in some way, but she saw no sign that anything was wrong. As it turned out, "Joey" was a vigorous eater, and he grew fast and strong.

All the mothers, father, and siblings loved their new baby, played with him, and tried to make him laugh. When Morgan had a little time at home, he liked to hold Joey and pretend to tell him about his day. He would say ordinary things, but in exaggerated tones, and Joey would stare at him with seeming fascination. The older children would laugh to hear Papa say, "Well, Son, I was glad to see my cows today. And I do believe they were happy to see me. They spent the winter in Arizona, and they enjoy that, but you know how it is, there's just no place like home." Joey would babble a few sounds, as though to say something in response, and that made the children laugh all the harder.

It was all rather complicated to have so many children of different ages and with different mothers. On the one hand, Ruth reprimanded her own children, but she felt just a little hesitant to say too much to Angeline's little ones. Angeline always told her she should never fear to treat all of the children as though they were her own, but Ruth raised children differently than her sister wives did. Angeline wasn't exactly indulgent with the children, but she was quick to regret a hard word, quick to take it back.

Mattie was a busy mother. Hannah was walking now, and very interested in her world, and Mattie liked to play with her as much as she could. Mattie was still full of fun, and she loved to entertain all the children, filling them up with her own good humor. That was not a bad thing, but sometimes she got them excited to the point of wildness and then had no idea how to bring things back into control. Ruth supposed Mattie would outgrow such youthful behavior, but for now, Ruth considered herself the dull one in the family, not nearly as exciting as Mattie or as able and powerful as Angeline. Still, she had her way of doing things, and she tried to make her children feel that they did have a mother of their own, that they weren't just part of a herd.

Jefferson was almost seventeen. He was finally getting tall, and he was filling out, too. The scrawny boy had turned into a muscular young man. And yet there remained something rather delicate in his spirit. He was kind to the children, kindhearted in general, and maybe a little insecure, as though he were not yet certain of his station in life. Ruth worried that he tried too hard to prove himself worthy of his stepfather. He liked to make something big out of any little thing he accomplished, and he especially liked to hear Morgan tell him that he had done a good job. But Morgan, for all his patience with the children, wasn't one to pour out praise.

When Jefferson had been younger, he had always hated to gather eggs from the chicken coop. Ruth had heard Morgan tell Jefferson, back when Jeff was nine or ten, "You can't take all morning to gather in the eggs. If those hens fight you a little, you can't let them scare you off. Just push them aside and let them know you're the boss." But the hens really had frightened him. He had always looked reticent when he left the house with the egg basket even though he never admitted to his fears. Certainly he didn't fear chickens now, but she saw some of those same qualities in him: especially his hesitancy to take on a new challenge. He still avoided the socials that the young people in town put on, and Harv Jones and Reggie Houston continued to treat him as though he were a little boy. He lacked their boisterous confidence and clearly didn't know how to talk to them. So mostly he stayed away. He prized time with his father more than with anyone, and his closest friend was still Morgy, who was five years younger than he was.

But Ruth was pleased with the way he was growing up. She knew that Jeff was not the type to become an Apostle or a stake president, but he was a lovely boy—as kind as Morgan, even if he wasn't as confident. What she liked to think about most was that he was nothing at all like his birth father. It wasn't his blood that would make him the man he would become; it was the example of a good stepfather. Being a second wife wasn't easy, but she had chosen right for Jeff, and she liked to think that all five of her children would grow up with Morgan's commitment to the Lord and to family.

Ruth was forty-five now, and she thought her fertile years were over, but the Lord had blessed her with a chance to be a mother in Zion, which fulfilled her hope in life. What she prayed for every day was that all her children—and all the children in the family—would grow to be worthy, righteous adults, and that she would live long enough to see them form their own families and create a fine posterity.

• • •

Morgan was feeling that it would soon be time to build another house. With eleven children, and with Jefferson growing up, it was time to build something bigger than a shanty for Ruth's family, and it was time for Mattie to have more room for herself. Her little bedroom barely allowed space for a cradle by her bed. No one in Orderville was supposed to build extravagant homes, but they could add space as their families grew, or as men married additional wives.

When Morgan's week with Ruth began, the shanty always felt crowded with Jeff and the four little ones all bedded in a single adjacent room. Jeff had also expressed a desire for some privacy from his brothers and sisters—and probably a little more distance from his parents.

One night after dinner, on the first night of the week in Ruth's shanty, Jeff slipped away to a corner of the children's room and sat on his bed, as he usually did, to read one of his few books. The boy never said much about his reading—certainly not when he was herding cows with his father and the other hands—but he seemed to live for the time he spent alone with those books. *Robinson Crusoe* was his favorite, and he had read it until the covers were falling off. Fortunately, the town had created a little lending library from books that members of the Order had donated, and that gave him some history and biographies he could read. But fiction was hard to come by, and it was what he loved the most. Sister Millard, who was one of the teachers in the town school, had once reported to Morgan that Jefferson was an indifferent student in arithmetic and science, but he liked to read almost everything. "If I let him go off in a corner and read, I hardly know he's there all day."

That was fine with Morgan, but he hoped the boy would assert himself a little more one of these days—show that he truly was becoming a man.

"I've been thinking," Morgan told Ruth, "it's time to ask the building committee to build a larger house for you. Maybe Mattie could move in here with Hannah, and you could have a place of your own with another room or two."

Ruth was sitting in her rocking chair, holding Andrew in her arms. Andrew had not wanted to go to bed until Ruth read him a story, but she had hardly begun when he had fallen asleep in her arms. Andrew was almost five, and a busy little boy. Morgan could see how much Ruth liked holding him now that he was peacefully asleep.

Morgan was seated not far away in the little room; he had been reading his Book of Mormon with a lamp nearby. He had expected Ruth to glow with joy at the mention of a new house, but instead, she looked concerned. "How far away would it be?" she asked.

"I don't know exactly. We couldn't stay in this same row, of course. It might have to be in a different part of town. It depends on what building lot the board would grant us." Ruth nodded, but he could see that she was troubled. "Wouldn't you want a little more room for yourself?" he asked her.

"Yes. Very much. But we're all together here, and, in most ways, that's nice."

Morgan chuckled. He knew plural families who preferred to separate themselves as far apart as possible.

"Is there a way to build three houses all together?" Ruth asked. "I like that we can help each other when new babies come, and we can all teach the children and look after them."

"I hadn't thought of it that way, but it might be all right with the board. New families keep moving in, and they could occupy these two places. If the building committee would build us a row of three houses—on whatever land was available—we could keep together better, couldn't we?"

"That's what I would like. Angeline and Mattie might like to be more separated as the children get older. I'm not sure."

"I don't think so. You help with their children so much, and it means you carry some of their burdens. Both of them tell me how much they love and appreciate your help."

Ruth looked pleased. "I know I'm the least interesting of your wives. In some ways, Angeline and Mattie are opposites, but they've found ways to make their sisterhood match up pretty well. Nothing pleases me more than to think that they feel all right about me. I just hope that we won't be pulled apart by the things that might be coming."

This was the subject on everyone's minds these days. There had been lots more bluster in Congress lately about ending polygamy. The new Republican Party was dead set on finding a way to stop the practice.

"The government can pass laws," Morgan told Ruth, "but they can't countermand God's laws. No federal officer is going to take you and our children away from me."

"They could take you away to prison."

"I don't think the Lord will let things go that far. But if it happens, it happens. For now, we have to live as though nothing will change. I'm going to talk to the board about building three houses, all joined."

• • •

Morgan received permission to have the new houses built on a little plot of land just east of the town square, not far from the shanties. He had a fairly clear idea how he wanted to design the houses, but Brother Stoddard, head of the building committee, had ideas of his own. Morgan knew he wasn't allowed to build the houses himself, and besides, he had plenty of work to do with the spring cattle drive under way, but he put in every spare moment helping the building committee workers, and the houses went up quickly. The houses each had three rooms when finished, with a kitchen in each. Morgan hadn't seen the need for that, but communal meals seemed unlikely to return, and Brother Stoddard explained that others might use the houses in the future. Different families might have different needs; the building committee had to create houses that would function for families that weren't joined in plurality.

These were not Morgan's houses; they belonged to the Order. No one knew that better than Morgan. But Morgan had built many homes, and it seemed unlikely that anyone cared as much about the design of a house as he did. He found it difficult to push his own ideas aside and follow the instructions of the committee.

But even as the houses were going up, and then as Morgan's families moved in, there was reason to wonder whether the arrangement had been a good choice. Every issue of the *Deseret News* that reached Orderville from Salt Lake City was full of news about the Edmunds Act. Not much was being done about enforcement so far, but Congressmen were quoted as saying that the Mormons would change their ways—and stop their mistreatment of women—or polygamous men would all end up in prison. By contrast, editorials by Latter-day Saint writers continued to claim that the courts would never sanction the law, and that was Morgan's hope. But the matter was a constant worry to him.

Morgan also worried that the Order might be heading for a breakup. Complaints and bickering kept increasing, and more members were deciding to leave. Still, a core of members remained committed to the way of life and still believed that they were carrying the banner for the law of consecration in the Church. Morgan was not about to give up on the idea he had championed so long, but he wearied of holding the organization together. He found himself thinking at times that he would rather drop out himself and no longer have to defend the Order before every man or woman who had become disillusioned.

There was usually much to do, however, and Morgan refused to occupy himself with all the arguing and accusing. Besides, his own life was good. The new houses had turned out well for his family. The children had more room, and yet there was still a large room in the center house where everyone could gather. The place was full of the noise and laughter of youngsters—and of course, sometimes the quarreling of the older children—but Morgan was all right with the commotion. What he hoped, more than anything, was that the government would never try to break up his family.

• • •

A year did pass without much attempt at enforcement of the Edmunds Act, but in 1883 federal deputies—called "Deps" by the Mormon people—began arresting, trying, and incarcerating any man who could be proved to be "co-habiting" with more than one woman. Many women were forced to admit to their co-habitation; others refused to witness against their husbands and were occasionally jailed themselves. More often, the Deps found other witnesses, and the Utah Territorial Prison in Salt Lake City began to fill up. But the year passed without any Deps showing up in Long Valley.

It was a relief not to be threatened directly so far, but a dangerous time seemed to be coming. It was not easy to concentrate on the love and harmony of the United Order when disorder was always lurking, ready to strike.

Mattie had a second baby that year, a little boy she named David. He was an easygoing baby, willing to be held by all the children, placid even when they passed him back and forth. It was this—the chaotic but joyous life in such a big family—that Morgan feared losing. It was hard to imagine that anyone could so completely misunderstand the goodness and rightness he felt or the life he and his wives and children were living.

In 1884, Apostle Erastus Snow sent word that he was coming to Long Valley to meet with the communities there, and word spread that the subject was an approach to dealing with the Deps, who were beginning to extend their "raid," as everyone now called it, into southern Utah. A warning system was set up to alert local members to the arrival of government agents. Men in danger were advised to prepare hiding places, or to slip away and head into Arizona, where, so far, the raid was not extending. Children would have to be taught what to say when asked who their father was, and wives were told how to answer questions *without* answering them.

"I know this is difficult," Apostle Snow told the people. "We aren't liars, so we don't know how to do it. But when a government turns away from God's law and threatens His covenant people, we have to resist in the ways we can. We will not use guns to take on this army of agents. We will not, generally, break any law of the land. But we cannot deny God's laws, so we must find ways to resist. We need not play into the hands of the Deps by admitting to the things they want us to say." He slapped his open hand on the podium. "We don't accept such treatment. We will fight these illegal searches through the courts and through Congress, but in the meantime, we must not be foolish enough to say the wrong things and get our men thrown into prison."

Before the meeting ended, Morgan had a plan. He still spent

much of his time in the canyon where many of the cattle were pastured. He knew of caves in the nearby cliffs. He could establish a little hideout within a cave and carry quilts and a stash of food there. He wouldn't be able to hide for more than a few days that way, but he could manage in a place like that if the Deps didn't stay too long. If things got worse, he would then ride off through the mountains and avoid public roads as he worked his way down to Arizona.

It was his children that he worried about. On the evening after the meeting with Apostle Snow, he gathered his family together. "All right," he said to all who could talk and give answers when questioned, "we are going to go for a walk together. Follow me."

It was nothing new for Morgan to take the children out of the house for a time on a summer evening, just to get them out from under the feet of their mothers, so the children saw nothing out of the ordinary in his request. Morgan led them down to the Virgin River bank, and then he had them all sit down on the grass while he stood with his back to the river. "I need to talk to you about some very important matters," he told them. He pointed at Jeff, who was standing behind the younger children. He had his arms folded across his chest and had taken on a serious look, as though he had guessed what this little meeting was all about. Morgy was standing next to him, even imitating his stance.

"I might have to leave our houses for a time," Morgan told the children. "And when I do, your mothers are in charge of the family, but Jefferson is the leader of the children. Do you all understand that?"

There seemed no doubt about that in anyone's mind. They were all nodding. But Ella asked, "Where are you going, Papa?"

Ella was fourteen and was maturing into a young woman. She was prettier than Ruth, her mother, but she had the same dark eyes. She had taken on some of Mattie's enthusiasm and quickness to laugh, but still, she was always the first to express her concern when difficulties came. She had clearly heard too much lately about the danger of the Deps coming after Morgan.

"There are people who might come around asking questions," Morgan said. "They are not our friends. They won't hurt us, but they might want to find out things about us that we don't want to tell. If they come, I might have to stay away from the houses for a while. But I won't be far away."

"Where will you sleep?" Andrew asked him. Andrew was only six and didn't understand much about the world outside Orderville, but he did like to be snug in bed under warm quilts. Morgan knew he was trying to imagine the discomfort his papa may have to suffer.

"I'll find a place. I don't want to say too much about that. Jeff will know where I am, and he'll be able to let me know if you need me for some reason. But everything will be fine. You don't have to worry. Still, there's something I want you to be ready to do."

Morgan wondered how he could say all this without scaring them. Naomi was only twelve, Suzanne eleven, Thomas ten, and Tabatha and Patience were still little girls. He didn't want to fill them with fear. He hadn't brought Joey or Mattie's two little ones, but the children he had brought were spread out in age, and he was not sure how he could speak to all of them at the same time. What he knew, however, was that he had to prepare them as best he could.

Morgan chose his words carefully as he said, "If your mothers decide you should hide, they might tell Jeff to bring you down to this spot here by the river. If you had to come here, where would you hide?"

The children all started talking at once, suggesting various rocks and trees.

"All right," Morgan said. "Those are good places, but I think you could hide best if you went into those reeds, close to the river. You would get your feet muddy, but no one could see you if you crouched down."

"Are Indians coming after us, Papa?" Patience asked.

"No. Just men who might want to ask a lot of questions. If you have to talk to them, don't be afraid, but it's better if you don't have to do that. You could stay here for a little while, and then Jeff would tell you when it was all right to walk back to your houses."

Morgan could see everything from concern to terror in the eyes of his children. Ella seemed to understand better than the younger ones, and she looked ready to cry. Morgy was stone faced, as though to hide whatever fears he had, but he certainly looked solemn.

"Why do we have to hide?" Morgan heard Ella whisper.

"Let me see if I can explain a little," Morgan said. "You have one father, but you have three mothers. God has taught us that this is a good way to live—and a good way to raise a big, happy family, like us. But some people don't believe that. They think a man should only have one wife. They disagree with God. But we don't care. We want to live the way God has taught us to live."

"Millie only has one mother," Ella said. Millie Stoddard was her closest friend.

"I know. Lots of men in the Church only have one wife. It's not wrong to have just one wife, and it's not wrong to have more. We do what the Lord tells us to do, and I was asked, by a bishop, to marry more than one wife, so we're doing what's right, and we all love one another. That's the important thing."

It was Jeff, in his man's voice, who asked, "What difference does it make to the government how many wives you have? You're not hurting anyone."

"Well . . . that's a good question. Some people just don't understand God's law. I guess sometimes they think it makes women unhappy to live the way we do. We know that's not true in our family. All the same, men from the government are convinced they have to stop us."

"Will they shoot you?" Naomi asked. She was tall like her mother, Angeline, but she had eyes the color of Morgan's. She had an innocent look about her, and Morgan heard that innocence in her question. It touched him.

"No. But they . . . well, they might want to put me in jail." He let that sink in just a little, and then he said, "So here's the thing. If one of these deputies comes around our home, he may ask you, 'What's the name of your father?' If that happens, just say, 'Papa is my father.' And if he says, 'But what's his name?' say, 'Papa.' Don't say anything else."

"Papa *is* my father," little Andrew said. "That's true."

"Do you know my name?"

"Morgan."

"That's right, but don't say it. It will be like a game. Just say that I'm your papa, and don't let a man like that make you say anything else."

"They'll ask me," Ella said. "Me and Jeff and Morgy. And they'll know we know your name."

"I understand that. But don't tell them any more than you have to. If you say your father is your papa, you aren't lying. Two of your mothers may end up hiding out too, and if that happens, say that all the children are your brothers and sisters, but don't say anything else. If you have to, just close your mouth and say nothing."

It was Ella who still looked the most troubled. "Why can't they just leave us alone?" she asked.

Morgan tried to think what more he could say. It was so hard for these children to understand the world that lay beyond their little valley. Finally, he asked, "Ella, which of you children do I love the most?"

"I don't know."

"Is it Jeff? He's the oldest."

"I don't know."

"Maybe it's you. You're a lovely girl. Do you think it's you?"

"No."

"Then which one is it?"

"I told you, I don't know," Ella said.

"Well, I don't either. I love you all the same. And it doesn't matter who your mother is, or who your aunts are."

Morgan took a peek at Jeff. He didn't say, *And it doesn't matter who your father is, either,* but he hoped his eyes would say that to his big son.

"So which of my wives do I love the most?" Morgan asked.

"All the same," Ella said.

"Is that just what you say, or is it what you believe?"

"It's what I believe. You're nice to all three."

"All right. That's what everyone here has to understand. We're a family. A family that God put together. And we all love each other. Someone, sooner or later, will try to convince you that it's wrong to have our kind of family. But they are the ones who are wrong. We love each other, and we will always take care of each other. We like our big family just the way it is." He laughed a little. "Except we might like to add a few more babies, don't you think?"

The children began to smile and nod their heads. They certainly did love the new babies that came into their family.

"All right. So we're happy, and we're proud of our family, and we'll always be together—in this life and the next. So let's just be careful what we say if deputies come to town. Don't say, 'My papa has three wives.' Just say, 'My papa loves my mama.' That will be the truest thing you can say."

Tears had filled Morgan's eyes. He hated to think what fear someone might bring into his home, what threats the Deps might make, but mostly he was moved by his own words. He did love their mamas. All three. And he loved all twelve of his children. He wanted more than anything to keep them safe and to keep them all together.

CHAPTER 17

Morgan was attending his board of directors meeting on a summer evening in 1884. He had served on the board for nine years now, and once again he was hearing what he had heard so often the last few years. Another brother—this time William Jessop—had asked to speak, and he had begun as so many others had: "I've decided it's time to take my family and leave Orderville. I'd like to receive a fair settlement so I can get started in a new place."

President Carrington crossed his arms over his chest. He looked down for a moment and didn't respond. Finally, he said, "Will, you've been one of our stalwarts. What's brought this on?"

Brother Jessop avoided everyone's eyes. The men of the board were sitting across from him, but he looked at their feet as he spoke. "It's not something that's just happened. I see the Order falling apart, little by little, and I think it's time to give up the whole idea. I used to raise my own crops, keep some cattle, raise a garden; it was a lot of work, but I was in charge of how things turned out. Now I farm a field with a big committee of men, and you board members tell us what to plant. And then you want to know why our yield wasn't what you expected. I don't—"

"Wait a minute, Will," President Carrington said. "That's not how it works. We ask your department head what he plans to plant, and he's supposed to ask all of you on his committee what you think. We approve the plan—or make suggestions—but we don't tell you how to farm the fields. We do have to coordinate with the other farms so that we balance out the various crops and everyone's not growing the same thing. That's the only 'control' we exercise."

"Well . . . I don't know about all of that. But I do think I can do better on my own than when I work with a dozen other men, all with different opinions. Half of 'em would rather argue than work anyway. The only way I know is to grab hold of a plow and start turning dirt. I don't like meetings where people just talk everything to death."

"You've been through everything with us, Brother Jessop," Morgan said. "I remember us down on the Muddy digging out ditches after windstorms. We worked hard, but we all worked together. There's no better feeling in the world than that."

"I know. It's what I felt, too." Will continued to stare at the floor. "But I don't know that it's in a man's nature to feel that way all the time. I don't think any of us feel the way we did back in those days."

"Here's what I want you to think about," President Carrington said. "After Christ visited the Nephites, they lived together in harmony for two hundred years. *Two hundred years,* Brother Jessop. They vowed that there would be no rich or poor among them, and they lived by that principle. From what the Brethren have told us, the same thing happened in the city of Enoch, and it happened among Christ's disciples after He was crucified. All that tells me that it's possible. But it's something we have to grow into, not quit as soon as we find out there are some challenges in it."

Brother Jessop let his breath blow out in a long sound of

exasperation. "That's what we've said all these years, but things are getting worse, not better. We've had a lot of new people come in, and about half of 'em came in lookin' for a free house and free food. I don't think they have any idea what it is we've been trying to do here."

"Are you sure of that?" the president asked. "Because I see a lot of good work being accomplished, and I see a society of people trying to prove to the Lord that we can live up to His teachings. I don't see much laziness. Maybe you're a little too ready to judge others."

"President, I know your opinion. You don't need to preach to me anymore. What I want is a settlement for all the work I've done, and then I'll leave, and all you *devoted* men will be better off without me."

"We don't feel that way at all, Brother Will. We want you to stay. We need you."

Brother Jessop shook his head slowly, still looking down. "Tobias, I didn't start thinking about this just a few days ago. My wife and I have talked and talked about it, and, to tell the truth, she's sick of all the ladies who tell her how much they love her and then share gossip about her behind her back."

Morgan knew something about this. Sister Jessop had shown her merits during the Muddy River days, and he knew she was a good woman. But she could be harsh. For one thing, she made no secret of her opinion that plural marriage was going to bring destruction to the Church. It was one thing not to practice the principle, but it was another to suggest to sisters that such marriages were not ordained of God. "Brigham may have liked having all those wives," she had told Angeline once, "but I think he got off track just as much as King David did, with a whole houseful of wives."

And there was something else. Sister Jessop had never liked to share all she had, and many knew that she had kept her own garden and used what she grew for her own family—even before the dining hall had closed. Comments had been made about that, and that was probably what Brother Will was speaking of when he talked about gossip. Morgan had never worried much about such small infractions, but that was part of the problem in making the Order work. Some were complete sticklers about the rules, while others hoped for a little more individual freedom. Those differing attitudes had not seemed too important at first, but more and more, people were offending each other, arguing about what was "allowed" and what wasn't.

"Brother Jessop," the president said, "can't you hold on with us a little while longer? So many are wanting to leave right now—all at once—that we're having a hard time making settlements with all of you. The Order will simply break down before long if we don't—"

"It has broken down. You men just refuse to see it. If I stay on, I'll end up with nothing, the same as you. That's why I demand a settlement, and I want it now."

"All right. We never have tried to force people to stay when they didn't want to. What do you feel you deserve?"

"For one thing, I want the property I put in when we first came up here. My wagons and animals, and all my tools—or something similar to what I had then. But I think, besides that, I ought to receive a considerable financial settlement. You keep telling us how we've prospered—all the farms and businesses we own. Well, if we've gotten ahead the way you say, share some of it with me."

"Brother Jessop, you know what we've done. All our profit has gone back into the organization. We don't have ready cash stashed away. But if you'd been out working on your own and you'd fed your family and had a decent house, what more would you expect? Take your wagons and mules and tools, and appreciate what you've learned and what you've shared with us. You've worked alongside good friends and brothers. Your children have been taught what's right, and they've lived among good people. What more is it you expect out of any period of your life?"

"I can see I'm not getting the money I deserve, but I want enough seed to plant this year, and enough food to keep my family going for a time, and I want harnesses and a plow. All I want is enough to make a new start."

Morgan finally couldn't keep his mouth shut. "Will, if everyone who leaves this place takes harnesses and plows, we won't get our crops in this year. You understood what the Order was all about when you joined it. The problem is, you don't want the same as everyone else. You want more."

"That's not fair, Morgan. Any man wants more than just enough to eat. He wants to move ahead a little, have a few nice things, feel like he's going somewhere. I'd like to build a nicer house, and my wife wants to have some decent furniture for once in her life."

"You keep thinking that way, Will, and when life is over, see how many trinkets you can take with you. See if Bessie can transport chairs and tables to the next world. If you're living God's commandments, living a holy life, you're accumulating the things that matter."

"Don't talk like you're so holy, Morgan. Brigham thought all this up while he was living in that big house of his up in Salt Lake City. But I don't need anyone telling me whether or not my wife can stick a few plants in the ground. And I'll tell you what else. I heard you say the same kind of things when we were living down on the Muddy."

"I know I did. And I regret some of the things I said. But all of that was before I saw what the Order could do for people, and what—"

"Never mind, Morgan," President Carrington said. "We've said enough. I suggest to this board that Will Jessop receive a wagon, draft animals, tools, adequate seed, and a wagonload of grain and foodstuffs." Then he looked at Will straight on. "But what I'm going to remember as you ride out of this town is that after all these years of seeming to be a loyal brother, you didn't accept the teachings of a prophet of God. Brigham Young went to his grave teaching us that we would never be a Zion society until we learned to live in harmony, all committed to one another. That's what I still believe."

"And I say, Brigham should have stuck with preaching the gospel, not acting like a king, getting into matters that have nothing to do with religion."

"*Everything* is religion," the president said. "Everything we do, every day, is part of building the kingdom and putting the principles of the gospel into action." He held up his hand when he saw that Will was about to respond. "I don't want to argue with you anymore. Let's part as friends. We wish you the best, Brother Jessop."

So the board members voted, and they gave Will Jessop more than Morgan felt they should. He was pretty sure everyone else felt the same way, but they wanted Will to feel their generosity and goodwill—and maybe some shame.

• • •

Mattie wondered why Morgan was so late. She was tired and wanted to go to bed, but she wanted to wait for him, since this was his week with her. She loved her house, and she loved that Morgan could sometimes spend an evening with just her and her children. Hannah was almost four, and very excitable. She loved to have her papa home to play with her, and she would even sit still to have him read stories to her. David was walking now, or at least trying, and everyone commented on how much he looked like his father. He also had a certain seriousness about him, as though he were trying already to be a little man.

Mattie longed for her children to feel a direct connection to Morgan, not always filtered through the noise and busyness of twelve children together. So every third week was sacred to her—and entirely different from those first months of marriage, when her thoughts had been only about the two of them and the joy of first love.

But it was quiet in her little house now, and after her children were down, she opened the door to the center house and peeked in to see Angeline and Ruth sitting together. Mattie decided to join them for a few minutes. It was a summer night, but cool at this hour, and pleasant. It was at times like this, when she could sit with her sister wives, that she realized how much she liked having the company.

Angeline and Ruth were sitting by the open window enjoying the breeze that swept down the valley on summer evenings. The room was illuminated only by the yellow glow of two coal-oil lamps. Mattie sat down with Angeline and Ruth, but they didn't talk at first. Angeline was rocking in her old rocking chair and humming, as she sometimes liked to do. "Abide with Me" was her hymn for the evening. She wasn't much of a singer, but her humming was not too far off tune. Ruth was sitting closer to a lamp, and she had her scriptures out. Mattie had noticed that Ruth loved to read the four Gospels in the New Testament, and she read them over and over.

Ruth looked up after a time and said, softly, "I wish I was more like Jesus."

That made Angeline laugh. "Oh, Ruth, you're more like Him than anyone I know. I'm the one who goes through life with my elbows swinging, knocking everyone down as I walk by."

"You're the only one who sees you that way," Mattie said. "You can shoot a gun, and you can swing a hammer, but inside, you're sweet as molasses. You just don't like to admit it."

Angeline laughed again. "'Sweet as molasses.' Oh, Mattie, no one has ever said that about me. You see the world through your own sweet eyes. You don't see evil even when it stares you in the face."

"What evil?" Mattie laughed, but she actually didn't like to be talked about that way. She knew she was optimistic, and she knew that she sometimes saw the world the way she preferred to see it, but she didn't think she was naïve. She knew there were bad things in the world.

"There's nothing wrong with your attitude, Mattie," Ruth said. "It's the right one. But you trust people a little more than you should sometimes. One of the things I've learned in my life is that people lie, and they make promises they have no plans to keep. You do have to learn to recognize those kinds of people."

Mattie wondered. She probably did trust people more than she should, but she didn't want to go to the other extreme. She didn't want to lose hope. She had heard Morgan talk with such passion and belief about making the United Order work the way it should. She wanted to believe that people could improve and finally fully embrace a life of unity and harmony.

Mattie had left the door open between Angeline's house and

her own, and now she heard footsteps in the other house. She looked over to see Morgan step into the room where the wives were sitting. He didn't look happy. He looked troubled.

"What are you all doing up this late?" he asked.

"Enjoying this breeze," Angeline said. "It's been very nice just to sit a little after a long day."

Morgan nodded, but he didn't say anything.

"What's wrong?" Angeline asked.

"Oh, just the usual kind of thing," he said. "Will and Bessie Jessop are giving up on the Order."

"It's Bessie," Angeline said. "She's been speaking out more all the time. She wanted out of here years ago. She's finally won Will over to her way of thinking."

"Well, yes, I think that's probably true," Morgan said. Mattie watched him look out the window into the darkness. "Will told us he thought the Order was falling apart and couldn't last much longer. What do all of you think about that?"

Angeline, as usual, was the first to speak. "I suspect he's right. People are saying that the Church has given up on the Order and it's time for us to do the same."

"But what's *your* opinion? Should we keep trying?"

"I'm not sure. The Order depends on people being a lot more like Jesus Christ than we seem to be. We've all been trying for a long time, but I think we're tired of the effort it takes."

Mattie couldn't see Morgan very well in the dim light, but she could see by his stillness, the stiff way he was standing, that Angeline wasn't telling him what he wanted to hear.

"What do you think, Ruth?" he asked.

"I guess I agree with Angeline. I don't want to give up quite yet, but I fear that it's just not in us to be quite so good as we need to be."

"I know that feeling, Ruth. But doesn't that come from the 'natural man' in us? We're like little children who say, 'That's mine, not yours.' Can't we outgrow that kind of thinking?"

"I think it might be possible," Mattie said. "I want to love every sister in this whole town. I want to work with them and build up the kingdom." She laughed. "The trouble is, I don't like some of them. But that shouldn't matter. We can love people we don't like so much, and then, if our hearts are right, we'll start to like them in spite of ourselves."

"Maybe," Angeline said. "But we've been trying that for quite a few years, and gradually, we're disliking each other more, not less."

"I don't want to believe that," Morgan said, but Mattie heard some finality in his voice. She sensed that he was giving up too.

• • •

By the end of summer, and on through the winter of 1884–85, Orderville was threatened by more than the failings of the people. More and more, leaders were receiving warnings about the spreading government raids. Federal deputies had begun to arrest "co-habiters" in southern Utah.

In the early spring of 1885, Morgan spent a long day with his cattle. It was calving time, and someone had to stay at the barn around the clock. It was almost ten o'clock when he let one of his assistants take over for the night, and he rode his horse back toward his home. But his worries had mounted lately. Deps had taken their time in working their way out to the smaller settlements, especially the ones in remote areas like Long Valley, but they had been spotted lately in nearby towns, and Morgan knew that with his three adjoining houses, his way of living was obvious. He had thought of leaving the area for a time, but his stubbornness kept him home. He felt that he was needed in the town, and he knew he was needed by his family. He found himself wanting to test the Lord. He had been loyal to the Order, and he had lived the principle that God had given him through the prophets. Now it seemed that it ought to be the Lord's turn to protect him.

He also knew that his own logic didn't hold. Brigham Young himself had been jailed, at least for a day, when the pressure against polygamy had first been building up. Now, several Church leaders had ended up in prison. If men of God—far better men than himself—were willing to pay the price for holding to the Lord's commandments, why should he expect greater protection himself? President John Taylor had been hiding out, according to the word that came to Orderville, and he was not a young man. What weighed on Morgan more than anything was the thought that the government was not letting up—that only the destruction of the Church would satisfy the politicians who had vowed to put a stop to the "evil" of polygamy.

Morgan wished that some of those Deps who were chasing polygamous men could spend one day with his family. The reality was that lots of men in America consorted with prostitutes or had mistresses. He didn't know why the Deps couldn't see that in plural families the men made a full effort not only to be true to their families but to balance the love and care they offered each wife, each child. He knew he wasn't the best man in the world, but he also knew how hard he tried to be a good husband and father. Adulterers were not thrown into prison, nor were men who beat their wives and children, but religious men who wanted nothing more than to build the kingdom of God were being locked up.

Morgan slowed as he neared his home, then stopped his horse. It was his routine every night just to wait and observe for a few minutes. He knew that Deps liked to post themselves outside the houses of suspected "co-habs" with the hope of catching them there with more than one wife present. So he sat on Lightning as she shifted from hoof to hoof, eager to move ahead those last steps to the little barn behind the houses.

Morgan was about to give Lightning her way when he saw a movement. A shadow seemed to drift to a corral fence just beyond the barn. He saw clearly that a figure—a man in dark clothing—had reached the fence, then crouched.

And then there was another motion on the near side of the barn. This time there was no mistaking. It was a man, all right, and the moonlight glinted off the rifle he was carrying. The man continued to the front of the barn, to a little row of poplars that Morgan had planted, and then he lay down on his chest and waited.

Morgan turned Lightning very gently, then spoke to her softly. "Walk along, girl. We're going back to the pasture." He pressed the horse's sides with gentle pressure, and Lightning walked on, but not with the steady gait of the homeward trip. Once they were a hundred yards or so up the road, Morgan urged the horse with more force, and Lightning did pick up her pace. What Morgan knew was that he would have to hide out that night. He only hoped that his wives wouldn't worry too much about him.

So Morgan rode back to the canyon where he spent most of his days, and then he turned Lightning loose in the pasture. He worked his way through the trees in the dark and found the cave where he had set up his hiding place. It was a cold evening, but the cave was a little warmer. Still, the ground was hard and the blankets not quite adequate to keep him comfortable. He waited, maybe slept a little, but spent the night primarily trying to think out his options. He could leave the area, hide somewhere for a time, and maybe avoid prison, or he could give himself up, accept that prison was inevitable, and start serving his time. The only other course was to split up his families and move two of his wives to other settlements. Maybe, after a while, all this harassment would end. Church leaders had been saying for a long time that members had to be true to the faith, continue to pray for a softening of attitudes in Washington, and prove to the Lord that they would not accede to the false values of a prejudiced people.

But what would it do to his family—especially his children—if he took any of those courses? He didn't want to leave, didn't want to send his wives away, didn't want to lose the unity that had grown up in their homes. In the last year he had felt more love than ever for his wives, and he had observed more love and kindness *between* his wives. Sometimes it almost seemed that he was becoming a better man, a better husband, a better leader—and now all this was being threatened by people who had no idea what his life was like.

He had made no decision by morning. He got up early, relieved to see the sun appear, and then went about his work. He didn't know how much the Deps knew about him, whether they would come looking for him in the canyon, but he kept Lightning saddled nearby, and he watched the road that led into the canyon. If men appeared, he knew he could ride into the woods and over the mountain. At that point, he would probably have to head south toward Arizona. What he didn't want to do, however, was to leave his family without letting them know he was going. There were things he needed to say, and he wanted to bless his family, give them some courage to deal with the test that was coming.

When the Deps didn't appear, Morgan finally made his way home again after dark. He watched for a long time without seeing anyone about. He knew that the deputies might have hidden better tonight, but he finally decided he would take his chances. He rode to his barn, put away his horse inside, and then went to Angeline's house. What he found was what he had expected. The whole family was gathered in the "center house," as they called it, and there was great relief when he entered the door. His smaller children all ran to him, and he hugged each one; then the older ones took their turns.

"Where did you go last night?" everyone was asking him at the same time.

Morgan wanted to be careful what he said in front of the younger children. He only asked, "Do you all remember what you're supposed to do if your mothers tell you to hide?"

"Go with Jeff and hide by the river," Andrew said.

"That's right. Do what he tells you." He looked around at his wives, who were standing back a little. "Right now, though, I want you all to go into Aunt Ruth's house. I need some time to talk to your mothers."

Jefferson, who was almost as tall as Morgan now, said, "Papa, maybe I should stay and hear what you have to say. If I'm going to be the one to—"

"I know what you mean, Jeff. But let me talk to you a little later. You look after the children in the other house for right now."

Jeff nodded, but Morgan knew he was insulted, and he also knew he would have to include the boy a great deal more now. If Morgan had to hide out, Jeff would be crucial to the survival of the family. Still, Jeff didn't understand everything about Morgan keeping his bonds with three wives. Morgan needed some time with them now, before he might be forced to leave.

So Jeff and the children walked next door, and as they did, Morgan stepped outside and looked around. He saw no movement in the shadows, didn't think the Deps were out there tonight. When he went back in, he walked to the fire and stood with his back to it for a moment.

"I guess you figured out that I spent the night at the cave last night. I came home after work, but I saw men out by our barn, watching the house."

"We knew they were out there," Angeline said. "Mattie's been keeping watch, and she saw them. We were glad when you didn't come in."

"But it was a long night," Mattie said. "We didn't know what men like that might do."

"They arrested Brother Peterson last night," Angeline said. "Brother Hart came by today to check on us. He said that the Deps watched Brother Peterson go into his house, and then they rushed the house, walked right in without knocking, so John wouldn't have a chance to skedaddle through another door."

"What about the bishop? Were they after him, too?"

"He got wind that the Deps were coming, so he left town. He's probably in Arizona by now."

"Well, that's good. But where are they taking Brother Peterson?"

"No one knows for sure. They think the Deps will haul him down to Kanab and try him down there. Brother Hart said that they didn't even bother to take his wives along to witness against him. Anymore, all they have to do is tell the judge that they found him in the house with more than one woman. These judges are working with the Deps, and all they care about is catching as many men as they can. They think that if they throw enough of us in jail, Church leaders will finally decide it's not worth resisting anymore."

Morgan didn't think the Church would ever give way to the pressure, but he did see terrible days ahead. The Lord certainly wasn't stepping in to end all this—at least not yet. He walked to the kitchen table and said, "Come here. Sit with me a minute. I have some things I need to tell you."

The three wives sat down at the long table, Morgan at the end, Angeline to his right, and Ruth to his left, with Mattie next to Ruth. Morgan took a moment and looked at each. He wished that he didn't have to tell them what he was about to say, and he tried for a few seconds to think whether he had alternatives. He was also surprised at the powerful emotions he felt. He had wondered, long ago, whether he could love three women, and he had wondered whether Mattie could ever fit into his family. Now, as he looked at each wife, one at a time, he felt connected, felt a sense of what they had experienced—what he had experienced with each woman and what they had all passed through together.

"I probably need to go away for a time," he finally said. "I've thought of all the options, and it's the only one that makes sense to me right now."

"What good will that do?" Angeline asked. "The Deps will be back. And they know to watch our houses. Whenever you come back, they'll be after you again."

"I know. But I keep thinking, if I can stay away for a time, this whole thing might finally blow over. It's hard to imagine that the government will keep after us year after year. The Lord will find a way to soften their hearts or—"

"That's what you always think," Angeline said. "We were called by God to go to the Muddy River, and you thought the Lord would see us through—because it was a mission. Well, it didn't work, did it? And you hang on to the Order because you believe it's what God wants, but Morgan, it's almost dead. With this raid going on, and our leaders on the run, there's no way we can keep it going."

Morgan sat back. He didn't want to argue—and more than that, he suspected Angeline was right. A third of the town was on the run, either the husband or his wives having left. How could any organization keep functioning under those conditions? But he still wanted to think that the Lord would intercede sooner or later. He couldn't accept that God had lost interest in what happened to His people.

"If I stay," he said, "I'll be taken to Salt Lake and thrown into prison. You three, and Jeff, will have to keep this place running. If I hide out, maybe I can at least come and go, help out for a time, and then go on the run again."

"And *then* go to prison."

Angeline wasn't being belligerent. He could see in her eyes that she was merely resolved—ready to face reality. "So what are you saying," he asked, "that I might as well get myself arrested now and just put in my three years?"

"Yes. That's what I think. We can manage here."

"But Angie, don't you see what they'll do? They'll tell me, after I get out, that I can't live with my wives. If I come back, they'll either make two of you leave or they'll arrest me again—and they'll sentence me all over again."

Morgan saw that these words struck home. Angeline looked down at the table. He had made his point, but now she did look broken. Morgan looked at Ruth. "What do you think?" he asked.

"Morgan, I don't know. There's no good answer. If the Lord is telling you to hide for a time, that's what you should do."

But Morgan felt too confused to claim that he had an answer from God. He looked at Mattie. "What do you say?"

"If you go to Arizona, you can find Church families there. You can find a way to live. At least it won't be prison."

"Morgan, the Deps can go anywhere," Angeline said. "They'll start looking in Arizona before long."

"I know. But I know people in Moccasin Springs that I've met on the cattle drive. They'll put me up. And if a Dep finds me there, he can't claim any proof that he found me with more than one wife."

"Well, then, maybe that's best for now."

Morgan shut his eyes, trying to find some clarity.

Angeline reached over and touched his hand. "Follow what the Spirit is telling you. But find a way to keep in touch with us, so we'll know where you are and what you're doing."

"I don't think I can send you letters. But I'll get word to you somehow. It might be better if you don't know too much—in case you're questioned. But I'll show up one night, after dark, and I'll see what's happening here. And then I'll leave before the next morning, if that's what I have to do." He sat and thought. He still felt no certainty, but the only thing that made sense to him was to head out of town the way so many other men across the Church were doing. "All right. I'm going to leave now. I need to pack a few things, and I need to talk to Jeff."

But the decision was even harder than he had imagined. It was Mattie who covered her face with her hands and let herself cry, but Ruth and Angeline also had tears in their eyes. And Morgan felt his own eyes fill up. "Let's bring the children back," he said. "I want to say a prayer—a blessing on all of them, and on the three of you. I'll leave you in the hands of the Lord for a time."

"Yes, do that. But don't worry about us," Angeline said. "We'll manage."

Morgan stood up. He took his wives in his arms, one at a time, and he told each, "I love you."

• • •

After Morgan pronounced a blessing on his family all together, he put his hands on the head of each of his wives, and on

Jefferson's, and he pronounced a specific blessing on each. He told Angeline that she had been his strength and power for all his married life. The words touched her. She thought about how different life had looked eighteen years earlier when they had married, but how much she loved Morgan and the great man he had become.

Angeline listened as Morgan told Ruth that she had come into his life in a way he hadn't expected, and she had blessed him with her steady goodwill. Then he told Mattie that although she was still young, she had wisdom beyond her years and was as good-hearted as anyone he had ever known. He told Jefferson that he was, indeed, his son, as much as any of his children, that he was a man now, and he would be needed to handle many things that a father usually took care of.

Morgan embraced all his children again, and then he walked out to the barn. Angeline was devastated, but she didn't want to show it. She walked to the window and looked out toward the barn. When she was certain that no Deps had been waiting outside for him, and that he had ridden away, she turned back to the family. The youngest children looked baffled, worried; the older ones, distraught. Most were crying.

"All right," Angeline said. "I think that's enough tears for one night. We're a strong family, and we don't let little things knock us down. I've seen many a Mormon father go off on a mission for two or three years—or more—and the families he leaves behind pick up the slack and do what they have to do. That's how we have to think of this right now. The Lord has called Papa away for a time, but he's going because he believes in the commandments of God and refuses to break the covenants he has made. We can all be proud of him—and we can be strong."

"I think we need to play a game," Mattie said. "Who wants to do that?"

The children stared at her for a moment, but then Ella said, "Yes, that's just the thing. What game shall we play, everyone? 'Ring around the Rosie'?"

"Yes, that's a good one," Ruth said. "We'll all play. Even Aunt Angeline."

That was not something Angeline liked to do. She had always left game playing to Mattie. But she knew the children would love to see her fall with everyone else when the words to the song rang out: "We all fall down." So she joined the circle, and she watched as the children's faces brightened.

But she was wondering when she would see her husband again.

CHAPTER 18

Angeline walked to the meetinghouse by herself. Ruth and Mattie had told her that she could represent the family. Angeline knew what the meeting was about. Everyone did. But she hated to hear the words. She knew how disappointed Morgan would be.

President Carrington had been in hiding most of the time lately, and he had been released as bishop, with Heber Ernst, a young man of thirty or so, having been called to replace him. But Tobias Carrington was still president of the United Order, and he had returned to town for discussions that had been going on for several days. Brigham Young Jr. and Heber J. Grant, both Apostles, had traveled to Orderville with the advice that it was time to dissolve the Order. There had been a great deal to consider, and many of the townspeople wanted to continue their way of life, but in the end, most of the discussion had come down to the mechanics of dissolving the corporation. Still, a vote had to be taken, and the current meeting had been announced as the opportunity for all to take part in the final decision.

Bishop Carrington looked out across the congregation—which was now diminished in size with so many of the men in hiding, some of them having traveled all the way to Mexico. "As you all know," he said, "it's been a struggle to keep the Order operating with so many of our leaders being chased and harassed. Now we've been advised by the First Presidency that we ought to consider disbanding the organization. The thinking is, when this federal raid finally ends, maybe something could be tried again, but so many have given up and left, or have been forced into hiding, that there's just no way to keep all the departments alive. With Elder Young and Elder Grant here, we've considered all the issues connected with dissolution—and tried to devise possible plans to avoid it—but we see no way forward. Therefore, it's the recommendation of your presidency and board of directors that the Order be unincorporated."

He scanned the audience, apparently to see whether anyone objected or wanted to propose a different course. But the room was still.

"Well, then, all in favor of ending the United Order of Orderville and—"

"What's that going to mean, President?" Lyman Hunt asked.

"Excuse me?"

"Who gets what? Do we keep our houses? Do we get a plot of land to farm?"

"Yes, of course. Possessions will be divided, and everyone who wants to stay here will receive a parcel of land. Certainly, you'll keep the house you've been living in. There are a lot of other things we're going to have to figure out. I know you'll want plows and wagons, draft animals, and all those things. The trouble is, we just don't have enough to go around. I guess I would say that cooperation among our people doesn't have to end when the Order ends. You can still share your equipment, animals, and the like."

Lyman nodded and ran his hand over his red beard, still

looking as though this sudden end was too much to comprehend. "And what if we leave?"

"I don't know, Brother Hunt. The only thing I can tell you is that we'll be fair and even-handed in making settlements, but I can't promise you that everyone will be happy with what they receive."

"It just doesn't seem right to send us on our way with nothing to show for all the work we've done here."

"We won't do that. I'm just saying that we can only share what we have, and we can't make everything exactly equal. But I want you to think just a little differently about what you'll take away from here." He paused. Angeline heard his voice become thick with emotion. "We've tried to consecrate ourselves to the good of the entire society and not just think of ourselves as individuals. In the end, I guess maybe you could say we failed, but I don't like to think of it that way. I'll never forget the feelings we've shared here. Yes, we've worked hard, but we did a lot more than that. For a few precious years, we lived a higher law. I felt a unity and love here I've never known anywhere else in my life. And we can take that with us. We may start to farm our own land, or set up a shop of some kind—or do whatever we choose—but I hope we won't forget what it was like to share equally and not place one person above another. We may not continue on in a supervised Order, but we can still carry that spirit. If someone is hungry, we can share our food, share our plows, share our skills and knowledge. We can teach young people a trade, but we can do more than that. We can teach them to love their neighbors, take care of each other, and live in harmony without backbiting and criticizing. We proved that we could reach that level of behavior for a time—before a lot of things started to work against us. I just hope we won't give up on the principles of the Order even if we dissolve the organization itself. I hope many of you will stay here, and we can remain a family."

President Carrington grasped both sides of his suit coat, just below the lapels, and he looked over the top of the people, as though it was simply too painful to look in their faces. "Some of the Saints who started out on the Muddy with us are gone now, and others of you have joined us since that time. But I think we've all benefited from these years together. Some of our people questioned why President Young sent us down into that desert on the Muddy, and all they could say was that we never should have gone there, that it was too hot, too dry, too windy. I admit that my family didn't move there until the latter part of that mission, but I'll be thankful all my life that I shared some of that experience with many of you, and that we worked together to make the best of things. We brought that spirit with us here, and I think that's why our Order lasted longer than the others."

Brother Carrington nodded a couple of times, but to Angeline he seemed to be stalling for a few seconds to control his emotions. "Now I'm hearing it all again. The Order was a bad idea, people tell me. Brigham Young asked us to do things we're not capable of doing. He was too idealistic. But if we weren't up to the ideal, that's our problem, not Brother Brigham's. And it surely wasn't the Lord's fault. What we've learned here is a better way of living, and I want that kind of life to continue even after we've divided up our land and possessions."

Brother Hunt was nodding. "I don't disagree with that," he said. "I was just wondering . . . well, how we'll manage everything at this point."

Angeline felt chastened. The Order had sometimes felt uncomfortable to her. She liked to serve, but she didn't like to coordinate all her efforts. Mormons believed in standing on their own feet, and most had little patience with those who for one reason or another couldn't keep up. But she had learned something here. For the most part, she had seen people do their best in Orderville. Some people were weak; some were negative or downright selfish. But the Order had asked for the very best in people, and most had risen higher than they would have any other way.

There had been plenty of talk lately about the "lazy" people in Orderville being too much of a weight on the system. And yet, Angeline had gone through times when her health had broken and she couldn't find the strength she had always prided herself in possessing. She had always thought people who let themselves "get down" were too soft on themselves. But she had been such a person at times, and others had carried her along. She would miss that spirit if it were lost.

So the vote was taken, and all agreed that the Order should be dissolved, and then Angeline walked back to the three houses where she and the other wives lived. Angeline tried to tell them what Brother Carrington had said. She wanted the children to hear it too. The United Order was now dissolved, but she didn't want them to give up the essence of what the organization had been about.

What pleased Angeline most was that after the meeting, Bishop Ernst, whom she had known when he was still a boy, came to visit her and the family. He told the three wives, "I'm sure you're wondering how you're going to get by, but I don't want you to worry. The leaders who are still here decided that we had to look after the families with husbands on the run. You'll keep these houses, and you'll receive five acres of land just down the road from here—the closest plot of land that's already plowed. You'll also be able to procure other things you'll need when the property of the Order is divided up."

The bishop and the three women were sitting at the kitchen table together, and Jeff had stayed close by. "Don't worry about us," he said. "My father has taught me enough that I can keep a farm going. I don't know how soon Papa can come back to us, but I won't leave my family. The older girls can milk the cow—if we end up with one—and the other children can help out in the garden. We'll all pull together."

Angeline tried not to smile. She was proud of Jeff, but he wasn't quite as knowledgeable as he thought he was. He knew the cattle operation, but he had actually never farmed. What she knew was that she could still handle a plow, and she could chop wood, even fell a tree if she needed to. Mattie had become a good cook. She could manage almost everything in the house, especially the children. And Ruth would keep the family on track. Maybe the Order was gone, but plural marriage was a kind of United Order itself, and she trusted that it would continue to work for them. She wanted Morgan to come home, but she didn't feel helpless. The family would be all right.

• • •

A few weeks after the United Order was discontinued, the board of directors organized an auction. Member families all received credits according to their time living in Orderville and their hours of work recorded in the log books. The big fields were divided, along with herds, farm implements, wagons, and work animals. Jefferson used the family credits to do the bidding for the Davis family, and he was able to procure most of what he wanted, based on the priorities he and the three wives had set. In addition to their five acres of land, they acquired an adjoining five acres, a wagon and ox team, a plow and harrow, and, to Jefferson's great satisfaction, old Lightning, the horse he had been using since his father had been gone. They also ended up with a cow, some chickens, and a healthy young sow.

Jefferson felt a kind of excitement he hadn't expected. Ten acres should be plenty to provide for the family, but Jeff would need a lot of help from Morgy and even Thomas, who was eleven now. In truth, Jefferson knew that Angeline would be his greatest help, but he wanted to prove that as a man of twenty, he could carry most of the load. Ella, Naomi, and Suzanne, now fifteen, thirteen, and twelve, could learn to make butter and cheese. Ruth was good at that and would teach them the art. Those girls could also help Mattie prepare meals, and the younger children could do chores too. Tabatha was nine, Patience and Andrew seven, so they could feed animals, gather eggs, dump the slop bucket in the hog pen, and do some housework. Even little Joey and Mattie's Hannah and David would start to learn small chores they could do.

Jeff had felt responsible for the family's well-being even before the Order ended, but everything was different now. If the crops failed or the animals weren't taken care of, he felt it would be his fault. He knew that friends in town would still help, even without a formal organization, but he liked to think that he would be the one looking after other families—the way his papa had always done—and that no one would feel that he was the one needing extra assistance.

But almost everything was changing. A lot of people from the Order were leaving the valley entirely. In the last little while, Jeff had watched many of the young people his age decide to leave. Harv Jones had gone away, saying that he was going to find a job in a mine. His plan was to work for a while, build up some savings, and then try his luck opening a business of some sort. It was all rather vague and full of Harv's usual overconfidence, but he believed in himself, and maybe he could do it. One thing was for certain: Harv would find a way to get himself some store-bought pants.

Orson Millard's family was also planning to leave. They were moving to Salt Lake City, partly to give Orson a chance to study—and work on his writing talent—at one of the Church academies. Orson seemed half frightened finally to face the possibility, and maybe afraid of failing, but at least he was going to try his wings, to see a new place.

Jeff didn't feel that he had any option but to stay with his family, but he had also made up his mind that he wasn't going to be jealous. He wasn't going to feel sorry for himself. He had to be a man of honor, and that meant looking after his family while his father was forced to stay away.

After the auction, Ruth and his aunts congratulated Jeff for his skillful bidding, and they walked home while he waited for the deeds and other papers he would need to show ownership. When he had what he needed, he stepped away from the table where board members had processed his paperwork, and he spotted Harriet Hart. "Oh, hello," he said.

"You think I was waiting for you, don't you?" Harriet said. "Just so I could admire how good-looking you are."

Jeff laughed. "Not at all. I—"

"Well, it's true. I was waiting. And you do look handsome—as always—and I was proud of you for the way you managed your bids and got just what you told me you wanted."

"Well . . . I did all right." He smiled and took off his hat. "And by the way, when it comes to being good-looking, it's my opinion that you shine the brightest in this whole valley."

"So what are you going to do about it?"

The question was more direct than Jefferson had expected.

The two had been sweet on each other for a long time, and they had been walking out for more than a year. They had talked about getting married at some point in their lives. But Jefferson didn't know how to answer her question. The day was mild and beautiful, the sky close and bright, and the air was full of the smell of newly turned soil. It all felt perfect. More important, he felt like he was truly grown up. He knew that his father would be proud of him for what he'd accomplished today. Still, Harriet's question had knocked a little starch out of him. "Let's walk just a little," he finally said.

Harriet nodded, still smiling, seemingly aware that she had flustered him. She took his arm, and the two walked away from the town square toward the river. Harriet had a few comments to make about the robins returning to the valley, and about a yellow butterfly she spotted, but Jefferson was trying to think what he could say to her. He began carefully. "I guess you know, I have more responsibility than ever right now."

"I guess I do know. And I guess maybe you're telling me we have to wait until your father comes home before you can . . . move ahead with your life."

"No. I'm not saying that. Not for sure. But I do have to figure out how to run a farm by myself. I can't run off and leave my family right now."

"I'm not thinking you should run off. Couldn't you run your farm just as well as a married man as you could single?"

"I guess I could. But it's not the right time to add another family to the dinner table, just when—"

"I don't eat much. Have you noticed how thin my waist is?"

She stopped, stepped away a little, and then spun about. She was wearing her gray homespun dress—which was rather baggy—but she gripped her hands to her waist and drew the fabric in close.

And it was true, she had the narrowest waist he had ever seen. Jefferson had been troubled trying to go to sleep at night sometimes, just thinking about the shape of her.

Jefferson watched her. He knew that she was teasing him, but at the same time, he felt frustrated that he couldn't give her a better answer.

"Harriet, now that I have a piece of land, I have to get it planted. It's such a busy time. I can't let my brothers and sisters think I'm only half committed to them. They have to see me leading the way, keeping things going. And my mother and aunts depend on me right now."

"I know. I understand. But how long do we have to wait?"

"Uh . . . well . . . come here a second." He walked closer to the river, and then down the path to the water's edge. There, with the high banks behind them and the willows hanging down, no one could see them. And it was then that he took her in his arms and kissed her.

"Oh, my," Harriet said. "You do that very well. Why don't you do it more often?"

"Because I don't want to wait either—and kissing you only makes the time seem longer."

"Then why don't we—"

"Harriet, I've thought this all through. Maybe if I can build one more house—maybe out closer to where our farm ground is, we could get married in another year or so. But right now, with the Order gone, and everything changing, I've just got to keep my promise to my father. I have to take care of my brothers and sisters."

"But maybe in a year?"

"Maybe. Maybe two. We'll see."

"If you wait too long, I might find someone else. Some of the other boys in town like to flirt with me."

"I do worry about that."

"Good."

"But you know what? I'm sure they don't know how to kiss the way I do."

"So what are you saying, that you've had lots of practice?"

"No. Not any. But it's my way of saying what I feel about you—and no one else loves you the way I do."

He took her in his arms again, kissed her again. All he wished was that they could marry that very minute.

• • •

That evening, after the auction, Angeline had arranged to have some friends over for a picnic. Eb and Mary Ann came with their seven children, along with Art and Susan Brooks, with eight children, and Lyman and Alice Hunt, with six still living. With all those children, and the twelve Davis children combined, bedlam ensued. All the children knew each other, and they collected into pockets, by age, the little ones laughing and running about, the older ones talking loudly enough to hear each other above the noise.

Angeline had never liked such wildness, but she looked over the scene and thought how wonderful it actually was that the couples who had traveled south to the Muddy, all newly married, had produced such a host of offspring. In another few generations, they would begin to be like Abraham's descendants, numberless as the sands of the seas.

Each family had brought chickens, new potatoes, carrots, and parsnips, and the Davis wives fried the chicken, mashed the potatoes, and boiled the vegetables. It was a mighty feast, and the myriad of children, preoccupied as they seemed, consumed great quantities of food. It was after dinner—served to the children sitting on quilts—that Mattie came up with a wonderful idea. She would take the children a little way out of town, where they could play Red Rover or Kick the Can—or "whatever games the children choose." Jeff—along with Ella and Morgy—rather reluctantly agreed to go along and help Mattie. So the older children from the other families joined in.

The din of voices passed away rather slowly as the children walked away, and finally, Angeline could hear only the faintest hint of laughter and hoots and shouts. "Oh, my goodness, Angie," Susan Brooks said. "I had no idea what a blessing a young wife could be to a family. I think maybe I'll have Art get us one."

Angeline let out a long sigh. The couples were gathered around the long table that Jeff and Morgy had carried outside. "Susan," she said, "I know you're joking. But Mattie *is* a blessing to us. She has the energy to work hard and still play with the children when evening comes. And she knows how to make all of us laugh."

"But I don't want Eb looking at any girls who are nearly so pretty," Mary Ann said. "I think I'll choose for him: a nice homely girl who's willing to do all my cooking and housework."

Ruth and Angeline glanced at each other and smiled, and then Ruth said, "I think you can imagine how we felt about Mattie," she said. "She knows just when to flash her dimples and make Morgan's knees go weak. But her heart is in the right place even if her dimples are an unfair weapon. I think we love her like a daughter, more than a sister, but we do love her."

"I've watched the way you three have come together over the years," Alice said, "and I think it's wonderful. But I'm glad—especially now, with the Deps chasing after all the plural families—that Lyman hasn't chosen to take any more wives."

"They wouldn't have me," Lyman said. "I'm not half so good-looking as Morgan."

Angeline wasn't sure what to say. All her friends knew how much strain she had gone through to accept these wives, and she didn't want to pretend that her life had been easy in that regard. But she remembered thinking after each marriage that her happiness had ended. And yet, she was happy now. Strangely, even happy with Morgan gone—and precisely because she had Ruth and Mattie and twelve children.

Angeline decided not to say any of that. She hoped they could feel that she was more contented than ever in her life, and once she got Morgan home, she thought her life would be just fine as she aged and watched her children grow into the people she imagined them becoming. "So, were you happy with the farm lots you received—and the other things?" she asked.

"Well . . . yes," Eb said.

Angeline took a careful look at him. She wasn't sure why he was hesitating. What crossed her mind was that Eb was not the same man she had known back in 1867. He still looked rather young for his age, but he wasn't baby-faced any longer. In fact, she saw lines forming around his eyes. She knew that he and Mary Ann had survived some painfully difficult years, but Mary Ann actually looked the better for it. She seemed truly grown-up now, and she had filled out enough to look healthy.

"Angeline, there's something we want to tell you," Eb said. Angeline waited, but she thought she knew what he was going to say. "We—all of us—have decided to go back to northern Utah."

Ruth said, "But why?"

"It's a little different for each one of us, but now that the Order is gone, there's no real reason for us to stay here. We came to this valley because our friends were settling here. And then, the Order seemed like the fulfillment of what we had come for. But everything is changing now. Most of the new people don't understand what we tried to accomplish."

Angeline had had inklings that this announcement was coming, but it saddened her to think of these friends leaving. She didn't want them to see her disappointment or hear it in her voice, so she said nothing for the moment.

"Angie," Mary Ann said, "you know how much I've always missed my family. I want to live near my sister—the one I'm closest to—and I want to be near my parents before they're gone."

"That's how it is for us, too," Lyman said. "We always thought we would go home from time to time, but the distance was always too great. We've already had family members pass away. We want to be closer now."

"I understand that," Angeline said. And she did. She too had always thought that she and Morgan would travel back to Farmington someday—for a visit—but they had never managed it, and she wasn't sure now, given the complications of their lives, that they ever would.

Ruth was also nodding.

"But it's you—and Morgan—we hate to leave," Art said. "Morgan has been my brother all these years—even in recent years when we've all been so busy with our own families. I hate to think that I might never see you two again."

"Don't you think about moving back to Farmington?" Eb asked. "We could all see each other from time to time that way."

"How can we do that, Eb?" Angeline asked. "The last time Morgan sneaked in and out, he was saying we should consider moving to Mexico. You can all live in northern Utah with your families, and no Deps will be after you. But if we continue to live the way we do now, Morgan could end up in prison."

"I know," Eb said. "But do you really think you'll go to Mexico?"

"I don't know. Maybe we'll have to spread out and live in different towns. We really don't know what we'll do."

"I'm sorry," Susan said. "It's unfair."

"Lots of things are unfair in this world. But we still feel blessed." Angeline stopped and listened for a moment. "Hear that howl, off in the distance. About half that noise belongs to our family, and they're all *ours,* not mine and hers. I prayed all those years ago that I could have babies, and now I have a multitude of them. And I guess some of them might need a good spanking, if any one of us had the heart to give them one, but we love all of them."

Everyone was nodding, smiling, looking a little sad, a little pleased.

"So when are you leaving?" Ruth asked.

"Soon," Art said. "Probably next week."

"You have property here. What will you do with it?"

"We would sell it now, if there were any buyers," Eb said. "But at least we have an asset we can maybe sell in time. We've come away with that much, anyway."

"And, I hope, much more," Angeline said.

"We've talked about that. I think we've learned more than we could have any other way. And our children got the right kind of start on life. We just hope they'll never forget this valley and how we lived here."

Angeline was nodding. "For a time, we made it work. We came close to being the society we wanted to be. I think for the rest of my life I'll miss the way we all felt—and acted—for those few years."

"We'll find it again," Eb said, "but maybe only in the next life."

• • •

Morgan, in the following months, visited his family from time to time—but never for very long. He had found an older man and his wife—members of the Church—near Moccasin Springs, Arizona, who had room for him to stay and who needed someone with a strong back who could help them farm their land. He was actually a blessing to them, but they understood that the day might come when he would return to his wives. They prayed with him every day that that would happen, but Morgan knew they were always relieved when he returned to them.

A year went by that way, and Church members continued to hope that conditions would soon change, that a favorable ruling would come in the Supreme Court, or that the Deps would finally give up the chase. But there were actually more federal deputies being sent to Utah or recruited from the Gentiles who lived there already. These men had learned that catching co-habs was tricky, and they were getting ever more clever in their techniques. They had their spies in towns all over Utah and southern Idaho, and if the Mormons had their signals of alarm, the Deps had a hired network of people who watched and would send word that a certain man was home and becoming more open in letting people see him there. And then the Deps would suddenly appear and arrest him.

Morgan had created a closet with a false back in it. It gave him just enough room to step to the back and pull shut a door that seemed nothing more than a wall. It was a tight space, and he didn't like to stand so still very long, but he had done it twice and avoided detection, and then he had sneaked out in the night and left town again.

But in the spring of 1887, Morgan began to believe that Orderville, especially now that a good many people had moved away from Long Valley, was no longer of much interest to the Deps. All winter and early spring, no one had seen agents in the area. Morgan began to stay longer, to attend church and walk down the streets of town. What he enjoyed most was harnessing his team of oxen and working alongside Jeff and Morgy. It was a simple life, now that he had no board meetings, no assignments away from his farm. His family was healthy and glad to have him with them, and he was happy to learn that Mattie and Angeline were both pregnant.

And then one night, not long after he had returned from his fields, he was sitting in the big room in the center house with all his wives and children around him. Everyone was laughing and talking, but Morgan, who had been reading his Book of Mormon, was slumped a little in his chair with his chin on his chest. Jefferson laughed and said, "I think I wore out the poor old fellow today. He won't admit it, but I can cut more furrows in a day than he can, and never break a sweat."

Morgan roused. He hadn't been quite asleep, and he had heard this comment. He was about to claim that he had more skill, rather than speed, when a knock came at the door. Morgan wondered. Maybe it was just a neighbor stopping by for a visit, but Angeline whispered. "Hurry, hide."

Morgan knew that was wise. He nodded, then hurried to the closet, and was glad he had done so when he heard a second knock, louder, just as he was hiding himself away.

CHAPTER 19

Mattie walked to the door. "Who's there?" she called out.

"Friends," a low voice said.

"Please come visit us some other time," Mattie said. "It's too late tonight."

Now the voice was louder. "Open the door or we'll bust it down."

Morgan had installed a wooden brace that swung down and held the door secure. Mattie thought of letting them have a try, but that wouldn't solve anything and would only heighten suspicions. So she swung the wooden arm away and opened the door only a crack. Two men were outside: Deps—there was no mistaking them. They looked disheveled, even dirty, as though they had been camping in the woods. Both of them were carrying rifles.

"What may I do for you?" she asked.

"Just move out of the way. We're coming in." One of the men, a bulky fellow with a full beard, more gray than black, pushed against the door, and Mattie had to step back. As soon as the men were inside, the big one scanned the room. "Where is he?" he asked.

"Do you mean—"

"Your husband. That's who I mean. We watched him come into the house."

"I'm sorry. You must be mistaken. I think you saw Jefferson here. He's full grown, but he's not my husband."

The women had agreed some time back that Mattie would handle these situations. Angeline was provoked too easily and always in danger of venting her anger on the intruders, and Ruth struggled to stay calm and unafraid. Everyone knew that Mattie possessed the skills to deal with men, and she was smiling now, drawing all the attention to herself. "You certainly don't think I'm married to a man the age of Mr. Davis, do you? I'm not really old enough—at least not quite."

The smaller man, in a ragged jean coat and a dilapidated felt hat—which he did not remove—said, "You're married to him, all right. We know all about you women. The old bull has himself a yearling calf to sidle up to on winter nights."

This was nasty talk in front of the children, and Mattie had difficulty controlling her temper when she said, "That's enough of that. I told you that Mr. Davis is not here. Now, I'll thank you to leave our house."

"He's here, and we'll find him," the larger man said. He seemed a little more respectful, maybe even more educated. "Everyone stay right where you are. Where does that door go?"

"Just to another house. A lot of the houses in Orderville are built like that—in rows."

"It's for other wives. Davis has three of 'em. And you three each have a house." He looked toward Angeline and Ruth, but they didn't respond.

Mattie got her composure back, tried to laugh. "You may think you know a lot, but I can tell you, Mr. Davis is not here."

"He's been back from Arizona these two months," the little

man said. He looked each woman over carefully. "And I can see one thing. Before that, he's been co-habiting with at least two of you." He made a motion with his hand, drew a half circle over his middle. "Either that, or you're hiding watermelons under your clothes."

"You *will not* talk like that in this house, sir. We don't accept such indecency here."

Mattie stared at the man, and he stared back, but he finally looked away.

"Just don't lie to us," the other man said. "Everyone stay put, and we're going to find him." He turned to his partner. "Look in all the rooms. He never left this house, so we've got him."

The partner walked through all three houses, and Mattie could hear him rummaging about, probably looking under beds. When he returned to the big room in the center house, he checked the closet with the false back. He didn't notice that the back was a secret door. Mattie took a breath of relief. She was watching all the children, who were clearly terrified. Only Jeff looked defiant, ready for a fight, but he had been instructed, over and over, never to take on a Dep, even verbally.

"I don't see him anywhere," the little man said. "He must have some way of getting down through the floor."

"Well, then, find it. Don't just stand there like an igner'nt fool, even if that's what you are."

"You find it, if you're so smart."

So the two of them worked their way around the big room, stomping on the floorboards, lifting rugs, always keeping an eye on everyone. Then the big fellow told his partner to wait, and he checked the floors in the other two houses.

Mattie could see that both men were getting frustrated. She knew she had to keep them from persisting and opening the closet again. When the man returned, she said, "One thing I've learned is that sometimes men hear that you're coming, and they sneak away before you come in. They head out of town—even out of state. That would never happen here, of course, but I'm just telling you, sometimes you men show up just a little too late."

"We watched him walk through that door, and not all that long ago."

"You watched all four sides of the house—and every window—and knocked at our door at the same time? That is a remarkable thing to do. You must each have two sets of eyes."

She saw the doubt come into the big man's dark eyes. But suddenly he spun toward the children, who were all huddled more or less together. "These children know where he is," he said. "Come here, little girl." He was using his finger to motion Patience closer to him. She didn't move, so he walked to her, grabbed her wrist, and jerked her into the center of the room.

Jeff took a sudden step toward the man, but Mattie shook her head at him. Jeff stopped, but he didn't back away.

"All right, little girl, I want you to tell me where your father is." Patience was nine, and shy. The Dep had seemed to pick her on purpose as someone he could frighten.

Patience didn't answer. She stood stiff, the color gone from her face, but she didn't say a word.

"Let me ask you an easier question first. Who's your mother?"

Again, Patience didn't answer.

"Let me help you, missy." The man eyed Mattie, looked her up and down. "This woman is too young to be your mother, so I'm going to rule her out. Why don't you choose between those two?" He pointed toward Angeline and Ruth.

Patience stared back at him, but she didn't speak.

"All right. I'll make it even easier. You look mostly like that one." He pointed at Angeline. "Is she your mother?"

Patience continued to hold her tongue, but Mattie could see that she was quivering, on the edge of tears.

"What do you call that woman? That one right there." He was holding his rifle in one hand, not pointing it, but Patience seemed to be watching the barrel as it waved about, sometimes in her direction.

When Patience didn't answer this time, the man stepped closer to her and grabbed her shoulder. "You're going to answer me, little girl. What do you call her?"

"Don't touch her," Jeff growled. Morgy stepped up next to Jeff. He was even bigger than Jeff now, and the two looked like a force to reckon with, even without weapons.

"And what is it you'll do about it, boys?"

"Just don't hurt her," Jeff said.

"Well, then, you answer for her. You're such a big, strong boy. Who's her mother?"

"I have no idea."

"So is that what your Mormon parents teach you—to lie to authorities?"

"They teach me not to help those who want to do harm to our family. Isn't that what your parents taught you?"

The man laughed. "Well, I see your point. But I'm thinking I'll take *you* to jail. Maybe a few nights in a prison and you'll decide you'd rather come back home to your mama. Which one is *your* mother?" The man brought his rifle up, aimed it at Jeff. "Now. If you think I won't pull this trigger, go ahead and take a chance. I'll say you threatened me—and I do believe you just did that—and no judge will put the blame on me." He pulled the hammer back with his thumb. "I'm going to count to three, and by then you—"

Mattie heard a bumping noise in the closet, and then Morgan stepped out. "Leave my children alone," he said softly. "It's me you want, and now you have me."

The two men smiled at each other. "Well, now, he's got a point," the small one said. "Let's take this holy Saint to jail and let these innocent children figure out who their mothers is."

"You're a despicable little worm, aren't you?" Mattie asked the man, her voice clear, intense. "Have you ever done one thing in your life as noble as this man—*my husband*—does? You take money for harassing God's people, but the day will come when the Lord will call you Judas and command you to depart from Him."

The man fumbled over some words and didn't really make sense, but his partner said, "Pay no attention to this little whore."

Jeff charged toward the man, but Morgan leaped and grabbed him, held him back. "Don't take the bait, Jeff," he said. "The family needs you here." Then he looked at the bigger man. "You can take me now."

"That's exactly what we'll do. Turn around." He nodded to his partner, who pulled a heavy cord from his coat pocket and tied Morgan's wrists together behind his back. Then he led Morgan from the house while the other man walked backwards, still holding his rifle ready, still watching Jeff and Morgy.

Mattie continued to stare the man down, but he only gave her one quick glance, as though he dared not look her in the eye again.

When the door shut, the room was silent for a few seconds, and then some of the children began to cry. Angeline said, "Don't worry. We'll be all right. Papa will come back to us someday. For now, we simply have to go on as we were. Jeff will help us run the farm, and all of us will do our share."

"Where will they take Papa?" little Joey asked.

"We don't know exactly," Angeline said. "But he'll be all right.

Papa's strong. And we'll be just fine. Let's have a prayer for Papa, and for all of us." And so the family knelt together, as they did every night, and Angeline called on Morgy to pray. He was almost seventeen now, and he surely didn't want to cry, but when he asked the Lord for help for Papa, his voice did break. And by the end of his prayer, everyone was crying.

Mattie, by then, was shaking, finally feeling the fear she had resisted when facing the Deps and starting also to feel her loss. Morgan was surely headed for prison, perhaps for years, and she would soon have three little children. She thought of Angeline and Ruth, and she was thankful not to be alone, but she had missed Morgan terribly when he had been gone before, and now there would be no visits. There was little to look forward to except work and survival until the government chose to release her husband. And what then? Maybe he could never come back to her.

• • •

It was two weeks before word got back to the family that Morgan had been convicted of co-habitation. Angeline had feared that she, or even all the wives, would be called to Kanab to witness against their husband. They would not have done that, but then they might have been jailed as well, and that was their greatest fear now. They needed to take care of their children.

The messenger, Bishop Ernst, said that he had been at the trial. He told Angeline, "They had an apostate come forward and say that Morgan had three wives, and he named each of you. But the man didn't even know you. He had been fed the information, and he spouted it, as he's done in lots of other cases."

"How long will Morgan be in prison?" Angeline asked.

"Three years is what the judge said. But he offered to cut his sentence down to a year if Morgan would denounce the practice of polygamy and promise not to go back to his wives."

"Morgan turned him down, didn't he?"

"He did. And he told the judge that he and the Deps were enemies of God—people who understood nothing about the ways of the Lord. He stood tall, didn't waver, and told the judge, 'I wonder if you have a wife. If you do, I doubt you treat her any better than I treat the three women I've married for time and all eternity.' And then he told the judge that he could put him in jail, but he couldn't take his wives away because you would all be together in the next life."

Angeline couldn't speak. She was moved by picturing Morgan standing like Paul before King Agrippa, refusing to back away from the truth.

"They're taking him up to Salt Lake to the federal prison. Morgan told me that he hoped you—all of you—will write to him."

Angeline only nodded. Of course she would do that. But three years. The tests in her life never ended.

Still, Angeline felt stronger than she had in a long time. Joey was almost five now and growing fast. He seemed to have more energy than anyone in the family. And she was happy that she would have one more baby. If all went well, she would soon be mother to six living children, with one waiting for her in heaven. She had to be strong for all of them.

But something else was also driving Angeline. Her husband was gone and would be for a long time, and that meant that she had to step in and lead the family. Jeff was a wonderful young man—as old as Morgan had been when she had married him—and he did well on the farm, but he couldn't do everything alone, so she would lead out in keeping the garden, and she would help in the fields.

Morgy was much like his father, tall and strong, willing to work long hours and get up the next morning and work again. He and Jeff worked well as partners; they got along well and seemed to welcome the responsibilities they were facing.

Still, Angeline was head of the family. Someone needed to keep the children going forward, doing their chores, their schoolwork, their gospel study. She was the one who reminded, organized, and, at the same time, kept up everyone's spirits. There had been times in Angeline's life when others had had to pick her up, convince her to carry on, but now she felt the need to provide that spark, that faith, that vision of where the family could still go, even without the presence of a father.

The truth was, Angeline sometimes wanted to curl up on her bed and cry. It wasn't just that she missed Morgan, but that she felt the heaviness of the load she was carrying. The government had decided to punish Latter-day Saints for believing in plural marriage, and it was making a full effort to destroy a way of life for a people who only wanted to trust in the Lord. She wondered what life might have been like had she been able to keep Morgan for herself, but it was too late to worry about that. What she needed to do was to live the Lord's law to the best of her ability, and she felt she was doing that—and so were her sister wives.

Orderville was a town now, not a United Order, and even though a certain degree of cooperation continued—and the bishop still looked after the people—those remaining in the area were gradually feeling more separated. It was not so bad to work hard and see the fruits of one's own labor, but Angeline worried about bad seasons coming, maybe grasshoppers again. She was not nearly so confident as she had once been that if hard times came, there would be unity in surviving with her neighbors. She was proud that her children were willing to do their share of the work, but that was not the same as relying on a whole community, all trying to help each other prosper.

• • •

A few weeks after Morgan's arrest, Mattie gave birth to a baby boy. She dealt with the pain more easily this time, or at least understood better what to expect. After, she lay quietly while her sister wives cleaned up the baby and then brought him to her. The little one was red and blue at the same time, and after his first protests of being brought out into a world full of air, he had seemed to fold into himself—and against her—as though he needed protection from a place he didn't understand.

She loved him instantly. She had felt that same deluge of emotion when she had first seen little Hannah, and again with David, and she had wondered all during this pregnancy whether she could ever love another child as much as her first two. But this little boy, battered as he was for now, seemed special to her. She wanted to believe that he would do great things in his life. "I want to name him Morgan," she told Ruth and Angeline. "I know we have Morgy, but this little one needs a name that tells him who he is—even if he won't see his father for a long time."

Ruth said, "But won't that—"

"I know. It will cause confusion. But I could name him Morgan Nephi, and we could call him Nephi. That would give him another example of manhood to follow."

"That sounds right," Angeline said. "Morgan loves his Book of Mormon and all those stalwarts, like Nephi."

"All right, then," Mattie said. "Morgan it is. Morgan Nephi. I'll write and tell his father." She looked at her son again. She wanted her husband to see him as her gift to him when he returned from prison. But Mattie had her worries about the future. So many families were splitting up to stay safe now. If Morgan returned, he might have to watch for Deps again, sneak into one of his homes and then steal away. He could only live openly with one wife, and the others had to use different names and even keep their secret from fellow Saints, just so no one would know enough to witness against them.

Most often the husband chose to live with his first wife, and her position took on even greater importance. Maybe, for a man with plural wives, the first wife was always the special one, the love of his youth. Mattie understood that, but she liked to think she had brought him joy, that he had a special feeling for her—even if he had never said that to her.

Now, however, she wondered how she could manage life if she had to live alone with her children, and Morgan might only visit from time to time. Would he be able to provide for her? She knew of cases in which the family had become so large that the husband couldn't bring in enough harvest, or cash income, to take care of everyone. Sometimes women had older children who could help a family get by, but this little Morgan—and Hannah and David—would not be old enough to help her for a long time.

• • •

One morning, when Morgan had been gone for just over a year, Angeline was pitching hay over a corral fence to the oxen and cow when Jefferson came up behind her. "I can do that," he said.

Angeline laughed. "You're too late. I'm finished." She turned and looked at him. "What are you going to do today?" she asked.

"I've got a few things to look to. Socks threw a shoe, for one thing, and I need to reshoe her." Socks was his new horse—or actually, a rather old horse he had bargained for after Lightning had become too feeble to carry a rider. "I'm just hoping the weather holds and I can start cutting wheat in maybe another week or so."

"We'll all help with that."

"I know."

"Are you feeling all right? You sound a little down in the mouth."

"No. I'm fine."

But he didn't look fine. The boy looked nothing like Morgan, and yet he had his stepfather's toughness, his resoluteness. He even had his mannerisms—the way he would stare away for a few seconds when she asked him a question, as though responses were never automatic to him. What she saw this morning, though, was a certain cloudiness in his eyes—not a sleepy look, but distance.

"We've put a huge burden on your shoulders, Jeff. We expect more of you than is probably fair."

"I like to work. That doesn't bother me."

"When Morgan comes back, you'll have your chance to do for yourself and not worry all the time about your family."

"I don't want to look at life that way. Papa may be back in a couple more years, but the Deps will be chasing him again. What I'm doing now is what I have to do. Maybe until all the children are grown and gone—or even after that."

"No, Jeff. You have to have a life of your own. You can't sacrifice your future for the rest of the family."

"What future?"

"You need to marry and start your own farm, your own family."

"There's no way I'm going to walk away from all of you and let you fend for yourself."

"Morgy is doing more all the time. He's someone we can depend on. And I'll work hard until I go to the grave. That's just the way I am."

"You can't always be out plowing the fields when the younger children need your help. Sometimes I wonder if little Gideon will ever know who his mother is."

Actually, Angeline worried about that, too. Not long after Morgan Nephi had been born, Angeline had delivered a baby boy she had named Gideon. Since Angeline was better at outside work than either Ruth or Mattie, she was the one who helped most on the farm, and Mattie had taken over Gideon, almost as though she were raising twins. Angeline didn't think either baby suffered under the arrangement, but she often felt guilty that she took so little time to hold the little fellow after she nursed him, or to play with him the way Mattie did.

At the same time, she needed to take some of the burden off Jeff's shoulders. She worried that she was stealing his life from him. "Are you doing what you want to do, Jeff?" she asked. "Do you want to farm? If Morgan could come back right now, and everything was all right with us, what would you do with your life?"

He turned a little and looked out across their fields. The corn was up now, maybe a foot tall, and the winter wheat was turning gold. A breeze down the canyon was making waves in the wheat—one of those little pictures Angeline never grew tired of seeing. "I guess I'll be a farmer—or maybe a rancher," he said. "I don't know anything else. I've always liked to read books, and sometimes I think I'd like to see some of the places I've read about. And then, maybe be a teacher. But I'm not likely to have the chance."

"Don't say that. Life won't always be the way it is now. Things will change."

"What will? The government won't change its mind about us,

and we won't give up polygamy, so everything's just going to get worse and worse." He took the pitchfork from Angeline's hand, apparently to put it away for her. "I'll tell you this much, Aunt Angeline, if I ever do have a family, I'm only going to have one wife."

"I understand why you would feel that way."

"No. I don't think you do. I feel about you almost the same as I do about my mother, and the same with Aunt Mattie. I don't feel bad about growing up the way I did. But we can't live in this world and always be different from everyone else. The Lord asks us to do things that everyone else considers wrong. We tried to live the Order, and it was too different, too hard. People laughed at us. And the Lord told our men to take extra wives, but the rest of the world has decided that's evil. We always say we're the chosen people, but that only seems to mean that God asks more of us than of everyone else. And what do we get for it? People hate us and the government punishes us."

These were all things that Angeline had said to herself at times. She had no idea what to say to Jeff. But she sensed that some deeper sadness was in him right now, coloring everything else. She thought she knew what it was. "Jeff," she said, "you need to get married. You can't put Harriet off any longer."

"Do you think I don't know that? She told me on Sunday, she's not promised to me any longer. There's someone else."

"Who is it?" she asked.

"I don't know. She wouldn't say."

No wonder Jeff looked so brokenhearted. Angeline knew, immediately, that she couldn't let this happen. "Then go to her today. No, this minute. Tell her you'll marry her now."

Jeff's eyes jerked away from Angeline's. "How could I do that?"

he asked, and then he turned and walked to the barn, unlatched the door, and walked on in.

Angeline followed him through the door. "Morgy's grown now. You've taught him well. And I can still do plenty to keep things going. I've never felt stronger in my life. We'll get by just fine."

"Morgy does all right, but—"

"You can have some of our acres, and you can farm right next to us. I've helped Morgan build a lot of houses in my life. I know all about it. I'll help you get one built, and you can move Harriet onto your own land. And you'll be close enough, you can guide Morgy when he doesn't know what to do."

Jeff hung the pitchfork on a hook, and then he looked back. The light was dim inside the barn. Angeline couldn't see his face clearly, but she knew he was thinking, not rejecting her idea.

"It would work, Jeff. It's what you have to do."

Jeff didn't answer for a long time, but finally he said, "I promised Papa that I would look after all of you—that I'd make sure you were all right. I can't go back on that."

Angeline walked to him, gripped his arm, waited for him to look at her. "Jeff, you've done all that. And if you're close to us, you can still help us. Go right now. Go tell her that you want to get married right away."

"I can't just—"

"Yes, you can. You love your family, but you can't sacrifice your own chance to be happy. We all have to move ahead, not stop hoping. If we lose hope, the Deps have won." She gripped his other arm and gave him a little shake. "Go right now. Don't think anymore. Don't change your clothes. Just saddle up Socks and go."

"Aunt Angeline, I want to, but—"

"Go now. Don't say another word."

He looked at her for several seconds. Tears had filled his eyes. He ducked his head; Angeline knew he was embarrassed.

"Go."

Jeff nodded, and then he walked from the barn. Angeline walked out too, and she saw that he was saddling his horse.

• • •

Jeff did marry Harriet, and by then, the whole family had helped him build a house. He was a new man in many ways, but he worked all the harder, keeping all the land under cultivation and guiding Morgy through each season's work. The time for Morgan's release gradually grew nearer, and the combined labor of all the family was inspiring to Ruth. She was proud of her Jeff, who had become stronger and more reliable than she could ever have expected. The other children seemed to model on him, and on Ella and Morgy. It was not difficult to imagine that all the children would soon be honorable adults and pass their strength to another generation.

But troubles didn't end. The raids on polygamous families did not let up at all. Congress continued to pass laws that would eliminate loopholes and offer additional means to prosecute co-habs. And finally a law was passed ruling that the government had a right to confiscate all of the Church's properties.

When word of this new method of shutting down the Church reached the Davises, Ruth was devastated. She had turned to Morgan so many years ago not because he had loved her, but because he had agreed to protect her. Now she wondered whether he could do that. The Deps would probably follow him from the prison, just to watch whether he returned to his family.

After supper, when the children were in bed, Ruth admitted her fears to her sister wives. "They aren't going to let us live this way, are they?" she asked them. "They won't let Morgan come back to us."

"No. I don't think they will," Angeline said.

"I don't think he'll want to go to Mexico," Mattie said. "He loves this valley. He said in the letter I got last week that this is where he wants his home to be. He said he'll never need anything else if they'll let him come back here."

There was a long silence after that. And then Ruth asked the question that had been on her mind lately. "Do you think plural marriage is wrong? Almost everyone in America thinks it's evil to have more than one wife. Maybe we're the ones who are misguided."

"I think about that too," Mattie said. "But look what they say about us—that men dominate us, and we're like a little harem. That just isn't true."

"I don't think people in the East, who think we're so evil, have any idea how much devotion it takes to make a family like ours hold together," Ruth said.

"The principle came from the Lord," Mattie said, "and we'll never give it up."

"Maybe the time will pass when the Lord commands it," Angeline said. She had heard more Saints saying that lately.

"But if it's from God, why would He take it back?"

"In the book of Jacob, what it says is that it's usually not the way to live, except when the Lord commands it. I would think that means those times could go away."

"But what about us?" Mattie asked. "If the commandment changes, what do we do?"

No one had an answer. And Ruth was worried. It was difficult to imagine a future of anything but trouble.

CHAPTER 20

Morgan hated almost everything about the prison where he lived. It was a cold place, dirty, and the food was revolting. He had made lots of friendships with fellow Mormons who were also convicted of co-habitation, but the atmosphere around them was hostile. They were reviled both by gentile prisoners and by most of the prison guards.

Morgan, however, was fortunate. He had expressed an interest in looking after the wagons and horses owned by the prison, used to haul food or to transport prisoners. He liked to tinker with the wagons and keep them in good repair, and, even more, he liked feeding and grooming the horses—large workhorses and some saddle horses used by the warden and some of his staff. Morgan liked the smell of the barn and the affection of the animals that had come to know him. The work gave him something to do a few hours each day, but above all, it got him out of the cell where he spent most of his time.

Morgan had three cellmates, one of them a stake president polygamist named Garner Fordice. But Morgan and he could rarely discuss the gospel or the state of the Church without hearing a rage of profanity and scorn from the other two men in their cell. These men were both thieves, both disrespectful, and they were filled with hate—especially for polygamists. So evenings were long. Morgan tried to use them to study his Book of Mormon, but his cellmates either polluted the air with filthy talk or harassed Morgan for reading scriptures.

Morgan had survived for well over two years, but every day was a challenge, and only in the barn did he feel some degree of comfort. And then one day, a guard came to the barn and said, "Davis, you've got a visitor. I guess it's your father."

Morgan's father had come twice before, and it was the one thing he loved more than anything. Morgan followed the guard to the visitors' room, where he sat down behind some bars, and then another guard brought his father in and motioned for him to sit across from Morgan.

"It's good to see you, Son," Brother Davis said.

"I'm glad you could come, Dad. It's hard to express how lonely I get."

They reached to touch fingers through the narrow bars, but the guard barked, "No reaching through. Pull your hands back."

So they withdrew their hands. Morgan wished that more visitors had shown up today. When more people were in the visitors' area, there was enough noise that the guards couldn't hear what any one pair was saying, but today, every word would carry through the room.

"Are you still working with the horses?" his father asked.

"Yes. I like that, but it doesn't take an awful lot of my time. President Fordice and I try to talk a little, but those two thieves in our cell hardly give us a moment's peace."

"Does anyone ever say how long you'll be here? Any chance that you won't have to stay the whole three years?"

"I don't know. I doubt it. No one ever says anything to us about that sort of thing." Morgan was noticing that his father appeared to have aged even in the few months since he had last seen him. "Are you doing all right?" he asked.

"I got sick a while back, and I can't seem to shake it," Brother Davis said. "It's in my lungs so bad that I have trouble breathing sometimes. It's been hard to keep the farm going. I wish you were back in Farmington. You could take over the place."

"What about my brothers? Do they help?"

"Yes, they help some. But they have their own interests. Jacob has his own farm to run—and four children—and his wife gets mad when he comes to my place for a day. I guess she thinks he's just loafing, but he's a hard worker, like you, and he gets a lot of things done that I can't do anymore."

"What about Sam?"

"He comes by once in a while. But he doesn't care a fig about farming, and he's got his own family to worry about. He's still a teacher, but he moved down to Provo now, to teach at the academy." Brother Davis laughed. "I don't mind that. He's smart, and he likes that kind of life. But we probably won't see him much at all anymore. We do see your sisters, and they've got good husbands. They help me with things when they can."

Morgan always had so many things he wanted to know, so many things he wanted to talk about, but now, with his father sitting across from him, he wasn't sure what it was he had hoped to discuss. Maybe it was the guard listening that kept him from talking openly.

"I've been wondering, Morgan," his father said, "what are you going to do when you get out of here? Won't the Deps keep track of how you're living?"

Morgan glanced at the guard, who didn't appear all that interested but surely had heard the question. "I think a lot about that,"

Morgan said, his voice lowered. "I know that I'm following the law of God, but I don't want to come back to this prison again."

"Don't take any chances. Your family needs you. It won't do them any good if you spend the rest of your life in here."

"I know. But it's all very complicated. Now that the Order has shut down, my family is on its own. Jefferson—the boy Ruth had before I married her—was running the farm, but he's married now. My son Morgan—the one we call Morgy—is trying to take charge, but he's young and inexperienced. A lot of the work falls on Angeline. What they need is for me to be there with them. But if my family stays together, and I live there with them, I don't know what the government will do to me."

"I know men who are living with one wife and just dropping by to help the others," Morgan's father said. "They bring some money, if they can, or food. But they know better than to . . . you know . . . live with every wife. And there's also lots that are still . . ." He glanced at the guard. " . . . just hiding out."

"The Church is in chaos," Morgan said. "From what I've heard, no one knows where President Woodruff is. Some of the Apostles are in here. There for a while, I used to see President Cannon when they let us hold church on Sundays. He got released, but I'm sure they would stick President Woodruff in here if they got the chance."

Brother Davis lowered his voice to a whisper. "The Deps hounded John Taylor right into his death—him running and hiding when his health wasn't good. And now, we hardly know we have a president, with President Woodruff unable to show himself."

"The rumor in here is that the government wants to confiscate the temple—and all the other Church possessions. They can't do that, can they?"

"Actually, they probably can. The whole country is in an uproar about polygamy, so no one, not even the courts, will stop something like that. And I'll tell you what, Morgan. I don't like to admit it, but the government is winning. The Church is going to go under if it keeps going this way. I don't see how we can cling to polygamy and survive."

"But, Dad, it's God's law."

"Well, I guess it is—even though I never had any interest in living it. But we also say that we uphold the law of the land. And the time might be coming when we have to choose between the two."

"We'll choose God's law. What else can we do?"

Brother Davis shrugged, but Morgan knew very well what he thought. He had always been a religious man—when religion meant living a clean life and doing good works—but he had never liked lofty theological debates. What he saw, no doubt, was what polygamy was doing to the people who practiced it—including his own son and grandchildren.

"There's something else I wanted you to know," Brother Davis said.

Morgan nodded and waited.

"Your mother's not doing too well. We're both over seventy now, and we don't manage so good as we used to."

"Is she sick, or—"

"No. Not exactly. But she doesn't remember things as well as she used to, and she gets a little mixed up sometimes. I told her I was coming down to see you, and it seemed like she didn't even know you were in prison. Maybe she just doesn't like to think about it, but I'm pretty sure it's more than that."

Morgan felt sick. "Dad, I was always going to come up from Long Valley to see her, but it was so far away, and I just never had a good chance to travel that far." He didn't tell his father that he had been as far as Salt Lake and hadn't traveled on to Farmington, mainly because he was under pressure to get back as fast as he could.

"Well, she does feel bad about that. But that's what I wanted to tell you. When you do get out of this place, come up to Farmington to see her before you head back south. And think about moving back home. That would help all of us."

Morgan didn't know how he could move. He would only be closer to where the Deps might find him. But he did need to visit his mother. "Dad, will she still be alive next year?"

"Who knows? We might both be gone. And you too. We never know, do we? But that's why you need to come up and see us if you can."

"All right. I promise I'll do that."

They looked at each other for a time, and finally Morgan asked the question that had been on his mind. "Dad, are you ashamed of me that I ended up in prison?"

His father's eyes opened wider. "Ashamed?"

"Yes. Do you tell your neighbors that you have a son locked up like this?"

"They know. But I'm not ashamed." His eyes had filled with tears. "Morgan, you are the best of the best. You were always a fine son, growing up, and you've lived a wonderful life. I know why you're in here, and it's not for anything you've done wrong."

"But you chose not to live in plural marriage. Maybe I should have done the same."

"You were called to it, Son, and you accepted the call—just like so many of our men. There's never been a day in my life when I haven't been proud of you."

Morgan nodded. "Thank you," he said. "It's hard not to be

ashamed of being locked up. I never thought such a thing would happen to me."

"That's all right. Keep your head up. This is just one more thing to get through. It will make you stronger than ever."

"I love you, Dad."

"And I love you, Son." It was something his father had rarely said to him in his life, and it meant a great deal to Morgan. "But you know what I want?"

"What?"

"Before I die, I'd like to see those fourteen grandchildren that I've never laid eyes on. I'd give just about anything to meet them all—and I know your mother would too."

Morgan understood. He had never thought, when he left his home, that he would not get back, or that he would raise so many children who would never meet their grandparents. He told himself that this was a wrong he would have to right, if he possibly could.

• • •

Angeline was shocked when the news reached Orderville. It was March of 1890, and President Wilford Woodruff had announced that the Church would stop teaching plural marriage to its people. The practice would end. A friend had brought her a copy of the *Deseret News,* and now she and Ruth and Mattie were studying every word of the announcement.

"I don't understand what it means," Ruth said. "The Church won't teach polygamy, and there won't be any new marriages, but it doesn't say that our marriages are canceled. What will the government say if Morgan comes back to us?"

"Will they release him now that this is over?" Mattie wanted to know. "Or will they make him finish out his three years?"

But no one had any answers. Only a few months were left in his sentence, but Angeline wanted to believe he would be released now. What she hated was to think that to a nation opposed to Mormons—convinced they were an abnormal, perverted people—this would seem an admission of guilt. She had been telling herself that God could choose to end the practice once it had accomplished its purpose, and she wanted to believe it was the Lord behind this change, but it seemed more as though the prophet were buckling under pressure and rescinding the law for political reasons.

What she also knew was that life under the raids by the government had been increasingly difficult, almost impossible. Women like Angeline and her sister wives were being forced to survive by whatever means they could, and the Church organization, in all its wards and branches, was almost impossible to operate with so many leaders in hiding. The unity that had once existed among the Saints in Orderville had almost disappeared. Too many women were making the best of their lives with little help from anyone.

Angeline liked to think that the government wouldn't care about the old plural marriages as long as new ones were not begun, but she didn't know whether that would be the case.

And so the wait was on: the wait to learn more, to find out what the prophet was saying about such matters, and, above all, to see what would happen to Morgan.

And then one night, a few weeks later, she heard a rap on the door and called out, "Who is it?"

The reply came: "It's Morgan."

She ran to the door, unbarred it, and threw it open, and finally she was holding him in her arms again.

• • •

Morgan could hardly believe he was home. He held Angeline for a long time, and then he took some time with Gideon. The little boy, going on three, was hesitant around him, but he sat on Morgan's knee and stared at his face as his father talked to him. The touch of this little child was precious to Morgan now. He hardly dared to squeeze him, aware that his own body was thin and hard, maybe too rough for such a pure little person.

The other children were in their bedrooms—or in the other houses. After a few minutes, Morgan said, "Can we gather the others now? Or is it too late?"

"No. It's not that late. Most of them are still up, I'm sure," Angeline said. He looked at her again. She did seem older. She was forty-seven years old now, and he saw tiredness in her eyes and considerable graying in her hair, but she was beautiful. He had forgotten how beautiful. It now seemed as though he had known her forever. So many things had been taken away from him, but Angeline, however difficult her life had been, was the one constant he had relied on. He wanted to spend time with her now, not talk about prison and about problems and worries, but merely hold her in his arms and maybe remember their life together, or talk about the goodness of the land he had returned to. More than anything, he wanted never again to leave her.

"In prison, I thought about you every day—and all the children. And Ruth and Mattie. I thought about this moment, when I would finally be here again."

"And I've thought about you. We prayed for you every day."

Once again his mind went back to the Muddy River Valley and his new wife working so hard to help him get the farm established. He thought of her anguish over the years, having lost her first babies, and then losing little Jane. He thought of her forthrightness, the fight she had in her. He didn't know how to rate love—he had no idea whether he loved Angeline more than he did his other wives—but he did know that the two of them had gone through the most together. Nothing he would experience in life could run deeper than what he had passed through with Angie.

Angeline went out and brought the other families in. It seemed a huge crowd now. Morgan embraced Ruth and Mattie and then looked around at all the children.

Morgy was a man, even taller than Morgan. He seemed hesitant to approach, but Morgan hugged him anyway. Then he stepped back and gripped his shoulders—strong shoulders. "How was the harvest?" Morgan asked.

"Good. Not as good as last year, but a big rain, early in the season, washed away some of the areas we'd planted."

"But you have enough for the winter?"

"More than enough," Angeline said. "Morgy's done a great job, and Jeff still helps us."

There was much more to learn about that, but Morgan went to all the other children, hugged the older ones, and then took the little ones on his lap one or two at a time.

Ella was a grown woman, twenty years old. Morgan knew, from letters, that she was engaged to one of the Houston boys, George. "When are you getting married?" he asked her now.

"I don't know for sure. His father has been hiding. George has had to work their farm—like Jeff and Morgy. But Brother Houston is home now. We're thinking maybe we can marry quite soon." She blushed, looking pleased, and Morgan could only think how lovely she was.

"I thought you wanted to move to Salt Lake and be an actress," he teased.

Now she blushed even brighter. "George and I met in a play," she said. "Maybe we can be in plays here, if we have any. But we want to live here with our families."

"That's good," Morgan said. "It's what I always hoped."

Naomi, Thomas, and Suzanne were greatly changed, all looking nearly grown. And Tabatha, Patience, Andrew, Joey, and Hannah were no longer little. Only David, little Nephi, and Gideon seemed children that Morgan could still raise. He wanted to talk to all of them, one at a time, find out who they were now. They had been writing him all through his incarceration, but he wanted details, wanted to get a feel for who they had become. "Let's have a prayer together now," he finally said. "And then it's about time for all of you to go to bed. I want to have a little time to talk to your mothers."

So after a prayer, the children went off to their houses, or to their bedrooms, and Morgan sat with his wives by the fire. He asked them about Jeff, about the town, and about each of the children, and then he said, "I need to discuss a matter with you."

He looked around at each of them. He knew that they were all waiting to understand what their marriages meant now.

"I don't know what the prophet would say about this, but the officials who released me from prison told me that co-habitation is ended. They can still come after me if this manifesto issued by the Church is ignored. In their minds, our marriages were never legal—except for the one with Angeline—and if we live together now, we're still breaking the law."

"Will they come here to watch us, the way they did before?" Mattie asked.

Morgan could see that she was the one with the greatest fear—and the most reason to be fearful. It hurt him even to look at her. He knew that he was about to break her heart.

"I don't know that they will watch us so closely now, but I do know this. If anyone but Angeline has a baby, I would have to answer for that. I suppose they would take me back to prison. At least they claimed that they would."

"I can't have any more children," Ruth said.

"I can't either," Angeline said.

Morgan understood that. He knew he was actually speaking to Mattie.

"But here's what I don't yet understand," he continued, "and I've been thinking about this all the way down from Salt Lake City. Does the manifesto mean that I should separate myself from Ruth and Mattie? I don't think anyone would say that I shouldn't provide for you and the children, that I shouldn't give you all the comfort and support I can. But maybe the leaders of the Church are saying that I should only think of myself as married to Angeline now—that a married life together with all of you is no longer sanctioned except in heaven."

Ruth nodded. He couldn't tell what she was thinking, but when he glanced at Mattie, he saw that tears were in her eyes.

"Mattie, I know you only have three children, and you would like to have more, but you see the problem, don't you?"

"No! I don't see the problem. Not if God is God and always the same. If I can't have babies with you now, that means that the ones I have are wrong."

"No, Mattie, they're our children, and I'll always care for them. I'll do everything I can to make your life what it ought to be."

"But we're divorced? Is that what you're saying?"

"No. We're still married forever. And in the next life we'll have more children."

"That makes no sense to me, Morgan. It's letting the government tell us what's right and wrong, and we always said we would never do that."

"Mattie, you've seen what was happening to the Church. The federals were about to confiscate the temples and all our other holdings. The government was not going to let up until the Church was dead and buried. This manifesto means we can start to move forward again. We always said that polygamy was to be practiced so long as the Lord made it our law, and what I believe is that it was God who rescinded it. Of course it was pressure from the government that caused the prophet to go to the Lord for an answer, but if God had told him to hold to the principle, no matter what, that's what he would have done. Maybe the purposes of plural marriage had been fulfilled. But think of the beautiful children we've created. Now we'll raise them up to the Lord and send them forth to preach the gospel—and they'll be free to do it."

Angeline was nodding. So was Ruth. But Mattie was staring back at him, clearly angry. Morgan had no idea what else he could say to her—or how he could let Mattie go and now become his wife in name only.

• • •

After Ruth went back to her own house, she felt lonely. Morgan was home, but he wasn't home. He never would be again. But she knew she would never say that to him. She would go on with life. It was what she had always done. At least Morgan would be there to farm and provide, and if she had to see him go home to Angeline every day, and not to her, she would give her attention to the children and not give way to self-pity.

But after a few minutes, much to her surprise, Morgan came to her house. "I just wanted to say good night," he said, "and I wanted to tell you how sorry I am."

This time he held her much longer, and the pain of that

touch was worse than the absence she had felt before. But she told Morgan, "I'll be all right."

She wondered, would he come to her bed sometimes? Did he still think of himself as married to her? Was the prophet saying that he *wasn't* married to her? She didn't know. But she was thankful that he still felt that he could hold her in his arms.

"You've done so much for me, Ruth. I thought, by marrying you, I was doing something for you, but you're the one who has blessed my life. And so has Jeff. He's been my strength these last few years, and you've been the one always keeping us on a steady course when Angeline couldn't."

"I'll always be here, Morgan. I'll do what I can for you. But please be a father to the children. That's my only worry."

"I will. I promise you that."

"Thank you," she said. One thing that Ruth had learned over the years was that Morgan kept his promises. But as he walked out the door, she realized that she had never felt so alone in her life—not even in those bad days before Morgan had asked her to marry him.

• • •

Mattie went back to her house and cried. She had longed for almost three years to have her husband back, and now he would be within sight, but he would not be her husband.

It wasn't long until he showed up at her house, and her first thought was that maybe he wanted to spend the night with her after all. But he only said, "Oh, Mattie, I'm sorry. I love you so much."

Mattie wanted to complain, even be furious with him, but she didn't doubt his love or his sorrow.

"We'll be married for eternity," he said. "It's only a short while, during the rest of our mortality, that we'll have to live this way."

But Mattie was too young to think that way. She could only think how empty her life would be. She wanted to give herself to her three children and to live for them, and that was what she had been telling herself she would have to do, but she needed Morgan's touch, his closeness. Now Angeline would be the only one who would have that.

Mattie broke down and began to cry. "I can't stand this, Morgan. How can I see you every day and not be truly married to you? I'll have to go away. I'll go back to Scipio and live close to my parents."

"But the children will—"

"I don't care. I can't live here. I just can't do it."

"But I want to be a father to our children. It's what you said you want, too."

"I know. But I can't live so close to you and . . ." She put her hands over her face and let herself cry hard. "Just leave now, Morgan. I need to think. I feel like my life just ended."

"We can talk about—"

"I don't want to talk. Just go."

"All right. I'm so sorry. I don't know what else we can—"

"Please, Morgan, just go back to Angeline."

"We'll talk again later when—"

"Get out of my house. Now!"

Morgan nodded. And he walked out the door.

• • •

By the time Morgan left Mattie's house, he had lost most of his resolve. He didn't know whether it would be wrong to give Mattie more babies. It didn't make sense that it could be wrong. He wasn't sure exactly what he would do about that. But he knew that, for now, he would have to live as though she were his friend, not his wife. And the same with Ruth.

Morgan knew he couldn't hurt Mattie and Ruth so much and then go about his life with Angie as though they had been returned to their original state—just the two of them. It was not just that they had a large family; it was what he had considered wrong for so many years: to treat one wife differently from the others.

When he stepped back into the center house, Angeline was sitting by the fireplace in her rocker, where he had seen her so many times before. The scene looked normal, the way life should be, but there was nothing normal about the way he was feeling.

"What are you going to do about Mattie?" Angeline asked. "You've broken her heart."

"I know," Morgan said.

"I never thought I would say this," Angeline said, "but it feels wrong to have you for myself. I can't stand to think what this will do to Ruth and Mattie."

Morgan pulled one of the chairs away from the table and moved it close to Angie's rocking chair. He sat down next to her. He had waited for so long to be released from prison and to be with his family again, but now, he saw no way forward. Taking on new wives had been difficult—an immense adjustment—but this, reversing everything, was worse. How could he and his wives put a stop to the love they had developed over time, and at such a great cost?

"Do you want to pray?" Angie asked.

"Yes."

So they knelt, there by the fire, and Morgan prayed that they could manage one more great change in their lives.

• • •

Morgan liked being in bed with Angie that night. He liked holding her, the two of them spooned together. But he asked for nothing more than that. His mind was too full of worry—and, in some way he didn't really understand, it seemed as though he would be untrue to his other wives. How could he think of them in pain, each wife lying in her own bed, alone, while he took comfort and pleasure close by?

He didn't sleep well, and he got up early. He walked outside and felt the goodness of an October morning. He walked to his fields and was satisfied with what he saw—grains harvested, the land harrowed and ready for the coming spring. He looked in on his animals, could see that they had been cared for. What he wanted was to feel at home, ready to start life again. But as much as things appeared the same, he knew that they weren't.

He was walking back to the center house when he saw Mattie open her door and step outside. He walked to her, stopped in front of her.

"I saw you out here, looking things over," she said. "Couldn't you sleep?"

"No."

"I couldn't either."

He nodded, and then he said again, "I'm sorry."

"I know you are, Morgan. This isn't your fault." She waited a few seconds and then said, "I'm not leaving. I'm not going home to Scipio."

"Good."

"If I went, the children would miss their brothers and sisters—and their aunts. They don't know any other life."

"I would like to keep our family together," Morgan said. "We can build new houses—bigger ones—and establish a bigger farm. As the children grow up, they can start their own farms, maybe close by. Maybe some will want to live somewhere else, but we can give them all a good start."

"Yes. That's what I would hope for. My children will be better off with you and Ruth and Angeline as examples—and surrounded by people who love them. I have to think mostly of them now."

"Mattie, this doesn't change how I feel about you."

"I know. But you'll forgive me if I feel like a very young widow."

"Please don't think of it that way. I'll be here. I'll support you and—"

"I know, Morgan. I understand. Don't worry about me. I'll be all right."

She smiled, but not in that quick way he remembered. She was no longer a girl. But she was painfully beautiful. "I never thought I would hurt you like this, Mattie. I—"

"Would it be wrong for you to come to my house sometimes and play with our children?"

"Of course I'll do that."

Then tears filled her eyes. "And could you maybe hold me sometimes, and kiss me good night?"

"Yes. I want to do that."

He wanted to hold her right then, but he thought better of it. This was all too poignant. He had to move away from her. "We'll find a way to make this all right," he said. "I'll do my very best."

"I know. And I will too."

"I'll see you every day. We'll—"

But he couldn't complete his sentence. He nodded, then stepped away. But he took only a few steps before he looked back. Mattie was still standing on the front step of her house, watching him. She smiled, but she was shaking with sobs. So he went back, and he did hold her in his arms, and he told her one more time how sorry he was. Then, once again, he walked away.

• • •

Later that morning, Morgan and Angeline walked out. Morgan wanted to see the town, greet a few people, feel at home. They did that, and then, as always, they ended up walking to the river. This was where he and Angeline and Ruth had been baptized into the United Order, and where he had baptized his children. It was the pure water he had loved since the first day he and his family had arrived in Long Valley. He wasn't sure why, but he felt something like surprise that the river was still running clear, still looking as it always had. So much change had come to his life that he felt satisfied to see something that seemed consistent, the same as it had been.

"Do you want to stay here?" he asked Angie. "Now that the Order is gone, I guess we could go anywhere."

"I like it here. I think I'd like to stay. Some of our friends have left, but lots of the people we love are still here—ones we've gone through thick and thin with."

"Before I headed down here, I borrowed a horse and rode up to see my family in Farmington. I saw some of your family, too. They all want us to come back. My mother's not well. She's not thinking straight, and something isn't right with her heart. And Dad's got trouble with his lungs."

"What do you want to do, move up there and help them?"

"I don't think we can. If we take our whole family up there, the Deps will be after us, I'm pretty sure, even if we live in separate houses. Down here, maybe they won't pay much attention. But I would like to take that trip quite soon. My parents want to meet their grandchildren, and your parents do too."

"I'd like that very much. But I don't know when we can do it."

"I know." Morgan watched the water flow, noticed the ripples, thought about what he had once told Ella, that we come and go in this life, and the ripples that we make fade away.

"Angie, do you wish I'd never brought you down here, never entered into polygamy, never joined the United Order? Every one of those things has been hard. Maybe we should have married in Farmington and just stayed there and lived a normal life."

Angeline didn't answer immediately. She too was watching the water. "I don't know how to think about that," she finally said. "If Brigham hadn't sent you home to find a wife, you might not have ever come calling on me."

"No. I would have. I believe it's what God wanted. I would have realized it, sooner or later."

"Well, I suppose. But I have a feeling we're both better for the experience, no matter what it has cost us."

"That's what I've been thinking too. In prison, I had lots of time to think, and every time I got close to the conclusion that we had made a mistake in accepting that mission to the Muddy, I would realize all over again that I needed to have those experiences, that we both did, and that we would have missed a great deal if we had never learned to love Ruth and Mattie, never had all our children together."

"So let's stay here, and let's live with all of them as best we can."

"We can grow old together now—all of us. But Angie, what I miss more than anything is who we were when we started out together. I wish we could have that back."

"I know. I've wished that all these years. But we have to be true to Ruth, and especially to Mattie. Life may change, but we have to make things right for them."

"I know. It's what I told both of them. And I don't know exactly what the Church is telling us now. Maybe I'm still married to Ruth and Mattie, no matter what the government says."

"I hope so. I know it's strange for me to say that, but it is what I hope."

Morgan tried to breathe normally, tried to let his muscles relax. He knew he couldn't live this way forever, always tense, always worried, always sorry. "Angie," he said after a time, "we have to trust in the Lord and in the prophet. It's been hard for me to accept their will at times, but it's what we have to do now. And there's something we have to believe, and always hold to. It's what we have to pass on to our children and their children. No matter what people think, and no matter how many accuse us of being evil, we know the truth. What we did—the way we have lived as a family—was not wrong. God called us, and we answered."

AUTHOR'S NOTE

A story, by its very nature, must end, but "real life" continues. Historical fiction is a hybrid: a story set in the flow of actual events. Maybe it's that mixed nature that causes readers to ask, "But then what happened?" I've written a number of historical series, and always, people tell me, "You can't stop there; I want to know how it all turns out." But life doesn't "turn out" at any given point. One event blends into the next, often with no clear resolution. What I set out to do in this two-book series was to tell the story of the settlers of the Muddy River Valley and then follow those same settlers to Utah, where they established the United Order in Orderville. Polygamy became an issue in both novels because many of those settlers were polygamists. The disincorporation of the Order and the end of polygamy were the natural endings to the stories I set out to tell.

You're probably still asking, "But what happened to Morgan and Angeline, Ruth and Mattie?" Unfortunately, the only answer I can offer is: "Nothing happened to them. I made them up. When the story ended, they ended." True, I could create more volumes, but I have to stop somewhere, and the story would only become more diffused as time and generations passed along.

But no doubt it's Mattie you're wondering about—and so am

I. If I were to write another sequel, I could choose a single path for her, but in reality, one of several things might have happened. The "Manifesto of 1890" announced that plural marriage was officially discontinued. No longer would the principle be taught, and no longer would plural marriages be performed. What the statement didn't explain was the status of marriages already existing. According to Kathryn M. Daynes, in her carefully researched history of polygamy, *More Wives than One,* President Wilford Woodruff testified in 1891 that the manifesto meant that "co-habitation" with plural wives should cease. She then adds, "In practice, each family decided for itself how to react to the new situation. Many men continued to cohabit with all their wives; others ceased living with all but one wife" (*More Wives,* 184).

I purposely ended my story at a time when plural families were left in confusion about their way forward. Government statements had implied that co-habitation was illegal, and polygamists would continue to be imprisoned. In reality, federal officials soon lost interest in pursuing the matter. It was not uncommon for polygamous wives to continue to have children. Perhaps out of fear that these births could create new problems for the Church, some of the children born after the manifesto was announced report being persecuted by members of Latter-day Saint communities (see *More Wives,* 186).

Another factor shaped polygamous families after the manifesto. A man who had several wives and, gradually, a huge posterity, was often in no position to support all those offspring. More often than not, older children helped their mothers. Most polygamous husbands tried to take care of their families, but others, especially as they got older, seemed to feel that they had done all that they could.

When plural marriage "ended," many Saints believed it was

still a true principle and was only rescinded because of government pressure. For that reason, some plural marriages continued to be performed—usually quietly or out of sight, as in the Mexican colonies that had been established during "the raid." As word of these marriages came out, the Church announced what has sometimes been called "The Second Manifesto," promising that all such weddings would stop.

So what would Morgan and his wives have decided to do? They might have adhered strictly to the official pronouncements of Church leaders. Morgan might have kept his family close, worked hard alongside them, and done all he could to help his children get a start in life. But he also might have trusted that his marriages to Ruth and Mattie were sacred and eternal, and, by that interpretation, he and Mattie might have continued to have children together. The Morgan I created gradually became committed to a life of faith and of trust in his leaders, but a certain independence persisted in him. So he would have been caught between a desire to obey and an impulse to make up his own mind. I'll let readers decide what decision he and Mattie would have made. I only feel certain that Morgan never would have abandoned Ruth and Mattie.

During the period of federal persecution of plural families, a narrative was created and spread across the land: Mormon men were lascivious deviants who collected harems of teenaged wives. They dominated these young wives and mistreated them. This account was simply not true, but it was widely believed, and politicians who sought to "free" polygamous wives used this narrative to seek legal and even extra-legal means to destroy the Church. What developed over time, after the manifesto, was a certain shame among Latter-day Saints. They wanted to escape a sense of being "the other," and they often accepted the false narrative, perhaps without realizing it. Many young Church members today don't like to mention this part of our past, hate to think about it, and wish the whole matter could be forgotten. Accounts of life in polygamy have become, especially for many young women, a matter of embarrassment and even disgust.

All this is understandable, and certainly few if any modern Church members would want to return to the practice. But we see that earlier era from a modern perspective, and we fail to understand that the early Saints also had great trouble accepting the principle when it was first taught. They entered into plural marriage because they believed they were called by God to do so. Most of those early adherents described polygamy as a great test. Some were thankful, in the end, for the self-discipline and cooperation they learned from living as they did; others wondered how so much could be asked of them. It was as hard for some of them to accept the end of plural marriage as it had been for them to accept its beginning.

We honor our "noble pioneers" for crossing the plains and building beautiful cities in the deserts of the West. They were asked to do many hard things, and one of those, for those so called, was to live a principle that demanded so much of them. Those strong, good people passed along to us the strength that has continued as our hallmark in the current world. Personally, my heritage includes several family lines of polygamists. I'm proud of that heritage, and I appreciate the noble traits that they passed on to me and that I hope to pass to my own children and grandchildren. We should never feel embarrassed or ashamed of people who faced a life that demanded so much love, fairness, trust, and patience. Rather, we should thank them and honor them for their devotion to the gospel of Jesus Christ.

For readers interested to learn more about plural marriage, many good books have been written. Some of the most helpful to me, in preparation for writing these books, were: *More Wives than One; Transformation of the Mormon Marriage System, 1840–1910*, by Kathryn M. Daynes (University of Illinois Press, 2001); *A House Full of Females: Plural Marriage and Women's Rights in Early Mormonism*, by Laurel Thatcher Ulrich (Knopf, 2017); *Mormon Polygamous Families: Life in the Principle*, by Jessie L. Embry (University of Utah Press, 1987); *The Polygamous Wives Writing Club: From the Diaries of Mormon Pioneer Women*, by Paula Kelly Harline (Oxford University Press, 2014).

Helpful sources on the history of the United Order include: *Not of the World: A Living Account of the United Order*, by Lucy Parr (Horizon Publishers, 1975); *Orderville Utah: A Pioneer Mormon Experiment in Economic Organization*, a monograph by Leonard J. Arrington (Utah State Agricultural College Monograph Series, Vol. II, March 1952); "Orderville: A Little Family," chapter 13 in *Building the City of God: Community and Cooperation among the Mormons*, by Leonard J. Arrington, Feramorz Y. Fox, and Dean L. May (University of Illinois Press, 1992); "The Orderville United Order of Zion," by Mark A. Pendleton, in *Utah Historical Quarterly*, Vol. VII (October 1939); *Orderville: Heart of the United Order* (Southern Utah Publishing, 1996).

Several biographies of early Saints who lived in Orderville provide rich details. The most useful of those for my research were: *Samuel Claridge: Pioneering the Outposts of Zion*, by S. George Ellsworth (Howe Brothers, 1987), and *Happy Is the Man: A Social Biography of Thomas Chamberlain (1854–1918)*, by Beverly Christensen Chamberlain (Brigham Young University Printing Services, 2009).

The archives of the Church History Library of The Church of Jesus Christ of Latter-day Saints contain many articles, family histories, and biographies that touch on the history of Orderville.

Some of these can be accessed online. I am grateful for the patient guidance I received at the library.

I have now published books with Deseret Book for over forty years, the first appearing in 1979. I have loved the people I have worked with there. I greatly appreciate the encouragement that Laurel Christensen Day gave me when I described this project to her. She told me that if I could write a book that would help her, and others, feel better about our history of plural marriage, that would be a great service. I hope I have achieved that. I am thankful that she, Celia Barnes, and Emily Watts have read my drafts, guided my revisions, and believed in my work. They care about my writing, but they also care about me, and they offer advice that sounds like love.

My wife, Kathy, has also read the book at several stages, as she always does. She is honest in her assessments, which I appreciate even when I don't want to hear what she tells me. She is great at spotting typos and mistakes, but, more important, she helps me think about my characters, my settings, my plots, and, ultimately, my goal in writing the book.